DEADLY POLITICS

A NICHELLE CLARKE CRIME THRILLER

LYNDEE WALKER

SEVERN RIVER
PUBLISHING

Severn River Publishing
www.SevernRiverBooks.com

This is a work of fiction. Names, characters, businesses, places, events and incidents are either the products of the author's imagination or used in a fictitious manner. Any resemblance to actual persons, living or dead, or actual events is purely coincidental.

ISBN: 978-1-64875-517-0 (Paperback)

ALSO BY LYNDEE WALKER

The Nichelle Clarke Series

Front Page Fatality

Buried Leads

Small Town Spin

Devil in the Deadline

Cover Shot

Lethal Lifestyles

Deadly Politics

Hidden Victims

Dangerous Intent

The Faith McClellan Series

Fear No Truth

Leave No Stone

No Sin Unpunished

Nowhere to Hide

No Love Lost

Tell No Lies

To find out more about LynDee Walker and her books, visit

severnriverbooks.com/authors/lyndee-walker

For DruAnn, Justin, Avery, Art, Tara, Aimee, Julie, Sarah, and Kristi, who believed Nichelle would get here.

1

Every story has at least two sides. Some have a dozen, some a hundred. And the truth always lies somewhere in the gray, murky middle.

A good reporter needs the objectivity to recognize facts peeking through thick curtains of perception. A great one needs the drive to keep digging when others abandon their shovels for the easy roads of official statements and press releases.

Finding truth in situations both ordinary and exceptional is my favorite thing about the news business. When a big story breaks, my universe narrows to the thrill of the chase. Caffeine becomes a food group, adrenaline a friend. Schedules evaporate. Sleep is for suckers who settle for second place.

I love every minute of it. But that rush has taught me to appreciate the quieter days, too.

Like a gorgeous fall Friday that kicked off with a salted-caramel white mocha and zero corpses waiting in my scanner app—pretty fabulous in its own right, even before I strolled into my editor's office for the news budget meeting two whole minutes early.

"Morning, kiddo." Bob clicked his monitor off as I dropped into my usual orange velour armchair like I was always the first in the door instead of the last. "What's interesting in your world today?"

I sipped my latte, tapping a pen on my yellow legal pad as I swallowed savory-sweet goodness that carried promises of short days and tall boots. "So far I have a robbery at a gas station in Church Hill overnight—no one dead—a shooting at a nightclub in Shockoe Slip—also no one dead—and court at one thirty. DonnaJo has spent the whole week hammering the meth lab guys from last spring. Should be a slam dunk for the CA's office, but one of the defendants is a minor, so the judge might lighten his sentence."

"Charges?"

"Manslaughter for the dealer who died, murder one for the kid, plus assault for the two firefighters who got hurt. And then all the drug charges. I'll have the week-one wrap-up for you today. Defense takes over Monday."

He nodded. "Good stuff. Sounds like a busy day."

"Only until five. I have a date tonight." I smiled and nodded hellos as the section editors trickled in, throwing Bob a wink and rapping my knuckles on the wooden arm of my chair. "I'll take this version of busy any day."

The features editor set a vintage orange Tupperware box on the corner of Bob's desk before taking her seat across from me. I leaned forward, the scent of spicy sausage and cheese making my stomach rumble.

"Eunice's breakfast bread, too? This day just keeps getting better." I snatched up a slice a split second before the rest of the room descended. Conversation ceased, chewing the only sound until a chorus of thank-yous pattered out a few bites in.

Eunice laughed. "My grandmomma always said a cook couldn't get a higher compliment than a quiet room full of people eating. Happy fall, y'all."

Bob swallowed and picked up his pen just as the door opened, Trudy Montgomery's auburn head poking around the frame. "Can I crash for a minute? I have something kind of big, and it'll be easier to talk about here."

Bob waved her in. "I was just about to start the rundown, so why don't you lead off?"

She pulled in a deep breath. "Some of you might have read that we have a high-profile congressman looking at the fight of his political life this fall, thanks to some creative redistricting that passed last winter."

I nodded, forgetting my coffee as she talked. Nobody outside the beltway had more information on Washington's inner workings than Trudy. Covering the White House had been my dream for practically my whole life before I'd moved to Richmond. This job was supposed to be a stepping-stone to it.

Nine years ago. I loved the crime desk, but politics still beckoned.

"Speeks has powerful friends who aren't going to let that seat go without a fight." Trudy clapped her hands together under her chin, flawless scarlet nails flashing in the fluorescent light. "So . . . the president is coming."

"Here?" Bob sat up straighter, clicking his pen out. "She hasn't been here since the campaign. When?"

I sipped my latte, trying to wash down the jealousy-green creeping into my complexion.

"Monday," Trudy said. "Here's the thing: it's big-guns time. She and her husband will both be speaking Monday night, at different venues across town from each other." She turned to me with a grin. "Which means I could use a hand. You free?"

I jumped and fumbled my cup, coffee and milk splattering caramel dots I barely noticed across the thigh of my cream linen trousers. "Me? Are you serious?"

"Because I'd ask anyone else?" Trudy winked. "I believe I still owe you a favor."

I bounced in my seat, turning to Bob, who nodded approval. Two years ago, I'd shared some information with Trudy that led her to an exclusive on a massive scandal ensnaring then senator Ted Grayson.

Still, this was one hell of a reciprocation. My face stretched into a grin so wide it almost hurt. "I'd be honored."

"I'll clear the Tuesday front and leave it to you two to figure out the details," Bob said. "Trudy, how late will they run? Do I need to schedule a hold for Monday night?"

She shook her head, her perfect chin-length bob swinging softly. "Both speeches are set to start at seven. They'll be wrapped by eight. We'll have copy to you by quarter to nine."

"Cutting it close, but doable." Bob scribbled something on his pad.

"Sounds like a plan."

"I'll have an advance for you by five." Trudy turned to me when Bob nodded. "Catch up with me later and we'll work out details?"

I nodded. I didn't trust myself to speak without gushing like she'd just handed me the key to a Louboutin warehouse.

The door shut behind her and Bob cleared his throat. "Well. Now that we have next week's big news all ironed out, what do y'all say we figure out the weekend?"

I half listened to the discussion around me, my brain still trying to wrap fully around the I-get-to-cover-a-presidential-speech thing. Or a presidential-adjacent speech, anyway. Mr. Denham was a former two-term congressman from Nebraska who had leveraged his position in the East Wing into some massive public program overhauls in just under two years in office.

The upcoming midterm elections held the fate of the rest of President Denham's term in balance, and she had pulled no punches lately in stumping for her chosen candidate in hotly contested races. Scribbling ideas and questions as fast as they popped into my head, I didn't even hear Bob talking to me until Eunice tapped the ebony toe of my new Jimmy Choo motorcycle boot with her foot.

"Care to rejoin the discussion about today's edition?" Bob winked.

"Sorry." I smiled. "I just—"

He nodded. "I know. I was saying, you said you have two crime stories and a trial recap coming today. Anything else on your list?"

"Not right this second."

"I have her feature on Southside's renaissance for tomorrow," Eunice said. "Lindsay got some fantastic photos. It'll make a nice section front."

"Nichelle wrote a feature?" It wasn't a real question—the sports editor followed his derisive tone with a curt laugh in case anyone missed his sarcasm. "What's our banner? A day in the life of a dope fiend?"

"I believe you're confusing my work with your training camp piece from August." I flashed my most Splenda-riffic smile.

"Enough, Spence." Bob shot me a *Don't feed the troll* look, turning back to Eunice. "I read it last night. It's a good piece. How many pages are you looking at for tomorrow?"

The rundown went on, and I floated back into my political daydreams. Would I get a chance to meet her? Or him? How did that even work? Did the Secret Service have to approve people? Of course they did. I had background clearance with the state, but I'd never been through a federal screening.

I scribbled more notes, my foot bouncing with excitement. I had to tell someone. Right now. Reaching for my iPhone, I clicked my boyfriend's name in the favorites and opened a text. *GUESS WHAT?* I typed. Before it finished sending, I fired off another: *Best. Day. Ever. And I'm not even to the part where I get to see you yet.*

I dropped the phone in my lap, jiggling one foot.

Robbery. Gunman. Exploding meth dealers. Focus on today.

Pretty damned near impossible.

Bob was on the business section, which had an inside tip on a merger announcement that could rock the financial world, when my phone buzzed. I smiled before I even looked at the screen. Joey has a way of making me do that.

A scanner alert bleated as I turned the phone over.

Not Joey.

Kyle.

Buzz. Now Aaron.

I skipped the scanner notification in favor of the rapid-fire texts from my favorite cops, my stomach closing around the breakfast bread and coffee.

"Nichelle?" Eunice sounded far away. "You okay, sugar?"

Reading Kyle's message for the third time, I started shoving belongings into my bag.

Damn, damn, damn.

"So much for knocking on wood. You're going to want to clear tomorrow's front, too, chief." I popped out of the chair, tossing my half-full latte in the corner trash can. "Aaron and Kyle have a body. I'll send you something for the web before TV can get it on air at noon."

"The PD and the ATF have the same body?" Bob's bushy white eyebrows shot clear to his receding hairline. "Where?"

Hand on the doorknob, I turned back. "In the governor's office."

2

Maneuvering around two state troopers and three RPD uniforms in a narrow alleyway five blocks from the capitol, I was pretty sure my fabulous Friday was about to take a sharp turn.

Good turn or bad turn, I couldn't tell.

I found a tiny space to wedge the car into and half ran toward the square, only slowing my stride as I closed in on the lawn. Nearly every emerald inch was obscured by camera riggings, TV reporters, or cops and firefighters.

I scanned the crowd for familiar faces, my phone buzzing again.

Joey: *What's up, baby?*

I stared at the little gray dot-bubble in the bottom corner of the screen that meant he was still typing.

Buzz. *Also, what's going on at the capitol? I think every emergency vehicle in the city has blared by here in the past half hour.*

I touched the screen to reply and a message alert rolled down from the top.

Kyle: *Are you here yet?*

Out front, I tapped.

Meet me at the corner of Grace and 9th in five.

Four blocks away. He didn't want anyone to know he was talking to me.

I surveyed the massive building, its white stone columns gleaming in the October sunshine. History practically thrummed in the air around it. Designed by Thomas Jefferson. Survived the Civil War.

What the hell was going on in there today?

I plopped my sunglasses over my face, turning for the corner Kyle mentioned. Maybe none of my broadcast colleagues had spotted me yet.

"Nichelle? Hey, Nichelle!"

Or maybe they had.

My foot froze in midair as I turned, fixing a polite smile on my face as Dan Kessler from WRVA jogged over.

"What do you know?"

"That an unresponsive person was found in the building this morning," I quoted the dispatch from my scanner app.

Kessler arched one perfectly waxed eyebrow, his troweled-on layers of pancake foundation creasing when his forehead moved. "And?"

"And what?"

"Come off it, Clarke. Everybody knows you're the detective's pet. Where are you off to?"

"I'm flattered that y'all give me so much clout with Aaron—truly, Dan—but most of it is in your head." I pointed to the Starbucks sign outside the hotel across the street. "You know how this works. They won't be out to give a statement for a while yet. I'm going to grab a latte—you want anything?"

He folded his arms across his chest. "Coffee. Right."

"It's October. Salted caramel is back." I smiled.

"You really have nothing?"

I spread both hands wide, blinking for effect. "I have the same statement you got." Every word technically true. "Can Charlie say the same?"

He spun back to the lawn, looking for the Channel Four crew. Poor Dan. He'd once been the crime reporter to beat in Richmond, but his station had recently fallen another notch in the local ratings thanks largely to his years of contentment with following me and Charlie to the big stories. Probably trying to hang on to his job.

But it wasn't mine to babysit him.

"Sure I can't bring you anything?" I asked the back of his Brooks Brothers jacket.

"No, thanks," he called, striding toward Charlie, who had planted herself half a breath from the lectern a pair of RPD uniforms were wiring mics to on the lawn.

I pulled my phone out and tapped, *On my way,* to Kyle.

He was pacing between the lamppost and the corner when I found him.

"Finally," he muttered, dragging me across the street to the park. He stopped behind a massive magnolia next to the statue of George Washington, running a hand through his burnished bronze curls as he opened his mouth and closed it again on replay.

I knew Kyle—in every sense of the word. Before he was a hotshot ATF special agent, he was my first love. Even way back then, he was pretty damned hard to render speechless.

"Kyle?" It came out an octave too high. I cleared my throat and tried again. "What's going on?"

He tapped a foot. Blew out a long breath.

I swallowed hard. "Who's dead?"

"I need your help," he said. "Off the offest, blankest record there has ever been."

I nodded, my eyes not missing a single tight, twitching muscle as he stared down at me.

"You remember Lakshmi Drake?"

My eyes fell shut. "Shit, Kyle."

Her face floated on the back of my eyelids. Long, thick dark hair. High cheekbones, straight nose. Wide, almond-shaped brown eyes. Last time I'd seen them they were scared, and Lakshmi was packing her things to heed my warning that the underground escort business funding her graduate studies was about to be dragged into the TV spotlight.

I opened my eyes and shook my head. "That was two years ago. And she said she was done with that life. Are you sure it's her?"

He ran one hand through his hair. "We're working on a positive ID for the remains. I need to know about your interactions with Lakshmi. Did she ever say anything about anyone besides Grayson? Did she mention any other clients to you?"

That's why they'd texted me. Even the detective's pet doesn't get the inside track on something like this without the cops asking a favor in return.

My teeth closed over my lower lip as I reached for the memories.

"I'm not sure?" I didn't intend for that to be a question, but the inflection was there all the same.

"I need you to try hard, because it could be important." He put a hand under my elbow and steered me back toward the capitol. "Really important."

I looked up at him as we waited for the light at the crosswalk. "What are you not saying?" I asked.

His lips disappeared into a thin white line. The light changed. Kyle shook his head. "Just see what you can come up with. Please."

"I want it first." I quickened my steps to keep up with his long stride. "If I'm helping with your investigation, nobody gets the story before we do."

"I'll see what I can do." He stopped on the corner and turned for a back entrance, waving me to the press corral on the lawn. "This is bigger than a headline, Nichelle. Bigger than the collar, too. Call me if you remember something."

Halfway back up the hill, I stopped when I realized what I hadn't asked him: Why couldn't they ID Lakshmi's body?

* * *

Aaron's press briefing was the most useless speech I'd ever seen him offer: an unresponsive person had been transported to St. Vincent's, and RPD was working closely with other interested agencies to get the matter resolved.

That was it. He didn't even try double-talk for lengthening effect. And his refusal to take questions before he disappeared back into the building put the entire Richmond media scene on high alert.

I dropped my pen and notebook back into my bag, turning to find Charlie Lewis's blue eyes fixed on me. They narrowed as she tipped her head to one side.

Behind her, Kessler watched us both. Thankfully, they were more than a football field away, so I waved and jogged toward my car, my fingers itching for a keyboard.

A dead (at least former) call girl in the governor's office? The political stakes hovered in the stratosphere. I couldn't print her identity without finding it elsewhere, of course, but once Aaron was back in his office, I could work on him. ID or no, a body in the capitol complete with cops crawling all over would eclipse everything else happening today.

Thanks to my history with Lakshmi and Kyle's trust, I had a jump on everyone else. But Charlie knew just as many people as I did. She'd have it before long. If I wanted to stay ahead of her, the clock was ticking. As always.

I tapped my foot through the elevator ride to the newsroom, nearly mowing down a photographer and two copy editors in my rush to Trudy's office. I slipped inside, then kicked the door shut behind me and leaned against it as she spun her chair around. She eyed my flushed cheeks and quick breathing, lifting her penciled-in eyebrows.

"You can't be that excited about covering a speech."

"Close. But no," I said. "Listen, I read every story you ran after the Grayson thing, but I know better than anyone that not everything we know always makes it into the paper. I need to know what else you had on him."

She tipped the chair back. "This wouldn't have anything to do with the Twitter alert Ryan just posted about a body in the statehouse, would it?"

I nodded, crossing to the chair in front of her desk and dropping into it.

"Interesting. Care to fill me in?"

The offest, blankest record ever, Kyle had said.

"I can't." I sighed. "You asked me once to trust you. I need you to return that favor today."

She clicked her nails against one another, holding my gaze for ten heartbeats before she nodded. "What do you need?"

"Was Grayson into anything shady that involved anyone in state government?"

Trudy shook her head slowly. "Not that I remember. He served on the security committee, though, and there's some overlap there with state agencies since 9/11."

I dug out a pen and notebook and jotted that down. Any needle in this particular haystack would do.

"I take it this means you're too busy to talk logistics today?" she asked.

I sighed. "I am so excited about this event—"

She raised one hand. "I know. I already put your name in for vetting with the White House. Once they get you on the list, the Secret Service will need a background check. They'll move fast because there's not much time, and she just added two appearances and a breakfast to her schedule for the day, which will have them hopping." She smiled. "How would you like to take her breakfast in the morning and his speech in the evening? If you have time."

I blinked. "I will make time." Pretty sure I managed to get the words out. To be in a room with the president—that was the literal manifestation of college Nichelle's every career dream. I shot out of the chair. "Thank you, Trudy. I'll do you proud."

"I know you will. Get Bob his scoop today and we'll circle up this weekend."

I scrambled back to my little ivory cubicle, flipping my laptop open before my rear hit the chair.

I had an email from Aaron at the top of my inbox. I clicked it and scanned the text. Press release from the governor's office. All members of the state assemblies and the First Family safe, many thanks to local law enforcement. So, nothing I didn't already know, but it would narrow Charlie's search a bit.

I didn't recall knowing Lakshmi's last name before, but Kyle said Drake, so I clicked to Google and typed it in.

Journalism in the Age of the Internet 101: the answer to almost anything can be found online. The tricky part is knowing where to look.

Social media accounts were the top hits, of course. I clicked Instagram first.

Her profile was public. Odd, for someone with her past, but okay. Last post was a week ago. She was on a beach.

I scrolled.

Before that, there were photos almost every day.

Lots of them featured a tall, dark-haired guy who'd rather look at her than the camera more than half the time.

Bingo.

I clicked to the tags.

There weren't any. Weird.

Back to Google.

Lakshmi's Twitter feed was full of retweets of love quotes and animal videos.

Facebook.

The page you requested cannot be found.

Huh?

Back to Google.

I copied the link. Pasted it into a different browser.

Got the same 404 error.

Leaning back in my chair, I clicked the pen in and out.

Why erase her profile there but not anywhere else?

I jotted the question down, put stars on either end.

Clicked her Instagram back up and stared at her wide smile.

She was happy. A week ago.

Next photo. She was facing the selfie camera, a serious pose this time, her gorgeous eyes wider than I remembered. Mine settled on the guy, the super intense gaze he had locked on Lakshmi, no hint of a smile. I loved it when Joey looked at me that way. Lakshmi's voice rang in my ears. *"Ted didn't like to share."*

What if Mr. Wonderful here didn't like her past?

I studied his face. Was it familiar, or was I making it that way because I wanted a lead? I couldn't tell. I tapped my index finger on the keyboard. What else did I know?

The governor's office.

How did she end up in there?

Her boyfriend was cute. On the skinny side, but handsome. Long nose. Strong jaw.

Oh hell.

Eyes wide, I went to pull up another photo.

404 error.

I clicked back.

Same screen.

But the photos had been there just minutes ago.

Instagram main page, search.

No such user.

Somebody was deleting Lakshmi Drake's online life right before my eyes.

I snatched up my phone. Clicked Kyle's name.

Why couldn't you identify the remains? Send.

Gray dot-bubble.

Buzz. *Too much damage to the facial bone structure for a positive without the lab. I still can't even figure out how the hell they got in here—it's supposed to be a secured area, but this place is a fucking jurisdictional nightmare today.*

My hands shook as I typed. *Try from the inside. I'm pretty sure Lakshmi's been dating the governor's son.*

3

Richmond Police and federal law enforcement officers are investigating a death in the Virginia capitol overnight Thursday. No details about the identity of the victim or the circumstances surrounding the death have been released.

A statement from Governor Thomas Baine's staff proclaimed the First Family safe and all members of the commonwealth's house and senate accounted for. The governor also thanked law enforcement for swift containment of the situation.

No arrest was reported as of 11 a.m. Friday.

"The First Family appreciates the concern of all Virginians as we move forward with the important business facing the commonwealth and let our fine first responders do their work," Kelly DeFazio, Governor Baine's press secretary, wrote in the press statement. "The governor has full faith in the ability of the men and women in our law enforcement agencies to resolve the matter quickly."

I stared at those two paragraphs way longer than I should've, twisting and untwisting a lock of hair around my fingers as I debated including the exact location of Lakshmi's body. Technically, nobody had said that information was off the record, and I had the texts to prove it. But my gut said I was the only reporter in town who got those texts, thanks to my history with the victim. So including it might tip Charlie and Dan to something they didn't know yet—and leaving it out would damn sure win me some brownie points with my cops, which could come in handy on a story like this. The statement from the governor's office was a hint, though it was hard to say how much of one since I already knew more than most folks.

Out. For now.

I'd better be right about being the only reporter in the know.

I filled the rest of my story with a bunch of history on the building and its architecture and information about Baine and the last legislative session, ending with Aaron's nonstatement before I opened an email to Bob.

Thin, but it's all we can print for now, I typed in the message I attached the story to.

Time for a caffeine fix. Halfway to the break room, I spun for Bob's open door when every ear in a three-block radius heard my name.

"You bellowed?" I stuck my head around the corner.

He gestured to his screen. "What is this horse shit? Two hours ago you said you had a murder practically on the governor's desk, and this is the copy I get?" He clicked his browser open as I stepped inside and shut the door. "Do I need Charlie Lewis to fill me in today?"

Wow. He wasn't known for his patience, but I usually got more leeway than this.

I kept my eyes from rolling upward as I sank into my usual chair, shaking my head. Every crease on his pinched face told me he was more scared than mad. And I was a safe whipping post because he knew I loved him. Months of scrambling to stay on top—and therefore off our weaselly publisher's shit list—had taken their toll.

I kept my voice even. Soft. "I'm trying to keep Charlie in the dark until I figure out what the hell is going on here," I said. "Pretty sure the only reason I know where the body was is because Aaron was in a rush and let it slip in that first text."

"And why do you think Charlie didn't get the same slip, exactly?" Bob laced his fingers behind his head. "I know you're White's pet and all, but the man still has to do his job fairly."

Good point. Except Charlie didn't have a history with the victim.

Bob's eyebrows went up, waiting for me to answer.

"I'm sure enough to risk it," I said. "Kyle and his team are neck-deep in this for a reason I'm not clear on yet, but I got something off the record from him, and I swear on my favorite Louboutins every cop in the state will give everything they've got to keep this as tight as possible."

Bob sat up. "What'd your friend give you?"

"Offest, blankest record there's ever been." Kyle's words ran through my head again.

I rolled my lips between my teeth, not breaking eye contact. "I can't tell you."

The words stretched between us in a silence heavy with what wasn't being said. I had worked a dozen people's fair share of sticky stories, and I hadn't ever refused to let Bob in on a lead.

He finally tipped his head to one side, clearing his throat. "You don't trust me?"

My eyes did roll that time. "Of course I do. This is just . . . complicated. I'd rather keep it to myself until I have a better handle on what's going on. It's really hard for me to say to you, chief, but it's the God's honest truth. I need you to trust me."

"You're sure we'll come out on top?"

I hated the tiny catch buried in his question. For nearly a year, my heart patient editor, the closest thing I'd ever had to an actual father, had lived every day worried he was about to be forced into retirement. And I had lived those same days determined to kick Charlie's ass on every lead so he could rest a little easier. Despite a couple of close calls, I'd always managed to pull out the win.

I could do it again this time. I didn't have another option.

"I'm sure. If by some chance I'm wrong about this, I have an ace in the hole." Kyle might kill me, but I could get confirmation on the victim ID from somewhere else, especially since I knew where to look. I stood, waving a hand to Bob's screen. "Ryan should get that on the web before noon."

"Do I need to hold more space than this on the front?"

I turned to the door. "Give me until four. I'll let you know."

* * *

An hour snuggled up to Google later, I knew the name of the governor's childhood dog, his college GPA, and how he liked his eggs—over easy—but the internet had officially failed me for the first time.

I had exactly jack shit on Baine's son. Other than confirmation that Hamilton Baine was indeed the boy from Lakshmi's Instagram, and I was pretty sure of that before I read about his dad for an hour.

Four campaign photos: two from the House of Delegates, one from the state senate, and one from last year's election. That was the sum total of what my computer could tell me about Lakshmi's adoring companion. I would've given my entire shoe closet to go back and screenshot just one photo.

"Now what?" I leaned back in the chair, stretching my arms over my head and trying to unkink my back. Governor Baine's family smiled, tooth-paste-commercial perfect, from my screen.

Dammit. Thomas Baine was a military hero, with a silver star and two Purple Hearts to show for his service in Iraq. A brilliant lawyer who'd started his career at a bank, but moonlighted helping out pro-bono in zoning and redistricting cases in economically depressed areas. A loving husband and father who still held hands with his wife in public and stood when she entered a room.

He was also only Virginia's second African American governor, sworn into office on the 235th anniversary of his great-great-great-great-grandfather's emancipation from slavery—a tear-jerking moment Trudy captured beautifully, straight from the we-can't-make-this-up files.

Baine was perfect. Poised to lead the commonwealth into the third decade of the twenty-first century with a strong economy and a commitment to top-tier education and technology access in every single county. And with early buzz about national aspirations, President Denham's reaching across the aisle to invite him to introduce her was a political coup, giving Baine clout with voters who would normally dismiss him out of hand.

Except now there was a dead call girl in his office. Whether Lakshmi had left her racier life behind when she walked out of that classroom after our chat two years ago or not, every talking head on every news channel in

America would label her a prostitute as soon as one determined reporter broke both of those tidbits.

The governor's whore. It was short. Scandalous. And it would stick, truth be damned.

I opened the bottom left drawer, eyeing the jumble of notebooks. I never tossed the important ones, so somewhere in there were the notes from all the conversations I'd had with and concerning Lakshmi Drake. Maybe I'd scribbled down something that could help me find a place to start.

If I could find it.

I pulled out a stack of five and started flipping.

Nothing.

Halfway through the second stack, a tap on my shoulder made me jump half out of my chair.

"Sorry, didn't mean to scare you," Shelby Taylor's high-pitched, whiny drawl came from behind me. I stretched my face into a smile before I turned. Shelby didn't know I knew she was screwing the publisher in her latest effort to wheedle her way into my job. She was still pretending to be my friend. Intrigued by how long she'd carry this on and what her end game could possibly be, I played along.

Slapping the notebook shut, I turned the chair and looked up at her— not far, Shelby's whole self only has a few inches on me when I'm sitting. "How's your weekend looking?" I kept my tone light.

"Eh." She waved one hand. "Solo ice-cream-and-wine fest. The usual. You have big plans with your mystery man?"

My smile didn't falter, thanks to a boatload of recent practice. Joey was a touchy subject in the newsroom. I'd kept our relationship quiet for more than a year because while I knew he wasn't a "bad guy," he was on a first-name basis with more than a few of them, and for a long time I wasn't sure I wanted to know why. But this summer, things got serious enough that I couldn't stay willingly ignorant of his life and continue to call myself any kind of smart. His official job title, director of transportation for a major trucking firm, wasn't an issue, but the darker, unofficial side of his days— making contacts and fixing problems for the Caccione crime syndicate— my friends wouldn't approve. Not that I did, either, but the situation was complicated, extraction from it dangerous, and I was well and truly in love with him, so I could deal. They would not. The questions hadn't stopped since he'd shown up at Parker and Mel's wedding last spring and swept me right off my glittery Manolos in the middle of the second dance. Pulling a trick from my years of covering cops and lawyers, I'd gotten good at deflecting them.

"Y'all will make a mystery out of anything. Even my boring personal life," I said with a wink. "What kind of ice cream and wine?"

She wrinkled her nose. The deflections wouldn't work forever, but I intended to keep the streak alive as long as I could.

"I'm thinking rocky road and Merlot."

Looked like it wasn't going to die today. I nodded, my gaze holding hers. She was every bit as full of shit as I was—she'd probably spend her Friday night doing things I didn't want to think about with Rick Andrews. I managed to contain a shudder, widening my eyes and murmuring, "Sounds good," instead.

"So, I heard Trudy Montgomery asked you to help out with the presidential speeches next week." Shelby leaned one tiny hip on the far edge of my U-shaped ivory laminate desk. "I walked over here half expecting to find you floating up near the ceiling."

"Still trying to wrap my head around it," I said, my fake smile spreading into a genuine grin. "The floating will come, I'm sure."

She nodded. "You've worked so hard for this, and I know how badly you want it. You'll kill it. No pun intended."

I tipped my head to one side, the sheen over her bright-blue eyes and drop in her pitch making me think she actually meant that. "Thanks, Shelby." Fake or not, it was a nice thing for her to say.

She eyeballed the notebooks. "What's all that? Anything to do with the dead person the cops aren't talking about from the capitol this morning? Charlie Lewis looked ready to spit tenpenny nails on the noon broadcast."

Ah-ha. Of course Shelby was really after the scoop on the hot story of the day. Which I probably would've gotten quicker if half my focus wasn't still on trying to extract the name of Lakshmi's math professor from my memory. I almost had it, my weirdly photographic brain calling up the door and the silver plaque, but I couldn't quite make out the name with Shelby chirping at me.

I shook my head. "Just cleaning out my desk." I picked up the top notebook and dropped it in my green recycle bin for show. "Aaron wouldn't tell anyone anything we couldn't get by watching the gurney come out the back door this morning. Whatever happened down there, nobody's talking about it today."

Saying the words out loud made me feel a bit better about having an edge on Charlie—for now.

"Bob had me proof your piece before it went live online." Shelby plucked at a loose thread on her blue silk blouse. "You . . . uh . . . you usually have a little more than that when there's an interesting corpse. And this one seems more interesting than average for sure." Her voice was carefully light. Interested, not nosy.

My teeth ground together as I swallowed a *Tell your boyfriend I'm onto your bullshit*. She was fishing, whether it was for Andrews or someone else —Shelby had a long habit of helping out anyone who was trying to cause me headaches with a big story. The trick this time was that I was supposed to think she was my friend. Telling her where she could stick that was more tempting than a Saks fire sale, but it wasn't the smart play. Yet, anyway.

"Like I said, they're not saying. At least not today." I stood, reaching for my bag and sweeping the notebooks on my desk into it. "But don't worry— I'll figure something out."

"You always do." She stepped backward and let me through. "Lunch plans?"

"I already ate," I lied. "But thanks. I have a trial picking up in a little bit."

I waved goodbye at the elevators and leaned against the back wall when I stepped inside. I did have a trial. But I also had just enough time before it started to swing through the math department at the university and see if I could find Lakshmi's professor.

4

Twenty-two doors on two floors of offices later, I spotted the right nameplate: Gaskins.

I tapped on the door and it swung open half a blink later, putting me eyeballs-to-mustache with a disheveled man sporting a bigger gut than I remembered and a coffee-stained yellow tie he might've been wearing last time we spoke. I stepped backward, my heel catching on the carpet. My nose said he'd splashed on half a bottle of woodsy cologne to make up for a few missed showers.

"Office hours today are from four to seven, young lady," he said, settling a stack of papers and workbooks under his left arm, his eyes never so much as passing over my face. "I'm on my way to a meeting just now."

Damn.

"I'm not a student," I said, extending my left hand so he could shake it with his free right one. "Nichelle Clarke from the Richmond *Telegraph*. I don't want to make you late for your meeting, but could I come back this afternoon?"

He pushed square, black-plastic-rimmed glasses up the bridge of his nose, which scrunched right along with his eyes when he squinted, peering at my face.

"You were here asking about Lakshmi before she disappeared," he said, his eyes popping from almost shut to white-all-around wide. "What did you do with her, you and your little whore friends?"

My eyes slid side to side as his voice gained decibels with every word.

"You have the story all wrong, sir." But he did have more of the details than I would've thought. "We can talk later, or if you have a moment now, maybe we should step into your office?"

He juggled the papers and glanced at his watch before he stepped to one side and waved me through the door. "Three minutes," he said, his eyes squinting again. "Did you say you're a reporter?"

I nodded. "I did come to see you a couple of years ago, and I did talk with Lakshmi that day, but it was to ask her for some information I needed and warn her that she was about to get in big trouble. She chose to leave school to avoid it, it seems."

So what the hell was she doing with Baine's kid?

He slumped back against the closed door. "I knew she was doing something she shouldn't be, and of course every male member of the faculty heard whispers about Dean Baker's little side enterprise. You can't keep something like that a secret in a group of academics. We're gossipy."

He wasn't the type I'd peg for being into coed call girls, but he sure seemed to like Lakshmi, so gossipy worked in my favor. I just needed to tread carefully—one offensive word and he'd shut right the hell up.

"She told me she needed the money to stay in school," I said. Neutral. Helpful.

Leading.

He nodded. "What happened to her father wasn't right or fair. And my God, she was a brilliant girl. Best grad student I ever had."

"You haven't heard from her since she left?" I watched his face carefully. Lakshmi had gone on and on the first time I'd met her about how brilliant this man was and how much she respected him.

Gaskins's lips rolled between his teeth, his eyes going up toward the ceiling.

There was something he wanted to say, but he wasn't sure he should.

"Professor? I'm sorry to be the one to tell you, but something terrible has happened. I liked Lakshmi. If there's anything you can tell me that might point me to where she's been for the past two years . . ." I let the words trail, keeping my tone soft, but urgent.

"Is she dead?" He didn't return his eyes to mine, the words falling heavy and monotone.

"I'm so sorry," I said. "Do you know anything that might help the police with their investigation?"

He stood up straight and looked at his watch again. "I have to go." He didn't turn to open the door, his eyes locking on mine for a good thirty seconds. I didn't blink.

"Lakshmi had a head for numbers like nobody I've ever met, and I've been a mathematician for twenty-six years. But numbers weren't enough. Too quiet. She was drawn to power. Action. She wanted to parlay her gift into a career in politics. And she didn't care what she had to do to get there." Gaskins turned for the door. "It's a shame. She was a brilliant, brilliant girl. Good day, Miss Clarke."

He charged into the hallway, leaving the office open as he rushed for the stairs. I shut his door behind me and followed him at a slower pace, his last words sticking in my thoughts.

The governor's son was a walking all-access pass to the political inside track. But what if Lakshmi wanted a more direct conduit to power?

* * *

I zipped my little red SUV into a parking space across the street from the courts building two minutes before the gavel was set to bang in DonnaJo's meth lab trial, which meant I wouldn't be able to see if she'd share anything about Lakshmi until later. If she knew anything to share. My friend was one of the most trusted senior commonwealth's attorneys in the state, but the cops were locking this down tighter than usual and no arrest had been made.

I got a smile and a wave through from the security guards. "Late today, are we?" Miles cocked one eyebrow as I scurried past the metal detectors.

Not unusual, but it also wasn't unusual for my morning to get hijacked by a body. I was just glad the judge had a personal matter that kept the trial from starting early today—otherwise I wouldn't know any more than Charlie did about what was going on at the capitol.

I slid into the end of the back row in the gallery just as the first witness, a seventeen-year-old drug dealer named Jerry Joe Stickley who went by "Sticks" on account of his bony legs, took his hand off the Bible and nodded to the bailiff.

His watery hazel eyes flicked between the defense table and his lap as DonnaJo approached the stand. "Jerry, can you tell us if there's anyone in the room that you knew before February twenty-third of this year?" She kept her voice low and soothing. The kid had flipped on his friends and solidified the commonwealth's case against them. But DonnaJo had worried over this moment for weeks—getting a ninth-grade dropout scared enough of prison to agree to testify against a drug ring when you had him in a room by himself wasn't hard. DonnaJo was smart and erudite, her unfaded former Miss Virginia looks aiding her gift for convincing folks to agree with her, whether they were in the jury box or on the witness stand. This was the final test, though: getting Jerry to stick by his word with three guys he was knock-kneed terrified of staring him down from across the room—that would take every reassuring smile DonnaJo could muster.

I clicked my pen out, the sound echoing in the silent chamber. Jerry didn't look up, muttering, "Yes, ma'am," into his threadbare blue button-down collar.

The stenographer shot the judge a look accompanied by an almost imperceptible headshake. The judge cleared his throat, but DonnaJo raised a discreet hand and leaned toward the polished cherry rail between her and the kid. "We're going to need that a little louder for the record, Jerry."

"Yes, ma'am, I did." His voice shook, but everyone heard him loud and clear that time. I squeezed my pen tighter. The tricky part was still on deck.

"And can you point out which people you're referring to, please?" DonnaJo's sleepy drawl cradled the words, her soft tone making the loaded question sound as innocent as an offer to take Jerry for ice cream.

He didn't move.

Not a twitch. Not a blink.

The entire courtroom held its collective breath. My eyes jumped from DonnaJo, to the witness, to the defense attorney, an up-and-coming junior partner at the city's largest firm. Craig was a nice guy, and a damned good lawyer, who'd taken the case on court appointment for reasons nobody could figure out.

Nobody except me, anyway.

Three weeks ago, I'd bumped into Craig accidentally-on-purpose at an upscale bar popular with the local legal crowd, and he'd told me flat out he didn't think his clients had a snowman's chance in Jamaica of avoiding prison. "This case doesn't have a damned thing to do with them," he'd said, leaning in over his Scotch. "The commonwealth has them dead to rights. DonnaJo Marsh is as good as it gets at sending guys like these away. She flipped a dealer and she has like ten eyewitnesses putting my guys at the scene." He'd shaken his head. "Nope. The win here isn't about a not guilty verdict. It's in the perception. People out in the suburbs or down in the Fan hear 'drug dealers' and they think 'black kids,' and so when an eighteen-year-old gets sent away for the years he might've spent in college for getting busted with an ounce of weed, nobody gives a shit. And that's just . . ." He waved one hand. "It's just stupidly fucking wrong. Especially when, statistically, white guys who kill people cooking up meth get lighter sentences. Not just in Virginia, but everywhere. There's not a scrap of justice to be found in that, Nichelle."

"So, you're trying to lose?" I asked.

He sipped his drink. "Not at all. I signed an agreement with the commonwealth to provide those guys the best defense I can muster, and I"—he winked, the effects of the Scotch starting to show on his face—"am very good at my job. They'll get service they couldn't pay for with five meth trailers running around the clock. But at the final gavel, the truth will prevail. As it should, really."

He drained his glass while I swirled the ice in my Midori sour with a swizzle stick. "I'm missing a piece of this puzzle, Craig," I said finally. "Guys like you are always in it to win—but so far what I'm hearing is basically that you know they did it and they deserve to do time, yet you're busting your ass for no return. Care to make that match up for me?"

He gestured to the bartender, not speaking until he had another double Scotch in his hand. "Your turn to tell the truth, Nichelle—the story is more interesting with me on their side, right?"

Yes, it was. Craig was movie-lawyer handsome with charisma to spare, and spent most of his professional life on some variety of moral justice crusade. His presence at the defense table had put these particular drug dealers front and center for every news outlet in the city for weeks now. Given them the run of the news cycle this week, too—until this morning.

I knew exactly why he was at that table.

It wasn't about the defendants at all. It was about the platform.

I wondered, watching Craig watch Jerry sit frozen on the stand, what he wanted the kid to do. Lawyers, especially good ones, are competitive by nature. Craig himself had played football at UVA. Could the desire to win overpower what he seemed to see as a larger social mission in this case, or was he laser-focused on Jerry because he was willing him to talk?

If he was, it worked. Jerry pulled in a breath I saw raise his shoulders from across the room before he pointed a trembling finger at each of the defendants. "Right there, ma'am."

I studied them, calm and still in the round-backed wooden chairs. They were dressed in navy suits for court, the leader's long red hair caught back in a ponytail, hands clasped in front of them on the table. Prison hadn't been kind to these guys—they looked thinner than I remembered, their hands red and chapped almost raw like they'd been scrubbing sheets over an old-school washboard. In lye.

DonnaJo drew my eyes back to the stand, firing questions for better than half an hour, letting Jerry's increasingly steady retelling paint a picture of hard men who cared more about skirting the law and cutting corners to turn a profit than they did about the safety of their friends, associates, or neighbors.

I swear I saw one juror swipe at the corner of her eye before he was through talking about the explosion.

"It was for real like all hell broke loose," Jerry said. "The thing I can't forget is the squealing sound when the metal walls of the trailer blew apart. Like somebody slaughtering a dozen hogs all at one time." He shuddered. I scribbled a star next to the comment, wondering if DonnaJo had coached him on the pause he followed it with.

"And did any of the defendants express remorse to you at any time for the lives lost?" DonnaJo walked to the projector screen, clicking the remote in her hand to display a picture of a freckle-faced redheaded boy on a tricycle. She touched the child's hand in the photo.

Jerry shook his head. "No, ma'am."

"No further questions, Your Honor." DonnaJo returned to her seat as Craig left his.

"Jerry, how close were you to the trailer when it blew up?" His tone was light, conversational. But I'd watched Craig work enough to know that slight smile was dangerous.

Jerry fidgeted, tapping his palms on the wooden arms of the chair. "A hundred yards, maybe? Close enough to get this." He held up his right arm, a still-pink scar running five inches down it easily visible from my seat. I scribbled notes, my eyes on Craig.

"And why were you on your way to the trailer that night?"

Jerry blinked. "They called me there. I was their best runner."

"They called you there." Craig walked closer to the box. "Why'd they call you there, Jerry?"

Jerry's thin lips disappeared altogether, rolling between his teeth. His hands picked up a beat on the chair arms again.

DonnaJo sat up straighter, watching Jerry for a silent minute before she scribbled something on the yellow legal pad in front of her and pushed it to her assistant. The young man read it before he turned to her and shrugged.

Oh shit.

Craig knew something she didn't know.

I scooted to the edge of my seat.

The judge leaned in to his mic. "The witness will answer the question."

Jerry's eyes went to DonnaJo, and Craig stepped smoothly between them. "Jerry?"

Jerry studied the ceiling. "Nobody ever got around to telling me that, sir. They went to jail before I talked to them."

Craig put his right index finger over his lips, nodding. He turned and walked back toward the defense table, where he took a swallow from his water bottle.

DonnaJo whispered to her assistant. He got up and hurried out the double doors behind me, his eyes on his shoes as he passed a gallery full of murmuring reporters and onlookers.

Craig let the pause ride, the crowd buzzing louder by the second, until the judge banged his gavel and called for order. I kept my eyes on Jerry. I could swear that was sweat gleaming on his forehead, and it was sixty-five degrees in the courtroom, tops.

The plastic of my pen bit into my fingertips.

"Jerry, how much did my clients agree to pay you for your . . . services?" Craig spun on the heel of one perfectly polished wingtip and crossed back to the witness box.

"A third of what I sold. Half for hooking a new customer." Jerry suddenly found it impossible to sit still.

"And how much were you making, say, in a week?"

Jerry's eyes cut to the defense table. Two of the three guys were stone-still, not even looking at him. The big one on the end facing the murder charge looked ready to snap the dealer's skinny neck.

"Maybe a grand. Probably." Jerry tugged at the collar of his shirt. "Usually."

"And how about if you add in what you were stealing?" Craig asked.

The gallery erupted, the buzz from a few seconds ago quickly growing to a roar. DonnaJo's spine went ramrod straight, her shoulders rising and falling with slow, even breaths that told me she was fighting to keep her seat—and control of her temper.

I made notes, watching Craig. He was good with the bravado. But the kid stealing from the defendants was almost expected—criminals will be criminals, after all. He was going somewhere with this. Somewhere besides here.

Jerry still hadn't answered that last question when the judge threatened to throw out anyone who didn't shut up. Craig didn't care. He kept his eyes on the witness and moved on. "Jerry, did you know Ben called you to come out that day because he knew you were skimming from his profits?"

Jerry's eyes fell shut. He nodded.

"We're going to need a verbal reply for the record," Craig said.

"Yes. Scooter told me they were onto me." The words were directed at the ceiling, Jerry's tone soft.

"Scooter, or Ricky Wayne Lesko, who was killed in the explosion that night." Craig clicked two more slides and a young man in a Kid Rock T-shirt, his long, stringy hair falling past his shoulders around a scruffy face, stared at the jurors. "Jerry, did you know Scooter would be there that night?"

"I did not."

"Jerry, did you tamper with the propane feed to the burners after you talked to Ben that day?"

There it was. Three of the jurors sat forward in their chairs.

Jerry shook his head, his slicked-back, baby-fine hair throwing loose strands around his face. "No, sir, I did not." He sniffled on the last, pulling a balled-up Kleenex from his pocket and dabbing at his nose.

DonnaJo's hand moved in a blur over her legal pad, her assistant still missing.

The judge let murmurs ripple through the gallery for less than thirty seconds before he banged the gavel again.

"No further questions, Your Honor." Craig returned to his seat. I could swear he winked at me as he crossed the floor.

I bent over my notebook, transcribing what had just happened like I was actually likely to forget it.

"Ms. Marsh?"

DonnaJo stood. "Not at this time, Your Honor, but the commonwealth reserves the right to recall this witness."

"So noted." The judge turned to Jerry. "You are excused, but you may not leave the building. Ms. Marsh, call your next witness."

"The commonwealth calls Special Agent Kyle Miller of the Bureau of Alcohol, Tobacco, Firearms, and Explosives."

My head swiveled to the doors the bailiffs were opening, my eyes following Kyle to the witness stand. He took the oath and his seat, his arms spread wide, body language easy and open. DonnaJo took only ten minutes to get a positive ID of the defendants and a firsthand account of the damage the explosion did not just to the surrounding trailers, but to the air the kids in the whole trailer park were still breathing. I starred that comment and jotted a note to look up the study Kyle quoted about exposure to chemical inhalants and lung disease.

"Agent Miller, who examined the propane tanks at the scene?" DonnaJo asked.

"I did."

"And did you find anything unusual about them? Any signs of tampering?"

Kyle's brow furrowed. "No, I did not."

DonnaJo smirked at Craig before she turned back to Kyle. "Thank you, Agent. No further questions, Your Honor."

Another murmur rippled through the gallery—quietly this time, with the scowl radiating from the bench—when Craig declined to cross-examine Kyle. I guess discrediting Jerry was easier than discrediting a cop with Kyle's flawless résumé, but it wasn't like him to give DonnaJo an easy pass on an expert witness.

The judge thanked Kyle and dismissed him, calling a fifteen-minute recess at DonnaJo's request. She followed Kyle out of the courtroom, Craig on their heels. I got stuck behind a circle of chattering Courtroom Clancys —that's what we called the retirees who hung out all day popping into different galleries to watch the action live. By the time I got around them, Kyle and both lawyers had disappeared into the recess crowd. Damn. I leaned against the wall outside the ladies' room and checked my phone. No new messages.

We were at minute twelve, the hallway clearing, when I spotted Kyle waiting by the elevators.

"You made quick work of that," I said, walking up beside him. "Though the star witness who came right before you was a little lackluster."

He raised one eyebrow. "Jerry? How so?"

I gave him the highlights as he punched the down arrow. He shook his head.

"It won't matter. They were still dealing, they were still cooking, it was still their trailer. That's admirable sleight of hand on the part of the defense, but it shouldn't create reasonable doubt in terms of responsibility. DonnaJo is smart. She knows that."

"You sound awfully sure. I saw a couple of the jurors react pretty strongly to the question about Jerry tampering with the propane."

"But nobody can prove that. I just testified that there was nothing wrong with the tanks." He shook his head, a hard edge on the words. "Those guys are going to prison. That's all that matters here."

"Tell me Governor Baine isn't about to join them, please." I lowered my voice, not that anyone was nearby.

He punched the button again. "No comment."

"Kyle, come on."

He stuck his hands in his pockets and rocked up on the balls of his feet, his eyes rolling toward the black plastic camera eye in the ceiling. "Sorry, Nichelle," he said. "It's just business."

Right.

I returned to the courtroom just in time to hear DonnaJo skip recalling Jerry to the stand. She walked around the table and looked every jury member dead in the eyes as she asked the bailiff to dim the lights and called up the photo of little Dakota Simpson again.

"Dakota Simpson should be finishing his seventh week of second grade this afternoon, ladies and gentlemen. Packing his Spider-Man lunchbox into his backpack and getting his desk straightened up to head home for the weekend as we speak. But Dakota can't do any of those things, because his life was cut short by the greed, thoughtlessness, and illegal activity of people his mother had the misfortune to live next door to," she said.

She paced as she recounted the child's life and family story for the jury —his mother working two and sometimes three jobs to take care of him, his love of superheroes and peanut butter sandwiches—every word skillfully directing their anger over the child's death at the men behind the defense table. "Now, Mr. Terry has done a good job today of trying to cast doubt on his clients' responsibility by disparaging a witness for the commonwealth, but you heard that witness deny responsibility for this tragedy, and you heard a highly decorated federal agent swear under oath that the propane tanks were unharmed. So as you listen to the defense, as you consider your recommendation to the judge, you mustn't be fooled by legal parlor tricks designed to make you doubt what you know is right. What you know is true. These men"—she swung one arm their way and pointed at each in turn—"are responsible for the death of this child. For the death of this young man." She clicked up the photo of Scooter, not pausing her speech. "And, in a way, for the deaths of countless drug overdose victims across the state. There is only one just verdict available here, and that is guilty on all counts."

She clicked the remote once more before she resumed her seat, leaving Dakota smiling at the jurors from the screen. Number six definitely wiped her eyes that time.

I followed the rest of the courthouse press corps out to the hallway for Craig's end-of-day statement. DonnaJo didn't care for splashy recaps, preferring to let her arguments stand on their own.

Tucking my phone into my bag and pulling out a notebook and pen, I stopped behind Charlie as Craig turned to face us.

"The commonwealth has done an excellent job of stating its case this week, and the evidence on their side is formidable," he said. "In light of the arguments presented today, my clients have agreed to change their plea. If you'll excuse me, I'm due in the judge's chambers for that discussion. Thank you all for being here today—I'm confident justice will be served."

Hand to God, he looked right past three people to find me in the crowd on the delivery of those last words.

5

Chaos.

We all expected Craig to put his hands up and walk away when the questions erupted, but they flew out of our mouths anyway, everyone trying to shout over the five people closest to them.

He left.

We whirled for the elevators. More than a little shoving and swearing ensued, trickling all the way to the front doors.

I strode outside, barely noticing the fiery red tips of just-changing leaves on the maples dancing in front of a clear, crisp cornflower sky—and those trees were one of my favorite things about fall in Richmond. The breeze carried the perfect level of chill: still warm enough to not be cold, but whispering the promise of cuddly sweaters and warm nights in front of the fireplace in Joey's new apartment.

I had three hours to get Bob the trial recap and still have it on the web before the TV stations went on air. I had two more stories to write in the meantime.

And all I could think about was Lakshmi Drake. Her gorgeous hair, light-up-a-room smile, melodic-bells laugh. There was more to that one than beating Charlie to the headline. More than keeping the publisher off

Bob's back, more than the adrenaline rush of putting a light on dark truths: I knew this girl. I had talked to her. Tried to help her. Liked her.

Why was she dead?

Hours closer to Charlie's next broadcast, I wasn't a bit closer to an answer than I'd been when I left the newsroom. At least I knew she'd been stuck in court all afternoon, too.

Like the thought conjured her, Charlie hustled past me, her quick steps shortened by her circulation-endangering pencil skirt.

She was just in a hurry to get the trial ready for air, I told myself, my feet speeding anyway. I sat behind the wheel of my car, staring at the front of the courthouse and wondering where Kyle had bolted to. And where I could look for a lead.

I thought going by the university would be helpful, but Gaskins didn't have much to offer. Or did he? Had Lakshmi put up with Ted Grayson for more than just the money?

She was smart enough to know politics traded in secrets and lies more than policy and principles. If her ambitions really were political, what secrets had she picked up on?

And did one of them get her killed?

I started the car and sped back to campus, parking near the math building.

Problem: I had no idea where to go next.

I dropped onto a stone bench under a maple, streaking sunlight creating the illusion of flame licking the branches. Pulling out my phone, I opened a text to Bob. *I don't think I'll have more on the capitol murder tonight, but clear space on the front for the meth trial: the defense is changing their plea.* Send.

I watched the screen while he typed. Buzz. *That'll move it up from Metro. Thanks for the heads up. Still three more pieces from you for tonight?*

I shot back a thumbs-up and tucked the phone back in my bag.

Everyone on this campus who knew Lakshmi Drake was probably long gone. Except the guy I'd already talked to, or people I didn't know to ask.

What I needed were names.

I stood, looking around for a campus map.

It looked like the library was about fifty yards the other side of the student union behind me.

Excitement hurried my stride.

I pulled the door open, the paint and plastic smell that said the building had been recently updated still overshadowed by the slightly musty perfume of old paper. I'd spent most of my childhood in the library across the street from my mom's flower shop. The smell was like a welcome home.

I found a computer catalog and searched for a Who's Who for the grad school from two years ago.

No results found.

Graduate directory.

Nothing there either.

Damn.

I turned a slow circle, rising shelves stretching for ceilings on three floors and miles of tables in the open atrium giving my search a true needle/haystack feel.

My eyes skipped over a pretty redhead in an Alpha Tau Alpha T-shirt and shorts that came dangerously close to showing more than most bikinis, and landed on the reference desk.

Lakshmi was in a sorority. That's where the call girl ring started.

I closed my eyes, trying to get my freakish memory to call up which one.

I'd typed it close to fifty times between the dean's arrest and the trial.

Kappa. Omega Delta Kappa.

I strode to the big U-shaped desk, flashing a smile at the petite brunette in the blue sweater behind it.

She smiled back, setting her book down. "What can I help you with?"

"I'm wondering if y'all happen to have copies of sorority yearbooks in your collection?" I asked.

She shook her head. "Most of our Greek houses don't even do electronic ones these days, because they all keep up with each other through social media."

My face must've fallen, because she frowned. "I'm sorry to disappoint you."

"No, it's—" Before I could get the "fine" through my lips, a guy in chinos and a rust-colored windbreaker sprinted through the front doors and straight for the desk, vaulted it, and swung the librarian off her feet in a circle.

She giggled quietly as a chorus of shushing floated their way, shaking her head as he put her back on her feet. "I take it it's here?" she whispered.

He pulled a magazine from his overstuffed backpack and waved it in her face before she snatched it.

"My first published study," he crowed.

More shushing. He ducked his head. "My first published study," he whispered, a smile playing around the scruffy corners of his lips.

"I'm so proud of you." Her eyes shone as she gazed up at him.

Mine went to the computer on her desk.

Published study.

Lakshmi was a grad student, and "publish or perish" was still a very real thing. Had she published anything that might tell me who else I could talk to?

I cleared my throat, snapping the girl's attention back to me.

"Oh, I'm sorry! Was that all you needed?"

"No worries." I nodded to the boyfriend. "Congratulations. Does the university have copies of all the journal articles published by students?"

The young woman nodded. "They're upstairs in the reference room," she said. "You can search the catalog in there if you know the subject or the author's name. Third floor, take a right and go straight and you'll see the room."

I thanked them and half jogged to the stairs.

I expected the reference room to be dark and empty on a Friday afternoon early-ish in the semester, and it didn't disappoint. I closed the heavy walnut door with a soft *click* and tapped the mouse on the computer directly across from it. The walls were lined with fat leather binders that contained collections of academic journals, curated by subject and date.

The computer screen came to life and I clicked to search by author. Typed in Lakshmi's name.

Twenty-seven hits. So, no danger of the "perish" part of that old saying.

I clicked the first one and looked through shelves until I found the right heavy binder. Statistics journals. I opened the first issue and skimmed a random article, finding less than five words in every fifty that made sense to me. Which meant I would need a translator to know what Lakshmi had been working on. Fantastic.

I found Lakshmi's article: *Modern Statistical Extracts*, summer issue. I pulled my phone out and took a snapshot of the page. Back to the computer. Next.

Fifteen articles later, my arms were more than a little weary of lifting the binders off of and onto the shelves, and I had fifteen snapshots of math jargon I could barely read to show for it.

I stretched my arms back over my head when I stood, flinching when my phone buzzed against the polished cherry table.

My lips tipped up when I saw Joey's name flash on the screen.

"Hey, you," I said, putting it to my ear. "I'm doing some research, but I'm still looking forward to dinner."

"I'm afraid I'm going to be late, princess." His voice was low, tight. Trying too hard not to tremble. I stood up straighter, my eyebrows drawing down.

"What's wrong?" I asked.

"Nothing for you to worry about." He tried for smooth.

Missed. Joey never missed.

"I'll see you tonight. Your place around eight?" he continued.

"But I thought we—" I stopped before I got the rest of that out. Duh. He didn't want me at his house for some reason.

"Sure." I forced brightness into my tone. "I'll be ready."

I frowned at the phone until the screen went dark after it beeped the triple-tone call end signal. All week, he'd been looking as forward to our weekend as I had. So what changed?

The doorknob rattled before I could think too hard about that. I spun, slapping the binder in front of me shut as the door swung open to reveal a broad-shouldered, business-suited wall of pecs wearing Ray-Ban aviators. Inside the library. In October.

If he was surprised to see me, I couldn't read it on the parts of his face I could see around the sunglasses.

"How's it going?" I flashed a smile.

"I—" Pause. His lips disappeared between his teeth. "There's not usually anyone in here."

Um. He didn't exactly look like the type to frequent this place.

"I'm almost done." I picked up my binder and returned it to the shelf, pressing the "Escape" key on the catalog computer as I walked past.

Turning to another shelf, I reached for a random volume like I knew exactly what I was doing and returned to my chair with it, smiling at Captain Sunglasses, who stuck out in this building way more than I did. Even his movements were jerky and uncomfortable.

My heart pounded twice too fast for the activity at hand, my fingers flipping pages, my eyes and ears tuned to the large man stepping into the room and shutting the door.

Shit.

Flip. Flip. Flip.

He fumbled with the mouse on the catalog computer. I risked a look up.

He tapped at the keyboard, his shoulders rigid. Feet shoulder width apart. Spine so straight you could level a wall off it.

That was military training.

Clearing his throat, he clicked the computer screen dark and turned to the shelves. I angled my face back down at the page in front of me—a political journal I understood, though I wasn't really reading it. Flipped more pages.

He moved into the far edge of my peripheral, murmuring under his breath as he read binding labels.

Flip.

I lost him when he moved to the shelf behind me.

Flip.

My heart hammered triple-time.

Flip.

A binder slid across the shelf, the leather-on-wood hiss familiar and somehow comforting. He was just getting a book. *Chill, Nichelle.*

He laid it on the table. I turned another page.

He pulled out a chair catty-cornered from mine, his big frame not really fitting in it when he moved to sit. Opened the binder.

My eyes slid to the cover of the journal and I sucked spit into my windpipe when my breath hitched in, dissolving into a full-on, teary-eyed choking fit.

He didn't move, didn't speak. Just watched. Flexed his fingers.

I swiped at the corners of my eyes and sat up straight as the bronchial spasms subsided. "Sorry."

"I think you'll live." He turned back to his binder. I feigned interest in mine. "For now." I couldn't swear on a Bible I heard the last two words with my ears or just inside my head, but either was enough to shoot me to my feet. I slapped the binder shut.

"Good luck with your research," I said, forcing myself to walk to the door. Thugs are like rabid dogs or hungry bears. Showing fear can get you killed.

He didn't reply, his log-thick neck bent over the pages in front of him.

I shut the door behind me and walked to the stairs, getting three down before I broke into a run.

It should take him a few minutes to find the article—about halfway through the fifth journal back, in the same binder I'd looked through an hour ago, because it was the first search result under Lakshmi's name.

* * *

By the time I slid into my car, I was downright annoyed with myself. Of course there were large men in suits hunting information on Lakshmi—she'd been murdered in the governor's office, for Christ's sake. If there was a state or federal agent in a hundred miles not working this case, I'd eat my shoes.

Not that a Louboutin sandwich sounded terrible right then, anyway—almost seven hours of nonstop murder and lies, and I was running on a slice of breakfast bread and a package of questionable peanut butter crackers. My head and stomach were starting to let me know it, too. Clock check: twenty minutes to five. Swinging through the Starbucks drive-thru for a latte and a protein box on my way back to the newsroom, I opened my Channel Four app while I waited. Charlie's story from this morning still led, with lame video of Aaron mostly shaking his head at that lousy excuse for a press conference. She hadn't updated her piece since noon. I checked her Twitter. No teaser for more information coming at six, just a mention of the trial.

So I had at least tonight to keep digging, and three hours until Joey would be free.

Shaking off worry over his weird tone on that call, I held my phone out for the barista to scan, checking my rearview and asking her to tack on the order for the blue Mazda behind me, too.

I didn't wait to get back to my desk to start shoving turkey and apples into my face, the whole box gone and my head a touch clearer when I stepped out of my car in the *Telegraph's* garage. Good. I had three stories to write, and an hour to deadline.

I started with the simplest first: the robbery. After clicking through the RPD site to the incident report, I scanned it for specifics and opened a blank file.

Richmond Police are still searching for a masked offender after a third convenience store in two weeks was robbed overnight in Church Hill. Witnesses said the suspect was armed with a handgun and wearing a rubber Halloween mask.

"The voice was low, but like someone was talking in a lower voice on purpose," the store manager told officers on the scene, according to the police report.

I added details from my stories about the first two robberies and a note for the graphics editor to make a map to run with the piece, then tacked Detective Chris Landers's phone number on the end for residents to call with information and reread it before I sent it to Bob.

Snatching up my desk phone, I dialed Landers's cell.

Voicemail.

I didn't leave a message because I knew he wouldn't listen to it anyway, clicking over to the text screen and thumb-typing instead. *Need to ask you about the nightclub shooting. Please call me when you get a minute. Thanks!* Send.

I wasn't his favorite person, but Landers was nothing if not meticulous about his job. He'd call.

And in the meantime, I could go find someone who understood numbers better than I did.

"Feel like helping me with something I'm not supposed to tell anyone about?" I plopped into a threadbare gray chair in Grant Parker's office and smiled when he swiveled his chair and stretched. He didn't even wince anymore as he put his long arms all the way out over his head.

Thank God. Almost losing him last spring had hit me harder than anything short of when my mom was sick. Some days, I popped my head into his office just to make sure he was still breathing.

"I think I'm obliged to help you with just about anything you want, short of, like, taking our firstborn or something." Parker's lazy Virginia drawl was half-playful, his emerald eyes smiling right along with the rest of his face.

My eyebrows floated up. "Is there news about a firstborn?"

He laughed. "Not as far as I know. She might tell you first, you know—saving the love of her life has earned you Mel's unending gratitude."

I shook my head. "Just being a good friend."

"Which I will happily do in return. What d'you need?"

I nodded to his screen, cursor still flashing in the middle of a sentence. "You need to finish your column before I start bugging you?"

Parker was a local legend. Our resident charisma machine's former UVA baseball god status and smelling-salts-required good looks beaming off our sports page twice a week sold enough papers to keep the place afloat. Bob wouldn't look kindly on me messing with his mojo, no matter how good a cause I had as an excuse.

"Tomorrow's copy is already in. This is a feature for Wednesday. It'll wait."

I pulled out my laptop, opened my Photos app, and brought up the ones I'd taken of the journal articles. I flipped the screen around so he could see them.

"I need to know what all this means," I said.

He squinted, pulling my computer closer and moving his fingers over the trackpad to make the text larger. "It's a journal article about math."

"I managed to get that much, thanks."

He read for a minute before he raised his eyes to mine over the top of the screen. "Do I want to know why you care about this? My sense of honor says I'm supposed to protect you, though my sense of logic says you do a decent job protecting yourself, and I tend to get myself shot when I try to help."

"I can't say right now," I said.

He sat back in his chair. "That means it's something to do with what happened at the capitol this morning."

My head tipped to one side at the drop in his tone. Parker knew everyone. Had I missed a connection to this story right inside my own inner circle?

"Do you know something about that I should know?" I let the words drop carefully—not demanding, just curious.

He shook his head. Maybe a little too quickly. "I just know you. And I know enough about how politics works in this town to know a body inside the capitol is roughly a *Titanic*-level clusterfuck, with possible Hiroshima implications depending on where exactly it was found. I worry. That's all."

Not like I hadn't given people reason to. I smiled. "I'm like a cat. I always land on my feet."

"Probably something to do with the shoes." He winked. "So, this looks like a study of varying statistical models on the same control groups, changing variables to see how it changed the results."

I pulled out a pad and grabbed a pen out of the Richmond Generals cup on his desk. "Slower for those of us who don't math well, please." It made sense that he'd minored in statistics in college, since baseball is obsessed with numbers.

He grinned. "I like knowing something you don't. Is this how you feel, like, all the time?"

"I think your intrinsic self-confidence plays a role in how it affects you." I raised an eyebrow. "Some of us minored in psych. Politics, and all."

He rolled his eyes. "I might be insulted if anyone else called me full of myself, but I know you love me. Anyway. This is basically a study on how pliable people's opinions are. These folks took two groups of average adults and gave each a list of facts designed to help them form an opinion. The facts they gave group A were in direct contradiction to the facts they gave group B. You with me?"

I nodded, jotting that down.

"Then they took a poll of both groups and recorded the opinion results. Three weeks later, they went back to the same people and switched out half of the facts for each group. They took another poll and recorded both raw results and how the results shifted within each demographic subgroup."

"Okay." I kept writing, something tickling the back of my brain.

"Then another three weeks after that, they brought them back, gave group A the fact list group B started with and vice versa, and redid the poll again. Same data sets recorded."

Fascinating. I stood and walked around to look at the screen.

"It's pretty interesting to see the shifts." Parker scrolled down, pointing to the screen. "Caucasian men between twenty-five and forty were the most susceptible to persuasion. A full thirty percent of that group completely about-faced their stance from the beginning of the study to the end. African American women were the least pliable, with only two percent shifting their opinion at all, and even then, it wasn't dramatic."

"Does it say what the facts were about? I mean, she didn't convince these guys the sky was green or the grass was blue, right? And were there black women in both groups? Because you said the facts were contradictory."

I laid my pad on the desk next to the computer. Parker scrolled.

"It's probably in an abstract somewhere. Is this all you have?"

I nodded. "I took photos. There are more articles, but not more pages of this one."

"I'm sure you could go back and look it up. It's fascinating research." He sat back and folded his arms across his chest. "Why do you care?"

I clicked to the next photo. "I can't say. Is this one similar?"

He leaned back into the screen. "Not particularly. It's a model on how pre-perception influences taste in food."

I raised the eyebrow again. He laughed.

"If I tell you escargot is gross and then serve you some, are you really less likely to enjoy it than if I tell you escargot is great, or that what I'm serving you is something else entirely?"

I scrolled down.

"But it's still kind of the same thing. How to influence people." I was mostly talking to myself, but Parker nodded.

"I suppose you could consider it that way. You're really not going to tell me why?"

"Come on, you know how this works." I resumed my seat, jiggling one foot when I crossed my legs.

"And you know journalists are inherently nosy. You have the battle scars to prove it, even."

I nodded, not really listening as I twirled my pen through my fingers.

I was missing something.

I got it just as Parker noticed the byline on the study.

"I'm going to be the next Nate Silver." Lakshmi's voice floated through my thoughts tinged with that bell-like laugh, her confidence that she could rival the undisputed king of modern political statistics heavy in the words.

Learning how easy certain swaths of people were to influence and what pushed buttons went past political polling analysis and into voter manipulation, though.

"Lakshmi Drake? The call girl from the RAU scandal you helped disappear?" That was Parker, slapping my computer shut. "What is going on here, Clarke? Is she . . . Was some politician . . . Oh, holy shit." He slumped back in his chair. "Bob said you told him the body was in the governor's office. The governor and the hooker?"

I sprinted for the door and slammed it a little too hard, leaning against it when I turned back to face him. "No. Not the governor. I don't think, anyway. And you cannot say anything to anyone about any of this. Not even Mel."

He clenched his eyes shut. "So it is her?"

"Parker, please. You have to promise me you'll keep this totally to yourself." I should've taken the time to black-bar her name before I opened the pictures. Hindsight, something something.

No time for regrets now, though. I had to stop Parker from costing me Kyle's trust and blowing my exclusive. Keeping big things quiet in a newsroom is hard. Journalists are nosy by nature—at least, the good ones are. But we're also busybodies at the core, taking the things we find out and retelling the story in a manner interesting enough to get readers a little nosy, too. Like Bob spilling the location of the remains to Parker, probably without a second thought.

He nodded. "Of course. Whatever you need. But you have to promise me something, too."

I waved a circular *Come on out with it.*

"I'm used to watching you run off after the truth without a thought to what's going to happen to you when whoever doesn't want people knowing what they've done finds you. But people who play politics at this level play for keeps. Be extra careful, and don't be too stubborn to ask for help. From me, or from the big dude who was glued to you at our reception that we all just pretend we didn't see because you won't talk about him."

I was kind of hoping Parker had been too hopped up on pain meds and romance that night to notice Joey. But I could deal with that later. The dead woman, the governor's political life, and my looming deadline were enough trouble for now. Subject change.

My phone buzzed in my pocket like it heard that last thought.

What now? A *Happy Halloween* from Michael Myers himself wouldn't have shocked me the way my day was going.

Landers: *No time to talk. Nightclub suspect in custody. Tyler Gaines, 21, RAU student. History with the victim, not random, no other injuries.*

Good. That would be an easy write-up. Easy, I could take, with this thing around Lakshmi Drake shaping up to be anything but. I tucked the phone away, turning back to Parker. As long as he knew what was going on, he might as well be a sounding board.

"The first time I met Lakshmi, she told me she was going to be the next Nate Silver." I crossed back to his desk and opened my laptop, reading the top of the food test results. "This study was done that summer, right before I met her."

I clicked back to the first page. Title, byline . . . date.

My eyebrows scrunched together.

"What's up?" Parker asked.

"This one, with the opinion-changing thing, was just published this spring. More than a year after she left her program at RAU."

"Maybe it took a while to find a journal to publish it," Parker said.

I nodded. Maybe. But Lakshmi had published several articles with this same academic journal, so not likely.

I reached for the pad and pen again and copied the other three names on the byline.

Could one of these folks shed some light on what Lakshmi had been up to?

6

Journalism in the Age of the Internet 102: social media will tell you a lot more about young people than they should ever want you to know.

One of the students who worked on the study with Lakshmi was in Africa, teaching in a school on the savanna. One was pursuing a PhD at Duke.

And the third was a friend—a close friend, from the number of Instagram photos—of Hamilton Baine.

Jackpot.

I put a star by his name and opened two blank files, pulling out my notes from the trial and Landers's text about the shooting. Thirty-six minutes to deadline. I work best under pressure.

The nightclub story was as straightforward as a crime story gets. Five paragraphs of nothing but facts with one quote from Landers (such that it was), it would fit nicely in the sidebar of our Metro front. I sent it to Bob and clicked the other blank window, shuffling facts in my memory and forgetting the rest of my harried day in the harmony of the story and the keystrokes.

. . .

Gasps and shouts erupted in the gallery of 13th circuit court judge Jeff Monroe's court Friday, causing Monroe to threaten clearing the room after the commonwealth's star witness admitted to stealing from the defendants in a murder trial stemming from a February mobile home explosion that left two people dead and three more, including said witness, injured.

But it was the fireworks in the hallway after Monroe adjourned that changed the whole case.

Moments after drawing an admission of guilt from Jerry Joe Stickley on allegations of theft, Defense Attorney Craig Terry said his clients were changing their plea. Details of the deal with the commonwealth weren't immediately available.

"The commonwealth has done an excellent job of stating its case this week, and the evidence on their side is formidable," Terry said. "In light of the arguments presented here, my clients have agreed to change their plea."

Before that, Terry hammered Stickley with quick questions during the cross-examination.

"Jerry, how much did my clients agree to pay you for your services?" Terry asked.

"I got a third of what I sold. Half for hooking a new customer," Stickley, who admitted to selling methamphetamine in a deal with prosecutors that guaranteed him house arrest, but no prison time, said. "Maybe a grand. Probably. Usually."

"And how about if you add in what you were stealing?" Terry asked.

When the courtroom quieted, Stickley admitted he knew the defendants had discovered his profit-skimming.

"Scooter told me they were onto me," he said.

Ricky Wayne Lesko, known to his friends as "Scooter," was one victim of the explosion. The other was six-year-old Dakota Simpson, who was sleeping in his room at the end of the mobile home next door.

I filled in the rest of the details, ran back through the story to proofread, and sent it to Bob with one minute to spare.

Now. Back to Wyatt Bledsoe.

I opened a notebook and my web browser, typing his name into the DMV database first. He lived about nine blocks west of my office, in a trendy building full of lofts popular with the upper-class hipster crowd.

Next, social media: he'd graduated from Madison in May with a master's in statistics, and was working . . . Oh, hell.

He was on Governor Baine's staff. Youth issues and voting rights.

I tapped my index finger on the edge of the keyboard, studying his smile. I needed this guy to talk to me. But he wasn't just friends with Hamilton—he worked for Hamilton's dad.

Which meant he wouldn't want to so much as be in a room with me.

I clicked back to his Instagram feed and scrolled through photos.

Hamilton and Wyatt at a bar. At the beach. Raising beers at a baseball game.

Maybe Parker could help me with this story after all.

I didn't get that written down before an email from Bob flashed in the corner of my screen.

Nice work, kid. Still no update to the actual big story of the day?

I rolled my eyes and stood, detouring through the break room for a Diet Coke on my way to his office.

"Nothing I can print yet," I said, tapping on the doorframe as I stuck my head around it.

"You're killing me, Nicey. And you'd better hope Charlie Lewis doesn't slaughter you."

I gestured to his computer, stepping closer to his desk. "She didn't have anything new at five. It's coming up on six. What are they teasing?"

He clicked the bookmark for the Channel Four site at the top of his screen. "Trial day four."

"She doesn't have my sources, Bob. I will get this first. But I have to make sure I get it right. I can't burn Kyle without making you regret that later as much as I will."

He shook his head. "I'm not asking you to burn your source. Just make sure you're not holding back."

"Have I ever had an issue with such a thing?" I put a hand on his shoulder.

"I don't suppose you have," he said. "Weekend plans?"

"It was supposed to be quiet. But it's looking busier every minute."

He clicked back to his design window, placing my sparse story on the suspicious remains in the capitol building below the fold on the front before he touched a few keys, added an image of the building with a credit to our photo editor, and dropped the file in the production department folder.

Pushing his chair back, he switched the monitor off.

"I'm going hiking in the mountains with a group from the Sierra Club tomorrow. I will likely be out of cell range." He gestured for me to walk in front of him to the door, pulling his battered black leather briefcase from under the desk. "Enjoy your evening. Get your story. Do not get yourself killed while I'm gone."

He winked as he shut the light off and pulled the door closed behind us. "I'm only half kidding."

"Which half?" I smiled. "Have fun on your hike. Don't overdo it, please." Two and a half years on since his heart attack, and I could still feel the terror of finding him in that chair not breathing like it happened this afternoon.

I carried my soda back to my desk and tapped the trackpad, bringing my screen to life, as I sipped it.

My email icon flashed in the corner again. Clicking the window up, I almost spewed soda all over my keyboard.

I didn't recognize the return address, but I damn sure knew that name at the bottom.

There are things you should know about Lakshmi. Come see me.

Signed Angela Baker, former dean of students at RAU, physical mailing address for the next quarter century or so: cellblock seven at Cold Springs, on nine counts of procuring sex workers.

Lakshmi's madam.

* * *

I couldn't get a visitor's pass for the prison until Monday, and needed a craftier angle—or help from a friend—before I tried Wyatt Bledsoe. That guy would spot a pump job at fifty paces, and I'd only get one shot. Had to make it count. Parker's office was dark and locked, so I wandered back to my cube and swiped my computer screen back to life.

I clicked the Channel Four bookmark at the top of my browser window and watched the first ten minutes of the six o'clock; Charlie didn't have anything on me. I had more detail on the trial by virtue of space. They didn't mention the murder at the capitol until after the second break, and then it was just updated footage of officers standing sentry while people milled in the background with a recap of the nonstory Aaron had offered before noon.

Not a bad end to the week.

I dropped my phone and my laptop into my bag, ready to head home for a glass of wine and a long, hot bubble bath.

Darcy bounced on the white tile kitchen floor, pawing my foot before I got a half step in the door. I stooped to scratch her fluffy ears, smiling when she twisted her neck to lick my hand.

"Hi, princess," I crooned, scooting her backward so I could put my bag down and kick the door closed. "I hope your day was quieter than mine."

She flopped onto her back and presented me with a pink belly to rub. I obliged, giggling when she grumbled low in her throat. "I've never heard of a dog that purred." I stood up straight, reaching for the purple leash hanging by the door. The bathtub would still be there in a half hour.

Darcy scrambled to her feet, lifting her chin so I could clip the lead to her collar.

"Me too, girl," I said, following her back outside.

We had a usual route, a one-mile loop around my little stone Craftsman in the Fan. The streets in my neighborhood aren't for the easily confused, the whole area named for the way it spreads at an angle from the central part of downtown, resembling an old-fashioned hand fan. Darcy, however, is an old pro. She knows exactly where to turn, which yards have the best chance of a squirrel sighting, and to stop and look for Mrs. Powers at the corner. The latter is almost always working in her flowerbeds, which have graced the cover of many a magazine—and every dog in the Fan loves her because she keeps peanut butter snaps from the dog bakery in Carytown in her gardening apron.

Darcy stopped at the foot of the steps leading to Mrs. Powers's sidewalk and yipped.

"Good evening." Her voice was deep and lilting with just a hint of a warble, her drawl dropping the final *g* and elongating the vowels. I couldn't tell if the greeting came from inside or outside, thanks to crisp evening air and open windows lining the front of the house. Darcy tugged at the leash, making for the right-side yard.

I followed, watching my step around the bright palettes of mums and petunias, blazing reds and yellows stealing the spotlight from the last few blue-purple hydrangea blooms of summer.

Mrs. Powers rounded the far corner of the house and knelt to pet Darcy when I turned the leash loose.

Darcy yipped again, nosing at the pocket on the left of the apron. "I know, sweetheart. Here you go." Mrs. Powers pulled off her gloves and fished out a little heart-shaped cookie. Darcy munched the treat as Mrs. Powers ran a hand through her long, rust-colored fur. The older woman smiled up at me when I stopped in front of them. "She's such a sweet one, Nicey. Nice to see you girls."

"Always good to see you, ma'am. The yard is breathtaking, as usual." I picked up the end of Darcy's leash and looped it around my wrist. "Such a lovely evening to be outside."

"I do love Richmond in the fall." Mrs. Powers shifted onto her backside and stretched her legs out in front of her, crossing them at the ankle. Her loose linen pants rode up to show an inch of skin starting to lose its summer tan. Darcy wriggled into her lap, resting her nose near the apron pocket.

"You are too much, you know that?" Mrs. Powers scratched Darcy's chin, shaking her head. "You don't spoil her at all."

"Not a bit." I grinned.

"Can she have another?"

"If it's okay with you."

"It's always okay with me." She winked, pulling another cookie out for Darcy and stroking her fur while she gobbled it. "So what's new in the news business? I haven't seen much of you lately."

I perched on the stone edge of a raised bed of fall-blooming coral azaleas and smiled. "I've been busy with things besides work, as it happens, but work is good. Tiring today. But good."

"Your gentleman friend is very handsome, if you like that tall, dark, and quiet type—and who doesn't?" She laughed. "His car hasn't been here so much lately. I was starting to worry. I'm glad to know you're happy."

"He got an apartment down by the river a few months ago. We spent a lot of the summer there—Darcy loves walking along the water and barking at the birds, and the view is just gorgeous."

She nodded, plucking a fading goldenrod flower from the mum next to her. "I saw on the TV this afternoon that there was a ruckus at the capitol this morning. You know what happened?"

"I can't really talk about that." The words dripped apology. "I'm working on the story and my sources are very sensitive."

"I suppose I'd expect that when there's a dead whore on the governor's desk." The dark words didn't match her sweet tone even a little, her fingers still working absently through Darcy's fur. "Shame about that. I like Thomas. I like his wife. And they've had enough trouble without another sex scandal."

7

I tried to get words out for a good minute, but damned if I could remember how to make my lips work.

Mrs. Powers smiled, scratching Darcy's ears and setting her on the perfectly clipped emerald lawn. "Tell you what. Why don't you come on in the house. I'm parched, and I have a fresh pitcher of tea in the fridge."

I nodded and followed her, Darcy trotting at my side sniffing the air in the general direction of Mrs. Powers and her apron.

Seated at a charming raw pine farm-style dining table in a breakfast room brightened by twin skylights overhead and a large picture window overlooking the back deck, I smiled and thanked Mrs. Powers when she set a glass of tea in front of me. She poured herself one, filled a crystal goblet with water and put it in front of Darcy, and took the chair across from mine.

I sipped my tea, watching her. I'd known Mrs. Powers since my second day in Richmond. Tiny puppy Darcy and I were exploring the neighborhood and got turned around by the crazy angled streets. The third time we passed her house, Mrs. Powers asked if she could help me find anything, made fast friends with Darcy, and told us how to get home. The next day, she was waiting with the fancy doggie cookies when we walked past.

And all this time I didn't know my sweet, dog-loving, flower-whisperer neighbor moved in powerful political circles? Some investigative reporter I was. But one thing I was sure of: whichever one of us talked first would lose here.

She let the silence stretch into awkward range before she spoke. "You know I was a preschool teacher."

I nodded.

"The part of that I always find too pretentious to tell folks is that I owned the preschool. I always hired someone to do the administrative things, because the little ones were my loves, and I enjoyed every minute I spent in the classroom. And my Harry, Lord rest him"—she crossed herself —"was a senior vice president at First Commonwealth Bank."

Governor Baine's first job out of law school was on the bank's legal staff, according to my research.

My phone buzzed an incoming call in my pocket. I clicked the power button to make it stop.

Thirty seconds later, a single vibration meant I had a voicemail or a text.

I nodded at Mrs. Powers. *Stay quiet, let her talk.* Everything else could wait.

She sipped her tea. I followed suit. Sweeter than I usually liked, but just the right hint of lemon made up for it. I took another sip before I put the glass down.

"Harry had an eye for hotshots," she said. "He told me the first time he met Thomas the boy was going to be someone special someday. I wish he had lived to see how special. He was the bank's chief counsel back then and took Thomas right under his wing, thinking he'd help him out. But Thomas didn't need Harry's help—if anything it was the other way around. He was bright. Quick. Made the department look good to the big bosses in New York. Two years on, Harry was promoted to VP mostly to get him out of the way so Thomas could take over legal. They played golf together. Thomas and Leslie got married and we'd spend weekends joined at the hip, the four of us. Thomas had a thousand questions about early childhood education, the benefits of what we did, and how it might help kids whose parents couldn't afford to pay. We'd stay up till the wee hours, talking out the finer points of giving kids their best start." She sighed, turning to stare out the window. "Nichelle, honey, when you get to be my age, you'll understand how the world works a little better. I wish I'd been better at under-standing it back then."

Uh-oh. I kept my face neutral, her "another sex scandal" comment rattling around my head.

I drained my tea glass. She turned back to the table and refilled it.

"Anyway. The next summer, Thomas filed to run for the school board. He wanted to start an early childhood education program in the city's poorest schools. Give those kids the same chance the kids he wanted someday would have. He won, of course, and by the time Hamilton was born, he was chairman of the school board and eyeing a run for mayor."

She stared at her hands. "It would have destroyed him."

Every muscle in my body tensed, keeping my ass glued to the chair when I wanted to crawl across the table and scream, "What? Who?"

I had the back of her train of thought by my fingertips, but I needed a little hand to get on board.

How did she know what had happened this morning when I'd practi-cally been threatened with jail should I let it slip? Surely the governor wasn't confiding in an old girlfriend.

I cleared my throat. "So you're still close with the family?" I asked when the silence had stretched around the house and back.

"Of course, darling." Her drawl swallowed the *g* again. "Hamilton Baine is my husband's son."

I sucked in a breath so sharp Darcy sat up and barked. "I . . . I'm sorry. What?" I stammered.

She rested her elbows on the table and leaned forward. "You're not putting any of this in the newspaper, now, are you?"

Shit.

That was a tricky question. On the one hand, she was my neighbor and this was obviously a complicated part of her life she was sharing with me. I liked Mrs. Powers. On the other, she knew I was a reporter and she never said it was off the record. The general rule is, you don't get to backtrack and take a comment or conversation off after you've said it. The terms are always on the table up front, and everyone has to agree.

But.

Was she sure she was talking to a reporter from the *Telegraph*, and not her neighbor Nichelle who had the sweet little dog?

I'd lean toward no. People who don't deal with the press on the regular don't know the rules. I wasn't at work. I didn't even have a notebook with me—the closest thing I could write anything down on was a doggie poop bag I'd tied to Darcy's leash.

Which meant it came down to one thing: What did my readers need to know? And I didn't have enough information to be sure yet.

"Nichelle?" She put her tea glass down. "I was supposed to ask you that before I started blabbering, right? That's the way they do it in the movies."

I spread my hands like a blackjack dealer, hoping like hell I didn't regret it later. "I don't have a notebook with me."

"I've just been so upset about this all day." She refilled her glass. "When I saw you and Darcy come up, I was hoping you'd know something that might help me calm down." She held out one shaking hand.

Poor thing. I wanted to help her feel better. I also wanted to know the rest of this story.

"Mrs. Powers, how do you know what happened this morning?"

"Ham sent me a note this morning. On my phone. Text, is what he calls it. About all I ever hear from the boy these days, he's so busy."

She pulled an iPhone out of her pants pocket, tapped the screen, and handed it to me.

A message thread labeled *Ham* at the top of the screen, three or four recent back-and-forths about the weather or a flower show followed by one marked 6:34 a.m.: *She's dead. Right on Jefferson's desk, and I wasn't even in there. I don't know what happened. What am I going to do?*

She'd answered him right away, as any sane person would: *What?*

She didn't get a reply to her question.

I handed the phone back. "Mrs. Powers, how did you know who Hamilton was talking about?"

Darcy put her front two paws on Mrs. Powers's knee. Reaching to pet the dog, the older woman shook her head at me.

"I told him she was trouble, that one. A beauty—Lord, yes—but trouble. From the second I laid eyes on her, I knew, but he wouldn't listen. His first big love, I think. He stayed right up underneath her, didn't like to be away from her almost from the beginning. Even when we found out she was a whore, he said there were reasons I didn't understand." She fed Darcy another cookie and sat up straight. "I understand plenty. She was after power, she finally got to Thomas, and something went wrong—that's what I think. But I'm afraid Ham will do something he'll live to regret if he finds out who killed her before the police do. He's a smart boy. Big heart. But a little awkward and very introverted."

I pinched the bridge of my nose, leaning my elbow on the tabletop.

"I'm sorry, dear. You've probably had a long day, and here I am mucking it up with my family problems. Can I get you something to nibble on? I made scones with the lemons from my tree yesterday."

Family problems. Boy, there was a story behind those two loaded little words. Idle political dirt or helpful information, I didn't know.

Only one way to find out.

"A scone sounds wonderful, Mrs. Powers," I said, sitting back in the chair. "Forgive me. It has been a long day, and I'm trying to make sense of all this." I wasn't telling her I knew Lakshmi—we didn't need yet another layer of complication. Time to start at the beginning.

"So, your husband passed away . . ." I let it trail, trying to remember how long it had been.

"Nineteen months and six days," she said softly, pulling the lid off a glass cake stand on her island. The scones inside looked like bakery showpieces—apparently the garden wasn't the only place she had a gift. She put one on a plate for each of us, brushing frosting and sugar crystals off her fingers before she brought them to the table and returned to her seat.

Darcy stood up and nosed at her hand. I clicked my tongue against the roof of my mouth and shook my head when she looked at me. "No more treats. You won't eat your food." The vet had her on a special diet for aging small dogs, as much as I hated to think about it. Darcy wasn't aging. She was fine.

Mrs. Powers scratched her ears. "I'm out, anyway, sweetness. I'll have to drop by the goodie shop this weekend."

I broke off a corner of the scone and almost sighed when the tangy sweetness melted across my tongue. "You are a heck of a baker yourself."

"I like to piddle in the kitchen." She smiled. "You have an excellent poker face, young lady."

I raised an eyebrow and she laughed.

"I know you must be dying to know about Ham and why he talks to me, why I talk to him, why Harry and I stayed married . . . But you're doing a very good job of keeping that to yourself."

I laughed. "You're a smart woman, Mrs. P. It is the nature of most reporters to be nosy, I'm afraid, and I'm sure you have a story to tell."

She picked up her scone and bit off a third of it, staring out the window as she chewed. Swallowing, she refocused on me. "How to explain such a thing to a young woman who's never been married? Who grew up in a time when women could be and do and have anything?" She shook her head. "In my day, a woman as the president of the United States was so far-fetched I'd have gladly laid money we'd put men on Mars first. Men who could breed flying Martian pigs. I never thought the day would come, let alone that I'd live to see it."

"I know things were different not so long ago."

Her lips tipped up the barest hint, her long, thin fingers going to the diamond band that still circled the third finger of her left hand. "Harry was a good man. We met the spring of my first year at William & Mary. He was a senior, getting ready to go on to law school and then take on the world. Change it. I was head over heels by the time he dropped me outside my dorm that first night."

Her green eyes took on a faraway sheen, cheeks flushing at the memory of long-ago first love. I smiled, Kyle's foot-shuffling lead-up to my first kiss filtering through my thoughts.

"He finished law school the year I finished my teaching degree, but I didn't really figure on ever needing to use it. I was a young attorney's wife. Harry wanted a big career, maybe politics. My job was to run a household and raise a family that would support that."

Her face changed, and I saw the next words coming before they hit my ears. They didn't have any kids.

"I couldn't give him children." Her voice thickened the barest bit, her eyelids fluttering blue white over tears she refused to let pass. "He said he didn't care. We looked into adoption, but the costs to find a suitable infant were too much for even Harry's salary. He focused on his career, and I opened the school so I could help raise as many babies as I liked."

I blinked hard at the pricking in the backs of my own eyes, breaking off another bit of scone.

"Thomas and Leslie were so sweet. So stuck on each other. They made Harry and me remember what it was like to be young and in love. I think that's part of the reason we were so close with them so easily."

"And you and Gov . . . er . . . Mr. Baine were spending all that time together talking about education," I prodded when she got quiet. She nodded.

"Harry and I never knew whether it was me or him, you know. I suggested asking a doctor when we kept trying and it didn't work, and he said he didn't want to know because it didn't matter. We were an us, he said, and if we couldn't have a baby then we just couldn't, it wasn't in the Lord's plan for us, and he didn't want to know why."

Her thin shoulders lifted with a deep breath. "So, it was me, as I learned when my husband spent one night, just the one, with another woman while I was busy running my mouth about access to education for kids whose parents couldn't afford it. Hamilton looks much more like his mother now, but when he was first born . . . well. Black couples don't often have babies with ghost-white skin and green eyes. Thomas was furious, but he kept it together. Leslie told him everything, and he threatened to sue any of the medical personnel in the delivery room who might talk.

"We all sat down together and agreed that nobody ever needed to know. Thomas's name is on Ham's birth certificate. But we all raised him. Together. He called us Auntie Sue and Uncle Harry. And when he was old enough to understand, we told him the truth. He and I have been close ever since—he wrote me a long letter once about how much he admired me being strong enough to stay with Harry. I never really thought about leaving. I have always believed things happen for a reason: we got Ham out of it, and I love that child more than I love breathing and coffee and good southern cooking. I prayed for a baby for ten years, and the Lord gave me one the only way nature would allow. How could I leave my husband over something I'd prayed for?"

I scarfed the rest of my scone, blinking harder when tears welled despite my best efforts. In nine years in the newsroom and five in and out of courtrooms, I knew better than most people twice my age that life can throw all kinds of impossible decisions at you straight out of the blue.

What you choose, which consequences you can accept, are deeply personal, defined by your psyche and life experience. I'd watched from the front row as impossible decisions saved lives, and ended them. I'd seen people go to prison for choosing poorly, and been personally hailed as a hero for choosing well. The thing I'd learned was there's often not a right or wrong—there's only what you can live with. Mrs. Powers sounded like she'd lived fine with the decision she'd made. She didn't need to justify a damned thing to me.

Back to today. "You didn't hear from Hamilton after this?" I pointed to her phone.

She shook her head. "I've been a nervous wreck all day. Can't stop thinking about it." She picked up my plate. "So. Is Tom screwing his son's girlfriend? Or was he?"

I tilted my chin up, locking eyes with her. Her hands still trembled enough to rattle the plates, her voice shaking the barest bit.

"I honestly don't know." Every word true. It seemed there were all kinds of skeletons in the Baine family's closets, and I had no idea which ones Lakshmi might've been part of. Yet.

What I did know: nine hours on, this was shaping up to be the biggest story I'd seen in a while. Maybe even ever. I liked Governor Baine. But I couldn't let that cloud my judgment. The truth—objective, good, bad, indifferent—that's what I was after. And I would get there before Charlie did. I had to.

"Will you let me know what you find out?" Mrs. Powers asked, her eyes filming over with tears.

"Of course, ma'am." The thought of this sweet lady fretting over a massive scandal she couldn't control any more than the weather made my heart feel too big for my chest. I stood, clipping Darcy's leash back to her collar. "Try not to worry, Mrs. P. I'm sure it will all work out just fine. These things look bigger than they are right at first."

I wasn't sure I believed the words as I said them, but they seemed to do the trick. She smiled, setting the plates in the sink before she spun back and enveloped me in a rib-crushing hug. "Thank you, darling."

I patted her back until she stepped away. "Of course, ma'am. You try not to worry and have yourself a relaxing weekend."

"I will try." She walked beside us to the polished walnut and leaded-glass front door and opened it. "I hope you get some time with your young man this weekend."

I led Darcy down the steps, checking my watch. I had about an hour to see what Google had to say about Mr. Powers. This particular curve, I was staying ahead of. Secrets are funny things: they have a way of slipping out of the shadows whether folks want them to or not, and often at exactly the wrong time.

8

Harry Powers was practically a choir boy.

Practically.

Google had thirteen hits, ten of them articles from our archives about charity work he'd spearheaded. Plus one profile on LinkedIn no one had taken down after his death, and two data site listings. Nothing shady. No hints of questionable business deals, cases gone wrong. He should've run for office; he'd have been the perfect politician. Except for the son he'd fathered through the affair nobody knew about.

His wife said he'd started his career with big ambitions. They must've evaporated the second Hamilton Baine took his first breath. No way a skeleton that juicy stays in a closet through a political campaign. I got it. There were days I read Trudy's stories and thanked my lucky stars for the crime desk: Politics had gone from a cerebral pursuit of the greater good to a no-holds-barred cage match of scandal and secrets. The farther below the belt the hits came, the better. Murderers and thieves are an easier bunch to read than most politicians, and a generally more sympathetic group, too.

When I thought too hard about the implications of that, it made me sad, so I let it go.

Setting my laptop on the quilt, I picked up my boots and plopped them into their spot on my shoe rack, shaking my head. For half my life, I'd wanted to write about politics because great speeches and big ideas inspired me. Sharing those messages, dissecting and explaining them to readers, helping compile the first draft of history from right on the front lines—I couldn't think of a more noble pursuit for a writer. Thomas Baine had given me hope for that again, watching him on the campaign trail as he listened to Virginians from all walks of life, and hosted upwards of a hundred events, from VFW breakfasts to packed-out town halls, in all corners of the state. He held himself above the cage match, looking at people instead of any given area's historic voting demographics. Patience, class, and nonpartisan handshaking and baby-kissing won the Virginia governor's mansion by a double-digit margin the Associated Press analysts called less than an hour after the polls closed. A bona fide landslide.

And here he was a year later, up to his Brooks Brothers Windsor knot in the kind of scandal most politicians don't come back from.

I closed my computer and picked up my phone to see if the message from earlier was from Joey. Strike one. Trudy, telling me to expect a call from an Agent Chaudry of the Secret Service. Holy Manolos. I couldn't help a tiny smile at that, even as frustrated as I felt. But my missed call was from a Cleveland number, not a DC one, with no associated voicemail. Do-not-call list, my scuffed patent leather boot.

I padded to the bathroom in bare feet and turned the spigots, watching water fill the massive claw-footed tub. I shook in a couple of drops of oil and some lavender bubble bath and went to the kitchen in search of a glass of wine.

Setting my red Moscato on the pink-tiled bathroom counter after one sip, I shut off the water and pulled in a deep breath, the sweet smell from the lavender letting my shoulders drop away from my ears a bit.

I was three more sips into the wine and up to my chin in the bubbles before the question prodding the back of my brain surfaced.

The wineglass shattered across the tile floor, shards flying, red wine flowing over the powder-pink ceramic diamonds.

Darcy came running and I scrambled to a sitting position, water and bubbles sloshing up the sides of the tub. "No!" She stopped in the doorway, tipping her head to one side with an *Excuse me?* look on her face.

"You'll cut your feet," I said, like she could understand. She backed up two steps and sat down on the scarred hardwood in the hallway. Hell, maybe she did.

"Good girl. Stay." I sank back into the bubbles, my mind still whirring through Baine's gubernatorial campaign.

Twenty-first century politics is outlandish Fashion Week spike-covered Louboutins ugly.

If Hamilton was enough to keep Harry Powers from politics, how in the blue hell did Thomas Baine make it all the way to the governor's mansion with that skeleton still tucked safely in his cedar-lined closet?

* * *

I still didn't have a good answer for that when I heard the deadbolt on the front door squeal out of its home, Darcy's claws clicking on the wood floor as she scurried to the foyer.

"Hey there, sweetheart." My stomach still did the slow flip thing when I heard Joey's voice, even when he was talking to Darcy.

"Nicey?" He sounded about two steps short of the bathroom door when he called for me.

"In here." I sank farther into the bubbles and smiled when he poked his face around the doorframe, his eyebrows already up. They inched up higher, a smile stretching his full lips over teeth that flashed bright white against his olive skin. Eight o'clock shadow peppered his jaw and chin, his tie loose, the top button of his starched blue cotton shirt undone.

Damn, but he was beautiful.

"Well hello there." His voice got deeper, his dark eyes widening. "Care for some company?"

"Watch your step," I said, raising one hand through the bubbles to point at the floor.

He shucked his jacket before he disappeared with a quick grin and a raised finger, returning with my broom and dustpan in his left hand and an old towel draped over his shoulder. "Can't risk bare feet coming out of the tub onto that."

He stepped into the room and I gasped when his right arm came around the side of the door. It sported a thick plaster splint and what looked like several layers of bandages. All I could see were his fingertips and three feet of taupe elastic wrap. That's why he'd sounded weird on the phone. He was hurt.

"That looks unpleasant," I said.

He shook his head. "ER overkill. I took a bad meeting out on my knuckles. They patched it up like my hand was in danger of falling off."

Um. What?

I sat up, wrapping my arms around my knees and fixing him with my best *You're not getting off that easy* stare. "Bad meeting?"

"Just some jackass hiding behind red tape. I needed some information, he said he couldn't get it, I know he could if he wanted to." He flashed the grin that still made my stomach do a slow rollover. "I'm sure you're familiar with the frustration. And the outlet." He made a punching motion with his hand.

Ah-ha. For all that we seemed so different on the surface, we had a lot in common: the abnormal level of life-and-death situations in our days required safe ways to blow off steam, so I had my body combat classes, and Joey had the boxing gym.

"Bag or actual human?" I sank back into the water.

"In my defense, he had a mouth on him like nothing I've ever heard, and that's saying something."

I shook my head, my eyes scanning his face. A tiny purplish spot under his right eye corroborated his story. Thank God for headgear—sparring was all good, healthy stress relief until someone's temper slipped away from him. But it could've been way worse.

"Is it broken?"

"Five X-rays and an MRI later, it's a bone bruise. I'll be good as new in a couple of weeks." He kept his eyes on the broom, moving the wet glass into a careful pile. "Something startle you, baby?"

"I had an epiphany about this mess at the capitol and dropped my glass." I sighed. "One of these days, I'm going to learn to stop saying it out loud when I've had an easy week."

He pushed a pile of glass shards into the dustpan and set about wiping up the Moscato. "You were so excited this morning, you were texting me in all caps. That wasn't about this corpse at the capitol?"

"Hold on. Do I actually have a story you don't already know the behind the scenes of before I even see you? I'm going to come back to the whole 'I know something you don't know' feeling in a moment, because no, it was not."

He dumped the glass in the wastebasket and dropped the sopping towel in the washer, which was nestled next to the end of the tub thanks to the 1930s plumbing. "Good as new." He went to work on his shirt buttons, slowly thanks to the clunky bandaged hand. "So what were you so excited about so early on a Friday, then?"

I watched his fingers work, distracted by the defined pecs they were revealing. He chuckled. "Princess? You were saying?"

I shook my head, my eyes not moving as he pulled the shirt carefully past the splint and hung it on the hook on the back of the door.

Frowning, he eyed his makeshift cast.

"Plastic grocery bags are in the box on the pantry floor," I said. "There's duct tape in the third drawer near the door in the kitchen."

He nodded and turned for the kitchen again, taking the broom and dustpan with him and coming back with waterproofing supplies.

"Scoot up," he said, the long fingers of his left hand moving to his Italian leather belt.

I pulled my knees up and hunched forward around them, focusing on the water faucet as he wrapped his hand, hung up his slacks, and slid into the tub behind me.

"How long have you been in here?" he grumbled, reaching for the hot water knob.

I pulled the chain on the plug, holding up my wrinkled fingers for inspection. "Too long."

His breath went in sharply as his bare back settled against the cold iron, and I scooped the warm water pouring from the faucet toward him with cupped hands. "Sorry. Better?"

He grabbed my shoulder with his good hand and pulled me back against his chest. "That is." He sighed, resting his chin on top of my head as he wrapped his arms around me. I didn't even notice the itchy wet plastic, every muscle going limp as I relaxed into him.

"I missed you this week," he said. "I've gotten spoiled to having you around all the time. Are you sure you don't want—"

I arched my neck back for a kiss, cutting off the rest of that statement before we could start down move-in-with-me avenue. It led straight to knock-down-drag-out-ville, and I wasn't interested in visiting again anytime soon.

Sitting in my bathtub kissing Joey was fabulous. Living with him was a great hearts-and-rainbows fantasy, but in the real world? Impractical.

Subject change.

"Trudy asked me to cover a speech the president is giving here next week!" I blurted when he raised his head.

Joey's arms loosened, for just a fraction of a second, his chest going still under my back. "She—" He cleared his throat when his voice hitched. "She what?"

A chill skated up my spine despite the hot water pooling around me. His face had gone pale with olive undertones, his eyes locked on the coral seahorse stickers on the tile wall, unblinking.

Shit.

"You can't go." His voice was flat. Hard.

"Excuse me?" I sat up, shutting off the hot water and splashing the last of the shrinking bubbles away from my ribs. I couldn't argue snuggled up to him in the tub. And ordering me to skip an assignment I'd dreamed about since forever was the express lane to an argument, which he damn well knew.

I blew my breath out in a *whoosh*, my eyes falling shut.

"What do you know, Joey?" I tucked my knees under my chin and swiveled to face him, leaning forward so I didn't catch my back on the faucet.

He blinked. Shook his head. "I can't have you in that room, princess. It's too dangerous. Haven't you been reading about the death threats in your own newspaper?"

Oh. I waved a dismissive hand. "She gets a hundred letters like that from crackpots a day. The Secret Service is the most highly trained security force on the planet. I'm probably safer in that room than I am sitting here with you."

He shook his head. "I'm sorry. I know how much you want this. But you can't."

Like hell I couldn't. I stood, reaching for a towel. "Something tells me this discussion is going to require clothing. And a lot more wine."

Stepping out of the tub, I pulled the towel tight around myself and tucked one twisted end under the other, wiping my feet dry on the small pink rug. "Why is it that whenever you want me to bail on an important assignment, you never will tell me why?"

I held out another towel. He sighed and took it, pulling the plug from the drain and getting to his feet. "Why is it you haven't learned to listen to me yet? Have I ever once been wrong?"

I planted my hands on my hips. No, he had not. But I also didn't regret ignoring his advice in the past. Anger bubbled up my throat. I swallowed.

Time out.

I strode to the bedroom, hoping the quick, jerky movements would alleviate some of my frustration. Joey knew things other people didn't. Sometimes bad things.

I shoved my arms into my robe, dropping the towel and yanking the sash so tight it pinched me. The more time stretched on, the tighter I clung to my secret fantasy that somehow this wasn't a one-way express to heartbreak. That he would find a way out of the Caccione family, that we *could* move in together, that there was a happily ever after in store for us somewhere.

I loathed any reminder of just how ridiculous a daydream that probably was.

Covering my face with both hands, I pulled in a deep breath. Darcy's claws clicked on the floor, coming closer behind me. Joey's hand landed on my shoulder.

"I'm sorry."

Two little words deflated my irritation. I sank back into him. "It's just—"

He slid his arms around my waist, the splint lying heavy on my hip bone. "I know."

And he did. I knew that, too. He'd risked just as much for me as I had for him. He'd uprooted his life and moved three hours south to be closer to me just a few months ago, and though he seemed fine with it, sometimes I wondered if it was everything he'd thought it would be. Did he come here thinking us moving in together was a foregone conclusion? Because how was that even remotely possible? I had spent weeks, since the first time he'd asked me about it, turning it every which way in my head, and it just flat wouldn't fit. Our lives were too different to try to mesh without risking . . . everything.

Why was he too stubborn to see that?

I wriggled, turning to face him and stepping back just enough to allow breathing space between us. "I cannot walk away from this opportunity. You know I can't."

"It's not safe."

"Neither is driving a car. Drinking coffee." I furrowed my brow, watching the muscle in his jaw that meant he was really annoyed—long reserved for moments when he had to breathe the same air as Kyle—flex in and out.

I took two big steps back, his arms falling away as he tipped his head to one side. "You okay?"

I shook my head so hard my hair half flopped out of its messy bun. "Do you know something, like really know something? Beyond what's been on the news? Why are you so intent on me skipping an assignment I've worked for half my life to get?"

He rolled his eyes. "You can't be serious."

That wasn't an answer.

"Joey. We still do a fair amount of don't ask, don't tell, and some days it's the only way we work. I know that. But if you know something about someone who's planning to . . ." I couldn't even say the words. It was too insane. People talk a big game, especially on the internet, but it's a once every other generation crackpot who's going to sacrifice their own life to try to murder the president of the United States. That wouldn't happen. Certainly not here. And if it could, Joey couldn't know about it and not tell anyone, for Chrissakes. He might have some shady business ties, but treason was a whole other level of shadow. He wouldn't.

He stretched one hand toward me. "I do not know anything more than you know." He paused. "Well. Maybe that's not entirely true."

I snatched back the hand that had started to creep toward his. "What?"

He shook his head. "And here I thought we were past the my-girlfriend-thinks-I'm-a-serial-killer hurdle."

My stomach didn't even do its usual flip when he called me his girlfriend. "How could you know something like this might happen and not alert the proper authorities? Call an anonymous tip line, for the love of God."

"I didn't mean I know something's going to happen." He sat down on the edge of the bed, retucking the aqua towel slung low on his hips. "I meant I see things in the everyday that you don't. Or won't."

Oh.

I sat next to him. "You see the Grim Reaper shadowing me with his sickle at the ready. To be fair."

He put his arm around me. "A more accurate picture is probably the Roadrunner. I see you walking blithely through trap after trap, danger after danger, and somehow managing to come out not too worse for wear compared to the people setting those traps."

It wasn't an unfair assessment from one perspective. But I deserved more credit than a cartoon bird.

"*Somehow* isn't chance, it's smarts," I said.

He turned, brushing a floppy hair strand out of my face. "I'm aware. I wasn't trying to insult you. I'm just afraid you're so excited about the opportunity here that you're not seeing the whole situation for what it is. Or maybe you are and you're too nice." He smiled when my eyebrow popped up at that. "You want to see the best in everyone. Believe me when I say that's one of the things I love about you. But I think it makes it hard for you to see real darkness in the world around you, too."

"So what darkness in the world am I missing today?"

He pointed to my laptop. "There are entire websites dedicated to photoshopped images of sick assholes doing horrible things to her. Politics today isn't the same game it was when she was a wide-eyed law student, when Reagan shook hands with Gorbachev, or when Clinton denied his dozens of affairs. The world has changed. We've had a front-row seat for it, and because of that sometimes it's hard to remember things aren't still the way they used to be. But they're not. Look at the headlines in your own paper.

Did the news talk about nutjobs shooting up schools and malls and churches when you were a kid?"

I shook my head, then laid it on his shoulder and put a hand alongside his face. He was working himself into a speech. "I know."

His shoulders dropped, his breath going out. "Then why don't you understand why I don't want you in a room with the most hated woman on the planet?"

"Oh, come on. She's never even been in the room with a single Kardashian. So I'm not sure that's a fair assessment."

"You would be if you spent thirty-five seconds on the dark web. And this is not funny." He tried to look stern. Didn't quite get there.

I sighed. He was just being his usual protective self, not the cryptic I-know-something-I-can't-really-tell-you mystery guy.

"So. The world is falling apart and bad people are feeding on each other's hate online, and there's not a damned thing we can do about it." I smiled. "Dinner, then?"

Joey's good arm tightened around my shoulders, and I snuggled my head into his collarbone. "I don't like fighting with you." My words came out muffled by his skin.

"Me either, princess. I just can't stand the thought of something happening to you. It's been a great six months being with you every day, you know?"

"I do." My voice was soft, the back of my brain conjuring a hazy fantasy of saying those words to him in front of our friends and family. I pushed it away.

This moment was all I needed.

I peppered his stubbly jaw with soft kisses, pushing his shoulder back toward the bed.

A low chuckle rumbled through his chest. "What was that you were saying about dinner?"

"I'm not hungry," I lied.

He fell back onto his elbows, his towel coming loose. I dropped my robe into a puddle of satin on the bed, twisting up onto one knee and settling astride his hips.

"I missed you this week." I reached up and pulled the few remaining pins out of my hair, letting it fall all the way down as I leaned forward. He sighed when it brushed his shoulders and chest.

"Me too." He put his hands on my knees, craning his neck upward as I covered his mouth with mine. His lips were soft, parting quickly, his good arm circling my waist and pulling me down to the comforter with him.

Fevered, deep kisses and strong hands and the scruff on his chin sent tiny shocks down my spine. Staying in the here and now. That was how this worked. I had all weekend to convince him I was right about covering the speech—and if I didn't, it wasn't like he could actually stop me from going.

"I really do love you, you know that?" he whispered.

I nodded, leaning in for another kiss. For tonight, I was right where I needed to be.

9

My coffee cooled on the counter as I pecked at my phone screen Saturday morning, my brow scrunched into hard creases no moisturizer would ever erase. Les Simpson. First thing on Saturday morning, blowing up my phone with bullshit questions about the "murder in the rotunda." Jackass couldn't even get the basics right, but somehow he was Bob's understudy.

I heard Joey's shuffling footsteps behind me and slammed the phone down on the counter, reaching for another fair-trade Colombian coffee pod.

"Morning, princess." He dropped a kiss on top of my head on his way to the fridge for the milk. "Why is your phone offensive this early in the day?"

"Bob is hiking up in the Blue Ridge," I grumbled, pulling a red ceramic mug from the cabinet and plunking it down as I punched the "Brew" button. The smell wafting from the machine settled my ruffled feathers a bit. I breathed deep.

Joey put the milk on the counter. "And you're pissed about that because . . . ? Is he feeling okay?"

I turned, the corners of my lips tipping up when my eyes landed on his bare chest. "I'm sure he's having a great time." I stepped into the circle of his outstretched arms and rested my forehead on his collarbone. "Les is, too, because he relishes any opportunity to be a pain in my ass."

"Ah." He ran his uninjured hand lightly up and down my back. "Doesn't he know it's Saturday? Why isn't he harassing the weekend stringer?"

I turned when the coffee maker beeped, pulled his mug out from under it, and added a pump of caramel syrup and a splash of milk before I handed it to him. "Emphasis on my previous statement."

I poured milk into my own cup and took it to the table, where the paper was already waiting. Joey took the other chair and reached for the business section while I flipped through the Saturday lifestyles, admiring the photos dotting my Southside feature. Lindsey had outdone herself. Joey struggled turning pages with his splint, so I reached across and flipped one for him.

We were so domestic it was downright cute.

My phone buzzed from the counter. "Go away, Les," I said.

Joey peered over the newsprint obscuring most of his face. "Seriously, what gives?"

"He's giving me hell about this murder. Acting like Charlie is going to beat me to the story if he doesn't nag me. Which is just stupid."

"We got distracted before you got to tell me about that last night. What the hell is going on over there?"

"Distracted? That's what we're calling it now?" I winked and sipped my coffee. "There's not a whole lot to tell yet, but I'm hoping I'll be able to dig up more today."

He tapped my story on the front page. "This isn't going to fly long if there's any politics around the corpse at all. Not that you don't already know that."

I put my cup back on the table. Shit. I did know that, but I hadn't framed the thought quite that way, and he was a hundred percent right. Virginia's law preventing consecutive terms in the governor's mansion meant Baine could be facing an assault from both sides. Charlie might not have better sources than I did, but a politician with sights on the governor's mansion? They knew how to dig up the rankest, smelliest dirt—and how to do it the fastest.

I jumped out of the chair and ran for my laptop. Opening it before I got back to the table, I typed Hamilton Baine's name into the browser search bar.

"Can I help?" Joey resumed his seat.

"You don't know who killed her, do you?" I flicked my eyes up at him and flashed a half smile. "Because that'd be super helpful."

He caught a sharp breath that sent him into a coughing fit.

I put the computer on the table and stood to thump him on the back. "You okay?"

He nodded, taking a couple of slow, deep breaths. "Good. Sorry—I didn't even know it was a her. Girlfriend? Secretary? Both?"

I returned to my chair and pulled the computer closer.

Joey touched the back of my hand with one finger. Not giving up, then.

How much should I say? I pinched my lips together. "What Kyle told me, he told me on deep, deep background . . . ," I began.

"Miller is in this? What did he tell you?" Joey's thick brows pulled together over his straight Grecian nose. "And why? I thought the state police protected the governor."

"Well, Kyle—" I paused. The more I turned that over in my head, the better a question it was. Like I didn't already have enough questions to juggle.

I looked up from the screen, shaking my head. "I don't know that, either." I puffed my cheeks full of air and blew it out fast.

My brain rewound through the press conference. Kyle texted me. Asked me to meet him way away from where the press corps was gathering. Aaron gave a crazy nonstatement, flanked by solemn-faced state troopers in wide-brimmed hats.

"I'm the only reporter in town who knows Kyle was there. So why would he tell me at all?"

Joey pressed his lips into a thin, pale line, tapping his index finger on the table. "What can you get that he can't? You say he told you something you can't tell anyone, and he knows you'll keep your word on that, so he's risking very little. For what reward?" His eyes stayed locked on me, dark and serious, as his good hand crept across the table to rest on mine.

"You are just full of insight this morning." I smiled.

"It's the endorphins. They're good for your brain." He winked.

I snorted. "I'll remember that."

"Experts will back me up." He leaned back in the little black bistro chair, his stoic expression relaxing a bit, his tone easier. "You need a sounding board?"

I tapped one finger on the edge of my keyboard, scrolling through headlines about the Baine kid. He was into sailing. Won a couple of regattas over the summer.

"You can't say anything to anyone." I stood, taking my half-full cup of cold coffee to the sink and rinsing both mugs before I put them in the dishwasher, mostly to keep my hands busy. Was this the right thing to do? I hadn't told Parker. I hadn't even told Bob. I turned back to face Joey, bracing both hands on the edge of the countertop and pulling in a deep breath.

"Of course not." His eyes roamed my face, mine flicking away when he tried to meet my gaze. "You can trust me."

The words floated on an undertone of hurt that pierced straight into my gut and twisted.

Joey wasn't a colleague. He needed me to trust him. And he was the kind of smart that had gotten him into and out of some scary situations.

What could it hurt to get his perspective?

"The body wasn't just in the capitol, it was in the governor's office." The words tripped out like I needed to say them before I changed my mind. "And the dead woman was a call girl I interviewed when all the shit with Senator Grayson hit the fan a couple of years ago."

Joey's face went the sort of sallow yellowish that results when the blood drains from an olive complexion. "Lakshmi? No." A tear escaped his lower lashes as he looked up. "That's what Miller told you? You're sure?"

I nodded, my eyes locked on the tear sliding down his cheek. I'd never seen him cry. I stepped forward. Back again.

What the hell did I not know now?

* * *

Joey didn't move, his face frozen in a mask of shock and grief I was sure would haunt my dreams in a nursing home someday. I swallowed hard. He was tough. Suave. And always, always in control. This was so utterly outside the realm of normal I had nothing for it, but comfort is a safe bet when someone you love is hurting.

I dropped to one knee in front of his chair, running both hands up his bare arms. "Baby? How can I help?" I asked.

He blinked. Shook his head. Focused on me.

"You're sure?"

I nodded. *How did you know her, and why do you care?* The words bubbled up the back of my throat. I swallowed them. Nope. None of my business unless he decided to tell me.

"I'm so sorry. If I'd known it was going to upset you, I wouldn't have told you. At least, not like that."

He shook his head again. "Not your fault. I just . . . I hadn't talked to her in ages. She told me once I ought to stay away from you if I didn't want to lose my heart. She liked you. Said you were special. Not the kind of woman you sleep with and forget the next day, she said."

I understood the words spilling out of his face, but not the context.

"She was a nice young woman who got caught up in a not-so-nice environment," I said. "I was glad I had the chance to help her. But sorry she had to give up her graduate studies. She was brilliant. We need more brilliant women in math and science. And politics." I tapped his arm lightly.

"She always said she was going to be the next Nate Silver." His voice had a hollow ring.

It almost felt like I was watching someone have this conversation with Joey. Sort of strange and out-of-body to be talking with him about another woman. Especially one he was crying over. Lakshmi was smart and gorgeous and special. I didn't know many women who wouldn't feel a little inferior standing next to her. I pulled my hands back. Joey's eyes widened.

"Oh, princess, no. You think I . . . that we . . . no." He shook his head. "She was a kid, for Christ's sake."

An unsettling combination of relief and confusion washed over me. He put one finger under my chin, turning my eyes to his. "Her family . . . did you ever ask her about them?"

"She said her dad lost his job, that he was a . . ." I reached back through my memory. "Something about him working for the government. Leaving to start his own company."

"Reynash Drake used to know a lot of very powerful people."

Oh. Like the kind of people Joey knew. So Joey knew Lakshmi because of her dad.

"Holy Mano—" I stood. Paced a few steps. Grabbed a can of Darcy's food out of the pantry and opened it, scooped it into her bowl, and scratched her ears as she nibbled at her breakfast.

A smart young woman with an eye on a career in politics and a father who moved in powerful political circles once upon a time, linked first with a disgraced US senator and now with a rising-star governor hiding some family secrets.

Charlie Lewis was free-falling down my list of concerns.

"Did, uh . . ." Joey cleared his throat. "Did Miller tell you what she was doing in Baine's office? How they found her?"

I shook my head. "She was dating his son, according to her now-deleted Instagram. I figured that's what she was doing in his office. Not that anyone's going to let me ask him. But it sounds like I have a lot more work than I thought, piecing together what the hell happened here."

He opened his mouth. Closed it again. Focused on the dog lying across his bare foot. "Looks like it's you and me today, Darce." He tried to force brightness into the words, but it just came out strained.

I returned to the table, tapped my computer screen back to life, and clicked my email open before I picked up the phone. Kyle answered on the second ring.

"I need a favor," I said by way of hello. "And I got my ass severely chewed yesterday thanks to your high-security tip I can't do anything with, so I'm hoping you'll take pity on me and pull a few strings."

"I'm not sure how strong my strings are today, but I could give it a shot." He sounded distracted. "What do you need?"

"A last-minute Saturday pass to Cold Springs. And a one-on-one unsupervised visit with Angela Baker." There were indeed things I needed to know about Lakshmi. Things that wouldn't wait for the pass I'd requested for Monday.

Things dean-slash-madam Baker might just be the perfect person to ask.

10

The visitor's gate at Cold Springs lives up to the name of the place: a wake in a cannibal enclave would be more inviting.

A slouching deputy behind the thick plastic window leered his way through a laconic once-over, his murky brown eyes pausing on my feet.

"Those could be classified as a weapon in some circles." His accent was more hillbilly twang than Virginia drawl.

My mouth flexed up in a tight, no-teeth smile. The red Manolos on my feet had in fact helped me out of a sticky situation or two. Not that I was telling him that. "I'm told height makes a person look intimidating," I said. "I always figure an extra three inches can't hurt, coming out here."

He twisted his mouth to one side, nodding. "I don't suppose you're looking to harm Ms. Baker, at that. You got some brains behind that face, don't you?"

"I like to believe so." I pulled my press credentials back through the slot by one corner with my thumb and index finger.

He flashed a crooked row of Big Chief–stained teeth as he signed a numbered placard for me. "Hope you get what you're looking for before you leave, now. Let me know how I can help with that."

I shoved my bag into locker number three and managed to exit the other side of the guard shack without shuddering, walking quickly, head up, to the door at the end of the hallway.

Facing the camera on the opposite wall, I held up the placard and clearly said my full name.

Thirty seconds, and the door buzzed, the jolting sound echoing off the painted cinderblock and tile walls.

Two more guards and a (cursory, because I also knew fitted clothing expedited entry) pat-down later, I was seated in a plastic chair at a metal table, watching a smaller version of Angela Baker than I remembered enter the little room through a door in the opposite corner.

She'd fallen through the prison time warp: her face was easily ten years older for the nearly two she'd spent here. Cheeks that were once enviably defined and supple looked sunken and sallow, her skin parched and lined. The carefully kept caramel highlights I remembered from her trial were still there, though. Sort of—the lemon juice version was brassy and brittle. Conditioner that fits prison substance regulations is nearly impossible to find.

The large guard who ushered her in backed out of the room and shut the door.

Thank you, Kyle.

Angela took the plastic chair across from me and nodded. "I like a woman who knows how to get shit done."

Her eyes were the thing that hadn't been changed by this place, a striking shade of deep blue hovering just to the cerulean side of navy, bright and curious as ever.

I struggled to keep my face blank. Two years ago, this woman was a young academic with a promising future. She'd gone from professor to assistant dean to dean by her midthirties, poised to take over for the chancellor who would retire in just a couple of months now.

Charismatic. Savvy. Brilliant. The words had filled the coverage of her arrest and trial, every person on the campus who wasn't turning tricks or looking to become one shocked at the revelations about their rising star.

"I have one hell of a convoluted story on my hands. I'm hoping you're going to help me untangle some part of it."

She shook her head, her eyes clouding over. "Lakshmi was a brilliant young woman."

And there was my first question. Even if she had a contraband phone or had been watching TV, nobody but me and the cops knew Lakshmi Drake was dead. I thought, anyway.

"Dean Baker, how is it that you know what happened to Lakshmi?"

She barked a short laugh, somewhere between amused and derisive. "Let's drop the formality. I'm Angela. You're Nichelle. I won't ever work at a university again, even when I'm done with this." She waved a hand. "I wouldn't hire me for the custodial staff at a school, would you?"

I pinched my lips together and shook my head.

"I hated you for quite a while when I first got here, you know." She watched my face carefully as she let those words drop.

A couple of hard blinks I couldn't help were the only reaction I showed. "A lot of people do. It goes with the job, I'm afraid."

Her thin face collapsed into a hundred lines when the corners of her mouth went up. "You are a tough one. Hell, I'd venture to say you'd do okay in here. It's a different world, for sure, and not the kind where book smarts help you too much."

I nodded, holding her gaze. I had been in and out of enough prisons and around enough hardened criminals to know repeating myself showed weakness. I wouldn't beg her to answer me. She had invited me here.

So I bit down on the *Back to Lakshmi?* and waited, staring. My chest felt too tight to hold much air.

She blinked first, pursing her lips and nodding slowly. "Okay then. So the way I see it, there are folks who think I'm the devil incarnate. I provided a service—a necessary one—to some folks, and for a long time everything rolled along and everyone was happy. Bright young women got through school with no debt. Marriages didn't dissolve over affairs because of things people couldn't or wouldn't talk about or do."

I nodded. Every conversation I'd had with Lakshmi Drake backed up her position. Mostly, anyway.

"I kept people's secrets. I was trusted in powerful circles." She paused there, her eyes moving to her hands, folded on the table in front of her.

I forced myself to stay mostly still, leaning toward her the tiniest bit instead of popping right out of the chair. Her tone said she was getting to why she'd asked me here. Journalism since the Invention of the Printing Press 101: Interviewing people is a tricky line between knowing how to ask the right questions and knowing when to let them talk.

"It never even occurred to me that anyone would get hurt. I never wanted that. Not Allison. Not Ted. Certainly not Lakshmi." She raised her eyes back to mine and, hand to God, they were bright with tears.

"I don't think anyone thinks you knew any of that would happen."

"Plenty of people hold me responsible for it," she said. "Secrets landed me in here. They've ruined and ended too many lives through all this."

Her thin shoulders, swallowed up by the drab gray scrub-like inmate uniform she practically swam in, lifted with a big breath. "It's time for some of those skeletons to come out of their closets. But I don't know whole stories, so I need a partner who can fill in the blanks. With the truth, not just with what's easy and palatable. Experience tells me you're my girl."

Partner? I laid my phone on the table. "You mind if I record this? I want to make sure I get everything right."

"Go ahead. I do, too."

I clicked the voice recorder on. "Tell me what you know about Lakshmi Drake."

"Lakshmi was a beautiful girl who found herself in a bind when her father lost his job." Another deep breath. She closed her eyes.

She wasn't sure she wanted to tell me this. The edge of the metal chair bit into my fingers, they closed around it so tight.

"Lakshmi's father's company went under because of Ted Grayson."

I sucked in such a sharp breath I choked on my own saliva. Coughing, I nodded, waving for her to go on.

She did not. "What did Senator Grayson have against Lakshmi's father?" I asked when my lungs stopped spasming, my voice low for no reason I could think of besides instinct telling me to keep this as quiet as I could.

She shook her head. "In politics, information is currency. Lakshmi's father worked for the federal government, once upon a time, most recently on a project nobody in DC could get information on. Grayson is nothing if not nosy. He wanted to know what was going on. But nothing worked.

Threats, kickbacks, all the usual suspects. They couldn't find anything to blackmail the guy with."

My head started bobbing. "But his boss, not so much?"

She flashed a half smile. "You are a smart woman, Nichelle."

I tapped one finger on the edge of the table, twisting my lips to one side.

"If Grayson had something on the boss he could use as blackmail, why didn't he just get that guy to tell him what they were working on?"

"Because that guy didn't know. He was a bureaucrat, not a scientist. No records were kept for anything they were doing. We're talking top, top, top secret stuff."

We were? "What kind of secret?" I closed my eyes, Lakshmi's voice whispering through my thoughts. "Experimental energy?" I asked. "Is that what her father did?"

Top, top secret experiment energy wasn't windmills or solar panels. Nobody would care enough to keep that kind of research quiet.

"Politically volatile energy research in Virginia probably means coal." The words trickled out slowly.

Angela tipped her head to one side. "You know, Ted said something once, about by-products, my business and Rey Drake's being similar. I told him unlike us, Lakshmi's dad was trying to save the world. He got this weird look and shut up, and he never said another word about any of it in front of me. Aren't the by-products of coal what's bad about it?"

"I think so." That might be a thing Grayson would want in on, given the weight the mining blocs carried in the southwest corner of Virginia and the money the coal companies pumped into elections. "But I don't get what Grayson accomplished by getting the guy fired. Didn't he lose his shot at finding out what Dr. Drake was working on entirely?"

She shook her head. "Ted excels at reading people. He knew Dr. Drake wouldn't give up on what he was doing, and sure enough, he funded the startup of his own company, right here in Grayson's backyard. The Drakes wanted to be close to their daughter, who was attending RAU as an undergrad at the time. The way I heard it, the lab ran for two years on the initial capital, with a plan of getting grants to continue once they had a research record to show."

"But Grayson made sure the grants didn't happen." I reached into my memory for that last chat with Lakshmi. "She said her dad's company went out of business in her junior year, right?"

Angela nodded. "Ted sent me after Lakshmi when her grant and loan applications all also got mysteriously denied." She arched an eyebrow and pieces of this puzzle rained into place in my head.

"And then he requested Lakshmi as his regular . . . um . . . escort," I said. "Did he think Lakshmi knew something?"

"He had his bets covered either way. Ted doesn't leave things to chance, and he likes to record every transaction." She hit the word *record* hard.

Oh hell. My eyes fell shut. "Tapes. So then he had something to blackmail her father with."

"Bingo. But here's the thing: Allison was the only person besides me who knew about his little setup."

Allison, the pretty blonde girl who ran Grayson's campaign office off campus and served as Angela's student point woman for the underground sex trade on campus, was long since dead.

And right there was why I was sitting in that chair.

"And now Lakshmi is dead and you're scared," I said.

"It's not like someone dies in here every week or anything, but do you know how easy it would be for someone with just a little money—not even good money—to make sure I stay quiet?"

I did. "So you figure the best defense is to talk?" I kind of wanted those words back as soon as they popped out. But I kind of didn't. I wanted the truth. I didn't want to help her get herself killed.

"The way I see it, the only defense is to bring the whole fucking thing crashing to the ground. I don't know what Ted found out about Lakshmi's dad, I don't know what the man was working on or what he's done since. But my bullshit radar has been pretty well perfected in here, and Lakshmi Drake, dead in a popular governor's office right before midterm elections that could be very good for the governor's friends and very bad for Ted Grayson's old buddies . . . something isn't right." She snorted. "A lot of things aren't right, I guess." She reached across the table and closed both her cold little hands over mine. I flinched. "Thomas Baine didn't have anything to do with that girl's death. I met him at several functions when he was the mayor. That man is the straightest arrow that ever was. Loves his wife. Believes in his state, in his country. He's the once-in-a-generation idealist who goes into politics not for power or money or ego, but because he believes he can help people and make the world a better place. That puts a target on his head when people like Grayson don't want their boats rocked."

I nodded. "I will do everything I can to help you, Angela."

She shrugged. "I am where I am. I'm smart enough to know this is, at its core, a giant game of beat the clock. And if I lose, well, I suppose that will suck for me, but you know, I'll be dead, so what will I care? I really never meant for anyone to get hurt, Nichelle. At least if I'm going out, killing me won't keep their damned secrets, right?"

I nodded. She pushed her chair back and I held up one hand. "You never told me how you knew what happened to Lakshmi," I said. "It's been the best-kept secret in town for better than twenty-four hours now, and I'm not seeing a prison grapevine that goes to the governor's mansion. If you want my help, I need you to be straight with me."

She blinked. "My lawyer came in and told me yesterday. You can check the visitor's log."

Her lawyer.

I let my eyes fall shut, back in a stifling courtroom last summer listening to thundering closing arguments. From Craig Terry.

She stood. "You know how to get me if you need to. Thanks for coming. Good luck."

A long, cold walk later, I strode back into the guard shack with my best smile in place, handing over my visitor's placard and opening the locker to retrieve my bag.

"Get what you need, now?" The teeth the deputy flashed were darker brown, a fresh wad of tobacco tucked in his lower lip. I swallowed hard, widening the smile and my eyes.

"Almost. Can I ask you a question?"

He blinked. "What would the news want from me?"

"I'm wondering if you have a list in your computer there that says who's been visiting a certain inmate?"

His forehead wrinkled. "I'm not sure I'm supposed to tell you that."

I put both hands on the counter. Leaned into the barrier. "It could be our little secret," I said in a loud whisper. "It would really help me out."

I didn't need to tell anyone where I got it. But Ted Grayson's name was way too wound up in the story Angela just told me for me to ignore. He couldn't do anything to hurt Lakshmi from inside the prison, though, which meant I needed to know who he'd been talking to.

The guard's eyes crinkled at the corners with a smile. "I guess it wouldn't hurt to help a pretty lady out. Who are we checking on?"

"Theodore Grayson." I kept my tone casual.

If the name rang a bell, he didn't show it, pecking keys with his index fingers. "G-R-A-Y-S- O-N?"

"That's it," I said.

He poked at the "Enter" key and stared at the screen. Scratched his head. Poked it again.

"Is something wrong?" My stomach turned a slow flip as I said the words.

"No listing found, it says. Are you sure that's his name?"

Two more stomach flips later, I nodded. "Did they relocate him?"

"This system searches the whole state." He clicked the mouse twice. Gave a slow nod. "Here it is—he's not here anymore. Got out three weeks ago, good behavior and house confinement."

Leaping Louboutins. Ted Grayson was out of prison and less than a month later, Lakshmi Drake was dead.

I managed to keep a straight face as I thanked him, rushing out the other door before he could get a coffee invitation out of his mouth.

Locked in my car, I pulled out my phone and found Angela Baker's email. Reply. *Did you know Grayson was out of prison? Is there anyone you think might have helped him hurt Lakshmi?* Send.

The whole drive back to downtown Richmond, three facts batted around my head no matter how hard I tried to ignore them: Angela Baker was afraid someone would kill her to keep this quiet. Ted Grayson was a quasi-free man with a whole bucket of powerful friends. And the prison visitor's log now showed that I'd gone to see Angela less than thirty hours after Lakshmi's body was discovered.

I'd just found myself another clock to race.

* * *

Walking into my favorite coffee shop a half hour later, I had turned the new puzzle pieces over in my head a thousand times, and all I could really tell was that I needed more to know what fit where.

The corner currently holding the most promise—or at least most of my interest—was Lakshmi's father's entanglement with Ted Grayson.

I believed Angela's story: Grayson had turned out to be the kind of slithering snake politician it was particularly gratifying to see in jail, because he got away with so much more than he'd ever be punished for. He was greedy, power-hungry, and lacking in anything resembling a conscience—I wouldn't put anything past him. Coal was decent business in western Virginia, and life's blood across the West Virginia state line. Money usually means power is somewhere nearby, and I was pretty sure I remembered that Grayson's campaign got truckloads of money from big tobacco and a few wheelbarrows full from the mining companies.

The more directions I turned that idea, the better I liked it. Coal companies would be interested in energy research, and might pull a paid-for politician's strings to get inside information. When Grayson couldn't deliver, he'd be faced with a whole lot of campaign funding drying right the hell up. The bait and blackmail plot Angela described fit his twisted personality perfectly.

I ordered a white mocha and sank into a plush armchair in the corner, the busy Saturday midmorning bustling around me. Couples. Groups of women planning shopping days and spa visits. Parents handing single Cheerios to little ones in strollers as they discussed yard aeration and home-improvement plans.

Just for a second, I wanted to be any one of them.

But only for a second.

Deep breath. Focus.

Kyle had texted me three times since I left the prison. I didn't know what to tell him (or not tell him), so I didn't look at his messages.

My phone buzzed again, but I didn't reach for it, closing my eyes to replay the talk with Dean Baker.

Question one: How the hell did Craig know Lakshmi was dead? I pulled out my phone and opened the contacts, touching the *T* in the margin and scrolling to his name. Cell. Call.

He picked up on the second ring. "Don't you ever take a day off, Nichelle?" he said in place of hello. "Looking for the inside scoop on the plea deal?"

I cleared my throat. "That'd be a nice bonus, but it's actually not why I called," I said. "I'm curious about how you know who the victim in the capitol murder was yesterday."

Crickets chirping in his neighbors' house would've come through in the silence that met my question.

I let it stretch. Thirty beats. Sixty.

"Craig?"

He took a breath. "Who—um—who told you that?" His voice was a full octave too high, maybe more.

"I'm afraid I can't share that," I said.

Another pause. "Nichelle, I don't always deal with the best society has to offer in my work. I know you get that. And attorney-client privilege says I cannot answer your question. I respect the hell out of the work you do, but trust me, you are in over your head. I wish I could unhear what I know. Powerful people will do just about anything to make sure their secrets stay buried."

"If I'm in over my head, an answer or two could serve as a life raft," I said. "Off the record."

"On the contrary, in this case, it might just serve as the anvil that drags you under. Back out of this now, Nichelle. Not as an attorney, as a friend, I'm telling you. Some secrets are better off kept."

He hung up.

I scribbled down everything he'd said before I forgot a word, furrowing my brow as I mulled over the bizarre conversation. Craig wasn't usually so cryptic. Dramatic, sure—he was a lawyer—but straightforwardly so.

Attorney-client privilege. I underlined that, clicked my browser open, and pulled up news results for his name. I scanned the headlines he was associated with, not seeing a single name that so much as breathed on an alarm bell. No politicians, no science types, no more prostitutes or madams. Clicking on random stories, I found mostly court appointments in his newsworthy cases: armed robbery, vehicular manslaughter, the meth lab, and three shootings (one fatal). Back to the top of the search results. More than thirteen hundred. Too big of a haystack to sort when I wasn't sure the needle was going to help me much.

Turning to a blank page, I dug out my earbuds and replayed my conversation with Angela, taking notes as I went.

Question number two: Coal. Was that the center of Reynash Drake's secret research? And what did Grayson know?

Not exactly my department. The real-world things I knew about Santa's naughty list gift of choice were few: it was the biggest source of electricity by a large gap, a lot of people wanted that to change quickly, it served as a decent part of the commonwealth's economy, and it was the backbone of West Virginia's. That was it.

I put the earbuds away and picked up my phone, ignoring the box on the screen that told me Kyle's text count was up to seven and clicking my browser open. Top secret government files weren't known for magically appearing in Google results, but I could go more generic and at least get an idea of what I might be looking for. Coal research. Go.

Sorting the articles by most relevant first, I found more than a hundred hits on clean coal technology. After bookmarking the top three, I scrolled through an article explaining carbon capture and gasification and a handful of other experimental technologies. A quick read told me if Lakshmi's father were somehow building a government case for regulations supporting these things, coal companies wouldn't be thrilled: it was good for their image, sure, but bad for their bottom line to the tune of tripling overhead for a fuel source whose sole draw was cheap access.

Back on the search results page, I spotted President Denham in a thumbnail photo and paused. Clicked. She'd spent sixty percent of her Virginia visits during the last election cycle in coal country, taking questions from and making promises to the strong voter base that had helped deliver her the commonwealth's thirteen electoral votes.

Would she be unhappy with clean coal research, too? I tapped her name and *clean coal* into the search bar.

Nine results. One interview where she said she supported carbon capture but wanted a cheaper way to do it.

Which told me nothing. Double-talk is its own language for politicians of her caliber.

And her upcoming visit was the only thing that put her in the same zip code as the rest of my story.

Back to more relevant facts.

Ted Grayson was absolutely the sort of man who would lure a college girl into escort service to blackmail her father. What he had never struck me as was a criminal mastermind. All his known forays into criminal activity were precipitated by someone else—he just followed along with the plan to satisfy his ego and his greed. So how did he even come up with such a thing, let alone manage to pull it off?

Wait.

Did he pull it off?

I sipped my coffee, tapping the fingers of my free hand on the arm of the chair, letting the stray question bloom in my head.

Lakshmi's face as she packed up her bag that day in the classroom. The article she'd coauthored just a year ago. Grayson, in somber navy and gray, being sentenced to four years as his secretary sobbed in the gallery behind him.

What if Lakshmi got out—or Grayson got caught—before he got to her dad with the tapes?

If Grayson hadn't gotten the information his donors wanted before he went to prison, what if someone got him out early to finish his mission?

I sipped my coffee.

New governor. New president. New challenges for and champion of the coal industry.

Desperate times and all—I didn't hate this goose's chance of sprouting golden feathers.

I clicked to whitepages.com. *Drake, R. Richmond and surrounding areas.* I crossed my fingers as I hit the "Search" button.

Fifty-nine hits.

Great.

I started scrolling. Number twenty-eight, for RM Drake on Westover Road, showed Lakshmi as a connected person. Age 60–65. Former city of residence, Burke, up in the DC suburbs.

Needle located.

If I could get him to talk to me, I might get something about this story to make a tiny bit of sense. I clicked the address for Mr. Drake, set my GPS, and placed my heavy mug on the dirty dishes cart on my way to the car. My questions weren't the sort I could ask over the phone, and surprise is often the best gate pass to sensitive territory.

11

"Damn, that's a big house," I muttered, pulling a fresh notebook from the console in my car and stashing the one with the notes from my chat with Angela in the glove box.

The place had to be four thousand square feet, sporting wide porches dotted with ceiling fans across both floors, everything faced in the wrought iron that was so popular in Richmond architecture after the Civil War.

The door chimes were ringing by the time I realized I had not the first damned clue whether or not these people knew their daughter was dead.

Fantastic.

The door opened to the round, pleasant face of a petite, curvy woman wearing a breathtaking gold-and-copper sari.

She didn't look like someone who'd just lost a child, and I have a hundred people's share of experience with that face.

I let a bit of the breath I'd been holding out and smiled. "Mrs. Drake?"

She smiled back, not moving to open the door or otherwise reacting to my words.

Okay.

I tried again. "Is Dr. Drake home this morning?"

She kept the smile in place.

For lack of a better option, I returned it, my eyes roaming the cavernous house on the other side of the iron-and-glass storm door. Gleaming, polished cherry flooring stretched behind her as far as I could see, the walls different colors by room, from deep cinnamon surrounding a silk-clothed dining table, to muted purplish blue in what I assumed was a study, to red in the great room across the back of the first floor.

A full minute ticked by. I took in as many details as I could without crossing to the rude side of nosy, wondering if this place had ever been photographed.

The other woman blinked, her smile faltering. "Are you looking for him, too?" Her voice was so soft I would've missed it with one brain cell less attention.

I leaned forward. "I'd like to speak with Dr. Drake if I can, please."

She shook her head. "Gone." Touched her chin to her chest. "All gone. All of them."

I stared at the silver strands weaving through the shiny dark hair at her roots, weighing my options. I didn't know who this woman was. Lakshmi's mother? Couldn't tell.

"Is he at work? Could I call him there?"

Her head bobbed. "His work. Always his work." A tear fell from her face, exploding a small dark splotch on her goldenrod top.

She fell still. Quiet. I put a hand on the outside of the glass. "Can I help you, ma'am?"

No answer.

With her head bowed, my eyes went to a coat rack behind her. A gray cardigan and an electric-blue fleece jacket hung opposite each other. The jacket had a logo in the top third of the front right.

A-L-T-C and a white star were the only bits visible, the way the letters played in and out of folds in the fabric. Company logo?

I repeated it silently until I was sure it had stuck.

"Ma'am?" I tried once more.

"All they asked about was him." Her voice was clear and flat as a Texas highway, but still directed at her feet. "Nobody asked about my Lakshmi. Just have I seen Hamilton. Where's Rey. Like she doesn't matter."

Wait. What? Someone had been here asking if she'd seen Hamilton?

Jiminy Choos.

"Who asked you? Mrs. Drake? Who asked you that?"

She raised her head and her right arm in tandem, pointer finger extended. "There."

I turned.

A black sedan was parked across the street.

Two dark suits, Ray-Bans in place, ties the sort of nondescript gray brown I'd never understand as a clothing choice, sat with their heads swiveled to the front of the Drake house.

What the actual hell?

Surveillance? At a murder victim's grieving family's home?

I pulled out my phone, turning back for the door just in time to see it close.

Damn.

I couldn't ring the bell again. That poor woman was on the verge of bona fide shock.

I jogged back down the long front steps, pausing three-quarters of the way, my hand closing tighter around my iPhone, heart rate picking up as I watched the suit in the driver's seat slide his shades down and give me a slow once over. I slid my thumb right to call up the camera, waving the phone in a long arc and hammering the bottom of the screen with my thumb, hoping it looked like I was just stashing it in my bag. Back in the car, I drove toward the river on autopilot, my thoughts tangled up in the bizarre half interview. Why would those guys be looking for Hamilton Baine? And how did that search lead to Lakshmi's parents?

I pulled out my key card for the garage when I noticed I was in front of Joey's building. Backing into a space along the far wall, I dug my phone out and dialed Kyle.

"Where the hell have you been?" He didn't bother with hello. "The guard shack says you left the prison over an hour ago, and I've been going out of my mind wondering if you got anything that might help me catch a break in this case."

"I've got a hell of a list of questions, starting with this one: Why hasn't the local media been alerted that Hamilton Baine is missing, Kyle?"

I waited.

And waited.

Pulled the phone away from the side of my head and checked the signal bars.

Still connected. I clicked the volume button. He was breathing, lightly.

"Kyle, don't bullshit me. I know y'all can't find him."

Easy hunch: because Hamilton flipped, killed Lakshmi, and took off. The simplest answer is usually the right one.

But then the only reason for the information freeze was that someone was trying to figure a way to spin the whole sordid mess to avoid hurting Baine's political career.

Which meant finding someone else to take the fall for it.

Kyle wouldn't have any part of that.

Right?

"Kyle, is he missing, or are you guys hiding him?" I half whispered the words, bitter as they crossed my tongue. Kyle was a good cop. More than that, he was a good man. Surely to God he wouldn't be party to covering up a murder.

"I—" He started to say something. Stopped himself.

My latte threatened to come back up.

"I have rarely wanted to be wrong about something so badly in my entire life," I choked out. "Kyle. Tell me I'm wrong."

He hung up.

I stared at my phone, forgetting to breathe. How had my fabulous weekend twisted so thoroughly into a nightmare with one murder victim? And who would help me figure this out without Kyle?

Aaron.

I clicked to my text messages.

The one he'd sent me yesterday morning, which I hadn't paid much mind to. It came right behind Kyle's, and they were clearly talking about the same thing.

Weren't they?

Come to the governor's office. There's a hell of a story attached to this body, but it's not going to be an easy one to get. For either of us.

I read it six times before I let my head fall back against the seat, going back through everything I knew about this mess.

Lakshmi used to sleep with men—some of them powerful—for money.

One of her clients was recently sprung from prison and might be looking to settle an old score.

Her father was a high-clearance-level scientist who lost his job and then his business because Ted Grayson wanted to know something Dr. Drake wouldn't tell.

Hamilton Baine was Lakshmi's boyfriend.

Hamilton's father was a sitting governor with an eye on the national political stage.

I pulled out my notebook and scribbled all that into a list, because this was already a stupidly convoluted puzzle, and I didn't trust myself to not lose track of a piece.

Okay. What else?

Hamilton Baine wasn't around. Or at the very least, people were looking for him. People traveling in dark sedans and matching drab, forgettable suits. I put the pen down and opened my photos, scrolling back through the most recent ones. Nope, nope, nope . . . blurry shots of sky and trees and a dark blob that might've been a car.

Damn.

I retrieved the pen. Next.

The Baine family, for all their greeting-card perfection, had a few skeletons in their assorted closets.

Wait.

My photographic memory retrieved the cell phone screen Mrs. Powers had shown me the day before.

"She heard from Hamilton yesterday morning," I breathed, tapping the pen on the paper and leaving behind a clump of little blue dots. The dim garage in front of me went wavy and unfocused, my brain lasering in on trying to make that piece fit. If Hamilton killed Lakshmi and disappeared, by choice or by design, why would he have texted my neighbor about her death? If he hadn't, where the hell was he, and why did Kyle hang up on me?

I had nothing. Except a whole list of weird things I couldn't quite see the connections between, and a situation that was producing more complicated questions practically by the minute.

Oh, and nobody to talk through it with.

Aaron's text message worried around my head. He wasn't known for being cryptic.

"Something is off. Way off," I said to the still silence.

It was about the only thing I was sure of, right then.

I put the car in gear and waved my key card in front of the sensor to open the gate before turning west for police headquarters.

Yes, it was Saturday. But if I was anywhere in the same neighborhood as right, Aaron wouldn't be able to keep his head out of the case any more than I could keep mine out of the story.

12

I nearly stumbled over my own Manolos when I walked into RPD headquarters, the new face attached to a mountain of muscle behind the desk pressing the brakes on my determined stride three steps into the lobby.

The guy looked more like a Manhattan bouncer than a Richmond cop, and certainly didn't spend a lot of time behind a desk, or anywhere else that wasn't a gym. His left bicep was as big around as my waist. And my best smile and chatty "Detective White is expecting me" didn't get me so much as a grunt. His thick arm shot into my path as he reached for the phone.

"I'm not sure Detective White is in today, miss."

I held up my press credentials. "Nichelle Clarke from the *Telegraph*. I can just go up and wait for him. I know my way around." I tried the smile again.

No dice. "I'm afraid I can't let you go up unescorted, miss." His face said the rest, which went something like *Which you would know if you really knew your way around.*

And while security at the department had tightened since Aaron's incident this time last year, I was still used to more leeway than your average civilian.

Not today.

"He's not answering," Captain Testosterone said.

I waited.

He nodded to the doors behind me. "Have a good day now."

"If Aaron's not here yet, I could talk with Detective Landers while I wait for him," I said.

He sighed and reached for the phone again. "Landers, you said?"

I nodded, not bothering with the smile this time.

He punched buttons, holding the phone to his ear for thirty seconds before he replaced it in the cradle. "He's not picking up." He didn't bother with the "sorry," either.

Fine. Big guns for the win. "Chief Sorrel," I said. Technically, my old friend Mike was the deputy chief, but brass is brass. The name-drop widened his eyes.

"What did you say your name was?"

"Nichelle Clarke."

He picked the phone back up. Punched buttons. "This is Officer Trenton at the desk. I have a Nichelle Clarke here from the newspaper, was looking for Detective White and now says she wants to talk with Chief Sorrel. Should I—" He stopped, his brows drawing into a V over the apex of his nose before he met my gaze. "Of course. I sure will. Yes, ma'am."

He put the phone down and pointed to the elevators. "She said you know the way."

I flashed a calmer smile. No gloating, just thanks and relief. "I do. Thank you." I strode to the elevators and pushed the up arrow, keeping my eyes on the flat steel of the doors until they opened.

Mike's office was on fifteen. Aaron's was on twelve. I touched that button first, but didn't press it. I'd love to go poke around and eavesdrop on the detectives' floor, or see if Aaron was just ignoring his phone, sure, but with all the weird around this place today, it might not be the best idea. Pushing the right button, I leaned against the back wall of the elevator. Mike was the only person in this place who was as big a workaholic as I was, so throwing his name out was a somewhat calculated last gasp at getting past Captain Powerlifting, but I had to go up to his office since he was now expecting me.

The bell dinged on twelve and my eyes went back to the buttons. I hadn't actually pressed it.

The doors parted and if I hadn't already been leaning on the wall, I'd have fallen over.

Aaron flinched back from the elevator, flanked by Detective Chris Landers—and a stubble-jawed, bloodshot-eyed Governor Thomas Baine.

"What in actual hell—" Landers didn't get his whole sentence out before Aaron recovered, holding one hand up in front of the junior detective and flashing a smile at me.

"Nichelle. I didn't expect to see you today." His tone said we might as well have reached for the same apple at the grocery store.

I rolled my lips between my teeth and bit down for half a second before I put a hand out. "Gentlemen," I said. "It's almost a crime to be stuck inside on such a gorgeous fall Saturday."

Aaron nodded. The doors started to close, and I put one hand on the right panel, arching an eyebrow. "Going up?"

The governor hadn't said anything, so I pretended I didn't recognize him for the moment. Mostly because I didn't have a way to open a discussion there that wouldn't piss off Landers more. Landers kind of stays half pissed off where I'm concerned. His dad was the sort of old-school reporter who devoted himself more to the story than his family. While I knew the feeling, I felt for Landers, too. This job doesn't exactly lend itself to family. Not that police work was better—but I wasn't in a position to point that out.

They stepped forward almost in unison, turning to face the doors and not offering another word as the elevator rose three more floors. I stepped off behind them on fifteen, and Landers whirled.

"What are you doing here, Nichelle?" He didn't yell, but the lines in his forehead said he wanted to.

"Going to see Mike," I said, raising one arm toward his office.

The little blue vein under Landers's left eye popped to attention.

So, not the response he wanted, then.

I slid my eyes to Aaron, whose face was so carefully blank it was hard to pull my gaze away. What had I lucked myself into when they wouldn't answer their phones? I would've never asked to talk to Mike if Officer Muscles downstairs had been able to get either of these guys. Probably not the best time to tell them that.

I tipped my lips up into a tight, toothless smile and stepped around Landers before his blood pressure could notch up any more.

Striding to Mike's door, I kept my head up and my eyes straight ahead, ignoring the murmurs around us, which were probably more on account of Governor Baine than Landers and his bickering.

I raised my fist and rapped twice on Mike's door. "Come in, Nichelle," his deep voice boomed from the other side. Turning the knob, I pushed the door open with a real smile. I didn't get to see him much since he'd moved upstairs. "It seems I'm not your only company today, Chief Bigshot," I said.

He stood, a grin flashing bright beneath a thick, dark mustache that was just starting to show the slightest hint of gray. "Long time no see, Lois Lane. I guess you've been too busy saving the world to drop in on tired old workhorses like me."

"You're one to talk." I shook his hand, forgetting the bizarre trio on my heels for a moment. "You miss your drug runners and snitches yet?"

"Only on slow days. I'll let you know when I have one." He winked, gesturing to a gray microfiber upholstered chair across from his. "Make yourself comfortable." He turned to the door. "You waiting for an engraved invitation, Chris? Shut the door."

Landers opened his mouth. Snapped it shut again. Pulled a rolling black leather desk chair from the table at the far end of the room over and laid a hand on the governor's shoulder. "Sir," he said, nodding to the chair.

"Thank you." Baine's voice was hoarse. Thready. I knew the mix of grief and exhaustion that caused that well, thanks to more interviews with folks whose quiet worlds had been upended by tragedy than I cared to count. I pulled my notebook out and flipped it open, casting my eyes down but trying to study the governor through my lashes. A dozen questions practically burned a hole in my vocal cords. Why was he here? What had him so distraught? Was he sleeping with Lakshmi? Was he worried about his career? This timing was God-awful, with the president's impending visit and the whispers of a national run for him. And perhaps most important: Where the hell was his son?

I swallowed them all, the waves of irritation radiating from Landers's tense form threatening an eruption he was only holding in check because of Mike. He might lose his temper if I spoke first, chief be damned.

I clicked my pen out and waited for everyone to settle. Governor Baine's chin rested on his chest, his shoulders rising and falling slowly with measured breaths. If he weren't so upset, I'd have thought he was asleep.

Mike cleared his throat, drawing my eyes up to his. He laced his fingers together and rested his hands on a thin butter-yellow file folder, the lone one in the center of his desk.

I tapped my pen on my notebook. Yellow was missing persons at the RPD.

Shit.

"It seems we have ourselves quite a problem here, gentlemen," Mike said.

And that was all it took to blow Landers's top. "Sir, we shouldn't discuss an open investigation with—" He got halfway to his feet, his voice getting louder with each word, before Mike stopped him.

"Enough, Detective." The words could've pierced Kevlar, and I blinked, my head swiveling slowly back and forth between the two of them.

Landers returned to his seat as Aaron coughed over a chuckle. Mike Sorrel was legendary for his temper and strict adherence to policy as a detective and then sergeant in the narcotics division, where he led some of the largest investigations—and secured some of the biggest busts—in department history. It seemed two trips around the sun on the command staff hadn't cooled his head.

"Nichelle has more than proven herself not only trustworthy but a damned fine investigator in her own right and an ally of this department," Mike said. "And I asked her here today. That will be the end of the discussion of her presence."

Holy Manolos. That was a loaded defense if there ever was one. There were cops in the room I considered friends, yes. But my allegiance was to the truth, not the Richmond PD, and Mike knew it. Furthermore, he'd only asked me because I presented myself via phone in the lobby.

Not that I was going to quibble over details.

"While we're on the subject, though, Nichelle, I see your notebook and I'm going to have to ask you to leave what's discussed here today off the record, at least for now."

I nodded. Of course he was. "We get it in print before it goes to the TV," I said.

Mike tapped his index fingers on the backs of the opposite knuckles. "I can't promise you first, because we have limited control over when something is going to get out about this, and I'm afraid I'm not up on who Charlie's got in her pocket around here these days. But I can promise you more. Exclusive interviews with the investigating officers, when we can."

"Deal." I put the pen down, pretty sure of what I was about to hear.

"I'm sure you've already managed to find out what happened at the capitol yesterday," Mike began.

I nodded. "Lakshmi Drake." My eyes went to the governor, who was looking at Mike. His eyes closed for two beats when I said her name, but if it bothered him more than that, he wasn't showing it.

"I know she was dating Hamilton Baine, though it seems someone doesn't want anyone else knowing that." I stopped there, lighting my eyes on each of the cops in the room in turn.

Aaron nodded slowly, but not at me. At Mike.

"Hamilton is missing." Mike lifted the folder in front of him, turning it so I could see the name on the tab and the small color photo of Hamilton stapled to the corner.

I widened my eyes and sat up straighter, because I didn't need them to know I had already figured that out. Yet, anyway.

"I'm so sorry, sir," I said, turning to Governor Baine.

A tear fell from the corner of one eye, a shiny dark mark across his cheekbone before it disappeared into the scruff lining his jaw.

"I just don't understand," he rasped, leaning forward and resting his elbows on his knees. "Any of this, really. What the hell is going on?"

Aaron put a hand on his shoulder. "That's what we're going to find out, Tom. I give you my word. We will get your boy back."

"Has there been a ransom demand?" My brow furrowed as the question popped out, because nothing about this made sense. For a missing person, and a high-profile one at that, where was the FBI? And for that matter, the state police oversee the First Family's security.

Landers tightened his hands on the arms of his chair, but he didn't tell me to shut up. Mike shook his head slightly.

Damn. So they didn't even really know if Hamilton was missing or dead.

I tucked a wayward strand of dark hair behind my right ear, frowning at Mike. "Don't take this the wrong way, but why are you guys handling this?"

He smiled. "I appreciate the vote of confidence."

I rolled my eyes. He knew I didn't mean it that way.

"Because I don't trust anyone else," Governor Baine said. "Aaron and Mike have been my friends since my first month on the city council, and I don't know what the hell is going on in my house, but I have a pretty good hunch that not everyone who's supposed to be protecting me and my family is actually invested in that mission."

I dropped my pen, turning to him.

Both eyes bright with tears, he was focused on Mike. "You have to help us."

Mike nodded, reaching across his desk to grip the governor's hand and raising one eyebrow at me. "What do you say, Nichelle? You in?"

"Of course."

There wasn't anything else to say. And I knew Mike was well aware of that when he dropped the question.

I could worry about what I'd just agreed to later. For now, maybe I could finally get a few answers if I was going to dig myself deeper into this story.

13

Chris Landers can lose his shit more spectacularly than a Real Housewife who's knocked back three too many glasses of chardonnay.

Apparently, even the governor and the deputy chief weren't enough motivation to keep it together once Mike asked me to do whatever it was he still hadn't explained.

"Are you goddamn kidding me?" The force behind the words seemed to launch Landers from his chair, pushing it hard enough to send it careening into the table with a clatter. "Who invites the fucking news media into a case we're trying to keep quiet? I had to leave my son's baseball game to sneak Governor Baine into the building, White says we aren't even supposed to talk to other cops about this, and you're just going to trust a reporter with it? Just like that?"

I kept my mouth shut. I'd spent a lot of years, and earned more than a few trips to the ER, chasing the truth around this town—and this building. But there are times to stand up for yourself, and times to let someone else fight that battle. This was the latter.

Mike didn't move. Maybe being a big boss had mellowed him out.

"I suggest you return to your seat and check your tone, Detective." Or maybe not: nobody in the room missed the deadly edge to his words.

Landers pulled in a breath so deep the buttons on his starched blue shirt strained across his chest. "But, sir," he began.

Aaron put one hand on Landers's forearm. "Chris. Sit." Quiet, but firm.

My fingers wrapped the arms of my chair so tight that I couldn't feel them.

"I don't believe in coincidences, son," Mike said, his eyes on Landers, who was retrieving his runaway chair.

I didn't either. This line of work will do that to a person.

"Nichelle called up from the lobby as you guys were on your way up," Mike went on when Landers was seated again. "And the fact of the matter is, we might be able to use her to get to the bottom of this."

"And we trust her," Aaron interjected, his eyes meeting mine, holding.

He knew I appreciated that. He also knew I took it seriously. It sounds great, in theory, being the reporter the cops trust. In practice, it's akin to walking a high wire backward in Louboutins. My first responsibility is to my readers. But how much I share, the effect it has on public consciousness and opinion—and my relationship with the cops who let me in on the information in the first place—that's where balancing can become a blind circus act.

I eyed the governor, my gut twisting with the feeling that throwing politics into the mix was about to add a hungry wolf to one end of my high wire. Or maybe to both.

Governor Baine stared at his hands, twisting together between his knees. I was sure nobody else in the room knew he wasn't blood related to Hamilton. Watching him, I was just as sure it didn't matter a bit.

"For now, our involvement in this is need to know, and nobody but the people in this room needs to know," Mike said. "Tom, you said you told Hamilton's detail you sent him out of town to his grandparents to grieve. How long can you make that fly?"

The governor shrugged. "A couple of days? Nobody was happy about it, but I told them he was inconsolable and needed to be with family."

Lakshmi's mother's teary, blank face flashed through my thoughts. "So maybe it was them who went to the Drakes' house," I said.

Aaron turned to me, waving a *Come out with it.*

"I talked with Lakshmi's mother this morning, and she said people kept asking about Hamilton, not about Lakshmi. Maybe his guards went looking for him there? Was Hamilton close with Lakshmi's parents, sir?"

The governor shrugged. "Not that I knew of, but that wasn't anyone from my detail. Yesterday was all hands on deck, and the whole team was in the house all day."

"Appears you haven't lost your instincts," Mike said to me. "Any theories on who it might've been?"

I pulled my phone out of my bag. "She pointed out these guys sitting outside. Nondescript sedan, dark suits, gross gray-brown ties they must buy in bulk online. I tried to get a picture as I was putting my phone away, but all I got were blurry blobs." I clicked up the recent photos and passed my phone across the desk.

Mike scrolled through, handed it back. "Tom, any idea who else might be looking for your boy?"

The governor shook his head. "I can't figure out a bit of this. I mean, Hamilton is grown. He was adjusting, I thought, though he never wanted to be the governor's son. He'd be happy stuck in a lab somewhere by himself all day. He likes helping people. But through science, where he doesn't actually have to talk to them. Especially women. Almost painfully awkward. That's why Lakshmi was such a godsend—he was comfortable with her. In control. A magician, that girl—no matter how hard I try, I've never been able to get the boy past his people issues."

That explained the devotion Mrs. Powers told me about. But it was the "in a lab somewhere by himself all day" that leapt out of that comment and danced.

"Governor, what kind of science was your son studying? Is. Is he studying." I stammered slightly over the quick correction, nearly biting my tongue.

"Nuclear energy alternatives." He didn't acknowledge my slip.

"Like for electricity?" Like coal, maybe?

Landers's teeth clicked together, his whole lanky form tensing in his chair every time I talked. I ignored it.

Baine's hand went to his temple, his index and middle fingers massaging. "I think? He doesn't like to talk about what he's doing, and I learned long ago that a smart father picks his battles."

My eyes slid to Aaron, whose brow was furrowing. He had two daughters in college and could probably tell you their schedules down to the minute. But he was also a cop. Seeing the worst of society at work every day lends itself to bubble-wrapping kids.

My fingers itched for a pen, but I couldn't pick it up without making the rest of the room uncomfortable. There wasn't much danger of me forgetting that Hamilton's work could be at least adjacent to Dr. Drake's, though. I didn't believe in coincidences any more than Mike did, so there was something to that. I just had to find out what, exactly.

"Where is he working, Tom?" Mike had a pen.

"Daltec." The governor didn't look up. "We have a . . ." He paused for so long Mike reached across the desk with a water bottle.

He took it. Cleared his throat. Twisted the cap off the bottle and sipped. "Sorry. We have a friend who got him an internship there. He's working on his PhD at Madison. Chemistry and physics. It's a special program. Hamilton is special. A brilliant kid."

Daltec, Daltec, Daltec, I repeated silently. Like Dallas, with technology. When I was sure I had it, I raised my hand.

Mike chuckled. "Yes, Nichelle?"

"Maybe we're going at this from the wrong side," I said. "Governor, could you tell us how well you knew Lakshmi? She was interested in politics—did she ever ask you for a job?"

"I think we're pretty well versed in how to question a witness," Landers said. "I'd like to continue talking about Hamilton, if you don't mind."

Mike nodded. "I appreciate your affinity for being thorough, Chris, but let's follow this for just a second and see what's there."

Baine sat up. "She's been on my staff since Hamilton first brought her to dinner during the campaign. I never saw a mind for strategy like Lakshmi's. She can dig truths out of numbers that men twice her age wouldn't find with a dozen supercomputers and weeks to work. I am so damned sorry about what happened to her . . ."

I watched him closely. His entire manner changed when he talked about Lakshmi. Stiff. Professional. Distant.

Aaron and Mike's faces said they saw it, too.

Landers continued to fume, so pissed I was there, he wasn't paying attention.

Mike toyed with his pen.

Aaron drummed his fingers on the arm of his chair.

Chickens.

I cleared my throat and let the words out in a rush. "Sir, I'm sorry for having to ask, but someone needs to. Were you involved with Lakshmi? Sexually speaking?"

You have to be blunt—and specific—with politicians. Years of listening to Trudy's war stories had taught me that vague questions about uncomfortable topics would give them windows to slip half-truths through, and then I wouldn't even be able to say they'd lied to me.

Mike and Aaron both suddenly found the ceiling fascinating.

Landers's breath hissed in, but he stayed still, side-eyeing the governor and waiting for an answer.

Governor Baine blinked. "You're asking me if I've been fucking a campaign strategist half my age, who happened to be dating my son?"

Not an answer. I closed my fingers around the arm of my chair and met his gaze, not blinking for so long my eyes dried out.

"Yes, sir, I am."

He shook his head, turning to Mike. "Do you think that's what I was doing? Do you guys think I—" He didn't finish the second question, shaking his head.

Mike sighed, running one big hand through his thick, graying-at-the-temples hair. "I don't want to, Tom, but she was on your desk, for Christ's sake. That indicates a level of intimacy with the room. We wouldn't be doing our jobs if we didn't ask."

"We didn't ask. Nichelle did." I flinched when the words came from Landers, turning my head. He offered an olive branch half smile. "We should've, though."

I returned the smile. Turned back to the governor.

"I thought you guys knew me better than that," he said, his head swiveling between Mike and Aaron.

Their faces told me they were thinking the same thing I was. He still hadn't answered the question.

That was a whole other level of not good.

Mike's lips disappeared into a thin, pale line.

"No. I have never slept with her," Baine said finally.

My teeth clamped down on the inside of my cheek. Aaron nodded. "Thank you."

I kept my eyes on the governor, his words playing in my head on a loop. He said he'd never slept with her, not that he'd never had sex with her.

Pretty fine hairsplitting. And I couldn't address it right then because they had accepted his statement and moved on. But I knew what Trudy would say about that if I asked her.

Window.

"Governor, do you know much about Lakshmi's background?" The words slid out quietly, because Kyle knew and I knew and Joey knew, but I had no idea what these guys knew.

Every eyeball in the room swiveled to fix on me.

Baine shook his head. "Brilliant young woman, degree from RAU, grew up near DC . . ." The governor spread his hands. "What exactly should I know?"

The room fell so silent I would've heard an ant sneeze.

I looked at Aaron. "You remember Angela Baker?"

His eyes popped wide. "No."

Landers shook his head when I just nodded.

"You going to tell us who she is, Clarke?" he asked.

Aaron sighed. "The madam from the RAU solicitation ring case."

"Wait. A prostitute? How? Why?" Baine slumped back in his chair. Shook his head. "Doesn't matter." He turned to Mike. "Just find Hamilton."

"Do you know of anyone who would want to hurt him?" Mike asked. "Had he said anything about being uncomfortable lately? Anything weird going on?"

Baine started to shake his head. Stopped. "The car," he half whispered. "Oh shit."

"What about it?" Aaron asked.

"I guess it was a month or so ago now. My security chief mentioned in the morning rundown that Hamilton had complained to his detail about his car being broken into. Outside his lab."

"Was anything missing?" Aaron asked.

Baine shook his head. "They said they went over the whole car with a microscope and couldn't find any evidence he was right, but it was almost like he was paranoid, insisting. That's why they mentioned it to me. He never did, though, and I figured they took care of it."

Landers leaned forward, resting his elbows on his knees. "Sir, does your son have a history of paranoid behavior?"

Baine shook his head. "He's very exacting about his studies and his work, but his mother tells me that's the scientist in him." Baine hammered a fist down on the edge of Mike's desk. "I should've asked him about it. Why didn't I ask him about it?"

Aaron's face creased into sympathetic dad mode. "You've been a little busy, Tom."

"Why does that take precedence over my family?" Baine's voice caught. "What if I missed something that might've prevented this? What if I let this hap—" He didn't finish that, his Adam's apple bobbing with a hard swallow. "Jesus. I don't care what Lakshmi had done, nobody deserves that."

"You didn't let anything happen," Aaron said. "If there's one thing more years in this place than I care to account for has taught me, it's that people never want to think the worst until it hammers right through their front door."

I nodded. True story. Real-life horrors are something average folks see on TV, read about in the paper. They make it through their days by believing it always happens to someone else.

Landers pinched the bridge of his nose, turning to Mike. "So can we talk to the head of Hamilton's detail? See if there's a recording of what he told them, or a report on the car?"

Mike tapped the pen on his desk blotter, twisting his lips and his mustache to one side. "Not right now, but let's note that for later. I don't want them knowing we're nosing around in this just yet." He nodded to the governor. "I think it's better all the way around if we keep it as quiet as we can for as long as we can. There are plenty of still-warm leads to follow here."

Landers's jaw tightened as he nodded, and I knew what he was thinking, because I was already there: just because Hamilton didn't want to tell them what was missing from the car didn't mean nothing was.

But he didn't want to press it just yet.

Baine stood and smoothed at the lines in the front of his slacks. "Speaking of security, I have to get back, gentlemen. This has been a hell of a long shower."

Aaron followed, guiding the governor toward the door and waving when Landers started to go with them. "I've got this," he said. "See what you can come up with on Hamilton and the girl."

The door closed behind them and Landers and Mike rounded on me. "What do you know about Hamilton Baine and Lakshmi Drake?" I couldn't even tell who the words came from.

Before I got my mouth open to answer, my phone erupted, ringing and buzzing a text arrival at the same time. I looked at the screen.

Les.

"I'm off today, you prick," I muttered, clicking the power button to silence it and tucking it away.

"All evidence to the contrary," Mike said.

I rolled my eyes. "Bob is out of town. Les Simpson seems to still hate me even though he's not sleeping with Shelby anymore. I don't think, anyway."

They nodded in unison.

"So?" Landers asked.

"I would advise y'all to start with putting cyber on who deleted Lakshmi's Instagram yesterday," I said. "That's about what I know right now. I found photos of her with Hamilton Baine on a beach, draped all over each other, yesterday morning. Ten minutes later they were gone."

Mike scribbled on his pad. Landers shot to his feet and started pacing. "What the fuck is going on here?"

He didn't expect an answer, because if any of us knew, we wouldn't have been sitting there.

"Thanks for coming up today, Nichelle." Mike pushed his chair back.

"Always good to see you, Mike. Good luck with this," I said.

"Let me know if you come across anything you think might help us," he said, opening the door for me.

"Of course." I didn't feel guilty for not spilling about Angela, because I knew nothing for sure yet except that Lakshmi's social media was gone, and I'd told him that.

I didn't check my phone until I got back to my car, expecting that Les had called when I didn't reply to his text right away.

Not Les.

Kyle.

The ATF has no official comment on yesterday's incident at the Virginia capitol, in accordance with our policy of not discussing ongoing investigations with the news media. Please direct all further inquiries to the office of public information.

I threw my phone across the car, watching it bounce off the passenger window and the dash before it clattered into the floorboard.

Like hell I would. Everyone I knew had lost their mind in the last twenty-four hours, but Kyle blowing me off like that wasn't . . . Kyle.

I worked my car out of the space and pointed it toward Byrd Park. When I stopped in front of the fountain, I retrieved the phone and replied with *Understood*. And a white dove emoji.

I pulled a notebook and pen out and started scribbling notes from my meeting at the PD as fast as my fingers could move, checking the parking lot entrance every three minutes until I saw Kyle's blue Explorer turn in. He parked at the other end of the lot and strolled toward the boathouse.

I put my notebook down and followed.

14

Kyle hadn't slept. At least all night. Maybe all week.

His icy baby blues were downright creepy, more blood red than white surrounding his irises, puffy pink eyelids rimming the whole picture for good measure. He'd looked harried and tired at the courthouse yesterday, but I'd blown it off, assuming he'd been at work in the wee hours because of the crime scene.

This was more than a dozen hours of lost sleep, though. My heart picked up speed, hammering against my ribs so hard I had to be visibly shaking. Nothing ever got to Kyle. That's why he made such a good cop. Practically un-ruffle-able.

I took in his scruffy face and rolled-up, rumpled shirtsleeves. Locking eyes with him, I laid one hand on his arm.

"Are you okay?" Story be damned, I was worried about my friend.

He shook his head, and the arm, sending my hand back to my side. "Keep your voice down," he hissed.

I glanced around. "There are five people here and none of them are within twenty paces of us." I fought to keep my tone normal, but tinges of high panic crept in around the words anyway.

He grabbed my hand and pulled me close, locking his fingers behind my waist and poking his nose so far into my face a sheet of paper wouldn't fit between us. "If anyone's watching us, they'll think we're kids making out."

I tried not to cough when the words rolled out in a cloud of stale garlic.

Hadn't brushed his teeth in a while either. Ick.

I fought the urge to recoil, worry plunging a sharp, stomping heel through disgust. "Kyle, you're scaring me." I tried to ration the words so I didn't have to breathe in as much. "What is the matter with you?"

"I screwed up." His eyes closed, his arms tightening around me the tiniest bit. "When I texted you yesterday. If I could take it back, I would—I should never have dragged you into this."

I pulled my head back as far as I could. He opened his eyes.

Tears brightened the redness to zombie-movie levels.

I swallowed hard.

He was scared, too.

I opened my mouth. Nothing came out. I closed it again.

I forced a smile and tried again. "It's not like I don't have some experience playing in the big leagues. I can take care of myself."

He shook his head. "I'm not sure I can even take care of you."

One tear escaped and slid toward the scruff lining his lip and jaw. "I'm so sorry, Nicey."

I swiveled my head, craning my neck as far as I could see in either direction, trying to catch my breath. It wasn't like Kyle still saw me as his high school girlfriend. We'd been through some pretty serious shit together in the past couple of years.

Which meant whatever was going on here was way bigger than I'd dared to think. Bigger than Ted Grayson. Even bigger than Governor Baine. What the hell had Lakshmi stumbled into?

"It doesn't seem there's anything for it now, does it?" I tried for cheerful but missed the mark by so much I just sounded nauseous. "I know what I know—which is a lot more than I've heard from you, I might add—so why don't you just go ahead and give up what you know about Hamilton Baine. Do you have a bead on where he is?"

He shook his head slowly, sniffling. "Nobody does." He pulled in a deep breath. "Listen, I told you to come here so I could tell you one thing: get the hell out of Richmond. Full stop. Don't pack, don't call anyone, don't tell me where you're going. Just go. I'll go get the dog. I can't have you in the middle of this one."

I squirmed, trying to take a step back. "I'm sorry, what?"

"Go. Not to your mother's, and try not to use your credit cards." He loosened his grip and I broke away, stumbling back over my heels until I was in the sun, staring into the shadows at my old friend.

"I have a job to do. A life. I can't just take off on a whim." I stammered over the words, my pulse rate fluttering like I was in the home stretch of the Suntrust Marathon.

"It's not a whim."

I furrowed my brow. What had changed in the past four hours? He wasn't particularly chatty this morning, but he'd helped me get into the prison. And then commenced blowing up my phone. Something happened while I was talking with Angela, because I'd swear this was a body snatcher if I didn't know every line of Kyle's face so well. His hands closed over my wrist, tugging me back toward him. "Please, Nichelle."

He had talked to someone. An interview was the only thing that explained the break in the insistent text messages, and his flip-the-hell-out about face.

And I had a pretty good idea how to find out who.

I let him pull me back, Governor Baine and Mrs. Drake flashing through my head. I had promised to help find out what happened to their children. Not to mention the fact that I liked Lakshmi. If I bowed out, who would stop her death from being reduced to a side note in yet another political sex scandal? Not Charlie. For damned sure not Dan. Lakshmi would be objectified in some circles and outright demonized in others.

I had to know where Kyle had been. I hugged him, running my hands up and down his back before I locked my arms tight around his narrow waist.

He folded his lips between his teeth. "You don't understand, dammit. This isn't the time to fight for the story. Be stubborn next month. At least you'll be alive for me to fight with."

"It's not about the headline. Not this time. It's about the girl. I'm the only voice she has, Kyle. What good is staying alive if it comes at the expense of being able to live with myself?"

His breath spread warm across my scalp as he buried his face in my hair, tears falling fast as he crushed my shoulders. "So goddamned stubborn," he whispered. "I love you, you know. Don't forget that, no matter what, okay?"

I nodded, fluttering my lashes over the telltale pricking in the backs of my eyes as I stepped back. "I'm always careful."

"You're always lucky." The words came out so soft I couldn't have sworn in court what he said.

I squeezed his right hand with my left. "Looks like you could use a little luck on this one, too, Agent. Take care of yourself, you hear me? We'll get dinner when it's all over. My treat."

He was still standing there, shaking his head, when I got in my car.

I turned the key and backed up, gunning it out of the lot and driving a few blocks before I pulled to the curbside under an orangey-yellow oak and opened my right hand.

"Stacy Adams," I whispered to Kenny Chesney, who was singing about nowhere to go. "Commonwealth Energy Alliance. Let's see if you can connect any of these pieces."

My fingers curled tight around the card I'd lifted from Kyle's back pocket when I hugged him, my throat closing around rising guilt. He always wore his pants too loose, and had a habit of palming cards when he did interviews and slipping them in his left hip pocket. The only explanation I had for the past twenty minutes was that somebody he'd talked to today had freaked him right the hell out, so I'd fished out the card trying to see who was behind his meltdown.

I was sure Kyle knew how to get ahold of Stacy again if he needed her. And maybe a sit-down with her would finally help part of this mess make sense.

* * *

I clicked my email open, looking for a reply from Angela Baker. Strike one.

Joey's face popped up on the screen before I could decide what to check on next. I sighed, my eyes going to the clock. Ten to five, on Saturday. Nobody was still in the office. And I couldn't keep ignoring him.

"Hey." I managed to keep my voice from shaking as I put the phone to my ear. "Sorry it's so late. What's going on there?"

"Starting to get a little worried about you. I'm not exactly used to sitting by while you go chase killers. You about ready to call it a day?"

Ah-ha. I hadn't had an all-consuming story like this since he moved to Richmond, and he wasn't really the stoke-the-home-fires type. I should call it a day.

"I need to write up a follow to shut Les up, but I can do that from anywhere. Where are you?"

"Still at your house."

"Be there in ten."

"I'll open the wine. Drive safely."

I clicked to my texts and touched Les's name. *Sending a follow on yesterday's murder shortly. Watch your email,* I tapped. Just because Charlie wasn't my biggest problem didn't mean I could ignore her.

Easing my foot off the gas, I took a right at the corner and let my brain wander back through the day as I navigated the tree-lined cobblestone streets, the dazzling yellows and oranges of the trees blurring into the gray of the buildings as the city zipped past my windows.

Sitting at a red light, I closed my eyes for a few beats, trying to sort a conclusion—or at least a theory or two—out of the tangled mess of information I'd taken in since this morning.

Kyle's teary, worried face kept pushing through everything else, sending panicked butterflies flapping around my middle.

"He's being overly cautious," I mumbled, putting my foot back on the gas when the light changed. I wanted to believe it. But I wasn't sure I did.

Something big was happening here. A senator devising heinous blackmail to get at science secrets. A dead woman who knew—in the Biblical sense—a whole bushel of powerful men. The governor's missing son—who had unfettered access to the murder scene and also worked in the science sector.

Not Lakshmi's research, like I'd thought this time yesterday, but her dad's. I turned into my driveway as the mission solidified: I just needed to know what Dr. Drake was working on. Because top secret energy science is easy to come by.

I climbed the steps and pushed the kitchen door open, smiling at the small bouquet of red and white roses in the center of the table. A plate of cheese and crackers sat next to it, two wineglasses completing the picture. My stomach rumbled, reminding me that my blueberry muffin was a long damned time ago.

"Hey," I called, kicking my Manolos off and picking them up. "Anyone home?"

I padded down the hallway in bare feet, peeking into the living room. Joey was sitting on the floor, tugging one leg of Darcy's favorite stuffed frog while she dug her toes into the rug, backing up and growling as she shook the toy by its head.

I smiled. "Y'all are so cute."

Joey looked up, a grin spreading across his chiseled features. "She's fun."

"She's spoiled rotten. But we like her that way." I crossed the room in three long strides, dropping onto the thick, geometric-patterned rug next to him with a sigh. "The table looks nice." I bumped my shoulder against his.

He pulled the toy away from Darcy and tossed it over her head, sending her skittering across the floor after it. Turning, he raised his good hand to cup my face. "I figured you didn't eat much after you left here. How was the madam?"

I shook my head. "Don't want to talk about it right now. Too much I'm still trying to process." I leaned in to plant a soft kiss on his full lips. "Dinner?"

His jaw flexed so briefly I couldn't swear I hadn't imagined it before his lips tipped up at the corners. "I ordered Vito's. When was the last time you went grocery shopping? All I could find in the kitchen was cheese, crackers, wine, and dog food."

"The cheese should still be good. Beyond that, it's a little fuzzy."

He stood, pulling me up behind him in one fluid motion. "Let's go see. Dinner will be here in about a half hour. Maybe some food will help you process faster." He did a good job covering the worried undertone—anyone who didn't know him like I did wouldn't have noticed it.

I followed him to the kitchen, where he pulled a bottle of my favorite Italian Moscato from the fridge and poured it into the glasses. I cut a wedge of cheese and grabbed a cracker, stuffing all of both into my face and chewing as I wiped escaping crumbs from the corners of my lips.

Joey took the seat across from me and sipped his wine, reaching for a cracker. I handed him the knife after I made myself a second one.

Nibbling the edge of the cheese that hung over the cracker, I studied him through lowered lashes. He wanted to know what I'd found out. Which wasn't unusual, even when the murder victim wasn't someone he had a soft spot for.

I just didn't know how much I should tell him.

Safer things first. "The governor's son is missing," I said, and bit into the cracker.

He froze with his glass halfway to his lips. "Who knows that besides you?"

I shrugged. "A very small handful of cops and the governor."

The muscle in his jaw twitched, and my stomach closed in around the cheese. "What?"

Joey sighed, setting his glass on the table. "I'm trying to figure out what kind of mess you're getting into here. Baine has some old friends at the Richmond PD. They're in a habit of being careful what they say where that kid is concerned."

I tipped my head to one side, chewing on the rest of the cracker. He didn't say anything else. I swallowed. "Care to elaborate?"

He leaned back in the chair, his face going flat. Unreadable. "You have a lot of friends at the PD, too, princess. How much do you want to know?"

Damn. I knew that look. It was the one that said he was protecting me by not telling me something. "I want to know the truth," I blurted, not sure the words were accurate as they left my lips. I walked a fine line in my relationships with my cops. They weren't supposed to be my friends, because it wreaks havoc on objectivity. But they kind of were anyway, particularly to the extent that I trusted them to want to do the right thing. And hoped that staying mindful of my fondness for a handful of officers would balance my view and keep me unbiased.

But sitting there looking at Joey, I felt much the same way as when Kyle started talking about the Caccione syndicate: afraid to hear things that would make me think less of people I cared about.

"You're not sure about that." Joey could read my face better than just about anyone.

I nodded. "You're right. But tell me anyway." Please God, don't let him say anything bad about Aaron.

"I'm not talking about shady deals and crooked cops—more like backroom political handshakes. But I wasn't sure you'd keep asking."

I sipped my wine. "What kind of backroom handshakes?"

"Back when Baine was the mayor, his kid was a handful. Things got resolved on the quiet, off the books, and Baine greased wheels at city hall for funding for programs the department wanted. Putting full-time officers in underprivileged schools, drug clinics, increased funding for child protective services. It didn't all directly benefit the department's budget, but what didn't helped lighten their workload."

I waved one hand. "And helped thousands of people. Hell, I'd sign on to keep the kid's name out of the paper for all that."

Joey's jaw flexed, his eyes going to the floor. "Not the best parenting tactic, though."

Because dad always pulling strings to get a troubled boy out of trouble might just make the kid think he could get away with literal murder.

Mrs. Powers's phone screen: *She's dead . . . and I wasn't even in there. What am I going to do?*

Grieving boyfriend, as I assumed the first time I read it? Or privileged young man who had experience covering his ass?

Kyle's red-rimmed eyes and stoic silence . . . Mike inviting me up into the middle of their conversation . . . Baine's rumpled and haggard appearance.

Puzzle pieces clicked in faster than I could keep up with. Were my cops hunting for Hamilton because they were concerned for his safety—or trying to help his dad with spin control? And how much did Kyle know?

Joey got out of his chair when I stood. "Where are you going now?" he asked.

I hurried to the living room, pulled out my laptop, and returned to the table. "Someone who had Lakshmi's passwords deleted all of her social media accounts," I said. "Hamilton looked well and truly into her, but he has a troubled history, right?" A history not one cop said a bitty little word about in an hour-long conversation. And while I was hanging on to that card for Stacy Anderson, it was also after I asked Kyle about Hamilton that he flipped his shit. "Something isn't right."

I clicked into my search history and found Hamilton's friend, the one I'd located the address for the day before. Copied it over into my notes.

Joey touched my knee, and I looked over my screen to find him kneeling in front of me. "Catch me up."

"Baine didn't know about Lakshmi's past today, when I asked him." I put the computer on the table and took a long swig of my wine. "But he also wouldn't give me a straight answer when I asked if he was sleeping with her. He looked like hell—which, I know, his kid is gone and there was a dead woman on his desk yesterday, but . . ." I paused for air. "But. You said yourself Lakshmi had a thing for older men. Powerful ones. Suppose Hamilton walked in on his dad and his girlfriend and went all Charles Manson?"

"They'd have no choice but to cover it up." Joey's full lips almost disappeared into a thin white line. "Hamilton would literally have dad's ass in a sling."

"Exactly. Thomas Baine is on the edge of vaulting onto the national political stage. State law here gives him a very narrow window for that—he gets four years as governor, and then he's out. The president is coming here. She likes him, party be damned. Everything is going his way." The faster I talked, the more sense this trail made. "Hell, he even said it today, that he didn't trust the state police as much as he trusted his old pals at the RPD. And Aaron and Mike bought every word."

"But what does he trust them to do, exactly?"

I nodded. "That's the question I didn't know to ask. Because if he trusts them to keep his career steaming ahead no matter what his kid has done, I have a serious problem."

Joey's brow furrowed. "How so?"

"I already lost Kyle. If I can't trust Aaron and Mike, I'm down all my best sources in the middle of the most complicated story I've ever seen." I slumped back in the chair. "So. Now what?"

15

"Lost Kyle?" Joey put his hands up. "What the hell are you talking about?"

Damn. I didn't mean to say that. Joey didn't like Kyle for obvious personal reasons, but under the jealousy, he respected Kyle's intelligence. Which meant under no circumstances could he know why Kyle wasn't talking to me about this case. I didn't need a fight on the home front piled on top of the teetering mountain of bullshit that had invaded our laid-back weekend. And I wouldn't put it entirely past Joey to try locking me in the bedroom for the duration of the investigation. His overprotective streak can stretch too far on occasion.

"He's really busy," I said. "This added to his caseload at an already inconvenient time."

Joey's eyebrows leapt to his hairline. "Since when is Miller too busy for you?"

It was a lame excuse, and felt every syllable of it. Before I could get my mouth open to try another, he laid both hands on my knees.

"If Miller is staying clear of you, there's a reason for it, and that probably means you're on the right track with your story."

I blinked. He didn't think I was lying to him—he thought Kyle was lying to me.

Which made me feel smaller than the pinpoint heels on my new emerald Louboutins. Joey trusted me. Really well and truly trusted me. And I didn't deserve it. Not right then, anyway. But keeping that to myself saved him a fight, too.

I twisted my lips up into a smile. "I hope so. This feeling in my gut that nobody else is going to give a shit if or how Lakshmi is remembered is getting bigger every minute. Getting it first is the best way to get as many eyes on my story as possible."

"Which means this just became a bona fide working weekend." He nodded. "I'm used to it. And I can't tell you how much I appreciate it." The last words were lost in an uncharacteristic choked-up cover cough that made my heart skip.

Jiminy Choos. Working weekend. I clapped a hand over my mouth, checking the clock. Five twenty. "I promised Les a story half an hour ago," I said through my fingers before I reached for my laptop. "The last thing I need is for him to be up my ass more than usual until Bob gets home."

The doorbell rang, and Joey stood. "Dinner's here. I'll get it. You write fast."

I turned the chair, sipped my wine, and retrieved my notebook.

Not much I could share, still. I clicked to Channel Four's website.

Banner headline: *A Death in Jefferson's Masterpiece.* "Dramatic much, y'all?" I grimaced, scrolling through Charlie's story. She didn't have anything new, and if she knew who the vic was, she hadn't published it yet. Her piece ended with a teaser for the six o'clock broadcast, though. Which gave me zero time.

Richmond Police and state officials continued their silence Saturday about the human remains discovered in the Virginia capitol early Friday.

"This is obviously a sensitive matter," RPD spokesman Aaron White said Friday. "We're going to be respectful of the state business that needs to go on, as well as the history inherent in this building, as we work through leads."

State police are working in concert with RPD detectives to resolve the matter as quickly as possible, White said.

White asked that any Richmond residents who were in the vicinity of Bank Street and 9th Street between 2 a.m. and 6 a.m. Friday please call Crimestoppers.

.   .   .

I finished up with a couple of useless talking head quotes and read over it twice before I attached it to an email and sent it to Les.

Closing the computer, I stood. "That's the longest dinner delivery I've ever heard of," I called, walking down the front hall. I paused in the living room doorway. "Are we having an indoor picnic tonight?" The smile the words filtered through died when I looked around. Empty.

"Joey?" I moved quicker, back to the hallway. "Darcy?"

No answer.

Bathroom? Nope.

Bedroom? Nope.

I bypassed the guest room on my way to the front door, my heart clear up in my throat as I jerked the thing nearly off its hinges and rushed out onto the wide, covered front porch.

No food.

No dog.

No Joey.

My fingers curled into a fist I pressed to my lips, holding a scream in by sheer force.

Deep breath. Calm. Think, Nichelle. Joey was not only a big man, he was a damned intimidating one. It would take a hell of a sneak attack or a real badass to make him do anything he didn't want to. I hadn't heard a peep, from right down the hall.

It had been maybe fifteen minutes. Maybe Darcy wanted a walk.

I padded down the steps and picked my way across the yard, still barefoot, to the driveway. His car was still there.

Spinning around, I surveyed the street.

A dark Crown Vic sat idle under a stunning scarlet maple three houses down.

I started for the street just as a Jeep with a Vito's magnet on the driver's door turned into my driveway.

"Delivery for a Mr. Clarke?" The stringy-haired teenage boy pulled a big insulated bag from behind the driver's seat.

That scream threatened to bust out any second.

My eyes stayed on the Crown Vic, just too far away and too in the shade for me to see inside clearly. I nodded. "Can you leave it on the porch?"

"But I need someone to sign," he began, and I stuck out a hand as he dug for the credit card receipt. I scribbled something that probably didn't look like anyone's actual signature and shoved the little slip of paper back at him.

"Thanks," I said, moving toward the street and then stopping.

I couldn't see if there was anyone in the car.

But if anyone was in the car, they could see me.

I put a foot out and pulled it back again half a dozen times. The kid put the food on the porch and climbed back in his Jeep, waving as he drove off. I stayed still, watching as his running lamps flashed across the windshield of the sedan.

A man's pale face registered behind the wheel, not enough time for me to see if he was wearing a suit. Because I was too busy staring at Joey, sitting in the passenger seat talking, gesturing with the hand that wasn't bandaged.

I backed slowly toward the front steps.

Joey trusted me.

But I seemed to be running out of people I could say the same about.

I left the food on the table next to the porch swing, shutting the door behind me and striding back to the kitchen. The wine bottle chilled my fingers as I grabbed it off the counter and refilled my glass—to the brim this time. I chugged it like a college freshman at a frat pledge party, wiping my lips with the back of my hand as I put the glass on the yellow-tiled counter.

Just thinking about Joey being involved in whatever the actual hell was happening had my skin crawling right up my arms. Things had been so good. Too good? Too easy, maybe? Had I fooled myself into getting too comfortable with our quiet little life?

I couldn't swear that guy was one of the suits from the Drake house. Couldn't swear he wasn't, either. A dark Crown Vic is a popular vehicle with federal law enforcement, which makes them popular with people who want to look official to avoid questions, too. I had a feeling those dudes were bad news. Not a feeling I could put a finger on, though.

Wait.

"Oh, holy Manolos," The suit. The sunglasses. The silent staring.

The guy who'd come into the library at the university the day before. That's where the creeptastic feeling I'd had floating around these guys all day originated.

I blinked. Poured more wine. Gave my world a second to settle.

"Just facts. No assumptions," I murmured.

I picked up the glass and swallowed more Moscato. Joey was so upset when he heard about Lakshmi this morning. Maybe he knew someone who might know something. Maybe he was trying to help. Certainly, precedent said he'd want to keep anything shady he might be involved in far away from me.

So I needed to jump back across this particular conclusion canyon.

I spun and looked back at the door. Still silent.

My cell phone buzzed on the counter. Thankful for any distraction from a problem I didn't want to face, I snatched it up.

Les.

Pushing the limits of gratitude there, universe. I clicked the gray rectangle.

Are you kidding? This is thinner than Andrews's hair.

I swallowed a snort. Les's comb-over was the stuff of newsroom legend —he had zero room to make fun of anyone's hair loss. But Andrews was also the only person I disliked more than Les.

I tried to come up with a tactful response.

Nobody is talking, I finally tapped. Close enough to true.

The gray dot-bubble that popped up immediately told me he wasn't done.

This is bullshit, Clarke. I won't run it.

I laid the phone on the counter before I typed something that would get me in trouble, stepping back two paces. I had enough of a mounting headache without a pissing war with Les. He was just being a jerk. If he didn't run my story, Bob would have his ass Monday morning, and he had to know that better than I did.

It buzzed more insistently, ringing this time. Was he kidding? I picked it up, finger on the button to dismiss the call. Not Les. Unidentified caller, Cleveland, Ohio.

"Seriously, we don't want any," I muttered, going back to the text screen.

Nobody else has more than I do, Les. We can't just not have a story on this, the whole city is buzzing about it. Send.

I watched the screen. *I thought you were supposed to be better than everybody else.*

Apparently even my superpowers only go so far. I wasn't letting him bait me into saying something I'd regret—on any front. Which meant I needed to be done with this conversation. *Look, run it, don't run it, that's your call today. But I wouldn't want to be you when Bob gets back if you don't print it.*

I clicked the phone locked, eyeing the clock on the stove. Joey had been outside for better than twenty minutes.

I moved toward the front door. Stopped. Took another step.

Took one back.

"This is ridiculous," I said to the empty house, marching to the door and yanking it open.

"That took longer than I thought," Joey said from the swing, Darcy lying across his feet and dinner spread picnic-style on the table in front of him. "Everything okay?"

I blinked. "I um . . . I was arguing with Les," I stammered, glad the wine wasn't making the words slur or my brain too foggy to put them together at a normal pace.

"I'm confident you won any battle of wits with that guy." He smiled. "Dinner okay out here? It's such a nice night."

I nodded, spinning back for the door. "I'll get the wine."

It took the whole walk to the kitchen and back for my pulse to slow sufficiently. I'd been all ready to ask him who the hell that guy was and what was going on.

But now? I wasn't sure. Maybe guarded and watchful was better. It didn't look like he had any idea that I knew he'd had company, and I could bury my whole house under the pile of mistaken assumptions I'd made about Joey. With uncertainty and mistrust around every solid corner of my professional life today, I didn't want to rock the personal boat.

If it was bad, he'd tell me. He trusted me. And it was past time I started having more faith in him.

I paused in the hallway, checking my face in the mirror near the old built-in telephone niche.

Even breathing. Bright smile.

My stomach snarled so violently Darcy barked from the porch.

My world might be trying to crash in from every direction today, but I had to eat something.

Maybe stabilizing my blood sugar would help my brain shake loose a way to figure out at least part of what the hell I was diving into here.

16

Two pasta bowls, a Caesar salad, and a whole heap of banter about my Cowboys beating Joey's Redskins later, I wasn't sure of much except that I'd made the right choice keeping my mouth shut. For now, anyway.

"Thanks, that was exactly what I needed." I sank back into the soft mustard-colored pillows lining the back of the swing, pulling my feet up to crisscross my legs in the seat.

He put his empty foil bowl back on the table and turned to face me, brushing a stray lock of hair off my cheek. "I like to think I'm getting pretty good at knowing what you need." The words dropped slowly, his voice deep. Almost raw. I leaned my cheek into his hand and met his eyes, warm and open and emotional.

"It seems that way."

He wasn't lying to me. I couldn't find even a trace of the closed-off, drive-Nichelle-batshit-crazy look I hated so much.

I closed my eyes, and his lips covered mine in a sweet, soft, warm kiss I leaned into and lost myself in. My arms floated up around his neck, my fingers curling into his thick, dark hair.

How many times had I guessed wrong where this man was concerned?

More than I cared to count. And I'd regretted it and sworn I never would again every time.

With everything in my world going sideways, I needed a place to land. To feel safe.

And I felt safe with Joey.

"I love you," he whispered against my lips as he sat back, pulling me close.

I snuggled my head into the soft spot between his shoulder and his collarbone and traced lazy circles on his bare forearm with my index finger.

"I love you, too," I said. Every word true.

Joey wouldn't do anything to hurt me. I had no proof the guy I'd seen him talking to had anything to do with my story, and I never asked him about his business "associates."

Best left alone, then.

He rested his chin on top of my head. "What do you feel like doing tonight? This was the extent of my master plan."

I giggled. "Decent, as master plans go."

He waved one hand. "Easy. You never remember to stop and eat when you're chasing a big story."

"You know me so well."

He chuckled. "And you know something? I like it that way. There's a thought I never expected to have. I do a lot of things I never would've expected because of you." His smooth tenor dipped to baritone again.

"I don't mean to be any trouble," I said.

He shook his head. "You're not trouble, princess. Some people, yes, but never you."

I planted a soft kiss on the curve of his jaw, drawing a smile. "Liar."

"Never."

He put a hand on my shoulder and sat me up, angling his chin down to meet my gaze. "I mean that. I will never lie to you, Nichelle. It's important to me that you know that."

I nodded, the downright earnest look in his eyes making my stomach twist. I kissed the tip of his straight nose and smiled as I stood. "Back at you. And how about a movie and a long, hot bath?"

He flashed a smile, something else skating across his face so quickly I couldn't match the flicker with an emotion.

"I can't think of a better way to spend Saturday night."

I couldn't, either. As we gathered empty food containers and wine-glasses, I squashed uncomfortable thoughts of all the questions I regretted not asking. In almost a decade in the news business, the list wasn't short.

But this also wasn't the same as a one-shot sit-down with a serial killer or a cagey cop.

I could always ask Joey later.

For tonight, hoping I wouldn't need to would do.

* * *

My bedroom ceiling fan blades spin forty-seven times a minute on low.

By 11:26, I'd counted it enough times to verify data that would stand up in any courtroom.

And I was no closer to figuring out where Hamilton Baine was or how Lakshmi ended up dead in his father's office than I'd been when I walked out of the police station.

After easing my shoulders out from under the safe, comforting weight of Joey's arm, I turned my pillow and pushed it between his bicep and the cool sheets before I tiptoed out of the room with a quick "shhh" at Darcy when she popped her head out of her bed.

I flipped on the kitchen light and then the coffee maker, and stuck a cup under the spout with one eye on the flashing light that told me the water was heating. It flickered off, and I pressed the "Brew" button and turned to grab my laptop and notebook. The kitchen filled with the smell of Colombian breakfast roast tinged with pumpkin and cinnamon. I added a generous splash of milk and carried the steaming mug to the table.

I had figured out one thing in going on two hours of watching the fan spin: there were too many trails to chase any of them properly.

I was frustrated and confused and felt like I was failing, because so much random shit kept happening, I couldn't tell what was and wasn't connected to Lakshmi's murder.

Flipping through my notes, I found a dozen things that would make a solid headline and earn a thorough story on a normal day.

My problem was, today wasn't normal. And it was a good bet tomorrow wouldn't be, either. I didn't have time to finish looking into one weird thing before another happened.

Journalism Even before the Age of the Internet 101: when a story gets complicated, a reporter needs to get organized.

I put the notebook down and stood, slipping back down the hallway and around to the guest bedroom, where I fished one of my friend Jenna's sketchbooks out of the back of the closet. She'd left it behind ages ago and told me repeatedly to keep it, and I kept forgetting to give it back. Score one for absentmindedness.

I folded the cover back to a clean page, snagged a *Telegraph* mug full of different-colored pens off the dresser, and returned to my chair in the kitchen.

Uncapping a blue pen, I wrote Lakshmi's name on one side of the top of the page.

With red, I wrote Hamilton's in the opposite corner.

I knew how the two of them were connected, at least lately. I drew a line from her name to Hamilton's with a heart above it.

How deep were they in with each other? How long had they been together? Either or both answers might help me find a way to why she was dead and he was missing.

I figured that partly because Lakshmi's online life disappeared. Someone didn't want people knowing she'd been seeing Hamilton. I put another star under her name and jotted that next to it.

Back on the other side, I changed to red again and noted Hamilton's disappearance. Another star next to his text about Lakshmi to Mrs. Powers —he'd still had his phone just before dawn Friday, but sometime in the next twenty-four hours, he disappeared and nobody knew how or why. If Aaron and Chris could've tracked his phone, they would've.

Working through my notes page by page, I listed every little odd thing I'd seen or heard in the past thirty-six hours, finishing with the quasi-gestapo unit that seemed to be nosing around under everyone's radar.

I pushed the cap back onto the end of the red pen, staring at the neat lines of facts on the wide, thick ecru paper.

Loads of crazy.

No links.

I was still missing something.

I clicked to Google. Typed Lakshmi's name.

And got a pop-up warning about explicit content from the *Telegraph*'s remote server.

Swallowing hard, I clicked the bar at the top of my screen and switched to my home Wi-Fi.

Angela Baker's words ringing in my head, I didn't want to look.

But I had to.

Videos. More than a dozen, from various adult sites both free and paid, with grotesque, demeaning labels in the titles.

I clicked the first one, watched about three seconds of her bound and gagged on a wide bed with dove-gray sheets, and closed my eyes. Jesus.

Swallowing hard, I opened my eyes, scanning the perimeters of the frame for her partner. Client. Whatever.

A man's bare middle two-thirds entered from the top left. He wound one hand into Lakshmi's long hair and forced her head back. Her eyes widened, afraid, as she looked up at him. I couldn't see his face.

Not that I needed to, really—I had enough pieces to plunk Ted Grayson dead center in this corner of my spreading web. I'd bet my favorite Louboutins one of the videos Angela had alluded to earlier was playing on my screen.

But why? I'd searched Lakshmi's name Friday morning and hadn't seen a single frame of this.

I clicked "Stop"—I couldn't take any more once he started hitting her, and Grayson was too smart to show his face. Watching would only lead to crippling nausea with a generous side scoop of white-hot fury.

I scrolled down. Checked the stats at the bottom of the page.

It had been up for fourteen hours and change. With over a quarter of a million views already.

Damn.

I clicked to the tax office website. Typed in Grayson's name and hit the "Search" button. He would either slam the door in my face or shoot me dead if I rang the bell wherever he was, but I at least needed to go see what he was up to.

No results found. I repeated the search in six surrounding counties. The immediate DC suburbs.

Nothing.

Who gets out of prison and vanishes into thin air? Someone who's up to no good.

My puzzle pieces all shifted at once as I closed the window and looked back at my chart.

Half the day, I'd been chasing Hamilton Baine, thinking he might've done something to hurt Lakshmi and then disappeared, with or without the help of the governor or my favorite detectives. Hunting political intrigue, musing about sex scandals and hot tempers.

But what if I was looking at it all wrong? That video wouldn't so much as ding a politician's reputation, especially with the care taken to keep the man's face off camera.

But Lakshmi?

Instantly branded with those subtitles. And *whore* was the kindest word I'd seen.

"They didn't just kill her. They're demonizing her before anyone even knows who's dead." Somehow saying it out loud, even in a whisper, made it less farfetched.

What if Lakshmi wasn't a political potshot at Baine—but instead she knew something that got her killed? And what if Hamilton wasn't in hiding at all? What if he was actually the last hurdle for whoever wanted Lakshmi not just dead but maligned and discredited to the point of immediate dismissal?

Not a brilliant mathematician. Not a rising political statistics star.

Not even a person.

A caricature. A demon.

A joke.

I picked up the chart and drew more lines. Scribbled more notes.

A corner of my mental puzzle took a dark, nasty shape as I wrote. Taking down Lakshmi's social media accounts, which would normally be the top results when someone searched her name, ensured that the harlot characterization was the first impression people got.

I once saw a tweet from a psych journal proclaiming that people make up their mind about you based on the first three search results your name produces. Less than fifty hours after she died, someone had worked hard to ensure that Lakshmi Drake would be scorned and hated, even vilified in some circles. Porn videos are the scarlet letters of the twenty-first century. The ultimate form of slut-shaming in a world where image can matter more than truth, and anything that makes it onto the internet is forever.

I stared at my chart until all the ink went fuzzy and unfocused.

It was the story of the year, a dead body turning up in the governor's office. Right?

Except . . . it wasn't. Secrets and "no comments" and official red tape had made the story about the act instead of the victim.

I'd worked hundreds of murder scenes. The victim is always the story.

Except when the body is found in what's supposed to be the most secure room in the commonwealth.

Downright diabolical, but clever as all hell. An idea shinier than the Swarovski-encrusted Manolos I'd been stalking on eBay.

Lakshmi Drake had just had the most private public death in the history of the world. Had she been found in the river, the woods, the gutter —everyone would've been writing about her, and before somebody had time to alter the Google-accessible narrative.

Because she was on the governor's desk, nobody was writing about her.

We were just writing about her murder.

Clicking my photos open, I scrolled back. And back. And back some more.

Weddings, Halloweens, and summers flashed by in a blur.

There: Lakshmi and I leaning on each other at the bar laughing, at the underground poker game where I first met her.

She had a beautiful smile and a brilliant mind. And if someone was trying to steal her voice, to redirect the spotlight to the darkest part of her story, the best way to fight that was to put her in the paper. Talk about her. Make her real. Gorgeous. Funny. Smart.

More than a handful of videos people would use to indict her character and dismiss her death.

I didn't have a comment on the record. I didn't know the rest of the story. I might tip my hand to Charlie.

But right then, none of that mattered.

This young woman, why she was dead, and why anyone wanted her dismissed and discredited in addition to dead, crowded my head until there was no room for anything else.

I spent my life chasing tragedy. Writing about the aftermath of horrifying events I had no way to control or predict. Tonight, with this, I could control something—maybe the most important something, if my hunch was on target.

Nobody had written or spoken one word about Lakshmi Drake.

So I could control her story if I told it first.

I opened a blank file. Clicked into my contacts and called Les. He mumbled something that might've passed for "hello" to someone who was really listening on the fifth ring.

"How much is a replate at this time of night?" I asked, my eyes on the clock.

I knew the ballpark: a lot, that's how much. It was after midnight. We'd be tossing half, maybe two-thirds of our press run. And for Sunday, to boot.

"Clarke?" My question was better than a mainline injection of espresso. Les was good and awake in less than a dozen words. "What the hell are you talking about?"

"You spent half an hour this morning yelling at me about the potential for losing to Charlie today. You want to kick everyone's ass tomorrow? Call the pressroom and tell them to watch for an email from me. We can replace the lead story on the Sunday front with an exclusive that will blow everyone else on the East Coast out of the water."

"You're talking about thousands of dollars. Can't we just put it online?"

"I've got her name, Les. Trust me, you want it in print."

"Send it to me first," was all he said before he hung up.

I put the phone on the table and started typing.

I knew all the way down to my bones this was bigger than even I had a handle on right then. Which is how I managed to ignore the downright obnoxious warning bells in my head.

Kyle's tears. Joey's mystery rendezvous.

The story on my screen was the riskiest thing I'd ever done, career-wise. I didn't have a quotable source. I was breaking a stone-set journalistic commandment. But standing up for Lakshmi took precedence over everything else as my fingers flew over the keys, my coffee still scenting the air with cinnamon spice as it cooled in the mug next to my keyboard.

I was one thousand percent digging into something I didn't yet fully understand, poking a bear I couldn't gauge for size or ferocity. I'd never jumped knowingly into harm's way. But some things were more important than safety. Wasn't that why Eunice climbed into a chopper that crashed and almost got her killed in Iraq? To get the story, even if it meant she didn't get to see it published?

I knew the stakes: If someone was trying to destroy Lakshmi Drake even after she was dead, and I put her on the front page of the Sunday paper, how long would it be before they decided to destroy me?

I was all in anyway.

17

Lakshmi Drake wanted to be the next Nate Silver. She liked bright colors and good wine and had a light, wonderful laugh that seemed to float all the way up from her perfectly polished toes.

Her professors described her as a "brilliant" young statistician. Studies and articles she conducted and authored suggest her gift was in seeing the patterns not just in numbers but in human behavior.

Lakshmi was found dead just before dawn Friday, her body discovered laid out across the wide oak desk in the center of Virginia Gov. Thomas Baine's private office.

I left out exactly what she'd been working on—there is a place where righteous crosses paths with stupid, but I didn't think I was there yet. Charlie could find that herself. The rest of the story filled out with the same stuff we'd had since yesterday, about tight-lipped cops and official investigations and a secured area. I scrolled back to the top and read it a third time, tweaking a word choice here and there and fixing typos before I copied it into an email. Cropping myself out of the selfie from the poker game, I attached the image of Lakshmi, gorgeous and relaxed and laughing.

Pressroom. Les. Send.

From my phone, I thumb-typed, *It's in your email.*

Hands shaking, I reached for my coffee and took it to the microwave, closing my laptop and leaning both hands on the counter.

What the hell had I just done?

And done it was—there was no stuffing that genie back in any bottle I had access to. Les would run it, no questions asked, because it gave him the chance to be the big shot and scoop the whole state while Bob was out of town.

I closed my eyes, picturing Bob's face, hearing his voice in my head.

He wasn't happy, even in my imagination.

Journalism Since Forever 001: important facts need attribution.

It's not optional. It's not a thing you forget.

It's a thing you do. Every time.

"This is definitely what you'd call a special circumstance, chief," I said out loud, opening the microwave and pulling out my cup.

Every word true. I believed it with everything in me.

If I'd seen another way, I'd have taken it. Taking the focus off the murder and putting it on the victim, making this story like any other murder story, was more important than following the rules today. Because it was the only path I could see to some answers. Even if said path led smack through the middle of a professional and personal minefield.

My phone buzzed. I put down the coffee and snatched the phone off the table. Les: *Holy hell, Clarke. I have to tip my hat to you. I'm not sure that's ever happened before.*

Jackass.

I didn't type that. *Thanks.* Send.

Buzz. *The uptick in rack sales on the Sunday issue will make up for pulling the plates and breaking the web. And the numbers will give me plenty of clearance for raising the ad rates for next week, too. Keep it up.*

I dropped the phone on the table, my nose squinching up as I wiped my hand on my *Telegraph* T-shirt, a crushing, breath-stealing urge to shower settling heavy around me.

When Bob was pissed even in my imagination and Les was sending me virtual high fives . . . well. My weekend had officially gone off the rails.

I laid the phone down and folded my arms on the tabletop, resting my head on them, my eyelids heavy. I could just close them for a minute.

Five hours later I bolted upright in the chair when Darcy pounced on my bare foot.

I scrubbed at my eyes with both fists, arching my back before I glanced around the kitchen. Damn. I'd slept too long.

The first rays of sunlight trickled in through the windows, the dog disappearing through the plastic flap leading to the backyard.

I opened my computer and checked the newspaper's website.

Exclusive screamed in seventy-two-point Times from the screen. Under that, smaller: Telegraph *learns identity of capitol murder victim.*

I scrolled down.

Les didn't miss a moneymaking trick. There was a paywall just on that story, and a note at the top that said full details and information could be found in the print edition of the Sunday paper.

Darcy's nails scratched on the back door, her tiny black nose poking into the kitchen, sniffing, before she scurried back to my feet. I stroked her head. She yawned and flopped across my ankle.

Draining the rest of my coffee, I opened my email. Stared alternately at my screen and my phone.

And nearly jumped out of my skin when the onslaught I was braced for came from the front door.

* * *

Joey met me in the hallway, still shirtless, heart-stoppingly sexy as ever in his boxers and disarrayed hair.

"Does nobody have any concept of Sunday anymore?" he grumbled, half stomping toward the door.

"No, I'll—" I didn't get the "get it" out before he flipped the locks and jerked the door inward. Just as Kyle raised his fist to bang on it again.

"Miller." Joey didn't step backward, blocking the way into the foyer, and most of Kyle's view of me. "Awfully early to have to deal with you."

Kyle ignored the annoyance in Joey's tone, only paying any attention to his presence at all because he was between us.

"What did you do?" His voice was high and tight, like someone had pinched off his airway. I couldn't tell if he was holding back anger or fear.

Or both.

"What I had to," I said when my voice would work, putting a hand on Joey's shoulder and moving him out of the way. "Come in. Let me make you some coffee and I'll explain."

Joey's head swiveled between the two of us for two full cycles. "Why do I feel like I missed something important?"

"I couldn't sleep," I said.

"So you decided you'd go on ahead and ruin everyone's life? That's a cure for insomnia I haven't heard of." Kyle stepped past Joey, his voice still weird but his eyes flashing.

"I did no such thing. And I didn't mention you at all. Why are you so pissed?" I turned back for the kitchen, waving for him to follow.

He pulled a folded-up front section of the paper out of his back pocket, brandishing it like a newsprint sword. "I trusted you!" Pretty sure he screamed it loud enough to rattle the beach glass on the hallway shelf. "After everything we've been through together, I thought you understood I was telling you something I shouldn't be. And then I begged you yesterday to stay out of this. And this is the conclusion you drew from that? To dive in headlong without knowing what the fuck you're doing?"

Kyle grabbed my shoulder and spun me away from the coffee maker to face him. "Dammit, Nicey, this isn't a game."

Joey lunged, good arm out stiff, shoving Kyle away from me.

Kyle staggered backward but kept his balance, his head whipping around as a low "Don't start with me this morning, I am not in the mood" slid between his teeth.

Joey opened his mouth and I raised one hand, keeping my eyes on my old friend. The last thing I needed was to referee a Joey/Kyle cage match in my kitchen on an hour of sleep and an empty stomach.

"If you trust me so much, why do you think I'm so stupid?" I asked Kyle softly, holding his gaze, unblinking.

He opened his mouth. Closed it again. The coffee maker beeped and I turned to retrieve his mug.

"I didn't say you were stupid," he said finally, the words huffing out on a long sigh.

I pushed the cup into his hands and crossed the kitchen to pull milk and cream from the fridge. "What else do you call barging in here at seven o'clock on a Sunday to scream at me about a story?"

He leaned against the counter, his chin dropping to the opening in the collar of his royal-blue polo. "I'm worried about you." He said it to his shiny brown loafers, but I caught it.

I could feel Joey pounce without him moving an actual eyelash. Kyle being worried would be enough to scare him. He crossed the room and stopped behind me, wrapping both arms around my shoulders and pulling me back into his still-bare chest.

Did he not realize he was having a conversation with a federal agent in his underwear?

"Would you fill me in on what the hell is going on here?" he asked.

Maybe he just didn't care.

Kyle pinched his lips into a thin white line and handed Joey the paper before I could get a word out.

He let me go and unfolded it. I scooted two steps to the left and turned my head away because I knew he was going to yell, too.

When I didn't hear anything after a minute, I peeked over my shoulder.

He stared at the page, the only clue that he was even reading his furrowed brow.

"I don't get it," he said. "We've been talking about this all weekend."

"Nobody's supposed to know who the victim was," Kyle said.

Joey let the paper fall to the floor. "Nichelle?"

I sucked in a deep breath. "I have a theory."

"Me too. You're trying to get yourself killed," Kyle barked. "I told you. Yesterday. I warned you. Hell, I apologized for calling you in the first fucking place."

I rounded on him. "You knew who you were talking to when you made the decision to call, though."

"I assumed you knew the meaning of the words 'off the record.'"

My cheeks heated. "Some things are more important than keeping your word. Not many. But some. And I left you out of it."

Joey put an arm out, pulling me into his side. "Time out. Why don't we let everyone's temper cool off." He glanced down. "I'll go find some clothes, and then someone is going to explain what kind of trouble y'all are talking about."

I felt my eyes start to roll back and managed to stop them, patting his shoulder as he turned for the bedroom. I couldn't be upset with him for worrying. It wasn't like I didn't worry about him plenty.

Kyle bent and retrieved his newspaper from the daisy-yellow linoleum floor, tucking it back in his hip pocket. He settled in one of the chairs, drinking his coffee and staring at me, but not offering a smile or a word of any sort.

Quiet closed in from every corner of the room, dense and accusing. The air felt thicker. Harder to breathe.

I picked up my coffee cup and refilled it, then changed the pod in the machine and made Joey some. It didn't distract from the silence.

But I wasn't sorry. Lakshmi was the focus here. She was the important one. I knew what I'd done would piss people off when I did it, but I had a reason. What I believed was a good one. Kyle would understand.

I hoped.

Breathing in the almost magical scent of the only pumpkin spice anything I cared for, I pulled Joey's cup from under the spout and added a splash of heavy cream.

He walked back in as I closed the fridge, his dark eyes stormy and concerned—but not angry. He took the cup with a smile and a thank-you kiss on my forehead before he sipped the coffee and turned to Kyle.

"What's going on?"

"I'm afraid I'm not at liberty to discuss an ongoing investigation. Especially not in present company." Kyle flicked his eyes my way.

"Don't flatter yourself. I can find out ten times what you know with three phone calls." Joey's voice was the kind of dangerous calm that meant he was reining in his temper. "I'm asking you why you're so out the ass about Nichelle's story."

"I think she knows."

I put one hand on Joey's bandaged arm before he lost hold of those reins.

"I told you yesterday that Kyle told me about Lakshmi on background," I said. "But I figured something out last night. Something that made me see that printing her name was necessary. And so I wrote a story and sent it to Les, and he put it on this morning's front page."

"But you said you didn't use his name," Joey began at the same time Kyle said, "Please share this urgent epiphany."

I reached for Joey's uninjured hand, lacing my fingers through his and picking up my coffee mug before I put it back on the counter without taking a sip. I pointed to my homemade crime chart, still lying across the chair opposite Kyle.

"I didn't use anyone's name except Lakshmi's. Making a decision to write the story is one thing, but betraying a source is a bridge I will not cross, even when I feel this strongly about something. It was never an option I considered." I kept my eyes locked with Kyle's, wanting him to realize I meant every syllable. I left out the part where Aaron and Mike and the governor himself had confirmed Lakshmi's identity the day before, because I wasn't ready to tell anyone I was in on that conversation.

He nodded. "I appreciate that. I didn't come here because I'm worried about me."

I crossed the room, picking up the chart.

"The last thirty-six hours have been extraordinary by any local news standard. I've covered several people's share of shitstorms, but I've never even seen anything like this. Before I can process one crazy thing, another chases right along behind it. I thought my weekend was about to be better than finding Jimmy Choos at a flea market when Trudy invited me to cover the president's breakfast Monday morning and her husband's speech Monday night, and since then I haven't even had time to wonder why the Secret Service guy hasn't called about my background check yet."

I was talking as fast as words came into my head, but I really ought to check in with Trudy on that.

"So you made lists," Joey said.

"And they made it clear that I was right. This is a whole lot of weird for a short span of time. It's like shock fatigue." I turned to Kyle. "If I haven't had time to look at one crazy thing twice before another pops up, you guys haven't either, right?"

He shrugged. "It's been busy."

Lord, he could pout better than a runway model staring down a Snickers bar.

"But the central thing, the craziest thing, the only thing I can imagine moving my attention from the fact that I'm supposed to be in a room with the president of the United States in just a couple of days . . . that was Lakshmi's murder. And I've written about a lot of murders. The story is always, always about the victim, not about how they died. That's how I always win the headline wars."

"Except none of your stories have been about Lakshmi," Joey said.

I snapped my fingers, pointing at the chart. "Because nobody was allowed to know she was dead. Which started me thinking that maybe there was a reason she was found where she was. It's like a master class in hiding in plain sight. If you want to make the discovery of the body the biggest story of the season, while simultaneously guaranteeing that nobody will know a thing about the person who was killed, at least for a while . . ."

Kyle sat up straighter in the chair. "You put a call girl on the governor's desk."

"Ding ding ding. You've won a one-way ticket to a mountain of bullshit, Agent Miller," I said. "Because even when the truth gets out, her background makes the chances that anything important gets lost in a political firestorm pretty damned good. So then I started thinking about all her social media accounts disappearing, and I looked online again, and there's nothing but amateur porn videos. The difficult-to-stomach kind. They didn't just kill Lakshmi, y'all. They assassinated her character for good measure."

Kyle's chin dropped back to his chest, his hand going through his hair.

"They who?" Joey asked.

I shrugged. "That's the part we still need. But it got me thinking that if whoever did this planned it out this far, it's because they wanted her name to drop after they'd had a chance to eliminate the respectable parts of her life from the internet. When the only thing people would see would lead practically everyone to dismiss her. Forget her. And I was playing right the hell into their hands by not printing her name or her photo. So I changed that."

"But in doing so, you put a big fat target on your back." Kyle was talking to me, but looking at Joey. "If someone who has the kind of brains to pull off what I saw Friday morning really wanted this girl gone and forgotten, they're not the sort of person you want to intentionally play games with, Nichelle."

Joey nodded, putting a hand on my arm, his gaze locked with Kyle's and his jaw doing the twitching thing again.

"Some things are bigger than making sure my ass is covered, gentlemen. Lakshmi was brilliant and funny and kind, and people loved her. She deserves to have her story told." I nodded to Kyle. "And maybe this will bring whoever killed her out from under his rock, besides."

"Out from under his rock and after you?" Joey asked. "No, thanks."

Kyle sighed. "Dammit, Nichelle. You should've called me first."

"Why? What do you know that you're not telling me?" I asked.

He shook his head, his eyes dropping to the floor. "This case is complicated. I don't like you putting yourself in the middle of it."

"Look," I began before Kyle's phone went bonkers, flashing and buzzing itself clean out of his pocket. He held it up, blocking most of his face, his eyebrows drawing down as he shook his head at the screen.

"What?" I asked.

He stood, starting for the foyer. "I don't fucking know. Apparently we've just moved to DEFCON 4." He threw a warning look over his shoulder at me. "I hope you're not why. I'll call you when I can." His eyes flicked to Joey. "Keep her out of trouble?"

I opened my mouth to object, but Joey laid his injured arm around my shoulders and pulled me close. "She's tough. But I do what I can," he said.

"I'll be fine, Kyle. You go get whoever did this."

He opened the door and jogged down the steps without another word or a backward glance. I swung it shut and flipped the deadbolt home, letting my head drop to the wood with a dull *thunk*.

Joey traced the line of my jaw with one fingertip. "I don't want you getting yourself hurt."

"Me either." I closed my eyes, inhaling through my nose for a ten count. "What I did last night was either brilliant or idiotic. I honestly couldn't tell you which right now. All I know for sure is that I felt strongly enough about the story to send it." I raised my head and met his eyes. "She was somebody. I couldn't let them make her disposable."

"Why would anyone want to?"

I shook my head. "There are too many possibilities for me to venture a guess, honestly. But politics is all about the end game. And I think I have an idea on who. I just don't know how."

He lifted one eyebrow.

"The videos I saw online. I'm highly suspicious, given some things I've heard, that they were made by Ted Grayson."

Joey's eyes popped wide, his head shaking. "What does he have to gain? He's locked up."

I shook my head. "He's been out for nearly three weeks. Good behavior, the official line says, but this reeks of too much coincidence. I haven't been able to find any trace of him, though."

He folded his arms over his broad chest, a smile playing around the corners of his lips as he brushed a wayward strand of dark, wavy hair from my face. "I don't like you rushing into trouble," he said. "But . . . it's sexy that you're so smart."

I laughed. "Brains not really your thing before, huh?"

He shook his head. "It's one of many reasons I'm so damned infatuated with you, Miss Clarke."

I smiled at the formality, a throwback to when we first met, electricity skating up my arm ahead of his trailing fingers. "You're not exactly stupid yourself there, sir," I whispered before his lips closed over mine.

Losing myself in Joey's kisses was easy—he was unmatched in skill, closing his injured arm around my waist while his good hand rested on the door next to my head and his lips brushed lightly across mine, whispering about love and cliffs and things he never thought he'd do. I ran both hands up his chest and over his shoulders, parting my lips under his. He pulled his head back, shaking it the barest bit, keeping the pressure light and sweet and utterly crazy-making. Twisting my fingers into his hair, I tried to pull him closer. He held his position easily, a chuckle rumbling deep in his throat. "My, my," he said. "I like a woman who knows what she wants."

My Sunday morning was getting a whole different kind of interesting when my phone blared "The Second Star to the Right" from the kitchen table.

"You should get that." Joey's lips went to my neck as he whispered, moving my hair back with quick fingers as I sank into the heavy mahogany door.

"Voicemail. This is what voicemail was invented for," I huffed between quick breaths, the morning stubble on his chin abrading my skin in the most delicious, tingly way.

He lifted his head and met my eyes. "Kind of a lousy day for you to ignore your phone."

I shook my head and ducked under his arm with a growl, loping back to the kitchen.

Les.

"This is not worth interrupting for," I hissed, clicking the green circle and putting the phone to my ear.

"I'm good at remembering where we leave off." Joey winked.

"Clarke," I said, swallowing a giggle.

"Turn on your TV." Les sounded pissed. But Les usually sounded at least annoyed when he talked to me, so I wasn't too bothered by that.

"Good morning to you, too, Les." I shrugged at Joey and walked to the living room, picking up the remote and clicking the set on. "What exactly am I looking for? I'm guessing you're not calling me about the Redskins pregame show this early."

"They're probably going to lose anyway. But I'll be too busy looking for a new job to care. Try Channel Four. Where the governor and his security detail are sitting down with Charlie Lewis. Calling you a liar."

18

I dropped the phone, stabbing a panicked finger at the remote, trying to suck air through lungs that didn't want to work.

Joey's footsteps sounded far away. "Baby? What's wrong?"

I shook my head, my eyes locked on Charlie's burnished-gold highlights as her back filled my TV screen. "Governor Baine, do you know how the *Telegraph* came by this faulty information?" She practically singsonged the words, glee floating around every one.

"Oh." Joey's fingers closed over my shoulder.

"I do not. I can promise you it came from no one here. I've never met Miss Clarke, and I've been assured that no member of my security detail has spoken with her, on the record or off."

"Bullshit." I didn't really mean to say it out loud, shaking my head. I stepped closer to the TV, studying his face. The bloodshot eyes were gone, the scruff replaced by perfect makeup, hair trimmed, teeth even and white.

His eyes looked straight into Charlie's camera and out of my TV, for all the world the tortured political victim of a reporter run amok.

But he was lying. I knew it. He knew I knew it, and he knew Aaron and Landers and Mike knew it.

So what the hell did he think his end game could possibly be?

I put a hand to my temple, rage pounding a heavy beat on the inside of my skull. What could he have to gain by lying to the whole city on live TV?

Time was the only answer I could muster.

But time for what? And what, exactly, had he said before I turned my set on? That she wasn't on his desk? That he didn't know her? Of all the cards I'd been prepared for anyone to play when I sent that story in, denial wasn't in the deck. I knew what I'd written was true. I hadn't used an attribution, but I trusted Kyle with my life. Literally. I'd spoken with Lakshmi's mother. I'd even talked to Governor Baine. He was brim-full of shit, but who would believe me if I told them that?

The way I'd run my story, it was my word against his. For now. But I had the truth on my side. The truth, and a better-than-average track record at proving it.

Every person I'd talked to all weekend had told me Baine was the real deal. And idealists only lie for one reason: fear. Which meant I needed to figure out what the hell he was afraid of, and right quick.

I sank back onto the sofa as the camera flipped back to Charlie. The couch dipped under Joey's weight as he dropped next to me, the fingertips of his banged-up hand going lightly to my jaw, trying to turn my eyes to meet his. I couldn't look away from the TV.

"This has been a News Four special report, live from the Virginia governor's mansion." I could just hear Charlie over the blood rushing in my ears. "Thank you for watching, and stay with us throughout the day for updates."

I slumped back into the soft pillows, my head swiveling back and forth like someone else had control of it. I spotted my phone on the floor and jumped to my feet. Bent to snatch it up just in time to hear Les's tinny little voice howling from the speaker. "Clarke!" He drew out the *A* so long I had to give him points for sheer lung capacity.

I waited until I was sure he needed to catch his breath before I put the phone back to my ear. "Yes?"

"Where the hell did you—you know what? Never mind. Andrews is on his way up here. He wants us both in Bob's office in twenty minutes."

"Thanks, Les." I clicked the "End" button and opened the browser, touching the bookmark link for Channel Four. Politics is all about nuance, and playing at Baine's level took downright wicked skills. Before I made another move, I needed to hear his actual words.

The video flashed up on my screen just as the phone started vibrating in my palm. Aaron.

Thank God.

I slid the bar across the bottom of the screen and raised it to my ear. "What the hell was that?"

"You owe me a day on my boat, Nichelle," he growled by way of hello. "A quiet one. Where nobody yells at me. And if you have an explanation of any sort for the phone call I just got from Tom Baine, let's have it."

"I was hoping you could help me with that," I said. "You heard him say all the same stuff I did yesterday. Didn't you?"

"I heard a group of people who trusted a friend let her into a meeting she'd have never been allowed in as a journalist," Aaron said. Paper rustled in the background. "And then this morning, I get up, I make my coffee, and I open my paper to see that we might've misread how much our trust meant to said friend."

He got quieter, tighter, with each word. I knew Aaron. Quiet wasn't what I wanted here.

"I wouldn't betray your trust. You know that. I didn't use anyone's name in the article." And I wasn't telling him about Kyle any more than I was telling Kyle about him.

"You are in a world of shit here, Nichelle. I shouldn't even be talking to you. But I owe you. Everything. And I don't forget the people I owe."

"I had a reason, Aaron."

"I'd love to know what the hell it could possibly be."

I glanced at Joey. "It's kind of a long story. Can I come see you?"

"Something tells me you won't be the most popular person around my office today."

"Coffee?"

He sighed. "Sure. Meet you at Thompson's in twenty minutes?" Yep. I had no intention of answering Andrews's summons. He'd fire me in a blink, no matter how thin Baine's denial might prove to be. I wasn't keen on the idea of losing my job today on top of my reputation. If I could save one, the other would follow suit. I hoped.

"Thanks, Aar—" I didn't get it all the way out before the doorbell rang.

"Jesus, what now?" I muttered.

Joey moved to the foyer, lifting up on the balls of his feet to look out the glass lining the top of the door.

"There's someone at the door. I'll see you in a few," I said to Aaron before I killed the phone call and hurried to the doorway. "What's going on?" I asked Joey, noting the lines creasing his forehead as he moved into the guest room and peered out the window.

"Cameras," he said, turning back to me. "Your pal Charlie from Channel Four and a few of her closest friends, it looks like."

"Oh shit." My hand flew to my mouth, and I backed away from the door almost involuntarily.

Of course. This was the biggest story of the day by far, and their job was to get both sides. I'd be looking for Charlie if that Louboutin were on the other foot.

I got it. But that didn't mean I was talking to them.

Striding back to my bedroom, I pulled a pair of soft, well-worn jeans and a light, muted-gray sweater with three-quarter sleeves from the closet shelf, and my favorite understated black Stuart Weitzman wedges from my shoe armoire. Dressed, I turned to the mirror and smoothed my hair back into a high ponytail I threaded through the back of a Generals cap, adding a pair of wide sunglasses that covered half my face. No time for makeup.

The door rattled for the third time in five minutes. "Nichelle, open the door. It's not like we don't know your car is here," Charlie called, three walls between me and the porch not muting her enough for me to miss that.

"And just because I'm home, doesn't mean I'm answering the door," I muttered, grabbing my bag and spinning for the kitchen.

"How can I help?" Joey handed me a full travel cup of hot coffee when I crossed the kitchen threshold. His dark eyes were worried, but I saw no trace of doubt. I swallowed hard and put the coffee on the counter, throwing my arms around his neck and squeezing tight.

"You help just by being you," I said into his neck. "Thank you for believing me, and trusting me."

He nodded, his prickly face rubbing against my cheek. "I'm not sure I'm built for sitting around while you chase murderers, but I'm giving it my level best. Take my car. Call me when you're leaving White, okay?"

I nodded, pulling away and taking his keys off the hook by the door. I paused with my hand on the knob. "Making a break for it."

"Don't run over any of your colleagues."

I flashed a smile. "Maybe just the really irritating ones?"

He laughed. "Go get 'em, princess."

I patted Darcy's silky head and rushed out the door—smack into Dan Kessler.

I sucked in a sharp breath and jogged sideways down the steps.

"I knew you weren't coming out the front," Dan said, signaling to his cameraman to start rolling. "What gives, Nichelle? Of all the people I've ever known in this game, I'd have put you at the very bottom of the list for making stuff up."

I clamped my teeth around the inside of my jaw.

The only way to win—or even push—in this game was to keep my mouth shut. For now. Any answer I tried to offer could be edited and spun to make the paper look stupid and me look like a liar, and I knew it. I shook my head and spun on one heel, pressing the button to unlock the car. It chirped just as Charlie rounded the corner of the house. "Damn, Kessler was right," she said, breaking into a run and hollering for her own photographer. "Nichelle! What made you decide to go with that story?"

I didn't turn around, pulling the door open and sliding into the car. So much for a quick incognito exit. Revving the engine, I put the car in reverse and shot Charlie and the new new girl from Channel Two (she made four in the past two years) a *Don't test me* glare as I laid my foot on the gas.

They jumped back, Charlie nearly knocking Dan to the concrete, and watched me peel down the drive before they scrambled for their trucks.

Dammit.

I reached for my phone, dialing Aaron again. "You okay?" he asked.

"We're going to have to rethink this unless we want an audience," I said. "The coffee shop will be overrun with the reporters who were on my lawn when I left in half a tick. We need somewhere they can't follow."

"I figured that when your doorbell rang before you hung up. You know where the Cavalier Club is?" he asked.

Swanky and private, it was on the top floor of the tallest building in the city. The kind of place power brokers made million-dollar financial and political deals over aged bourbon and Cuban cigars. I was surprised Aaron knew where it was. "Can you get us in there?"

"They extend special courtesies to local law enforcement," he said. "The elevator code is five nine six one—push those buttons in sequence and it'll bring you to the top floor. I'm already here waiting."

I hung up and checked my rearview, Charlie's van closing in from behind me on the left, Dan's not far behind her on the right. I slammed on the gas when the light at Monument and Boulevard turned to yellow, leaving them stuck as I turned to weave through side streets. I sped past houses and cars and gorgeous fall reds and yellows drifting from the oaks, keeping my eyes on the road and hoping the light cycle was long enough. I just needed time to get into the building before they caught up.

Swinging into the parking lot four minutes later, I didn't see a news van for blocks. Point Nichelle.

I kept my head down as I scurried inside, tapping one block-point toe as I waited for the elevator to creak and rattle down to me. The place was gorgeous—all striking dark tones of walnut and hunter green accented with white marble and copper—but carved-wooden-doors-on-the-elevators old.

They slid apart with barely a whisper, an invitation into a secret society. I stepped in, pushed the buttons as Aaron instructed, and watched them slide closed just as Charlie made it up the sidewalk to the one-way-glass front doors. I sent up a silent thank you for small favors.

Soft music, classical of course, floated from a speaker somewhere above my head, the scents of expensive cologne, rare cigars, and old, well-oiled wood seeping from the walls of the tiny box around me. Elevators weren't built for moving people efficiently back in the day, or people were built smaller, one of the two. This thing might fit five adults, and only if they were all in decent shape.

The doors slid apart to reveal a long, dim hallway lined with deep-green jacquard wall coverings, shiny, scarred walnut wainscoting, and the occasional painting of one of the half-dozen Founding Fathers who called the commonwealth home.

I stepped out, the cigar and wood smell fading into wafts of good booze laced with a touch of cinnamon.

"You made it." Aaron stepped out of the corner next to the elevator.

"Beat Charlie through a light and wove through Carytown. But yes." I smiled. "This place is gorgeous. And just the right touch of creepy."

He chuckled. "They throw the best Halloween party in town." He started down the hall, waving for me to follow. Neither of us spoke again until he'd ushered me into a burgundy box of a room with five round felt-topped card tables dominating the center of the floor and a bar in the back right corner. Not unlike the basement where I'd first met Lakshmi.

Shutting the door behind us, Aaron waved me to a chair facing the windows at the nearest table and took the one next to me. I swiveled mine so I could look at him. "I would never—" I began, and he held up one hand.

"I have always trusted you, Nichelle. When I shouldn't have, when it got me in trouble, when it didn't make sense to. But I'm not sure you have a firm grasp of what you've done here, or the trouble you're about to cause yourself and a handful of people you're supposed to care about. I consider you more friend than colleague, which is why I'm here at all. Exactly what in the blue hell were you thinking?"

I drummed my fingertips on the table, the felt muting any noise from them.

"She mattered," I said finally, looking up to meet Aaron's striking baby-blue eyes. "That's what I was thinking."

"Where did you even get her name?" he asked.

"I can't reveal my source."

"Miller?" He cocked an eyebrow skyward. He was a good detective, after all.

I kept my face blank. "I can't tell you that, I'm sorry. But you know I'm not lying, because I listened to the four of you discuss her yesterday. Which I also haven't told anyone else, just for the record."

He opened his mouth. Shut it. Shook his head. "Nichelle, there's more going on here than anyone can tell you. This is an extremely delicate situation. There are a lot of important things, and important people, involved in this. You can't make assumptions or flip decisions based on your personal sense of justice here."

"I saw her mother yesterday. Read the research she was working on. She mattered. And everyone's acting like she didn't." I met his eyes. "She was almost the same age as Alyssa, Aaron."

"That's a cheap shot and you know it."

"I'm not throwing shots. I'm trying to give you a way to see the other side of this." I closed my hands around the arms of the chair. "You've worked hundreds of murder cases in some capacity. What's the focus of any murder case? From the minute someone is missing or a body is found. What do you look at first?"

"The victim," he said. "The quickest way to the killer is somewhere in the victim's story."

"Exactly. And the victim is always the center of my story. Except this one. This one has been all about the governor and his son from where you sit and all about the place the victim was found from where I sit. That doesn't strike you as odd?"

He twisted his mouth to one side. Paused. Steepled his fingers under his chin.

He was weighing his words.

"It's not normal," he said finally. "But nothing about this is normal. There are special considerations."

"Why? Because the guy is the governor, or because he's your friend?"

He flinched. "I thought I'd earned more credibility with you than that. I wouldn't let a murderer walk because of personal feelings."

"I'm not saying the governor killed her," I said. "I think she was found where she was found because someone wanted her lost in a bigger story. And I don't know that I've ever seen a bigger story than this."

His silver-speckled brows drew down.

"I'm going to need you to elaborate."

I tapped the unlock code into my phone and pushed it across the table. "Search her name."

He picked it up and poked at the screen, sitting back in the chair after a few minutes, his eyes staying on the screen. "Explicit content? Why are you showing me this?"

"She was a brilliant, published statistician. She was twenty-six years old. Friday morning, the top hits were her social media accounts."

He put my phone on the table. "How would someone even go about changing that?"

"Her social media has been deleted, across every platform. Which makes sense for this since those are always the top hits when you search a name, unless the person has a website. All someone would need is her password to take care of that." I sat back in the chair. "It seems that someone didn't just want her dead, they wanted her dismissed. I didn't break a confidence for the hell of it, and I damned sure didn't do it to beat Charlie. I did it because she mattered, Aaron. And whoever has masterminded this thing doesn't want her to matter. I'm not giving up until I figure out why."

He leaned one elbow on the table, resting his chin on his palm and curling his fingers over his mouth. "I thought it was a political stunt. Someone out to disgrace Tom—even the timing works, the president is coming here day after tomorrow." I watched his face, the way his eyes were on the window. He wasn't talking to me.

I stayed quiet.

He sighed, shaking his head and gesturing to my phone.

"So you thought when people started looking for her name . . ."

"They'd label her a whore and that's all she'd ever be. Unless someone got in front of the story. Made her a person. Brought her to life for readers and made them care about her and what happened to her." My voice was soft, my throat scratchy.

"You do excel at that," he said.

"This isn't about beating Charlie." I shook my head.

"But that doesn't change the fact that you're in a hot mess of trouble. The governor's media spin people are running around like the damned sky is falling."

I nodded. I had expected that. "But what do they think lying is going to get them, exactly? I know I don't usually cover government, but it's not like these people don't read the paper from front page to obits every day. I've built a reputation for being stubborn. Why would they think I'm going to just let this go? He looks worse when he gets busted for lying on top of having the call girl on his desk."

Aaron reached across the table and laid a hand on my arm. "That's part of why I came to see you. They've already talked to your publisher, Nichelle. You don't work at the *Telegraph* anymore, effective immediately. And the attorney general is drawing up papers as we speak to have a restraining order placed on you to keep you away from any state-owned buildings, or any room the governor is in. They also want to petition the court to force you to reveal your source. If you won't . . ."

"It's as good as admitting I'm lying," I said, letting my eyes fall shut, his words hitting like he was talking about someone else until my temper rose to meet them. So much for avoiding Rick Andrews.

First Lakshmi, now me. Every bit of this was about controlling the story. Yesterday, they thought they had it in hand. This morning, I disrupted that.

They were pushing back harder than I thought. But they weren't as smart as Kyle gave them credit for if they thought I was just going to give up, either.

"They could put you in jail," he said softly. "Miller wouldn't want that."

I studied Aaron through rapid-firing lashes.

He was my friend. He said he owed me. But that was the second prod at getting me to admit Kyle gave me Lakshmi's name. Did he ask me here to talk through the case, or to pump me to reveal my source for his buddy Baine?

I swallowed hard, the increasingly familiar feeling of not knowing who to trust wrapping its tentacles around me with suffocating precision.

Subject change.

"I thought you said you knew this guy. You asked me to help him." I shook my head. "I hate to have to break it to you, but your old pal Baine is kind of an asshole."

Aaron's lips tipped up at the corners. "He's a politician. I think that automatically means he's not an angel. But . . ." He let it trail off, shaking his head.

"But what?"

He sighed. "He's a good egg, as political types go. He's invested in doing as much good as he can for as many people as he can."

"Present company excluded?" I raised one eyebrow.

"Come on, Nichelle. If you thought it'd help a thousand homeless people for you to give up your job, you'd quit in half a second. I know you.

This is no different. Politics is entirely about weighing risk and reward. Sacrificing one thing to gain something bigger."

"Not entirely. But either way, actually being the lamb makes a person feel a little differently about those sacrifices, it seems. And you're not counting all the people I help, either."

"You're not saying you have bigger reach than the governor?" His baby blues popped wide, smoothing the creases at the corners.

"Of course not. Simply pointing out that putting my career on this altar comes with a higher collateral damage bill than the loss of one person's job and credibility. Nothing personal or pouty about that. Just a fact."

He leaned back in his chair and laced his fingers behind his head.

I knew Aaron. That told me he was thinking.

Sitting forward again, he steepled his fingers under his chin. That told me he was uncertain.

"You don't have much of a choice," he said. "If you don't give up your source, you're giving up everything you've worked so hard for."

I met his eyes.

He didn't want me to do this. Which left only one reason he would ask me to.

I shook my head. "Giving up my source will cost me more than a job, Aaron," I said, standing. "At least this way, I walk away still proud of who I am and what I do."

He smiled around the next words, the face fitting his sharp tone like Chuck Taylors fit a little black dress.

"Pride isn't going to pay your rent," he said.

I nodded. He couldn't help me. But he'd decided he didn't want to be there, too. Loud and clear.

I put one hand on Aaron's shoulder, my fingers resting over a scar I'd never forget, because I'd held blood inside him and prayed for paramedics who liked to speed after he'd been shot last year. Leaning in, I spoke straight into the collar I'd seen him tape a mic under a hundred times. "Governor Baine is a powerful man, and he has some powerful friends. But burning a source to cover my own ass isn't in my DNA. He can continue to deny the truth. I'll go look for it. We'll see which one of us is on our game."

Before he could get another word out, I turned and strode out the door.

I was on my own. Likely without a job. Chasing the cleverest killer I'd ever come across. My brilliant, burly cops were afraid to tread where I was headed.

But I would figure it out, because I had to.

Backwards in high heels, if it came down to it.

19

My legs carried me all the way to the car before they started shaking. Two knock-kneed blocks away, I glanced in my rearview—and almost plowed into a parked catering van.

"Kessler! Are you kidding me?" I choked out when I could breathe and the car was pointed in the right direction again.

"What gives, Nichelle?" He didn't even blink, like he broke into people's cars every day. Which I knew damned good and well he didn't—he'd beat me to stories way more often if this were part of his regular playbook.

I swerved into the empty parking lot in front of the biggest law firm in town, my knuckles going white around the steering wheel as I tipped my head back, staring at the towering gray marble building and inhaling for a slow ten count.

Talk about a morning. I was more than a little scared and a whole lot mad, and confident I could wring Dan Kessler's skinny neck in less time than it took to reapply my lip gloss.

But I didn't want to hurt Dan.

Yet, anyway.

"Come on. We all know—" he began, putting a warm, sticky hand on my shoulder.

"I would take that back before I lost it if I were you." The words slid through teeth clenched so tight I wasn't sure how sound made it out.

He snatched it away.

Another breath.

Another ten count.

I closed my eyes and opened my mouth. "I am not having the best day ever, Dan." Even I was impressed with how calm and (honestly) sane I sounded. "And I have no intention of spilling my guts to anybody, but even if I had gut-spilling plans, why in the name of Christian Louboutin would you think I'd confide in you?"

He cleared his throat, his suit rustling against the leather seat as he squirmed. I checked the mirror.

"You can talk now," I said.

"If you'd let me finish my sentence, what I was going to say was, we all know you didn't make up the thing about the dead whore."

My head snapped around. "Watch it. Her name was Lakshmi."

His hands flew up in mock surrender. "Lakshmi, Lakshmi. Didn't know you two were buds."

"I have to be buds with someone to remind you not to be a demeaning, misogynistic ass? Since when?"

"Now hang on," he said. "I wasn't trying to be insulting."

"Yet you said not a word about the men who were in any of those videos." I arched one eyebrow.

He was quiet for three blinks. "Point taken. Truce?"

I nodded.

"I mean, I can tell Charlie's hoping you've cracked, but even she knows better, deep down." He leaned forward, practically rubbing his hands together. "The truth is your whole deal. A person's inherent personality doesn't just change overnight." He flashed his I-belong-on-the-anchor-desk smile.

I sighed. "What do you want, Dan?"

"I want to know how you knew about her. We all know the cops tell you juicy stuff they don't tell anyone else, but with the governor saying you're wrong, I smell a rat. All I'm trying to figure out is where it's rotting. Come on, Clarke. You help me, I'll help you? We can do this on air after the game if you want. We'll have twice the viewers Charlie got this morning."

I shook my head. "I appreciate the vote of confidence, but I can't. I won't burn a source for a decision I made myself."

He sat back and folded his arms across his chest. "See? Moral compass." His eyes narrowed. "But is the rat Baine himself, or someone in his security detail?" His head tipped to one side. "You know the thing I can't figure out? I would've pegged you for a Baine voter any day of the week. I'm rarely wrong about people's politics." He snapped his fingers. "It is him, isn't it?"

"No comment. And I didn't say I didn't support him—careful putting words in people's mouths."

"You tried to ruin him less than twelve hours ago," Kessler said.

"Did I? I guess I missed that part." I pointed to the door. "Out the way you came in, please. And Dan? Don't do this again. Next time you'll leave with some battle scars." I flashed a Splenda-sweet smile as he kicked the door open.

"Got you to talk to me, didn't I?" he grumbled, smoothing his slacks and jacket. "You're really not taking me back to my car?"

"It's nice out. Stretch your legs," I said.

"I hope you know what you're getting into. And I hope I can figure it out before Charlie does." I couldn't tell if he was talking to me or to himself, so I just waved as I pulled away.

I made it to the light before my phone buzzed.

Putting my foot on the brake, I picked it up and touched the gray box with Joey's name in it.

The light turned green. Yellow. Red again.

I was still staring at my screen when it flipped back to green.

Don't come home. Go to my place. I'll take Darcy to Jenna and meet you there when I can. There are four state troopers on the porch with a summons for you. The kind that'll turn into a warrant if you refuse to go.

Leaping, flipping, circus-trick-performing Louboutins.

Aaron had warned me. But I thought it would take longer.

I clicked the reply line. *Jenna and Chad are on a cruise for their anniversary. Just bring Darcy with you. And thanks.*

I swung the car left toward the river instead of right toward home, thankful for Charlie and Dan and their spectacular knack for pain-in-the-ass-ery that made me leave my car at home.

Tapping my fingers on the wheel at the next light, I eyed my phone the way a normal person would a coiled copperhead resting in their cup holder. I reached for it. Shut it off. Stuck it in the console. Checked the mirrors, a Big-Brother-is-watching tightness making my skin feel two sizes too small.

Every traffic camera was suddenly the enemy. I'd watched Kyle check footage. I knew just how closely they could track a person by plates.

I just never thought I'd be on this end of the checking.

For once, the fact that Joey and I had to keep our relationship quiet was my friend. I had no doubt whoever was looking for me would find out eventually, but I'd bet our careful sneaking around for the past two years had bought me at least a day.

Turning into the garage under Joey's building and putting my sunglasses back on in the dark concrete basement, I hauled my laptop bag out of the back seat and slipped into the elevator, hoping a day would be enough.

* * *

Stacy Adams was a dude.

A wiry, geekishly handsome dude with a prominent Adam's apple and black horn-rimmed Buddy Holly glasses covering hazel eyes that looked greener thanks to his hunter-green-and-sapphire plaid button-down.

But his photo wasn't what had my jaw slack, eyes locked on my laptop screen.

And neither was his job title. Energy innovation manager. I'd seen it on the business card and dismissed it as one of those business-speak things that gave someone a label without actually describing their job.

It was his bio. A bio that touted a meteoric rise to R&D at Daltec straight out of grad school.

That didn't just jump out at me. It wrapped around my throat and squeezed, screaming in my ear.

I clicked to their website, grabbing a spiral off the table next to my favorite chair and starting a new chart.

Daltec's home page sported the logo I'd seen on the windbreaker at the Drake house before Lakshmi's mom shut the door in my face. Hamilton Baine worked in nuclear-alternative research at Daltec. And now this dude Kyle was talking to just before he went batshit was a former hotshot scientist there.

I drew a line and jotted the most obvious label. Kyle went looking for information on Hamilton from an old colleague.

Right?

Except Aaron and Chris were supposed to be looking for Hamilton. I still didn't really know what Kyle was looking for here at all, and it was a pretty good bet he wouldn't tell me after this morning. When, by the way, I'd let him in and out of my house without finding out what he knew about Hamilton's vanishing act.

Dammit. Supposition for the win, then.

The easiest thing? Kyle was looking for information on Hamilton. The most interesting? Fishing for information on Dr. Drake's work. Which might lead to why Lakshmi was dead, if Angela Baker knew her stuff.

Staring at my notebook, I realized that two days brim-full of crazy had gotten past me and I still didn't have an answer to the most basic question. The one Bob asked before I set one boot heel on the lush capitol lawn: Why was Kyle even there?

Nothing about a politically charged murder gets Kyle's special agent pinky toe in the office door. At least not in an obvious way. Nobody in Baine's inner circle was selling bootleg cigarettes or bathtub gin. Weapons, then?

I pulled out my notebook and flipped back. He'd said her head and face were too badly beaten to ID her. But he didn't say that was how she died. So had someone used some sort of illegal gun on her? Military-grade assault rifles, sawn-off shotguns, specialty weapons like 3-D-printed plastics—that was ATF purview. And while I couldn't see how anyone would get a machine gun or a shotgun into the building, concealed and open carrying were both legal in our capitol, so the specialty train might go somewhere. I just didn't have anyone to ask at the moment.

I made a note and went back to Daltec's site. Scanned the menu at the top of my screen.

Innovation. Projects.

Clean coal.

I made it through three pages of high-level science that might as well have been written in Farsi for all I could comprehend, before I clicked the logo again to return to the home page.

Scrolled.

Scrolled more.

Stopped and stared.

Lakshmi's dad. And Thomas Baine, before he was Governor Baine. Each held the end of one of those big cardboard cartoon checks. I clicked the photo closer. Grant money, given by the environmental caucus of the House of Delegates to Dr. Drake for research.

But what kind?

The caption on the photo said it was a year and a half old, and that Drake was on the leading edge of clean, abundant energy research.

Vague much?

I clicked the search bar. *Clean* and *abundant* and *energy* and *Virginia*. Go.

Over a thousand hits. Sorted by most relevant. I didn't see the word *coal* until twenty-six.

The top twenty?

All nuclear.

Holy Manolos. What if Angela Baker heard wrong? Or misinterpreted what she heard? What if Dr. Drake wasn't working on making coal better—but replacing it?

That could motivate some executive to pressure Grayson to shut it down by any means necessary. Desperate times—and Ted Grayson had nothing left to lose. I picked up the chart again, drawing zigzag lines between words and phrases.

Grayson wasn't stupid. I'd never really pegged him for the diabolical genius type, but I had underestimated folks before. Baine was for pretty much everything Grayson was not. If Grayson had somehow formed and implemented a plan to blackmail Drake out of his research by using his daughter as a sex toy, it wasn't even a long stretch to think he might've found a way to take down a rival politician headed for superstardom and get back at Dr. Drake in the process. Kill Drake's daughter, put her on Baine's desk, and alter her online narrative. It was pretty simple, as evil plans go, so there had to be a bigger why at the core—and coal could be it.

So many moving puzzle pieces. So many trails. Had I found the right one?

Sex or money, almost every time. And this road had both: Google said coal was a roughly $200 million annual industry in the commonwealth.

Aaron had clearly been ordered to see me earlier, and while Grayson might have fallen from his white marble pedestal, he still had plenty of powerful friends. People with power do heinous things every day and get right away with them, because political titles and friends are damn-near unbreakable shields. Cops, prosecutors, journalists—power and money insulate secrets from everyone whose job it is to drag them out into the light. Red tape, missing files, and corporate boards worried about already-shrinking profit margins are the sorts of everyday obstacles that keep monsters hidden.

Aaron and Kyle and DonnaJo had bureaucratic hurdles to clear in the race to Lakshmi's murderer. But I didn't—not anymore. Staying out of jail would be nice, of course, but my lack of a job meant journalistic rules no longer applied. Nobody had to talk to me on the record for me to figure this out. I didn't care anymore because I had nowhere to print it. And I didn't wear a badge, so people would talk to me who refused to talk to them.

I looked at my chart. At my screen.

Found the common denominators.

All three of my surest, best-traveled trails led to or through Hamilton Baine, two of them by way of Ted Grayson.

Kyle's red-rimmed eyes flashed on the back of my lids with every blink, Governor Baine's broken, hoarse voice zipping through my head as one more big piece of my puzzle slipped into place: Hamilton and Grayson were both off the grid, but Hamilton's text to Mrs. Powers hadn't said he was planning to disappear. The governor said there'd been no ransom demand, asked for my help, then called me a liar on live TV less than twenty-four hours later.

So many contradictions.

I needed to find the governor's son. The more I thought about it, the surer I got that when I did, I'd find my least favorite ex-senator, too.

And my money said the place to start the search was with Mr. Adams over at the power company.

I grabbed my bag and dug for the card. Cell number. Bingo. Pulling my phone out of my pocket, I crossed my fingers, dialed, and pressed the "Talk" circle.

20

Voicemail.

Of course.

I didn't leave a message; better to try again than be ignored.

I laid the phone on the table as the lock clicked behind me. Joey slipped in, Darcy in his arms. "You are in some kind of serious shit," he said by way of hello, locking the deadbolt behind him.

I jumped to my feet, my long legs gobbling up the black floor tiles between us, and threw my arms around him, hiding my face in his shoulder.

"It seems I'm developing a knack for that." The words were muffled by his shirt. The dog yipped, wriggling. He put her down and she ran for the bed he kept in the corner.

Joey straightened, wrapping both arms around me so tight he was practically hugging his own shoulders, resting his chin on top of my head. The slow, steady beat of his heart invited my breathing to match it.

"What did White say?"

I kissed the tip of his nose and turned for the kitchen. "You thirsty?"

"Is it too early for bourbon?"

I snorted. "Church isn't even out yet."

"So no, then?" He winked when I looked over my shoulder.

I pulled a cut-crystal snifter from the bar cart in the corner and took it to the counter to pour Joey's drink before I picked up my glass and squeezed a lime over it, adding ice and Diet Coke.

"I'm in no place to judge anyone's choices today." I sipped the soda and handed him his bourbon. "Something's off with Aaron." I put my glass on the counter and boosted myself up next to it, letting my feet dangle in front of the cabinet doors. "He was weird. I'm as sure as I can be without actually having laid eyes on it that he was wearing a wire. Oh, and he did the honors of firing me for good measure."

Joey's eyes popped so wide I could see white all the way around his dark irises. "Firing you?"

I rolled my eyes. "Andrews got away with it for a whole day last time. I think this is going to be a regular thing until he gets one to stick. I'm so tired of that guy and his bullshit. If it weren't for Bob, I'd tell him to shove his ungodly hours and ridiculous pay straight up Shelby Taylor's ass and see how far it gets him. He's all blustering and very little backup. I need to save my reputation and get the story, and the board will force him to take me back. Again." I hoped.

Joey shook his head. "I thought White was supposed to be your friend. You saved the man's life, for Christ's sake."

"He kept trying to get me to tell him Kyle was the person who told me about Lakshmi."

Joey shook his head. "Throwing Miller under the bus, too. No sense of loyalty."

I raised one hand. "But then he kind of tipped me off that he was doing that. Which, if he was really laying a trap, makes zero sense. Aaron White could draw a murder confession out of an innocent priest and have the bishop believing it was true. He bumbled this morning on purpose."

"So he was there as someone's lackey."

I pointed, putting my soda down. "Exactly. He did tell me he'd talked to Baine this morning."

"The governor is probably not a good enemy to have, princess."

I shook my head. "I'm not sure yet who's friend or enemy here. Politics is its own universe, with its own bizarre rules. What I do know is that Baine is scared. And to be fair, I forced his hand by running that piece this morning. I didn't expect a subpoena at the time, but it's a brilliant move. They hit back hard. I mean, even if I can prove I'm right—hell, even if I find the killer, where do I get that information out without a newspaper to write for? It's a bit too long for an Instagram story."

"You just said the board would make Andrews take you back, just like last time." Joey sipped his bourbon, his eyes on my face.

"Probably." I blew out a long, slow breath. "That's probably right." In truth, it depended entirely on how many board members Andrews could convince that I was more liability than asset. And the longer it took me to find an answer, the more time he would have to yak at them.

Tick-tock, Nichelle.

"Does anyone but the governor have enough pull with White to make him do something he doesn't want to where you're concerned?"

I nodded. "A handful of people, I'm sure. He's awfully close to a thirty-year pension to go pissing off too many powerful people. But all the local politicians lead back to the governor."

Joey tipped his head to one side. "Except all the ones who hate his guts."

Holy Manolos.

I'd seen Aaron with Baine the day before, I'd listened when he said he talked to him today. And I'd completely disregarded the possibility that he could be influenced by a political enemy of Baine's.

The question wasn't even really if, because it was as possible as me coming home with new shoes on a given day. The question was who, and why.

If Grayson was trying to make the governor look bad, this was a genius backhanded way to go about it. I'd sure made it look like I was out to get him already . . . between his interview this morning and my chat with Aaron, it wasn't unthinkable that I'd be guns blazing after him by now. But Aaron wouldn't listen to Ted Grayson. Not directly.

Neither would Thomas Baine. If it was true that Baine had an enemy influencing the course of this day, it wasn't someone from the other side of the political aisle.

It was, as he'd said yesterday, someone in his own house.

Which changed this entire game.

I grabbed my notebook, flipping to a fresh page.

The interview. I'd taken off to meet Aaron before I saw exactly what the governor said.

I crossed the room and planted a long kiss on Joey before I ran back to my laptop.

He took a seat on the sofa, swirling his whiskey around the glass and smiling. "That's my girl."

I winked at him as I opened the browser and clicked my shortcut for Channel Four, then I pulled up the video of Charlie's live interview and replayed it five times.

"The Richmond *Telegraph*'s report on the death of Lakshmi Drake is untrue." Baine's voice was flat. Controlled. "I'm unable to discuss details of an ongoing incident investigation, but I assure you, Miss Drake did not leave the building in the coroner's van yesterday."

"Then where is she?" I asked. "If she's not dead and she's so valued, why not bring her on camera and prove me wrong?"

I clicked "Play" again. When the intro music started, Joey cleared his throat. "I could just recite it for you if you need. Are you having some sort of masochistic fit? Because I'm getting weary of listening to that guy call you a liar."

I shook my head, shushing him, my eyes on the screen.

Every time Thomas Baine said my story wasn't true, or he didn't know how I had come up with that, or any variety of untruth, he cleared his throat.

Every. Single. Time.

Nobody has allergies that specific.

He was uncomfortable. A wholly different person than the man I'd spoken with. Watching the segment sans panic, that was painfully plain.

"Someone made him do this." I was talking to myself, and Joey knew me well enough to notice and keep quiet. "But how does anyone make the governor do anything?"

I put the computer on the table and picked up the notebook, looking up at Joey.

"The big pillars of weird here are Lakshmi, this interview, and that the governor's son is missing. So maybe someone has something political on the governor, or maybe someone has his son. But either way . . . it's got to be someone close to him. To have pulled off all three of these things, a person would have to be on the inside."

Which meant it wasn't Ted Grayson. I closed my eyes and inhaled for a ten count. He was the easy villain. I wanted it to be him. But I couldn't ignore facts that didn't fit my preferred narrative if I really wanted the truth.

If there was a power play going on in the governor's mansion and the other side was pulling Baine's strings, the governor needed help.

And if I was the only person who'd put this together with nothing much left to lose, I might be his only hope.

No pressure.

21

I needed political dirt. From someone I could trust, at least relatively speaking.

Bob was still hiking, because he wasn't blowing up my phone with expletive-laden refrains of "What have you done?"

Which put me on Trudy Montgomery's wide, stately Monument Avenue front porch, juggling fresh lattes as I pressed the doorbell and crossed my fingers.

I heard footsteps, soft, before a gasp, not so soft, and the deadbolt squealing a protest as it slid back.

She jerked the door open and closed one hand around my wrist, yanking me into her foyer and slamming the heavy oak and leaded-glass door behind me so fast it took me a minute to adjust to my new position.

"Have you lost your mind?" Trudy raised one hand. "Don't answer that. Of course you have. But why do you want to take me down with you? What in the name of all hell are you doing here, Nichelle? People in this town talk, and my street isn't exactly light on the political scene."

I held out the latte, fixing a smile in place and trying to remember that Trudy moves in a world where perception is everything and loyalty is a rare —and not highly prized—commodity.

"I come in peace. I'm telling the truth. I'd think after our last go-round with this, you'd give me the benefit of the doubt."

She took the cup and turned, padding barefoot down the cherry-paneled center hall and waving for me to follow her.

Seated on a velvet divan in a charming navy-and-white conservatory off her living room, she pulled her thin legs up and folded them under her oversized William & Mary sweatshirt, waving me into an antique green jacquard-uphol-stered armchair opposite her. Fixing shrewd eyes that had seen through more than their share of bullshit on me, she twisted her mouth to one side before she sipped the coffee, tapping one scarlet talon on the side of the white paper cup.

"People are my job, Nichelle. Reading faces. Summing up personalities. It's my gift. It's what makes me so good at what I do."

I smiled. "I guess we have that in common."

She kept talking like I hadn't spoken. "But I don't get you. And every time I think I have you figured out, you do something crazy and throw me off. You have to know you're going to be political poison in this town at least until this shakes out, and possibly forever," she said. "And everyone knows Rick Andrews is gunning for you. I know how stupid Les is, but I didn't peg you for beating him to the dunce cap. What the hell possessed you to write a piece like that with no backup?"

"I trust my sources. I know I'm right," I said. "And everybody was so busy theorizing about politics and talking about a murder in the capitol that nobody was talking about the girl." I felt like I'd never stop saying it: "She mattered."

Trudy waved a hand. "I know where you knew her from, and I'm sorry that you liked her, but, honey, girls like her are a dime for two dozen in DC, and they are ultimately . . . disposable." She shrugged. "So no, she did not matter. Certainly not enough for you to risk your career over."

I blinked. Opened my mouth. Closed it again.

Where would arguing with her get me?

Kicked out with no information and no help.

What had she told me?

That she was way more callous than I'd have thought ten minutes ago —and that she didn't know I'd been fired. Yet.

And if Trudy didn't know, neither did anyone else. She was our resident gossip queen, and in a newsroom, that's a tall mountain to climb. Eunice liked to say you couldn't shit at the *Telegraph* without Trudy knowing what color it was. And she was right. Gross, but right.

"Agent Chaudry says he's having hell getting ahold of you, so I'm not even sure I can get you into the speeches you were supposed to cover now." Trudy narrowed her eyes. "And if Bob tries to send Shelby Taylor, I might as well abdicate and let Richmond get all its political news from the *Post*."

Good Lord. She should sell tickets for drama like that.

I could wonder what Bob would do about the speeches later. Damned if I would've ever thought covering a presidential speech would drop on my priority list, but here I was.

"How well do you know Baine's inner circle?" I asked, shifting gears with a smile so bright I was betting she'd think I'd been properly chastised and move on. Trudy liked to flaunt her insider knowledge of every facet of politics, sprinkling important names into everyday conversation such that I didn't even acknowledge it anymore.

She took the bait. "Tommy?" she tossed her hair, wavy and uncoiffed and falling around her cheekbones. "He's an absolute doll, if a bit of a do-gooder. Which is funny, because he doesn't seem to like you much, and yesterday I'd have said you two were peas in a tiny little pod. He's plainspoken, direct, and determined. Surrounds himself with smart people, even when they disagree with him." She paused. "Maybe especially when they disagree with him. Why do you want to know?"

I pounced on that last part. "Who's close to him that didn't like him before he won the election?"

She sipped her coffee, watching me. I tried to sit still. Didn't manage it, fidgeting with a puffed button on the arm of the chair.

"Why?"

I tapped one toe. "I think someone is setting him up. If I'm right, figuring out who is the only way to fix this."

Her eyes popped wide, but she still didn't speak. Toying with the paper cup, she nodded. "It's not impossible. And like I said before, I doubted you once and regretted it. I don't like feeling stupid." She reached into the pocket on the front of her sweatshirt and pulled out her phone, tapping at the screen with one thumb a few times before she flipped it around.

"See the guy in the back? The tall one, in the blue suit?"

I squinted at the screen, reaching for the phone.

Oh hell.

Wyatt Bledsoe, Hamilton Baine's buddy I hadn't ever gotten around to tracking down.

"You know him?" Trudy's eyebrows lifted as she studied my face.

"I've seen his picture before." I handed her phone back without elaborating.

I blinked. Smiled. Tried to look normal. I needed her to say why she'd shown me the kid's photo, and then I needed to find him.

Like yesterday.

Literally.

"I've always respected Tom's insistence on surrounding himself with dissenting voices," Trudy said. "He's been that way since he was on the city council here, going to Junior League teas and sitting with old-money attorneys at our most exclusive golf clubs regardless of the eyebrows it raised."

She paused.

My knee jiggled, my ability to sit still crumbling even as I tried to hang on to it.

"Well, there's too far, even for a guy like Thomas," Trudy said with a sigh. "He's always looking for the best in people. But sometimes, people are just going to hate your guts no matter how hard you try." She nodded to me. "As you well know."

I did indeed. I also thought I knew what she was going to say next.

My eyes stuck to her lips, watching the words come out so I could be sure I wasn't imagining it.

"Wyatt was out of a job when Thomas was elected because he worked for Senator Grayson. And Ted Grayson hates Thomas Baine and everything he stands for with a burning passion most people reserve for the bedroom. He lost a school board seat to him, once upon a time."

Jiminy freaking Choos. I blinked. Don't let her see.

But it all made sense: this Bledsoe guy was a Grayson mole in the Baine administration, with bonus dude bro access to Hamilton.

What if Baine's son really had been kidnapped? Or worse?

I jumped to my feet so fast my coffee sloshed out and dribbled over my knuckles. "Thanks, Trudy. I have to run."

"I better be the first to know what you find," she called after me. "And please, for the love of God, don't leave me stuck with Shelby tomorrow."

I waved over my shoulder, my heart taking off like a jackhammer.

If Grayson was pulling strings on a man inside the governor's mansion, Baine was in way more danger than I'd imagined.

And in the world according to Ted Grayson, it was my fault he'd spent the past fifteen months in a cell. Which meant he might be gunning for me, too—in more ways than one.

* * *

I drove three blocks with my hoodie up and my sunglasses on before I stopped in the lot at Cary Court and picked up my phone. Not that I knew who to call.

I didn't have time to freak out. I didn't have time to be scared.

What I did have was a thickness in my middle growing heavier every second with the certainty that none of the things spinning around me were unrelated, but the threads of the web were too gossamer-fine for me to make out.

I let my head fall back against the seat, closing my eyes.

Grayson was at the center of this shitstorm. I knew it in my bones. But I needed proof. Locked down, nailed in, airtight, hurricane-ready proof, especially after this morning. Which meant I had to find him. It was the only way.

I knew how Grayson and Lakshmi were connected in more detail than I cared to consider. I'd bet my brand-new boots if I found Grayson, I'd find out what happened to Hamilton Baine. Wyatt Bledsoe connected Grayson to the governor—and Hamilton—and Angela had given me the reason for Grayson's grudge against Lakshmi's father.

Angela.

You know where to get me if you need me, she'd said. But then she never replied to my email.

I raised the phone and clicked the little blue envelope on the screen, checking the junk mail folder for good measure. Nothing.

But I hadn't deleted her original message yet, either. I tapped the reply arrow again.

No salutation, no formality. Short and to the point: *I need to know where Ted Grayson would go to hide. Country house, family estate, anything you can think of. Please answer me ASAP—the governor's son may be running out of time.* Send.

Good. What next?

I still wanted to know more about Dr. Drake's research. I reached into my bag and came up with Stacy Adams's card. Flipped it over. Traced the cell number written on the back. Crossed my fingers. Dialed.

"Adams." His voice was smooth. Soft. Relaxed.

I pasted my brightest smile in place. It's an old trick that helps me sound happy and professional even when I'm fighting back nausea making a phone call. Mostly, it comes in handy when I have to bug a victim's family. Here's hoping it would work when I was afraid for my life, too. I started talking before I lost my nerve or my window.

"Hi, Mr. Adams, this is Leigh Mays with the *Virginia Environmental Digest*. I'm so sorry to bother you on a Sunday, but my editor got your contact information from someone in Governor Baine's office and just passed it on to me, and my deadline is pretty tight." My voice didn't even shake, the lies rolling out smooth and easy. I was too scared to be bothered by that. "Is it at all possible that we could sit down this afternoon and chat about what you're doing to protect Virginians and their land and water?"

I stopped talking and closed my eyes, concentrating on breathing normally.

It was a long shot.

But the promise of good publicity from an environmental magazine was pretty good bait.

"Of course, of course," he said. "Thank you so much for calling, Leigh."

Pretty good bait indeed.

"Great!" That came out maybe a little too loud, but I hustled past it. "Can I meet you at your office? What time is good for you?"

I wanted inside that building. So I preempted an offer of lunch or coffee while I had the chance.

"Will an hour from now work?" he asked. "Do you know where we're located?"

"Perfect." I let out a long breath. "I sure do."

"I'll meet you at the front doors and walk you up," he said. "Security is tight, it'll be easier that way."

Easier, I would take. Especially today.

"See you soon." I clicked off the call before he could change his mind and opened a text to Joey.

You don't need your car back, right? Send.

The dot bubble came right up. He was worried.

Take as long as you like. You need anything? You okay?

I smiled. *Fine. Have a lead. And an interview.* Send.

I couldn't tell him about Grayson until I knew more.

Buzz. *Be careful.*

Always. I added a heart and hit "Send."

I was trying, anyway.

I ticked through corners of my puzzle, looking for holes and realizing I didn't know anything about how the president fit into this. But suspicion gnawed at my insides with the whisper that it wasn't a coincidence, all this craziness preceding her visit so closely.

Clicking my mobile browser, I searched her name. Found the biggest virtual haystack I'd ever seen.

I had forty minutes to sift through needles. I didn't peg her as the type to be in with Grayson, but there had been enough surprises with this story, and ignoring my gut had been nothing but trouble so far.

I clicked to the news articles first and started reading.

She won West Virginia by promising the mining companies more lax EPA restrictions. "Coal is king, and we will make it profitable again," she said at a campaign rally steps from a mine shaft during one of twenty-nine visits to the Appalachians in seventeen months.

So she and Grayson had something in common. Not that it meant anything, really.

After the twentieth article, I put the phone down and started the car, letting my thoughts wander as I navigated the familiar streets to the industrial triangle between Church Hill and Scott's Addition.

Commonwealth Energy Alliance was a research outfit with fingers in everything from home automation, to windmills, to carbon recapture, but it was the *other cutting-edge technologies* line on CEA's website that had me curious. In the corporate world, backhanded bragging on something you won't identify usually means the PR department doesn't want it getting out. Which means it's not a thing you ought to be bragging on in the first place.

Parking twenty feet from the door, I scanned the lot.

Four cars.

I looked up the front of the building. Counted nine floors. And at least twenty windows just on this side of each one.

Going to see strangers alone had gone badly for me on enough occasions to give me pause.

But this Adams guy was kind of skinny and his voice hadn't sounded capable of threatening a mouse.

Time for Leigh to get him talking. The trick was to make him feel comfortable.

A feature. Practically a publicity piece. Adams had no reason to be on guard.

Journalism Even before the Age of the Internet 102: People who are flattered by interview requests often develop loose lips.

I kicked the car door open and turned my flattery gauge to overdrive, striding to the front doors. Adams opened them with a wide smile, extending his hand. I put mine out before my eyes went past him.

To the taller guy in the navy suit behind him.

Good news: I'd found Hamilton's friend Wyatt.

Bad news: Hamilton's friend Wyatt had found me.

22

My mouth went drier than Death Valley and forgot how to work.

"Thank you so much for coming, Leigh," Adams was saying, waving me inside.

I nodded, not taking my eyes off his companion.

Adams noticed, turning and putting both hands out. "Have you two met? I thought it might be helpful to have someone here who could let us know what the governor would like covered in the article."

My eyes stayed locked on Wyatt's. She who blinks first shows fear. And politicians feed on fear like well-groomed, toothpaste-commercial-smile-sporting succubi.

He blinked. Smiled.

I stuck my hand out. "Of course. I don't think we've met, but thanks so much for letting me interrupt your Sunday in the interest of my deadline. I'm Leigh Mays."

He shook my hand, his warm and almost sticky. "Wyatt Bledsoe."

I kept my smile in place, my posture easy.

I wore not a speck of makeup. My hair was stuffed under a ball cap, my jeans and sweater hiding my figure and my low wedge shoes making me shorter than I usually looked.

I wasn't Nichelle from the *Telegraph*, current commonwealth political enemy number one. I was Leigh. A freckle-faced, practically petite do-gooder environmental reporter.

The fundamental political truth that perception is reality was suddenly in my corner. All I needed was for them to believe I was Leigh, and I was. One person's truth, colored by their own experience and expectation, wasn't necessarily the next person's.

It was a basic tenet of human psychology my friend Emily always said I needed to understand better in my job. Standing there, I promised myself I'd consider it later if I could use it to get myself out of this building sans handcuffs now.

"No problem." Wyatt's lips tipped up in a tight smile, his eyebrows flashing skyward to match. "My job doesn't exactly keep regular hours."

"I do understand that," I said.

"Why don't we head up to my office?" Adams asked. "I think we'll be comfortable chatting there."

I nodded, swinging one arm wide in a lead-the-way gesture.

"Ladies first," Wyatt said with a nod. I fell into step beside Adams, high walls of gleaming tinted glass, steel, and stark white rising around us through an atrium so modern it looked like a set for an eighties sci-fi movie version of the twenty-first century.

"I can't tell you how glad I was to get your call," he said. "We've been so anxious to share some of our advances with your audience, and I appreciate you taking the interest." He looked over his shoulder. "And of course we appreciate the governor's confidence."

Wyatt nodded. "He's been impressed with your research." He had? Lucky break, since I'd big fat made up the name drop to make the interview sound important.

"Of course, he's a little busy today." Shit. Did Wyatt's eyes flick my way when he said that? I focused on my breathing, keeping my shoulders relaxed. Kyle always said they were my nervous tell, pulling so tight they crept toward my ears. Wyatt kept right on talking. "So I didn't have a chance to ask him for specifics, but I'm sure your editor shared that with you, right?"

I glanced back, nodding. "I think I have a good handle on what I'm here to get."

We stopped in front of a bank of elevators—glass, of course. Adams pressed the button, holding it for two blinks too long to be normal. "Up, please."

Like he could read my thoughts, he slid his eyes to me and smiled. "Fingerprint and voice ID. Our security is top notch."

I smiled, nodding as I stepped through the doors when they opened. "I'm sure folks around here will rest easier knowing that."

We shot skyward at a stomach-unsettling speed, my hand closing around the rail when the elevator took off.

"Takes a bit of getting used to," Adams said. "I don't notice it anymore."

I wondered if the elevators were turbo-charged in case of accidental gamma ray leak or something, but didn't ask. Better off not knowing, since my closet was fresh out of lead-lined outfits.

I kept my eyes on the gleaming steel floor. They couldn't be producing actual nuclear energy in here. The neighbors would've raised a ruckus I'd have heard about if that were the case. Right? Right.

We slowed to a seamless stop that reminded me of one of Jenna's new kitchen drawers when you shoved it closed, and a soft *bing* was followed by a sultry robot voice that said, "Ninth floor, Mr. Adams," before the doors opened.

Fancypants.

I followed Adams off the elevator and into an office every inch straight out of *2010: A Space Odyssey*, all bright white ten-foot walls and clean-lined white or clear-and-chrome furniture. He even had the egg-shaped chair behind his wide glass-topped desk.

The only art in the room hung opposite the desk, a wall of photos I didn't notice until I turned to get a bead on my friend from the governor's office.

I squinted at the prints, walking closer.

Jesus. My breath sucked in sharply, and not on purpose.

Stacy Adams spent his days staring at death. Disaster.

Names of places made famous by tragedy landed behind me.

"Chernobyl. Three Mile Island. Fukushima," Adams said.

I ripped my eyes away from the anguished faces of the people affected by the dark side of nuclear energy, turning back to the two men and shaking my head.

"Those are . . . jarring," I said.

"They're supposed to be." Adams waved one hand toward two clear plastic chairs on either side of a white oval table, taking the one at the head for himself. "Do you know what radiation sickness does to people? Constant vomiting, insurmountable fatigue—and those are the best symptoms. Folks lose their hair. Their skin, too." He pointed to a photo of a tiny boy with huge raw blotches on his chest. "Nothing in this office commands your attention except the images of the reason we do what we do. Working for a better future, a cleaner planet, where we don't have to fear meltdowns and waste disposal."

Damn. I didn't know a thing about any of this, but he had my attention. The guy was a good salesman, at the very least.

Wyatt nodded, leaning back in his chair and crossing his left ankle over his right knee.

"So tell me how you're going about that, exactly?" I pulled a pen and notebook from my bag.

He glanced at Wyatt, then back at me. "Did the governor's office fill you in on our thorium research?"

I nodded, scribbling *thorium* and clearing my throat. Not the first damned clue what he was talking about. "But the specific scope of the project, the hypothesis for outcomes, timeline—that's what I need to get straight from you." I blurted words as fast as they came into my head, glad I had to sit through the news rundown with the business and technology editors five times a week. I was well and truly out of my element talking to these guys, and letting them figure that out could set off a meltdown disaster of my own.

Adams nodded. "Of course." He pulled a tiny remote from his pocket and clicked it once. The lights went off. The surface of the table lit up with an image of a field dotted with buttercups.

"It's actually not terribly expensive to build a small test MSR unit," he said. "And we have a site that was donated last year, the requisite twenty miles from any home or school." He gestured to the table.

I kept my head down, my hand flying over the paper, not missing a word. I circled the acronym, not daring to ask what it was, but not really grasping what he meant, either. I had my homework cut out for me. But I also had the feeling this might actually get me somewhere.

"We're looking at a total cost of just under one billion to get up and running, with the potential of cleaner, safer energy that could serve the whole state—in a few years, the whole mid-Atlantic—with zero carbon emissions."

I kept my hand moving, my eyebrows going up. "That sounds . . ." I let it trail, raising my head as he clicked another button, bringing a line graph up on the table.

"Too good to be true?" He smiled. "You know the crazy part of this is, the government has known about this for almost a hundred years now."

I forgot to move my pen. "You're kidding."

He shook his head. "Back me up, Bledsoe."

Wyatt was so quiet I'd almost forgotten he was there. "I would've expected an environmental journalist to know that," he said, sitting forward slightly. "But it's true. Since right after World War II."

I nodded, "Oh, no, of course" tripping out of my mouth as I reached into cobwebby areas of my brain, hunting a history class, any history class that covered the war years, as I pretended to jot notes.

"The Manhattan Project," I blurted.

They both nodded, Wyatt relaxing his pose again. "The aftermath, anyway," Adams said. "The bombs led to the development of the energy technology. But the thing is, our way was on the table back then. They said it was a function of the slower replication rate for the fission that made them choose uranium. Well, that and the gamma ray production. But even when faced with the facts—that the gamma rays can be eliminated, and the MSR is safer—they went with the uranium."

I kept my eyes on my paper. Was I supposed to know this already, too? Because I didn't, and that was a hell of a claim. But the *Why?* stuck in my throat for fear of tipping my bluffing hand.

I kept quiet, scribbling nonsense under a light line when I ran out of notes to make and hoping Adams would keep going.

Just when I thought I was sunk, I looked up and he smiled. "It's one of Washington's dirty little secrets: they wanted their weapons. They chose the more dangerous option based on hokey-at-best science so they could quietly use money designated for energy infrastructure for side research projects on weapons. And so it went, for better than seventy years."

Seventy years that included Dr. Drake's top secret government research?

Holy Manolos.

I kept my face blank, nodding. "But you're looking to change that."

He shrugged. "Everyone who gets into this business dreams of changing the world. Very few people get to. But I have a shot. I'm planning to take it, yes. My biggest hurdle is getting Virginians to understand this so we get the support we need in the House of Delegates, which will lead to support in the private financial sector—that's the key. Which is why I'm so glad to have Governor Baine's support, and to have you here. So, what questions do you have?"

Shit.

I grabbed the first thing I could think of, turning again to the back wall. "At the end of the day, most folks want the same basic things, regardless of their political leanings. Plenty to eat, a warm, safe place to sleep, and to feel like their family is well cared for."

Wyatt nodded. "Astute of you." He laced his fingers behind his head, uncrossing his legs and recrossing them the opposite way. "But try having a candidate say 'nuclear power' around here. They get it from all sides: the tree huggers scream Chernobyl, and the EPA haters scream coal. It's a no-win."

"Which is why the governor hasn't made his support for this public," I said, trying not to let the end go up in a question.

"He has not. Which makes me wonder exactly how you found out he does support it?" He didn't move in the chair, but his voice dropped half an octave at the end, the blank look folding back over his face as he studied me.

No-win.

Play dumb.

I widened my eyes and stretched my face into an innocent smile I'd practiced in front of the mirror a thousand times, because sometimes the best way to get people to talk was to pretend I had a hollow cavern between my ears. But if Baine was on board with this plan and Bledsoe knew it, that meant Grayson knew it—which I'd bet meant the coal executives did, too.

"My editor is the one who told me that, not the governor himself or anything. You'd have to ask him. I assumed he'd heard it from the governor, but I might be wrong. He didn't really say, come to think of it." Widen the smile just a hair at the end. Blink. Don't break eye contact.

Wyatt nodded again, slower this time.

He didn't trust me—that wasn't my imagination. He was throwing up obstacles. But so far I was Indiana Jonesing the hell out of his gauntlet. I tried to keep the self-satisfaction to a minimum, turning back to Adams. Were they running some sort of good science nerd/bad political strategist schtick, or did Adams really believe me?

No way to tell for sure. But if he was faking his ease and excitement, he ought to at least consider moonlighting at the community theatre.

I picked up my pen, clicking the tip in and out. "So how do you keep it safe? For the planet and the neighbors?" I asked, forgetting for a split second that I wasn't really writing this piece. His points were fascinating, and when I had time, I'd like to dig into the story deeper.

Adams's face widened into a grin, bringing out adorable dimples that cut a straight line with the tip of his nose. "We bury it." He put the remote on the table, leaning on both hands and casting a squatty shadow over the graphs. "A single midsize reactor will power a city the size of Richmond easily, and we can sink it two hundred feet into the earth and leave it for thirty years. Because there are no waste isotopes to expel or dispose of, once it's running, it will just work."

I jotted every word, underlining the last ones before I looked up at him.

"It does sound too good to be true," I said. "Where's the catch?"

He shrugged. "I've reviewed all the research from as far back as 1942, and done thousands of hours of my own, and I can't find one. Except . . ." His eyes slid to Wyatt.

He cleared his throat and sat up. "Washington doesn't like doing things differently than they've always been done, Miss Mays. You've heard the phrase moving mountains, but in DC terms, we're trying to push a whole range. It takes time."

And money.

I nodded. "So, what's the next step?"

"If we can get approval from the House of Delegates during this winter's session, we'll be able to start construction of the first operational salt reactor on US soil in almost sixty years," Adams said. "It will take two years to have it up and running."

"And then?" I raised my eyebrows.

"And then we show the world what we can do. Then we go global."

I glanced back at Wyatt. "All on Governor Baine's watch. With his blessing. Two years is good timing for y'all, isn't it?"

He leaned forward again, nodding as he said, "The governor is interested in what's best for Virginians, not what's best for him and his career."

But if this guy was anything like Ted Grayson, he wasn't interested in either. I smiled. "Can I quote you on that?"

He tipped his head to one side. Smiled a bare, cold smile. "Of course."

I scribbled, looking back at my notes.

Still couldn't read him. But the longer I sat there, the more my legs seemed of their own mind to get up and move far away from him.

He glanced at his Rolex and rose with a polite half smile. "I'm afraid I'm out of time for today," he said. "I hope you have everything you need, Miss Mays." He lingered on the last two words, I swear. I ignored it, nodding and extending a hand.

"Thank you for being here."

"Anything for Governor Baine."

Adams cleared his throat, standing up straight. "Leigh, could you excuse me for a moment?" He looked at Wyatt and tipped his head toward the door. "I'll walk you out."

Wyatt's eyes shot to me, then back to Adams. He lifted his shoulders in a small shrug. "Suit yourself."

Hunching back over my notebook, I watched them go out and shut the door from the corner of one lash-veiled eye. Counted to thirty as their footsteps receded down the hallway.

My breath picked up right along with my heart rate as I stood, laying my pen on the notebook and tiptoeing across the tightly woven flat-gray industrial carpet, keeping the backs of my wedges off the floor and soundless as I moved.

Creeping behind the desk, I peered through the glass and spotted a laptop in a drawer beneath the glass surface, the screen facing up, displaying the charts that were projected onto the surface of the table.

Mouthing a thank you at the ceiling, I slid the tray above the drawer out and touched the trackpad on the shiny white keyboard, bringing up Anderson's directory.

He had a file for every dollar he needed for his pollution-free reactor.

Damn.

I scrolled, no idea what the hell I was looking for.

Tick-tock. Tick. Tock.

I could feel time racing past, my ears perked for the bing of the elevator or footfalls in the hallway.

I spotted a folder labeled *MSR*.

It was password protected.

I stomped a silent toe, biting blood out of the inside of my cheek to keep a frustrated scream in.

The guy had told me just enough to make me think I knew something. But I still didn't know anything particularly helpful. I cleared the screen and slid the keyboard back into place, turning to the drawers in the sleek white credenza behind me.

Why would a man who so clearly loved his technology keep paper files?

To cover his ass, or to make sure other people kept his secrets. Maybe a little of both.

I tried the drawer. Locked.

Examined it. There was no keyhole.

What the actual hell?

I ran my fingers around the seams.

Nothing.

Wait.

My eyes went back to the big table across the room.

His remote was still there, a foot from my notebook.

I raced back, my calves protesting the tiptoe-running, and snatched it up.

Six buttons.

Forward. Back. Lights on/off.

Open. Close.

Open. Close.

I held my breath, pointing the little wand at the credenza and pushing "Open."

The top drawer slid out. I scurried back.

A neat row of white folders full of white paper.

Except one.

A single black folder hung in the center, the little label reading *u 233* in tiny black type.

Always go for the standout.

My hand closed over the folder as the elevator binged down the hall. Shit.

I yanked it free, plopped it on the desk.

Footsteps. Slow, not quick. One set. Maybe he was looking at his phone.

I fanned the papers wide, and fired off a dozen or so photos with mine.

The steps paused.

Sweeping the papers back into a pile, I closed the folder and dropped it into place. The steps picked up pace, stopping outside the door.

Sprinting, I fell into my plastic chair and hit the "Close" button as I picked up my pen. Adams tucked his phone into his pocket as he strode back in.

"Sorry about that," he said. "Busy, for a Sunday. I hope you got everything you needed. Did you think of any more questions for me while I was gone?"

Yep. What the hell is a u 233?

I didn't say that.

Smiling, I shook my head. "I really appreciate you taking time out of your weekend to talk with me."

I stood, hoping my legs weren't shaking enough to be noticeable.

I didn't know what to make of anything I'd heard or seen in the past hour and a half, but surely there was something in all this that would be helpful when I had a bit of time alone with Google.

He smiled, gesturing a *Ladies first* toward the door.

"Anytime. I'm a big fan of your work, Miss . . . Clarke."

23

So much for my clever cover story.

Spinning slowly, I tipped my head to one side.

He folded his hands behind his back, rocking up on his toes.

"Did you really think a ball cap and some jeans would do it?" he asked. "I'm a total news junkie. I've been following your stories since that boat crash on the James two summers ago. I've seen you on TV a dozen times."

I didn't have time to think.

I folded my lips between my teeth and nodded. "I'm flattered. I think?" My hand went into my bag, closing around my pepper spray.

"I'm not interested in hurting you," he said, his eyes on my wrist. "If I was, I'd have ratted you out to Wyatt. His boss is none too happy with you today. Ballsy, dropping his name when you called me."

"I'm trying to . . . figure something out." I sighed. "I needed to speak with you, and I didn't think you'd consent to an interview if there was nothing in it for you."

He backed up two steps, pulling his glasses off and pinching the bridge of his nose.

"But there is something in this for me," he said. "Because I'm hoping if you figure out what the hell is going on at the capitol, you'll find Hamilton."

I stepped toward him, the raw anguish in his voice catching me off guard.

"He can't be dead. Not yet. I would know." His whole body shuddered with a sob. "He's my soul mate."

Oh.

Boy.

I couldn't stop my hand from clapping over my mouth.

Adams looked up, wiping at the corners of his eyes under his glasses. "Don't tell me I've shocked you. Surely after everything you've seen, the governor having a son who swings both ways doesn't even rate as the most shocking today."

I shook my head, letting my hand fall back to my side. "Not even close." Every word true. And I didn't give one damn who Hamilton Baine wanted to sleep with as long as it was consensual.

"When was the last time you talked to Hamilton?" I tried to keep my voice calm. For the first time in two days, I had someone in front of me with a seemingly pure interest in the truth. Maybe he would tell it, too.

"Thursday night. We met for drinks at a little place we like down south of the river. Pretty safe for us to be seen at if we're careful. Drinks turned into dinner. We went down to the water and walked a while. Talking." He shook his head. "I was stupid. Demanding more than he could offer. I knew that. But I couldn't help it. I love him. I know he loves me. Have you ever been in love and done something dumb?"

Like telling Joey I didn't want to live with him? Every fight we'd had over that in recent weeks played in my head on fast-forward. I was afraid of getting too close. He thought my job was more important than him. But watching Stacy tear up over Hamilton, I finally got it: it didn't matter. Live with him, don't live with him—I loved him, and my address wasn't going to change that.

Holding Stacy's watery gaze, I just nodded. This wasn't the time to dwell on my romantic issues.

He sniffled. "He liked Lakshmi. A lot. And he's not exactly big on the ladies as a general rule. But I mean, hell, I liked Lakshmi. She was gorgeous and so fucking smart . . . the kind of girl you could talk to for hours. Marriage material, Hamilton's dad always says. Brilliant. Interesting."

So Baine really didn't know about Lakshmi's past. Interesting. Because if Wyatt worked with Grayson, he sure did.

"But Hamilton didn't want to marry her," I said.

Adams shook his head. "His parents pushed him to propose. Hamilton was stuck. He said he wasn't sure he could be happy forever with her, and they damned sure wouldn't be happy with me."

"But—" I began, and he laughed.

"There's a big difference between walking in the pride parade for the cameras and standing up with your son while he pledges his heart to another man. Which I'm sure you realize, now that I've made you stop to think about it. It's not personal. It's political. Bad optics, you understand." He deepened his voice and stuck his chest out in a half-decent imitation of the governor on the last.

"I see. Where did he go when you left dinner? Do you know?"

Adams shook his head.

"I never asked. I told him we were through if he was so ashamed of me. And now all I can think about is how much I want to talk to him, put my arms around him . . . and they're not telling me anything. Wyatt knows how crazy this is making me, and he shut down when I asked him just now." He shook his head. "Why I cared what those fucking rednecks thought, anyway . . . like it was worth it." The words fell so softly I wasn't convinced I heard him right.

"Rednecks?"

I stepped closer, letting go of the pepper spray before I pulled my notebook back out, clicking my pen.

"They came into the parking lot in a big pickup as we were walking back up from the water. Three guys. The one who was driving spotted us and called out to Hamilton. He knocked my hand away from his arm like I'd sprouted vipers for fingers."

Huh. "And you didn't recognize them?"

He shook his head.

"Do you remember anything else about these guys? It might be helpful if I could talk to them."

"Why?"

"They were among the last people to see Hamilton before he disappeared, right?" I lifted one brow.

He shrugged. "Those guys weren't smart or strong enough to do anything to him. The one who seemed to know him, I mean, I could break that guy in half over one knee, and I'm not exactly the poster child for the gym. Overconfident, for a scrawny little balding dude. What hair he had was stringy and limp, but he didn't look old enough to be losing it."

The plastic of my pen bit into my fingers as a picture formed in my head.

No way.

"Oh, and he stuttered. Pretty bad. I thought maybe he'd already been drinking."

Oh. My. God.

I scribbled.

"The other guys?"

He shook his head. "I'm sorry, I was pissed and they didn't come over. I didn't really get a good look at them." He paused. "Except, one was a big dude, with a stupidly unruly beard that was missing big patches. Looked mad, his face was all red when they got out of the car. And the other was dressed like he was trying out for a Vineyard Vines ad. Didn't fit in with the other two. He even had a bow tie."

I made sure I didn't miss a detail, tapping my index finger on the side of the pen when I stopped scribbling.

"Anything else?" I didn't want to wonder if I'd led him into remembering something wrong. The human brain is an imperfect thing. "I don't suppose you saw a plate number or anything definitive."

He snorted. "Better. Their pickup is painted like the *General Lee*. You know, from *The Dukes of Hazzard*? No shit."

Leaping Louboutins. I reached for my phone and clicked up my story from yesterday. Double-tapped the picture of Jake Stickley. "This guy?" I asked, passing Adams the phone.

He took it, his eyes widening when he held the screen up to the end of his nose. "Yeah. Yeah, that's him. That's even the same shirt he was wearing, but he didn't have the tie. Who is he? How did he know Hamilton?"

I took my phone back before he could zoom out to the rest of the story, ignoring his first question.

"I don't know." Understatement of the month. "But I am going to find out." Every word true.

I handed him a card. "Call me if you remember anything?"

"Is this why the ATF guy was up my ass the other day about where Hamilton and I had been and who we'd talked to?" I wasn't even sure he was talking to me, his eyes on the floor as he took the card. "I thought he was some sort of political spy and I didn't tell him anything, but now I'm not so sure."

The meth lab was Kyle's case. He'd been on it since before the explosion.

Had he come here, not chasing leads on Lakshmi, but because he thought Hamilton Baine was somehow involved with the drug runners? Damn, what if Hamilton's disappearance really did have nothing to do with Lakshmi's death? And how come every time I thought I finally had a piece of this down, everything around it shifted?

I tucked the notebook back into my bag with a smile. "I hope things work out well for you, Stacy. All the way around." I liked him, and my people radar is rarely wrong.

He walked me out of the building, the space-age elevator lowering us back to the ground floor nearly as fast as it had shot us to the top.

At the front door, I turned back with one more question. "You and Hamilton met when you worked at Daltec?" Assuming nothing seemed a safe bet.

He shook his head. "I got him that interview, actually. Lakshmi introduced us at a party when I was a grad student at Madison."

Wait.

Lakshmi's last study.

I closed my eyes, willing my cluttered photographic memory to action. L. Drake, S. Adams, and W. Bledsoe.

I'd found a Stephanie Adams in the school directory and tracked her to Africa through her social media.

I was wrong.

"You worked with her in the statistics department?" It popped out before I could stop it. I leaned on the wide steel counter inside the door.

This thing kept wrapping back in on itself. I needed to stop chasing new ideas and start trying to find the intersecting trails that made sense of the ones I already had.

He flashed a smile. "I've always been a big math and science nerd. Took me a while to pick one to stick with. A long while, if you ask my dad. He's still complaining about the tuition bills."

"So Lakshmi knew Hamilton before she worked for his father?"

He nodded. "She was a whiz with the political stuff. She was testing a hypothesis about identity politics and harnessing it to influence elections with social media. She knew Wyatt from way back . . ." He trailed off. "Though now that I stop to think of it, nobody ever really said how."

I knew how.

"When did you guys actually do the study?" I asked. "I know it was published last spring."

"We worked on it from April to September of the previous year," he said.

During Baine's campaign. Had her influencing research helped put him in the governor's mansion? And how ethical was that, if it did? Would someone kill her to keep that quiet?

One more goose I didn't have time to chase.

"Lakshmi brought Wyatt in to give advice on the methodology and help find subjects, and he brought Hamil to a party we had when we finished up the research and the numbers supported her idea." He shrugged. "Politics doesn't matter much to me, honestly. I'm too black-and-white minded to see all the gray Lakshmi went on about when she got revved up about it."

"Did people at Madison know anything about Lakshmi's past?" I asked.

"I didn't know much of anything, though I never thought about it. She was a smart woman and a hard worker. She didn't talk a lot about her family or her personal life. Hell, I didn't even know she was Reynash Drake's daughter until I went to work at Daltec."

I fired off a half-dozen rapid blinks, trying to keep my brain from spinning any faster.

I needed to think this through. But not here in front of this guy.

I pulled a slow breath through my nose and put out a hand.

My phone buzzed in my bag. I flicked my eyes down. Not now, Ohio.

"Thank you, Mr. Adams," I said. "Let me know if you think of anything else."

He closed both his hands around mine. "Find him." He said. "You're good at making things right. And pulling off the impossible. I know Governor Baine isn't your favorite person today, Miss Clarke, but believe me, he's not Hamilton's favorite, either."

I just nodded before I stepped out the door.

I couldn't promise him something I wasn't sure I could deliver.

24

The troopers waited until Adams was out of sight before they closed ranks around me, about a half-dozen steps into the parking lot.

I scanned for familiar faces. Not a one.

"Miss Clarke, we're going to have to ask you to come with us," the tallest one said.

The other three folded their arms across their chests, forming a wall between me and Joey's car.

So I hadn't really fooled anyone. Or they'd linked me and Joey and tracked the car. Either way, I didn't need the extra complication today.

I turned to the one who was doing the talking. His nameplate said Davis. "Do you have a warrant, Officer Davis?"

He pulled an envelope from his back pocket and handed it to me. "I have a subpoena. From the attorney general of the Commonwealth of Virginia. Ma'am." He tipped his hat and took a half step back.

"What could the attorney general possibly want with me?" I knew, because Aaron had told me. But I could also tell this guy wasn't sure he wanted to be here, and the stripes on his shoulder told me he was a commander. So I wanted to make him say it out loud.

"I'm sure it's all there in the summons." He shifted his weight from one foot to the other, refusing to meet my eyes.

Fine.

I ripped one corner of the envelope, specks of the shiny gold seal in the corner falling to the concrete.

Shaking the thin paper out, I held it up.

Matters involving state secrets.

Were they kidding?

I hadn't ever actually met the attorney general, but people I trusted had always had good things to say about him.

Surely he wasn't accusing me of treason against the commonwealth for printing a story they damn well knew was true, no matter how much they disliked it.

I looked back at the trooper.

"It seems I'm an enemy of the state today?" I let my voice go up at the end.

"I'm just doing my job, ma'am." He still wouldn't look at me.

I let my head fall back, a puffy white cloud drifting lazily overhead. Looked kind of like an elephant.

Good metaphor for my day. Elephants filling all the rooms, sitting on my chest . . . and now flying overhead, too.

I didn't really have any options. They weren't asking me to go with them. They were telling me. There were three of them and one of me, and it wasn't like I was outrunning them all, even in wedges.

"Okay," I said, spinning to move toward the gray state patrol cruiser to my left. One of the silent troopers jumped in front of me and I stumbled to a stop, eyeing him.

"I said okay." I raised my eyebrows, folding my lips between my teeth and biting down to keep words I shouldn't say in.

He moved and waved me ahead.

Another officer, who looked to be the youngest one, opened the back door of the cruiser for me, putting a hand out to make sure I didn't hit my head. Reflex, since they'd spared me the ridiculousness of handcuffs.

The commander slid behind the wheel, the youngster taking shotgun. Nobody turned to look at me, the silence in the car heavier than the kettlebells my body combat instructor was so fond of these days.

Oh hell no.

They weren't getting around this without talking to me.

I laced my fingers together in my lap. "Do either of you gentlemen have a sister?"

Crickets.

"A daughter?"

The commander's eyes shifted to the rearview.

Bingo.

"Lakshmi Drake's mother was beside herself when I saw her yesterday. Her little girl—and my mother tells me no parent ever stops seeing a child as the small person they once were, no matter how old they get—was murdered. Rather viciously, from what I've been able to find."

I paused.

Waited.

The commander put the signal on and turned the cruiser into the shoe-box-sized excuse for a parking lot at the corner 7-Eleven.

He turned in the seat, shooting the other trooper a wordless glare that sent the kid scrambling out of the car.

"Need some coffee?" I asked, keeping my voice calm as he rounded on me.

"I know your game here, and I'm not playing," he snapped.

I blinked. Okay then.

"You can't tell me you don't know how that woman feels," I said. "Look, I work with law enforcement every day. I count a lot of those guys among my friends." Or I thought I did, anyway. "I'm not trying to piss you off or get you fired. But every cop I know well has one thing in common with all the others: a desire to do the right thing. Sometimes it's hard to tell what the right thing is when you're faced with a thousand impossible decisions on every shift. But this—hauling reporters in for questioning based on a polit-ical vendetta—isn't why you do this job, is it, Commander?"

He rested his right arm along the back of the seat on the other side of the glass. Sighed. Dropped his chin to his chest.

"The governor says you're lying." The words tumbled into his lap so fast and soft I wasn't sure I was supposed to hear them.

"Yet something is telling me you don't believe that." I snapped my mouth shut. Silence is a good tool when someone is conflicted.

"I wasn't there Friday. Not even his personal detail was allowed in the office. Listen, I never wanted any part of politics." He lifted his head. "I have to take you in. It was made very clear to me this morning that my job depends on it. But no, this isn't me. This isn't supposed to be the function of this organization."

His shoulders fell, his whole broad chest deflating with a long exhale. "Look. I don't know exactly what you put yourself in the middle of here, and to be honest I don't really want to know. But whatever it is, you've got people flipping the fuck out. Important people. People who pull the governor's strings."

Hitting the "Lock" button on his door, he put the car in gear and pulled back onto the road. "No need to bring a rookie along for the ride."

He wasn't talking to me.

But the words sent ice shooting all the way to my core.

I reached for my bag.

Pulled out my phone.

Clicked the text messages.

Kyle. Joey. Aaron. Bob.

I closed my fingers tight around the plastic.

Charlie. Dan.

In the back of a state patrol car, subpoena from the AG citing matters involving state secrets. Commander who's driving seems reluctant to take me in. Scared, even. I'll take the questioning, I deserve it. But this guy is making me nervous.

Back. New message. Mom.

You are amazing and brilliant, and I love you. So proud to have you for my mom. It wouldn't alarm her to see that—I get mushy where she's concerned pretty easily, and . . . well, bases covered. Hopefully the first message would keep the second from being more than a smile in her Sunday morning.

I hit "Send" as Davis turned into a back lot at the capitol building and stopped at security.

I tapped my email open. Come on, Angela. I swiped down.

No new messages. Damn.

Davis opened the door to my right as I dropped my phone back into my bag.

I stood, tipping my head back to look up at the stark white stone against the clear cornflower fall sky.

These folks were awfully intent on keeping their secrets.

I walked in front of Commander Davis to the door, where another uniformed officer took my bag and placed it on a shelf behind the metal detectors and X-ray machine without scanning it.

"You'll get it back when you leave." The words were clipped as he waved me through the metal detector.

I nodded. Stepping through the thing, which seemed like some sort of portal to an alternate dimension, I felt another chill.

These people were supposed to be the good guys.

Which left me wondering who, exactly, the bad guy was here.

* * *

Wesley Cameron's office looked a lot like Wesley Cameron himself: proper, bright, and understated.

Three walls of floor-to-ceiling bookshelves were lined with thick leather-wrapped legal tomes. The lone drywall surface, a soft ecru color, was dotted with ornately framed diplomas and certificates. A credenza along the awards wall held framed photos of Wesley with every visiting dignitary from the president to the Duke and Duchess of Cambridge. I studied them, Commander Davis watching from the doorway.

"Feel free to have a seat," he said. "I'm sure he'll be up momentarily."

"I'm good, thank you." I didn't turn around.

The guy smiling out of these photos didn't look like he had it in him to kill anyone.

But could he order it?

No idea.

Which had me so unnerved I couldn't tell if my hands were trembling from that or the anger I was trying to keep from directing at the cop guarding the door.

I closed my teeth around the inside of my jaw and crossed a few feet of thick goldenrod carpet to the bookshelf.

Copies of the Code of Virginia from every year back to 1946 on the middle shelf.

Up one higher, a thin layer of dust lined the front of the shelf, which held fat books on everything from tax law to real estate regulations. Perusing the titles, I noticed a drag mark in the dust and looked up at that book.

Executive Power and Privilege: Checks and Balances for State Legal Systems.

Awesome.

So he might be trying to figure out how to limit the governor's power.

Or how to make me shut up for good.

Before I had time to consider that enough for the sour bubble of terror to crawl all the way up the back of my throat, the door clicked open.

"Sorry to keep you waiting."

Cameron, starched and buttoned up in a navy pinstripe suit, walked to the desk without offering a hand.

I strode to the chair opposite him and put mine out. "I'm more than a little confused about why I'm here, Mr. Cameron. But it's nice to meet you."

He met my eyes and reached for my hand in inching degrees, his gaze flickering between my face and the bookshelves on either side of us. "Thank you for coming in on a Sunday." His hand was cold and damp, almost slimy feeling, when it closed lightly around mine. I fought the urge to draw back, my eyes going to the door, where Commander Davis had just disappeared.

"I wasn't made aware that I had a choice in the matter."

He pulled his hand back and sank into his big leather chair, gesturing to the one behind me.

"You've put us in a very unusual situation," he said, folding his hands on the blotter.

I leaned back in my chair, forcing my shoulders to relax and opening my arms. Nothing to hide here. Which was true. It was the "cool as a pitcher of cucumber water" part I was faking for all I was worth.

"It seems to me that whoever killed Lakshmi Drake put you in a very unusual situation," I said.

He plucked a pen from the marble holder next to his clock and rolled it back and forth between his long fingers. "And therein lies the problem.

Miss Drake is alive and well, as the governor told Charlie Lewis this morning. And as her father will tell Charlie Lewis at five o'clock." He held my gaze through the whole spiel, watching my face go slack.

"You have been played, Miss Clarke, and we need to know by whom. It's a matter of high urgency. Who told you that Miss Drake was the deceased found in the building yesterday?"

I shook my head. "I'm afraid I can't tell you that, sir. But I do have a question for you: If Lakshmi wasn't the victim yesterday, who was? And why on earth would the governor or her father need to talk to Charlie—why not just have Lakshmi sit for the interview herself?"

I blinked, letting out a slow breath that kept my nerves from showing.

The backs of my eyelids played Nichelle and Kyle's greatest hits, from a gangly boy with slightly long hair shuffling his feet and handing me a bouquet of daisies in my mom's foyer, to the night I lost my virginity, to him showing up in a warehouse in Shockoe Bottom, to Friday morning . . . and yesterday afternoon.

Kyle would've seriously cut out his own tongue before he'd lie to me. Until this guy marched Lakshmi into a room where I could see her speak and hear her laugh, he was the liar, not Kyle. And I damned sure wasn't throwing a friend under a runaway political bus on the threats and assertions of a stranger.

I sat up straighter in the chair.

Cameron did likewise. "Someone is lying to you," he said. "You do realize the governor could sue you for libel?"

I sucked a deep breath through my nose to keep my voice even, his dodge of my simple question not lost on me. Anger and fear were not my friends here, though.

"Mr. Cameron, no disrespect, but people lie to me almost every day. This presents the rare instance when I'm not quite sure who is lying about what, and I'm dealing with people who use lies as their stock in trade," I said. "As for a libel suit, well, best of luck with that. My story said nothing about Governor Baine being a suspect or connected to the victim or her death in any way."

"You said there was a dead prostitute in the governor's office." He shook his head. "If that's not political warfare, I'm not sure what is."

"We'll have to let a judge decide that, I suppose," I said.

He sighed. Planted both hands flat on the edge of the desk and stood, leaning forward. "I'm not sure you understand the stakes of the game you've wandered into here, so let me explain: Someone is out to ruin Governor Baine. Not just his career, him as a human being. And they pegged you as an effective vehicle for that. Rightly so, it seems. I'm not going to let that happen." His face contorted into an ugly, borderline cartoonish mask flooded with ruddy color from his hairline to his bright-white collar. His voice dropped two full octaves as he spoke, coming out in almost a growl. "You will either tell me where you got that tip, or you won't tell anyone anything for a very long time."

My heart took off to the races. I closed my fingers around the smooth, cool polished wood of the chair arms, scooting back in the seat.

Raising my chin, I forced my mouth to make words. "I won't betray a source."

He reached into a drawer behind the desk.

I threw myself backward so hard I toppled the chair, my head bouncing off the thick carpet, the wind rushing out of my chest with the impact.

I wriggled, my sweater sticking my shoulders to the carpet and my hips and legs still bent around the C-shaped chair, flailing in midair.

I was stuck. As good as a turtle on its back in the mud.

Cameron charged around the corner of the desk, and I threw my hands up like it would do any good, my eyes pinching shut and refusing to open.

I'd been in some dangerous situations, and more than anyone's share of ridiculous ones, too. But to have it all end here, in cold blood on ugly carpet because I was stuck in a stupidly designed chair . . . Kyle better be telling the truth. And he'd better get whatever he was after when he pulled me into this bullshit, too.

25

The door rattled in its frame, someone pounding it half-down from outside.

"What?" Cameron roared.

I forced one eye open enough to see him stomping away from me. It didn't appear he had a weapon.

I rocked side to side, trying to turn the chair. No dice.

Fine. Throwing my knees toward my nose as hard as I could, I flipped backward out of the seat, the momentum carrying me until I ended up on my knees in an awkward heap, my ball cap askew, hair half-falling out of my ponytail and covering my eyes.

I shot to my feet, backing up to the credenza as I swiped at my face.

Cameron's hands were indeed empty. My eyes flicked to the desk. Nothing there, either.

Breathe.

Cameron jerked the door inward.

Commander Davis.

Had he been standing outside the entire time?

"I thought I was clear that you were dismissed for the day," Cameron said.

"Sir, Dan Kessler from WRVA is down at security." Commander Davis looked over Cameron's shoulder, his eyes finding mine with a nod so tiny I couldn't swear I didn't imagine it. "He says he knows Miss Clarke is here and he'd like to speak to someone about what she's being charged with, or when she'll be ready to go."

Cameron ran one hand through his copper-colored curls and turned to me.

I folded my hands behind my back, standing up as tall as I could and thanking God for Dan Kessler. There was something I never thought I'd have cause to do. Specifically, at any rate.

Cameron turned back to the door. "Obstruction of justice," he said. "Take her down the street and have them put her in a cell." He turned back and gave me a once-over. "A holding cell. No calls except to me." He nodded. "When you're ready to talk, you let them know. They'll be able to reach me anytime."

He walked back to his desk and watched the commander cross to me. "Make sure Mr. Kessler knows where Miss Clarke is headed. Just in case he has any half-baked ideas of his own." He nodded to me. "Smart, Miss Clarke. But I'm still smarter."

I walked out of the room in front of the commander.

We'd have to see about that.

* * *

Holding cells are gross on an average day.

On a Sunday morning? Downright disgusting.

Twenty-six people crammed into a twelve-by-twelve space that reeked of cheap perfume, BO, and vomit. The fragrance cocktail was right up there with decomposing human, but it seemed everyone else was either still too blitzed to care or had gone nose blind to the stench. I was hoping for the latter, because then maybe I would too, if the shallow breaths didn't make me pass out first.

Since all my belongings were back at the capitol building, where Commander Davis assured me they'd be well looked after (pretty sure that was code for "the cyber unit is trying to crack your phone as I speak"), it took about seventy-five seconds for the deputy on duty to process me—

fingerprints, mugshots, and a pat-down were completed with clipped precision.

Davis stayed on the front side of the desk when the deputy took my arm to lead me to the little overstuffed room. She was probably thirty-five, with flawless café au lait skin, long lashes, and the kind of hips most of the women in my body combat classes abhorred carbs and killed themselves in the gym trying to get. The thick hair that cascaded halfway down her back in dark waves was flat-out unfair. She shot me a side eye as she strode down the hall half towing me. "The hell did you do to get in here on order of the state police? Selling your kid's Adderall? Your mother's Oxy?"

I snorted, my hand floating to my face. "The dark circles are from work, not kids." Apparently I had exceeded my best-by date for leaving home sans concealer. "I'm a reporter at the *Telegraph*." Recently, anyway. The matter of job security was still a bit fuzzy, and low on my priority list. "They want me to tell them something I'm not willing to share."

She stopped. Turned to face me. "No shit? Like, some Woodward and Bernstein type stuff right here on my shift?" Her eyes flew open wide, the lashes hand-to-God brushing her bangs. I wanted to know what kind of mascara that was, but this wasn't the time to ask for makeup advice.

I flashed a smile. "I'm not bringing down a president anytime soon, but protecting a source is protecting a source, so . . . kind of?"

She glanced over her shoulder. "That holding cell is a bad place to be."

"I've seen more than a few. I'm not scared." Mostly true. I wasn't afraid of being there so much as how long they'd keep me there. Legally, seventy-two hours is the maximum in Virginia without an arraignment. But if the *Telegraph*'s attorneys didn't come to the rescue, I could find myself in actual prison, depending on the judge's view of the fourth estate and how much of a case Cameron could invent in two days.

I wasn't ready to think about that. Or about the fact that Dan Kessler was my current best hope for avoiding it. Lord help me.

She shook her head and unlocked the door, still the old-school bars style, letting go of my arm and waving me inside. "I'm right outside if anything goes wrong." She turned stern glares on a few of the folks in the crowd.

I slid past a woman with smooshed-down big hair and smeared too-bright makeup clad in a miniskirt and a faux-fur jacket, scooting into a corner.

She turned on one boxy knee-high boot heel and followed. "What are you doing here, Mary?"

I resisted the urge to roll my eyes at the childish backhanded insult, keeping my gaze locked on hers instead. "Being crossways with the local cops, same as anyone else here." I put a hard edge on the words. A jailhouse brawl wasn't on my bucket list, and a dash of bitchiness can go a long way toward avoiding physical conflict in some places.

She reached a hand toward a lock of hair that had escaped my hat, and I tossed my head, dodging her fingers but not breaking eye contact.

She stepped back. Tipped her head to one side and folded her arms across her clearly braless-under-her-halter-top chest.

Her eyes narrowed as they traveled from my hat to my wedges and back again.

I narrowed mine right back.

She shrugged. "Whatever. Hope you're comfortable standing. Lucky puked on the mattress in three places, so she's got the bed to herself today."

I nodded, my eyes going to the ball of spandex and sequins on the narrow cot against the lone solid wall. It seemed most of the stench was emanating from her, on closer inspection, so I picked my way around bodies both sitting and sprawled on the concrete floor until I could lean against the bars on the opposite side of the cell.

Or not. The metal cut into my shoulder blades, sharp and unforgiving. I stood up straight, looking around at long, pale faces and hollow eyes. I'd worked the crime desk long enough to guess what better than half of these women had done to end up here, from drugs to solicitation. And then there was the one in the far opposite corner everyone else gave a wide berth to, arms around her knees, sharp chin resting on her elbow. I didn't see or smell a reason for the space, which told me she was here for hurting someone. Maybe worse.

I'd interviewed hundreds of criminals, some of them en route to a lethal injection at the hands of the commonwealth (one on his way to the chair, when I'd first started, even). But being in here without my credentials, without a deputy behind me . . . it was unsettling at best, and when I looked to the corner with the lone occupant, it cranked all the way to scary.

I focused elsewhere, lacing my fingers in and out around the bar behind my back and finding a crack in the cinderblock wall behind the smelly cot to keep my eyes on.

Lord knew I had plenty to occupy my brain.

Roughly a truckload more information than I'd started the day with rattled around my head. It was figuring out what was true and what wasn't and how to discern between the two that made it hard.

Cameron was freshest in my memory. He was passionate about his job, all right—frighteningly so in some ways. But I couldn't shake his words about Dr. Drake. They gnawed at the back of my mind no matter how I turned them. I'd talked to the man's distraught wife. I'd talked to the governor, for that matter. They'd both told me Lakshmi was dead. So why were they telling Charlie otherwise today? I figured the governor was intent on covering his ass, but if Cameron wasn't bluffing about Lakshmi's father, which I'd know in a few hours . . . well. I had missed something gargantuan.

Back to looking for elephants.

I rewound the past few days, analyzing every conversation, every revelation, looking for the links.

Kyle couldn't have lied to me. There were a whole lot of things I'd buy before I believed that. New puzzle pieces took shape, the crack in the wall fading into the background as I concentrated.

I spent my life looking for the truth. And no matter how I liked to spin it, it wasn't just my job. Joey was a hundred percent right: it was my identity. Somewhere, back when, journalism started out as something I wanted to do. A way to meet interesting people and write for a living.

But in the nearly ten years I'd been at the *Telegraph*, the profession had become my life, the newsroom home, the staff my family. I knew all that. I just didn't want to admit the first part when it was pissing Joey off, because I also didn't want it to be different.

It was a noble pursuit. Game-changing on the best days, simply difference-making on most others. I didn't just get to meet people, I got to help them.

The truth. An honorable thing to seek by any account.

But what if the thing I was hunting was my problem here?

The door at the end of the hallway buzzed. Clicked open.

Officer Doe Eyes appeared, skipped her gaze around the cell until she found me and nodded, putting a key in the door. "Jerri. Viv. Your friends pitched in bail money. Let's go."

A petite woman curled in the fetal position on the floor next to my left foot sat up, poking a lanky girl who couldn't have been old enough to buy a legal drink, which her padded push-up bra and slinky black dress did a poor job of disguising. The girl's eyes fluttered open.

"We're sprung," the older woman said. "Get up."

They followed the deputy out, leaving a space on the floor. I sank into it before anyone else could spread that way, wrapping my arms around my knees and falling back to my thoughts.

The truth can be a subjective thing.

From a hundred uncomfortable courtroom benches, I'd listened to DonnaJo go on about that for hours on end.

But I'd never really believed her.

What if, though?

What if Kyle was telling the truth, but so was Cameron? And so was Governor Baine?

How could that be?

Pinching the bridge of my nose to fight the headache this rabbit hole was spawning, I inhaled sharply.

Any single person's version of truth is shaped by how they see an event. The lens through which they see the whole world is shaped by their history and experiences.

Which is how two different people can see the same thing two completely different ways.

Most of the time this manifests in opinions, which are easy for me to dismiss.

But.

Backing all the way up to Friday morning, what did I have?

There was a body in the governor's office.

Kyle said Lakshmi was the victim.

The governor's son was missing.

Kyle said he shouldn't have told me and actually cried as he begged me to step out of this story. I had only ever seen Kyle cry once—at his grandfather's funeral.

What Kyle never did say after that was why.

And he never said anything else about Lakshmi.

Lakshmi, who someone was running an at least mildly sophisticated smear campaign against online.

Whose mother was morose and angry and seemingly close to shock—but had she actually said her child was dead? No. She'd been angry that the suits who came to her house were talking about finding Hamilton Baine. She said they acted like Lakshmi wasn't important.

The governor had been focused on his son, mentioning Lakshmi only as adjacent to Hamilton.

Kyle's disgusted, clipped tone from Friday morning bubbled through my memory.

The videos.

Advance spin control.

Oh.

My.

God.

I bolted up straight so fast I whacked my head on the iron bars behind me hard enough to see actual stars.

But for the first time, I wondered if I didn't also see what the hell was really happening here.

And just how royally I had screwed up.

26

"She's not dead."

I clapped a hand over my mouth, blinking back tears I couldn't attribute with any certainty to the head injury, what with the blinding realization that Wes Cameron was right, at least in the big picture: I got played.

My lens, shaped by a hundred other murder stories, showed me a warped version of the facts that sent me chasing after the wrong truth altogether.

Ohmygod ohmygod ohmygod.

The woman sprawled on the floor in front of me turned her head, her glassy eyes still too dilated to focus properly.

"Yes, she is. I heard it from three different people last night. Word travels fast."

I only half heard her at first, my brain stuck in a panicked loop because I was suddenly sure that everything I thought I knew about this story was 180 degrees wrong, and my entire world had just been flipped on its end.

The words filtered through eventually, though, and I looked down.

Torn fishnets, cheap spike stilettos, faux-leather pull-on skirt—topped with a satin blouse three seasons Donna Karan past and a diamond lavaliere.

I studied her face.

High cheekbones, caramel-colored hair. What slivers I could see of her pupils were bright green.

Slight lines around her eyes, just barely visible. No roots or gray in the hair.

"Who?" I asked.

"Who? Who?" She folded her arms clumsily over her bare midriff, cackling. "Are you an owl?" Her face went slack again. "My mom used to like that one. When she talked to me. So smart. She thought she was so frigging smart. Keeping it secret. Nobody on campus." She shook her finger, the words slurring and then fading.

"Did you say someone is dead?" I leaned closer.

"Dean Tricky," she said. "That's what we called her. Because we turned the tricks. But she ran the show." She laid the finger across her lips. "Don't tell," she whispered.

Jiminy Choos.

"What're you doing, talking to her?" The words were almost shrill, the voice high.

I looked up to find the spandex-clad girl, still splotched with vomit that sent waves of stench rolling off her, leaning over the side of the cot with her hand outstretched. "I told you not to tell anyone that!"

"Who's she going to tell?" Pupils waved a hand at me. "Look at her. She's not our kind of people."

My eyes shot between the two of them, both about the same age, which I would peg as younger than me, and then to the older one in the fake fur sitting against the other wall.

"Were you two students at RAU?" I asked Pupils, ignoring Vomity Spandex for the moment. "Are you talking about Angela Baker?"

Her head lolled up and down, her eyes drifting closed to reveal masterful smoky shadow and liquid liner.

I raised my eyes to Spandex. "Is Angela dead?"

She rolled to face the wall.

Shit.

I swallowed hard, the stench in the air fading as my own stomach turned itself inside out.

She'd told me she was afraid. And I was at least close to the last person on the registered list of folks she'd talked to.

Bonus: thanks to possibly the dumbest thing I had ever done, I was a sitting. Damn. Duck.

I had to get out of here. Had to get to Bob. Had to apologize to the governor.

And I had no way to do any of it.

I steepled my fingers under my chin. "What have I done?"

I didn't need anyone else to answer that. I got cocky. I trusted the wrong source, all right, but it turned out the wrong source was me.

Kyle said "victim," and I assumed murder. That one bitty little snap choice changed my lens, colored the way I'd heard every word people had said since, the way I followed every lead, and the worst decision I'd ever made.

I had to make this right.

The buzzer sounded again, the door at the end of the hallway clicking open.

"Clarke?"

I didn't look up until I heard my name. Deputy Doe Eyes had company.

A large gentleman in a boxy gray suit with an ugly brown tie I'd seen twice already on similarly built men this weekend.

I shot to my feet.

She unlocked the door. "You're free to go." She nodded to the suit.

My fingers closed around the bar behind me, my eyes looking for something I couldn't find with his sunglasses still in place.

I pulled in a deep breath. Regretted it when my stomach recoiled from the holding-cell stench.

He scooched the shades down the bridge of his nose. "You coming or staying?" His voice was deep, his eyes flat and unreadable.

I shuffled forward.

Stepping out, I looked back at the girls in the cell, then up at the muscles in the suit, who had settled his shades back in place. We were in the basement.

Frying pan, or fire?

I chose the fire.

Given my gut's record of late, I wasn't sure it was safer, but at least it smelled better.

Suit didn't speak again until we were outside.

"Over here." He turned for a black Ford sedan. Didn't wait to see if I was following. Stopping at the passenger door, he opened it and nodded to me.

I paused a few steps back, studying the mountain of barrel-chested man in front of me. He could probably crush my skull like a walnut without straining a tricep. And I didn't miss the slight gun bulge beneath the jacket under his left arm, either.

I tipped my head to one side.

"Why did you come get me? And why is Cameron letting me go?"

"Probably because I didn't ask him," he said, his face keeping its stony blank expression. "You are a difficult woman to get in touch with."

Difficult . . . I blinked. The weird repetitive calls?

"Agent Chaudry?"

He nodded. Just the once.

"You know your phone shows up with an Ohio area code? And voice-mail is a thing for a reason."

The words drifted out on autopilot, my brain trying to change this gear and figure out what the hell the Secret Service had to do with any of this.

"I wanted to schedule a meeting with you in person. You've made that difficult."

I slid into the car, shaking my head. "If this is about my background check, I'm afraid you've wasted a trip, but I'm thankful for the Get Out of Jail Free card."

Same blank expression as he shut my door and rounded the front of the car. Was he training for the guard at Buckingham Palace or something?

He slid behind the wheel and pressed the button to start the engine. "Your background check is done and filed. I wouldn't be here about a back-ground check." He flipped the turn signal up and took a right at the corner. "But since you brought it up, I gotta say: you have made your share of enemies in the past few years, but your background is about as clean as it gets. You could practically have your own superhero slogan. Truth, justice, and exclusive news." He glanced at my floorboard. "Or something about the shoes, maybe? You spend a lot of money on shoes for someone who earns what you do. NewsGirl: Truth, justice, and good shoes." He sort of smiled at his own joke. It looked like he was in pain.

Not anymore. I didn't say that out loud.

"There's been a lot going on here, Agent. I'm running on very little sleep and even less caffeine. You're going to have to just tell me why you want to talk to me."

He stopped at a light.

"What do you know about Lakshmi Drake, Miss Clarke?"

Sweet cartwheeling Jesus.

"Honestly? Right now I have not the first clue."

"Now who's not being straight with who? You splashed her name and photo all over the front page this morning."

I nodded, blowing a long breath out through flappy lips.

"I'm not so sure I was right about that."

I ventured a sideways glance up when he didn't answer after a few beats. He put his foot back on the gas when the light changed, and nodded.

"You are a smart woman. I knew that from reading your file."

"What, do y'all pull SAT scores for background checks?"

I tried to keep my voice even, but it sounded too high anyway. This was the freaking United States Secret Service. He probably knew what kind of ice cream I liked best and why I'd named the dog Darcy. Which meant he also knew about my history with Kyle.

Whatever else was going to come crashing down around this, I didn't want Kyle's career destroyed because of me.

He chuckled, his eyes staying on the road. "Fourteen-eighty. Impressive. But I was talking about your FBI file."

"My . . . my what?" I stumbled over the words.

"You don't piss off powerful people without becoming more than a blip on the government's radar," he said, his voice still stoic and smooth. "Don't worry. There's nothing troubling. Well. I guess it depends on your point of view. But from yours and from mine, you're good."

And he seemed to still think that, having mentioned my story from this morning.

I looked out my window, the art deco buildings lining Broad Street blurring together as the car sped up when the light turned yellow.

"Where are we going?" I asked before I snapped my fingers. "Damn. My bag is still at the capitol building."

He answered my question with a question. "Lakshmi?"

If Lakshmi was alive, but the governor couldn't put her on TV to refute my story, Baine didn't know where she was. Which spawned a whole herd of new questions, led by: Who did? And what did Hamilton's disappearance have to do with it? My money was still on Ted Grayson, but I wasn't betting the house anymore.

"I'm pretty sure she's not dead, if that's what you're asking me. I know I screwed up. I'd like to try to make it right, but I'm going to need my purse and my phone and my laptop." And a bit of luck, too, not that he needed to know that. I managed to sound confident. Controlled. Not a trace of the panicked regret churning my guts into mush came through in the words.

Small victories.

He stopped at another light, putting on his turn signal.

My brow furrowed. "Are you . . . ?" I didn't finish the question, watching as he wound through the Fan, shaking my head when he turned onto my street.

Seriously. What the actual hell was going on?

He pulled into my driveway behind two cars I knew and one I didn't, shutting off the engine and turning to face me in the seat. "Shall we?"

Fear didn't override my desire for answers.

I strode to the door ahead of the agent, turned the knob, and shoved so hard it rattled on the hinges when it bounced off the baker's rack.

Kyle and Joey looked up from their coffee, and a jeans-and-Nike-T-shirt-clad Chris Landers unburied his head from my fridge.

I stopped short.

Chaudry did not. His chest hit right between my shoulders, sending me stumbling forward. Joey shot out of his chair and put a steadying hand out that I swatted away as I caught my balance, a fiery rage settling in my chest before it erupted out of my face.

"I haven't slept. I haven't eaten. I was very nearly puked on, I spent the better part of the afternoon in a cell, and I'm pretty sure I've managed to trash my career. One of you better start spilling some guts. Now."

27

"Calm down." Landers put a carton of milk on the counter and closed the fridge before pulling a box of Oreos out of the cabinet overhead.

"Go on and help yourself, Detective." The words dripped so much sarcasm they oozed through my teeth. "I don't mind at all."

He rolled his eyes. "I thought you might be hungry, and Miller said you like sweets when you're upset." He reached into the dishwasher and pulled out a small plate, dropping a half-dozen cookies in the center and pouring a glass of milk.

Kyle scrambled out of his chair, picking up his mug.

"Sit. Eat."

I turned a puzzled squint on each of them as I scrubbed the jail off my hands like I was about to operate on somebody. Taking the chair as Landers put the milk and cookies in front of me, I picked up one sugary disc and dipped it, cutting my eyes to Joey.

Of everything that had happened today, walking into a room full of cops he was sitting and chatting with was the weirdest by a middle-of-nowhere backcountry mile.

Not that I could ask him about that without making it even weirder.

He reached across the table for my hand and closed his fingers over mine.

I focused on Kyle, standing next to my chair with his arms folded over his chest, his brow furrowed, and his clear blue eyes brim-full of concern.

"Are you okay?" he asked.

I chewed and swallowed the cookie. "I know Lakshmi's not dead. I'm betting you have her stashed somewhere. And that's making me wonder if you don't also know where the governor's son is." My eyes skipped from him to Landers. "What in the ever-loving hell is happening here, gentlemen? And who left the building in that body bag yesterday? I owe the governor one massive boldface front-page apology, and I want to make sure I have every fact straight before I start writing it."

"We don't have anybody stashed anywhere." Landers looked between Kyle and Chaudry. "Right?"

"We do not." Kyle didn't look at Landers, raising an eyebrow at Chaudry. Got a nod.

Threw up his hands. "Hell, I'm not even sure where to start."

"How about with the part where you lied to me? The first time."

He shook his head hard enough to make his gelled hair move. "I did not. I specifically removed myself from the situation so I wouldn't lie to you. I begged you to bow out." He laid one hand on my shoulder. "It would've been easier to lie to you, but I can't do it. I've never been able to tell you anything but the truth. It's like your superpower." His lips tipped up in a smile I couldn't stop myself from returning. But he wasn't off the hook.

"Even if you didn't realize I thought you meant Lakshmi was the murder victim when you did your little Deep Throat schtick on Friday morning." I stopped, glancing between Landers and Chaudry. Shit. I'd spent the whole weekend and hours in a gross cell to keep from spilling that, and my temper got the best of me. This was really not my finest collection of hours.

Kyle waved a hand. "We're all on the same page."

I looked at Chaudry. "What do you have to do with this, anyway?" Back at Kyle. "Do you know who he is?"

Kyle patted my shoulder. "Brad was on my team until about three months ago. It's fine, I promise."

My head whipped back. "You were ATF?"

"Secret Service agents don't just spawn ready to take a bullet for world leaders, Miss Clarke. I was a trooper before I went to the ATF, like Kyle here was Dallas PD. Most of us work in law enforcement for years before we land these jobs." He put his shades on the counter and grinned at Kyle. His face was handsome in a John Cena sort of way when he smiled. "I still had my suit and everything, chief."

I blinked. "The suits are ATF?" Damn, was there anything I'd been right about here?

Back to Kyle. "It's not like I had to reach, Kyle. Dead body plus talk of a victim usually equals an ID."

He nodded. "But I did not lie. I let you think the wrong thing."

My hands curled into tight fists. I swallowed a scream. "But why?" It was still many decibels too loud. Joey ran a thumb over the backs of my knuckles.

"Because I know you. I knew if you thought she had been murdered, especially for political reasons, you'd start digging. And sometimes you come up with stuff we don't." He waved agreement out of Landers before he sighed and ran a hand through his hair. "You said it yourself, yesterday. There was a reason she was on his desk. I'm pretty sure she was supposed to die, but not a hundred percent on why. And we're running out of time."

Joey's thumb moved faster as I nearly came up out of my chair.

"Kyle David Miller, if you make me ask one more time . . ."

"Damn. Middle name and everything," Landers muttered. "You're in trouble, man."

Kyle squatted, resting his elbows on his thighs and lacing his fingers together between his knees.

"The president is coming here tomorrow. Brad and I have been working a weapons case for over a year, and we got a break last week that came with a credible threat to her."

I slumped back down into the chair.

No. No way.

Joey's pleading eyes and uncharacteristic freak-out when I said I was covering the speech. I glanced at him. He wouldn't look at me.

I turned to Chaudry.

"Credible." My voice sounded far away. "Threat."

Holy fucking Manolos.

Chaudry nodded. "Someone is going to try to assassinate the president of the United States tomorrow night, Miss Clarke. And we're hoping you know something you don't even know will help us stop it."

* * *

There are moments in a reporter's life when nothing seems real. For most people, they come when they're interviewing a childhood hero, or a Sahara-in-the-summer-hot movie star.

I was having one in my kitchen.

With cookies.

"I—" That was it. All I could manage.

Darcy pawed at my foot. Kyle laid a hand on my knee.

Everyone's breathing was downright deafening.

I shook my head. "No. This isn't happening."

Joey's fingers tightened on mine.

Kyle patted my knee. "It really is, Nicey. Now look, I'm sorry about all the shit you've been dragged through, but it's serious all-hands-on-deck time here."

I looked up at Chaudry. "Don't let her come. Why is that hard?"

He shook his head. "In the first place, I work for her, not the other way around. We can advise about threats, but we don't have the authority to cancel an appearance. Haven't you ever read a book on JFK?"

"About a thousand of them." And he was right. The Secret Service tried to talk Kennedy out of going to Dallas. He wouldn't even put a bubble over the damned car. "But I'm sure she has, too. Why would she still want to come here?"

"Because she's a stubborn lady who sees the best in people."

"You wouldn't know anything about that," Kyle said.

"I don't intentionally . . ." The rest of the words stuck in my throat when Kyle and Landers and Joey all coughed over laughs.

"Fine. I get her. So, move the speech?"

"Not possible. The venue has to be secured and checked, the staff vetted. There's no time to get another place checked out. She cut it close this time as it was."

I closed my eyes. Cleansing breath. Calm thoughts. What did I know that they might not?

Angela.

I opened my eyes and met Kyle's. "Angela Baker didn't answer my emails this weekend because she's dead, according to the jailhouse grapevine. The only person I know who had an interest in shutting Angela and Lakshmi both up is Ted Grayson. Who, as a bonus, has a former employee working for Thomas Baine, and a burning hatred for our governor. It seems he got out of prison a few weeks ago and has kept quite a low profile."

Chaudry waved a hand. "He was released on good behavior to a suite at the Jefferson—sort of a posh version of a halfway house. I checked his every biorhythm on that bracelet readout. Grayson's a black-hearted, selfish bastard, but he hasn't so much as breathed in the direction of the street in front of the hotel."

That's why I couldn't find him. Hotel guest registries aren't public record.

"Phone calls?"

He shook his head. "Clean. Some of the rest of us are decent detectives, too, Miss Clarke."

"I wasn't suggesting otherwise."

Dammit. All roads led to brick walls. Except, of course, the one Kyle apparently thought was about to lead to a dead president.

I got up and went to the living room in search of a notebook. "I really wish I had my stuff," I said over my shoulder.

Landers disappeared as I walked back into the kitchen. He returned with my purse, laptop bag, and the sketch pad I'd been making charts on in the wee hours of . . . damn, was that just today?

I took it. "Um. Thanks."

I resumed my seat, focusing again on Kyle. "This whole damned thing started with you telling me Lakshmi was the victim. She was. But it was a sexual assault, not murder, wasn't it?"

I thought I had it pretty well figured out, finally: those horrifying videos were spin control, a whole new high-definition level of "What was she wearing?"

Except if Lakshmi wasn't dead, there was a twist in this particular story. I kept my eyes on Kyle. "That means your actual murder vic was her attacker. So who did she kill? And where did you put her?"

"She didn't kill anyone." Kyle nodded as he spoke. And the last piece of this puzzle corner clicked into place.

"Hamilton." I felt my eyes widen. "He walked in on someone attacking her, and he killed them."

"No." That wasn't Kyle.

Every part of me, from my hair to my toenails, went cold and numb.

No.

Oh God, please, no.

I turned my head.

Joey didn't look at me, talking to his hands, one folded over its bandaged mate on the tabletop.

"I did."

28

No.

Just . . . no.

I couldn't think anything else, couldn't see, damned sure couldn't speak.

My boyfriend was sitting in my kitchen confessing to murdering . . . somebody pretty fucking important, judging by the lengths that had been stretched to keep it quiet.

And not even just confessing to me.

Confessing to a cop and two federal agents.

I closed two fingers and a thumb around the skin of my forearm and squeezed with everything I had. Watched a blood bruise rise and redden under my skin.

It wasn't a nightmare.

Except it had to be. This could not really be happening. Not in the actual world.

I scanned the room. Chaudry remained leaning against the counter, examining his neatly clipped fingernails. Kyle had shifted to a one-knee crouch next to me, his hand on my arm, head bending to catch my eye.

Landers was chewing an Oreo.

Not a damn one of them looked concerned about what they'd just heard.

Because they already knew.

My ass sprang out of the chair with enough force to knock Kyle back onto his.

"National emergency. Personal crisis. Anything else you guys want to dump on me? Just go ahead and say it while I'm still in shock from the other two."

"Princess." Joey half rose from his chair before I put one hand up.

"Don't you 'princess' me." I shook my head. "How did you even get in the middle of this? And why the hell didn't you tell me? You." I took a step back. "You were so believable, when I told you Lakshmi was dead. You told me that whole story, and I bought it."

I could feel my stomach again, just in time for it to twist and send a jolt of nausea through me. "What else are you lying about?"

Kyle stood, brushing the seat of his light pants off, and stepped forward. "I think everyone needs to cool off and refocus."

Joey shook his head. "I don't lie to you. I don't tell you things I think you wouldn't want or don't need to know, but I don't lie. I told you I hurt my hand punching a guy with a foul mouth. And I didn't know if she was dead or not after I left the building."

I whirled on Kyle. "How long have you known about this?" Landers. "Or you?"

Landers raised both hands. "I just found out this morning. I thought I was looking for Baine's kid, until Miller here called and asked me to coffee."

Chaudry cleared his throat. "No offense, but the big picture here is the thing that's the most important. The governor can wait for his apology. Everyone and everything is on the back burner as of right now. Miss Clarke, your, uh, friend here is in a difficult situation. Someone with his background involved in a situation like this one would usually already be on deck for a long stay at Cold Springs. He was protecting Miss Drake, which her statement on the scene and the surveillance video corroborate. Except. His history and her history combine to create a possible political tsunami. A"—his eyes slid to Joey—"career criminal, let's say, murdering a United States congressman in defense of a former paid sex professional." He raised his thin eyebrows. "The optics are abominable."

I didn't need him to tell me that. But since nobody had Joey in handcuffs, I figured it best to keep a lid on my temper.

"A congressman?"

My mental political rolodex flipped. Virginia had seven men in its congressional delegation. Three of them were of an age that would probably require pharmaceutical assistance for any sort of sexual activity, and might well put them at risk for a stroke.

Chaudry shook his head. "That's not important right now, either. The president, her safety, is what I need all your focus on. Help us with this." He spread his hands. "And other things can be made to disappear." He nodded to Joey. A dangled carrot cloaked in a coded *Stop asking or else.*

Fine.

I turned to Kyle, who nodded agreement. "We've kept it quiet this long."

"Someone is going to start missing a sitting congressman, Kyle."

"It's being handled." That was Chaudry again. "Now please. What have you found out about Miss Drake? Her research, her connections, her family? Anything could be helpful, so I need you to really focus."

"What the hell does Lakshmi have to do with the president being shot? I thought you said weapons? Why aren't you checking recent rifle purchases?" I asked.

"Because whoever is after President Denham isn't coming armed with a rifle. We know how to stop a gun," Chaudry said, his voice strained.

Kyle stepped forward, his hands out. "Nicey, we're looking for some sort of experimental weapon, and we think someone was using Lakshmi to get access to her dad's research and what Joey walked in on was a plan to get her out of the way. What we don't know is who. Or how."

Ted Grayson, that's who. I eyed Chaudry, who had dismissed that suggestion once already, as I reached for my laptop and my sketch pad. My gaze flicked to Joey, smaller and quieter than I'd ever seen him. He hadn't been himself all weekend, and I'd blown it off as him not knowing how to deal when I was buried in a big story, one more for my list of reasons why living together was a lousy idea. Wrong again.

I couldn't let that tug at my heart right now, though.

Saving him meant saving everything else, too. I glanced around the room. These guys were smart. And they were most of the way there. They were taking one hell of a chance, bringing a reporter into the middle of a case like this one, but they were in a corner, and they had Joey to hold over my head.

I swept an arm over my counter, knocking the dish drainer and the flour canister into the sink and spreading my charts out as I clicked my screen to life.

I needed to get these guys to Grayson on their own, not because I said so. I could start by answering Chaudry's question.

"Lakshmi Drake likes to talk about being the next Nate Silver. And leaving her program at RAU didn't mean she gave up on that." I pulled up the images of her recent studies. "She was researching the impact social media can have on influencing people's political preferences, and then she started working for Baine's campaign."

"And dating his kid," Kyle said, stepping up to peer over my shoulder.

"No, the governor said Hamilton took her to dinner during the campaign. She knew him first. So her connections with the campaign and the family got her into the office, I assume."

"But why she was in there without her boyfriend or her boss, we still don't know?" Chaudry tapped a thick fingertip on the countertop.

I shook my head.

"Maybe he just found her in there," Landers said. "If she was waiting for someone else. The video footage shows her hopping up on the desk and hiking up her skirt."

I tapped my space bar. Why would she do that?

"Y'all are sure she wasn't waiting for Hamilton? Was he in the building at the time?"

Landers shook his head. "The last place his Visa card was used was at a bar across town that he couldn't have gotten back from."

And I knew from what they'd already told me that Grayson hadn't left his hotel room. Maybe she really was sleeping with Baine. Or something. But if it was a weapon of some sort they needed, Lakshmi wasn't the trail we should follow. I didn't think.

"Kyle, you said 'experimental weapon.' Can you elaborate? Like a fancy plastic rifle that will get past security?" I asked.

Or. No.

The letters on the screen blurred in front of my eyes. "Dr. Drake's research, that Grayson went to prison to try to get close to." I leaned on the counter. "What if Lakshmi's father wasn't researching nuclear alternatives to coal at all, but some sort of nuclear weapon?"

Kyle offered a slow nod. "He used to work for the DOE. Had a security clearance that's above my pay grade—I couldn't find much on his work. But his political donation and primary voting records tell me he's not plotting to kill President Denham, so I dropped it. If Baine were the target, it might be a different story."

"I think someone might be trying to set Baine up," I said. "Not sure what Drake's motivation would be for that, but it's the lead I've been chasing all day."

"Having a direction to point the finger when the president dies is pretty damned powerful motivation." Chaudry's lips disappeared into a thin line. "Let's say your science guy is in this, and he hates Baine because Baine really is screwing his daughter. Can't hurt to ask the man a few questions, right?"

Kyle shrugged, jerking his head at Landers. "They live over in Church Hill, by the park."

Landers started for the door. "I'll call you when I've got him."

I bit my lip, staring first at Chaudry, then Kyle. Neither looked inclined to dismiss the possibility that we were looking for a rogue nuclear fucking weapon.

That was crazy. It was the plot of a dozen movies where Liam Neeson or George Clooney spends two hours getting shot at while he tries to save the East Coast from a nuclear explosion/winter. High testosterone, low suspension of disbelief.

I put one hand on Kyle's arm. "We're not seriously talking about this?"

He smiled and patted my shoulder. "Just running down a lead. Nothing more until we know it's more. We need to work fast, but we can't ignore anything. That's all."

Nothing about any of this had been straightforward. But I flashed a tight, toothless smile and nodded anyway. Flipping to another page in my notes, I glanced at the clock. The president's speech would start in twenty-three hours.

Tick.

Tock.

* * *

At nineteen hours and counting, Landers was trying to hunt up Dr. Drake's lab because the house was dark and quiet, and the rest of us knew way more than we ever wanted to know about everything and everyone connected to Thomas Baine or Lakshmi Drake.

We'd searched from atomic physics to zoning records, and the issue wasn't too little information—it was too damned much.

I shook my head at my screen. We'd wrestled a spreadsheet for the past hour, trying to sort data that was too tangled to be sorted. It blurred into a useless blob of letters and numbers. "This is a level of crazy I don't think I've seen before, and I thought I'd seen them all."

I opened the photos of the mystery file from Stacy Adams's office for the third time, wishing I'd had time to try to get the pages more in focus.

"He swore this didn't have weapons capabilities." I wasn't talking to anyone in particular.

"I'm telling you, it doesn't," Kyle said for the third time in as many hours. "At least, not ones anybody would be stupid enough to try to use if they had access to the equipment it takes to produce them. I did a bit of reading on Adams and his thorium salt reactors last night: he's not totally wrong, but it's not the superfuel he makes it out to be, either. The irradiation process produces tiny bits of a highly toxic, gamma-ray-emitting compound called uranium-232. No sane person would subject themselves to the toxicity in order to try to make a bomb, and the stuff has to be handled carefully within a reactor to keep everyone safe." His tone had an edge that I knew meant he was frustrated with the situation, not with me.

"But you can't use that stuff to make a bomb?" I asked.

He shook his head. "If we're looking for a nuclear weapon, it's an experimental take on plutonium, which you still cannot buy at the corner store, no matter what Steven Spielberg said in 1985. But tracing it is proving to be problematic." He gestured to his laptop. "It seems those records are kept only on triplicate paper forms."

So we needed another road to our possible mad bomber. For someone to despise a public figure enough to risk handling radioactive material, and be okay with killing a whole lot of other folks as collateral—that was pure. Focused.

I pushed the computer away.

I'd spent the whole weekend looking at everything about this fiasco entirely wrong.

Was my lens right this time?

"That kind of hatred should be easy to spot," I said, mostly to myself.

"Huh?" Chaudry asked.

"What we know that we know: Lakshmi Drake was attacked in the governor's office late Thursday night. But the assault was interrupted, and the perpetrator was . . ." My words stumbled to a stop. I glanced over my shoulder. Slumped over in the chair, Joey didn't look up. My heart twisted itself right around in my chest, my legs aching to move to the side of his chair and cradle his head and let him talk until he didn't have any more to say.

Later. When we weren't in a room full of cops and there wasn't an impending nuclear disaster. And if we didn't manage to skirt it, it wouldn't really matter.

I cleared my throat. "And Hamilton Baine is still missing."

"What about your neighbor?" Chaudry asked. "Do you think she's telling the truth, about the Baine kid? I mean, that's a hell of a secret for people to keep for this many years in that sort of a spotlight."

I shrugged. "Who could make that up? She's seemed lonely since her husband died, and I feel sorry for her. But she showed me texts from the kid." I pushed the computer toward him. "Can't you get to his vital records? She told me the governor's name is on the birth certificate, but it might be worth checking. Maybe someone found out about Hamilton and is trying to get something from Baine."

I couldn't fathom a coincidence this massive, but Kyle said every lead. So better to check this box off.

Chaudry shrugged. "Anyone got a DOB?"

Kyle scrolled through his iPhone screen. "August fourteenth, '97."

Chaudry pulled my laptop across the counter and started pecking at the keys.

Scrolled.

Frowned at the screen. Pecked some more.

"What?" Kyle and I asked in unison.

Chaudry ran one hand over his clean-shaven head. "His medical records. The file is big. But it's locked down so tight even I can't get in."

"That's not typical of politicians and their families?" I asked.

He shook his head. "Let's assume the old lady is telling us the truth. What did her husband die from?"

"No idea. He was in his seventies."

Kyle pulled out his phone. "Let me see if I can pull some strings from this side. If Hamilton has some sort of serious medical condition, our sand just started running through this hourglass faster. But knowing what we're dealing with could help."

Damn. Was that why the governor was so freaked? Because his son was sick?

I owed the Baine family. I couldn't keep sitting here rehashing facts with Kyle and his friend if I might be more helpful somewhere else.

I moved to the door, slipping my feet back into my shoes before I grabbed Darcy's leash.

"Uh, baby?" Joey spoke for the first time in hours, looking up at me with a furrowed brow. "I can take her out."

Kyle put his phone down and opened his mouth to protest that, snapping it shut when I glared at him.

I shook my head at Joey. "Thanks, but Darcy's my ticket in. I'm going to go ask Mrs. Powers about Hamilton's medical history."

29

Mrs. Powers had plenty of dog cookies, plenty of questions, and no idea why Hamilton had a fat medical file, but loads of worry over it after I told her.

Which meant the governor and his family had another big secret—one they didn't even trust this woman Hamilton treated like family to know.

Joey's comments about my cops keeping the kid's name out of the police reports mingled with Governor Baine's hoarse assertion that Hamilton liked to keep to himself, and the governor had to pick his battles.

What if Hamilton wasn't physically ill, but mentally? Depression would explain a fat, ultra-secured medical file. But it was obvious Mrs. Powers didn't know. And I couldn't tell her—at all, by personal preference, but certainly not without more proof than a file, an interview, and a hunch.

So Darcy munched her fourth peanut butter snap as I sipped coffee and smiled. "I'm sure he's going to be just fine, ma'am. I didn't mean to upset you."

She shook her head. "I just don't understand. He was so agitated when he was here yesterday. Not like himself at all. Kept talking about some girl named Stacy ruining his life—'blowing everything up,' the young people call it. I've never seen him so mad when he wasn't talking about his mother

—and then he asked me how much cash I had in the house and he just left."

I sat up straight in the chair so fast it rocked forward. Darcy popped her head up, eyeing me for three blinks before she returned her attention to her cookie.

Mrs. Powers leaned forward. "Are you all right, Nichelle?"

Deep breath. Slow smile. Nothing wrong here.

Hamilton wasn't a missing person. Not if he was here yesterday crying about his breakup and looking for cash. So where the hell had he been? And why did the governor think he was in trouble?

His work. The governor said he buried himself in his work.

And Hamilton said Stacy was "blowing everything up." What if his word choice wasn't hyperbole?

Shit. I liked Stacy. And why not? His save-the-world counterpoint to Grayson's greedy, suspicious former assistant was guaranteed to build rapport.

Maybe that was the whole point of Wyatt Bledsoe being there in the first damned place.

That black folder flashed in my head like it was swathed in pink neon.

Had Hamilton Baine been suckered into an assassination plot without realizing it until it was too late? Stacy Adams knew Hamilton better than anyone, and he'd spent the whole weekend trying to find out where Hamilton was from everyone he could think to ask—including me. If Stacy was good enough at bluffing to fly under my bullshit radar, he could have played on Hamilton's mental health issues or even tinkered with his medications to make him think he was imagining things, even get his help without him realizing it. And killing Lakshmi and sticking Hamilton with the blame was pretty good revenge for a jilted lover, too.

"Mrs. P, did Hamilton say anything else about why he was upset, or anything about where he'd been?" My voice was too high, but it was the best I could do. She didn't seem to notice.

She shook her head. Paused mid-shake. Raised one finger. "He did say something about all his hard work being a lie."

Bingo.

"I don't understand," she went on, shaking her head. "I read your article this morning, and I know he was seeing that woman. If his girlfriend was murdered, why didn't he say something about her? And why on earth did Tom go on TV and say you were lying in the newspaper? I was offended by that. You wouldn't do such a thing."

I didn't have time to climb onto that horse. "I'm afraid nothing about this story has been normal, even for me," I said. "And that's saying something." I stood, reaching for Darcy's leash. "Thank you for talking with me, especially so late."

She rose to walk me out. "You'll figure all this out, won't you, honey? Ham will be okay?"

Lord, I hoped so. If he was trying to stop Stacy Adams from blowing up half the city or selling a weapon that would, I really hoped so was the best I could do.

I nodded as she opened the door. "Goodnight, ma'am."

I clicked my photos open before I got to the foot of the steps, pulling up the file folder I'd found in Adams's office.

Kyle said uranium-232 wasn't weaponizable.

But that black folder label didn't say 232. It said 233.

I hadn't even noticed it earlier.

Kyle said we didn't have time to chase the production goose. What we needed to know wasn't how the weapons were made, but who to track down to stop one from getting near the president. He and Chaudry could work backward from there, after disaster had been averted.

He'd studied this thorium thing for days now and I was jumping in for a crash course, but the little nagging voice in the back of my brain kept getting louder. Stacy Adams was hiding something.

I opened my browser and typed *uranium-233.*

Google, don't fail me now. My fingers trembled as I hit "Enter."

Google never disappoints. I clicked the top result.

Read ten words.

And dropped my phone.

* * *

I was out of breath by the time I got home, rushing up the mostly empty driveway into the kitchen and kicking off my shoes before I'd made it past the table.

Where the hell did they all go?

"Anyone home?" I called, charging toward my bedroom.

Joey appeared in the doorway. "Miller said to tell you to wait here for him to call. Their phones went crazy and they took off."

He wouldn't look at me.

I unclipped Darcy's leash, dropping it on the dresser before I put one finger under Joey's chin and turned his eyes to mine. "I'm not mad at you. But I'd like to hear what happened. From you."

I don't think I've ever meant a handful of simple words more. And I wanted to know how Kyle knew about this and didn't have Joey in some basement cell somewhere, but for the moment I was content to be thankful for that, especially in the face of impending national disaster.

He shook his head, his lips shrinking into a thin line as he leaned one shoulder against the doorjamb. "It's going to sound so stupid, but I don't really know. It's kind of a blur. I remember the meeting. It was late, after midnight by the time we were done, because . . . well. Because I don't go to the capitol for meetings during the day."

He'd told me he had a business thing Thursday night. I nodded.

"I was on my way out, and I stopped in the restroom, and then I got turned around coming out, all the long hallways in that place, and then I heard a scream. Not even a scream. More like . . ." He raised a hand to his temple, his eyes falling shut. "More like a high-pitched whimper, and it just cut off so suddenly. I doubled back and when I opened the door, I got an eyeful of some guy's bare ass and started to shut it again. Didn't want to interrupt. You know?"

I nodded again. I would've thought the same.

I put a hand on his arm. "It's really okay."

His Adam's apple bobbed with a hard swallow. "No. I don't think it will be. But it is done, and there's nothing I can do about that. Hell. I don't know that I'd do it differently if I could go back and see it more clearly. I just remember seeing her leg kick in the air before I got the door shut, and she whimpered again, and the guy said—" He paused. Waved his bandaged hand. "Not important. He sort of snarled something I won't repeat to you at her and pulled his fist back and punched her. I heard his knuckles connect with her face, a sort of muffled cracking sound followed by another yelp. I didn't even know it was Lakshmi until . . . until after. I ran—the room is pretty big—and I grabbed his shoulder and spun him around." He shook his head. "This guy's face was twisted up into something that didn't even look human. Ugly, deep red, even before I hit him. And then I hit him, just four times." He held up his bandaged hand. "But something went wrong."

Jesus. What he had done here—certainly, it was wrong. But looking at his face, pale and pained, I didn't think he meant to kill the guy.

"I didn't mean to," he said, like he could read my mind. "I just wanted to stop him. Put him on the floor for long enough to help the woman on the desk. But I caught his nose wrong with my ring, Miller's coroner friend said." His eyes went wide, his hands closing around both of mine as best he could with the bandages. "I've done some things I'm not proud of, Nichelle, but this . . . I didn't mean to. And they moved me out of the room so fast I didn't know what happened to Lakshmi after that. So yesterday when you said she was dead, I thought I'd done it for nothing. And I wanted to tell you, to help you, but Miller told me to keep my mouth shut. Watching you try to figure this out and knowing what I knew has been a special kind of hell the past few days, but I was too selfish to risk losing you."

I shook off his hands and looped my arms around his neck, pulling him close.

"I trust you," I said, burying my face in the starched cotton shirt covering his chest. "You're not going to lose me. And we will figure this mess out later. I swear." I managed to avoid choking on the words. One panic attack at a time. I had spent considerable time and energy in the past two years trying to make sure Kyle and Joey's worlds didn't intersect any more than necessary. And once the immediate crisis was contained—I hoped—Kyle would be right in the middle of a manslaughter investigation, at the very best. Jesus, if they'd taken prints, who knew what he'd found already?

Nope. I couldn't.

Not now.

"But right now, I gotta go." I planted a kiss on the tip of his nose and turned back to the mess at hand, my brain thirty steps ahead of my feet.

I grabbed my gym bag off the chair in the corner and pulled out my sneakers, then looked around for socks as I wriggled out of my sweater. Two layers of form-fitting tanks and a hoodie later, I was lacing up my Nikes when the bed dipped under Joey's weight. "You're going to the gym? Now?" His brow furrowed when I turned my head to look at him.

I only wore those shoes to the gym. Ever. It was a fair assumption.

And for a split second I considered letting him continue to assume it. I didn't have time to explain, and he would just freak out and try to make me stay out of it, anyway.

"Where did Kyle go again?" I answered Joey's question with one of my own.

I'd sprinted home intending to rally Kyle and Chaudry for a nuke-finding expedition. Stacy Adams said the reactor he wanted to build would power the whole city, and that the donated land was twenty miles from any home or school. When I'd seen that in my notes halfway through hour two of our brainstorming session, I'd checked the requisite distances. Zoning records told me there was almost exactly four square miles of land close enough to town that fit the distance requirements Adams mentioned. Tax records revealed that a large plot of it was owned by SAE Limited. Chaudry and Kyle had dismissed it, because his reactor was a theory, not an actual device. My entire life—and maybe a lot of other people's—currently rode on my guess that Stacy was boring enough to name his shell company with his own initials, hadn't waited to build his reactor, and had somewhere in that black folder that a tweak in his process would produce uranium-233. A tiny bit of that stuff makes a big blast, Google said.

Federal agents or no, I was going out there for a look.

Joey shrugged. "He doesn't exactly keep me in the loop on what he's doing. They left together. If someone's really trying to kill the president here in town, I assume every cop in a hundred miles is up to their neck in that until tomorrow night."

Probably not, actually. Federal agents aren't exactly known for their loose lips. Now that he mentioned it, Kyle and Chaudry talking so freely in

front of Landers was downright weird. It just hadn't stuck out in the parade
of unbelievable that had been my day.

And it wasn't important enough to worry with now, either.

I stood. "If he comes back, tell him I went . . ." I clicked zoning photos
up on my phone and flipped the screen around. "Here."

Joey leaned closer, squinting at the screen.

"Tell Miller you went to a vacant field in the middle of the night in your
running clothes. Why do I need to do this?" His gaze shifted to my face.
"What is that? Where is that?"

I turned for the door. "I'm going to drop a location pin on the map when
I get there and I'll send you the coordinates," I said. "I am betting it is not
an empty field. Anymore, anyway. But the only way to find out is to go look,
and I'm the only one free, so I'm going to go look."

"By yourself? Like hell you are." He stood, jaw set and eyes hard. "You
know what I did and you're still here. Damned if I'm letting you out of my
sight again before this is over."

He had a point. He also had a gun, somewhere. Which really would
make me feel safer, especially since he knew how to handle it. But I didn't
want to drag him into something that might be dangerous, either.

The look on his face told me there was no dragging about this.

I nodded. "I can fill you in on the way out there. Bring your handgun?" I
flashed a smile I hoped was reassuring. "Just in case."

I didn't fool anybody.

"You don't like guns," he said. "And Miller took mine."

I thumped the doorframe with the side of my fist. Dammit, Kyle was
working my last nerve today. "Why did he do that? Why did you let him do
that?"

I swiped my phone off the dresser and touched Kyle's name in my
favorites.

Straight to voicemail.

I opened a text. *Call me when you see this, taking J on a wild bomb chase.*

"Pissing him off isn't exactly in my best interest right now," Joey said.
"He . . . well, he did something that means I'm not currently in a cell. So he
asked for my gun, and I gave it to him."

Something tickled the back of my brain.

Commander Davis.

"Not even his personal detail was allowed in the office." What was Kyle doing there in the first place? And who had barred the state police from a scene that should have been their job? I put a hand on Joey's arm.

"Did you see—" I stopped. Of course he hadn't. He'd probably been in shock. "You know what? Never mind." I strode to the kitchen, grabbing my bag on the way through and switching my focus back to the task at hand. "I have pepper spray." And a decent hope that the place we were going would be deserted this time of night on a Sunday, because if Stacy Adams was building nuclear weapons, pepper spray wouldn't do jack shit to help us, and Joey's punching hand was out of commission.

I paused with my hand on the doorknob. I had chased enough stories into danger in the past couple of years to know what I was letting us in for. This—the actual catching of bad guys and saving the world—wasn't my job. It was Kyle's and Aaron's and Landers's and Chaudry's. It was Sunday night, and I still wasn't sure whether or not I had my actual job to head off to in the morning. But I was damned sure I'd like to be alive to find out.

I tapped a finger on the doorknob.

Lakshmi.

Hamilton.

The president. If the first woman to hold the office ended up splattered all over downtown, what would that do to the country? To every little girl who'd spent the past two years thinking she could do that someday, too?

I turned the knob and stuck a hand out for the keys to my car.

If I stayed home and a tragedy happened tomorrow night, I'd never forgive myself.

I'd rather go down trying to do good in the world than end up hating myself for living a long life sitting down.

30

A solid twenty minutes after we'd passed another car, human, or house, Joey reached across the console and laid a hand on my knee. "Are you sure this is the right way?"

No, I wasn't. I had a pile of random information, a tip, a hunch, and a large assumption that my super-hurried search had yielded correct information. But it was all we had to go on, and Kyle still wasn't answering me. I peered into inky darkness so thick the high beams could've been a flickering candle, praying for a break.

"It's the best lead I have," I said.

He squeezed my knee. "You really think they're going to try to kill her, don't you?" The words were halting. Incredulous. "Jesus."

"If they're going to try what I think they're going to try, she won't be the only person dead. Not even close."

I swallowed the panic and shifted my thoughts so it wouldn't well back up. There was no time for freaking out. And this whole damned thing was so crazy, I could convince myself I was making it up if I just didn't think about it too hard.

My GPS blipped.

You have arrived at your destination.

I slowed the car, pulling to the side of the deserted two-lane road. Squinted past Joey into the dark.

Couldn't make out a single thing past the end of the car.

Okay then. I killed the engine, fished my phone and keys from my bag, stuck the former in my pocket, and closed my hand around the pepper spray hanging from the latter. I was more worried about bears than wannabe homegrown terrorists. For the moment.

We made it less than fifty paces before that changed.

"It's a wheat field, baby," Joey was saying from my shoulder, half jogging to keep up.

My eyes fell on the dark structures in the distance, the earthy, grassy smell surrounding us laced with a sour stench.

"I hope you're right." I turned, plunging into one of the rows.

"What the hell is that smell?" Joey coughed over the last couple of words, the stink closing in on all sides as we moved through the fields.

"Grains," I said. Growing up in Texas, I'd driven past and through many an unharvested field. "Rotting grain."

"Why would they plant it and let it rot?" Joey paused. "Oh. Because it's not really a farm."

I caught sight of a light up ahead and took off running, then stopped so short Joey charged right into me, knocking me to the ground. Looking up at the diamond-dot stars, shadows whispering along the darkened ground behind me, I shook my head.

It was not really a farm.

Being smart is fun, for the most part.

But damn, some days it really sucks.

Joey pulled me to my feet with his left hand. "If they're not harvesting it, what's with the silos?" he stage-whispered.

I laid one finger across his lips as I looked up at the gleaming metal cylinders, stretching probably five stories toward the sky.

They were harvesting something, all right. It just wasn't growing out here above the ground.

Waving for Joey to follow, I crept through the edge of the field, keeping the tall stalks around us as cover. I didn't see any cars. Or hear any voices.

Fairly satisfied that we were alone, I stepped into the clearing. My second foot wasn't even on the ground when the whole field lit up brighter than noon on the Fourth of July, the huge lights spotted around the perimeter obviously on a motion sensor.

Shit.

* * *

We froze in tandem, staying still long enough for my heart rate to drop from the stratosphere before we turned to each other at the same time. "I think we're clear," I said at the same time Joey murmured, "So how do we get inside to find your proof?"

I tipped my lips up in a smile, my head whipping between the silos and the field.

I was right. I was sure of it without seeing inside.

I could call Kyle and plant my ass right back out at the road in my (locked) car and let him come save the world.

It sounded awfully damned appealing.

Except he still wasn't answering, and I had no idea if we were too late, or if we might be able to stop this from happening if I didn't chicken out.

Bonus: there was nobody around.

I started forward, Joey's hand warm on my lower back as he walked beside me.

I pulled out my phone, opened the map and dropped a geo-locator, and clicked to send the pin to Kyle.

I think I found your weapons factory. It's quiet right now, we're going in to check it out. Send.

We circled the building until we found a door. Flat, blending into the curve of the wall, but there.

On the ground.

Joey pointed to the stairs winding up the side of the building. "I'm a city guy, but in the movies the doors to these things are up high."

I nodded, running my fingers along the cracks, hunting for a catch.

Joey smiled and pulled out a positively frightening-looking pocketknife. "Maybe this will help?"

I took it with a grin, letting it lie cold and heavy and reassuring in my hand. Better than pepper spray. Way, way better.

"Miller only asked for my gun," he said. There was the weird reading Nichelle's mind thing again.

"I love you, you know that?" I squeezed his good hand with my free one, peering up at him. "Whatever happens in here—death, radiation poisoning, heroic acts of patriotism—I need you to know that."

"I do." He smiled—soft, brief, but heart-stopping in the middle of the chaos all the same. "And back at you."

I slid the knife into the left-hand side of the door a bit above center and pushed the handle back like a crowbar.

It broke.

Bending to retrieve the pieces from the dirt, I saw the shoes before anything else.

Prada.

Eggplant. Box heel. Gorgeous.

This season.

I followed the long legs up, past the pencil skirt and the designer silk blouse, my eyes pausing on the gun trained on us before they settled on her face.

"Nichelle." Her voice was low. Hard. Not at all the way I remembered it. "Joey."

I felt the wind go out of my chest and my sails.

We got played.

Again.

* * *

"Lakshmi." I forced the word out over the lump of disgust and disbelief blocking my throat, looking over her shoulder. "And Hamilton."

Jesus.

The governor's son nodded and held up a shiny gizmo, pressing a button. I looked over my shoulder. The door slid silently back into the wall behind me, a stairwell leading underground on the other side. Not how I wanted to find that. I slid my hand into my pocket, dropping the blade and fumbling with my phone. I swiped up from the bottom of the screen and tapped the bottom center twice, crossing my fingers I'd hit the right spots. If we didn't make it out of here, maybe my phone would.

"Let's go inside, shall we, folks?" Hamilton Baine's smile was fifty degrees colder than the evening air. "Chilly out here tonight."

Lakshmi waved the gun, her eyes darting from the weapon in her hands, to the doorway, to her boyfriend anxious-rabbit style, never staying on one thing for more than a split second.

She wouldn't look me in the face.

She wouldn't even look in Joey's general direction.

My fingers brushed over the lump in my pants that concealed the pepper spray canister, my eyes measuring the distance between Lakshmi and Hamilton.

It was too risky. If I sprayed her and she shot blindly, she might hit us. Or he might get his face turned away and get the gun before we got into the field, even at a sprint. And if I sprayed him, she would probably just shoot me.

I couldn't get close enough to reach them with the knife.

So the smart move was to play along. For now, anyway.

I turned for the door.

Joey shot a hand out to stop me, his eyes on Hamilton.

"Leave her alone, man. I'm the one you want. Let her go."

Hamilton snorted. "Are you on something? You want me to let a newspaper reporter famous for sticking her nose where it doesn't belong and fucking things up out of my sight on the eve of the most important night in American history since a bunch of drunk assholes chucked some tea into Boston Harbor?" He smirked. "Chivalrous of you, but I'm gonna go with no." He grabbed my arm for good measure. "Let's go, sweetheart."

Joey lunged forward.

I put an arm out to stop him, but didn't get it all the way to him before Lakshmi's gun whipped through the air, butt first, the blunt end connecting with the elbow on Joey's uninjured arm. He stumbled backward with a guttural moan, managing to keep his footing as he cradled the arm and glared at her, his eyes going flatter, colder than I'd ever seen them. I'd have been shaking in those pretty pumps. She just stared back at him.

"I appreciate that, but I don't need an attack dog," Baine said, not bothering to look at her.

"I've seen what he can do to someone with his bare hands," Lakshmi whispered, her eyes still on the dirt. She righted the gun in her hands, resting a light finger on the trigger, and gestured to the door. "We should get them inside. You're going to run out of time."

Hamilton's fingers sank into the skin around my bicep until I was fairly certain my hand was no longer getting blood, half dragging me forward as Joey walked in front of Lakshmi, still holding his injured elbow with his bandaged hand.

We proceeded down so many spiraling stairs we had to be a good bit of the way to China by the time we reached a long sterile hallway with smooth white walls, overhead florescent lights, and a door at the far end.

Hamilton let go of me and strode to the door, waving for us to follow. Lakshmi stayed between us and the foot of the steps, blocking the only exit and keeping the handgun trained on our backs.

I shuffled my feet forward, drifting in a fog of disbelief I knew wasn't doing me any favors, unable to shake it.

The very people I'd spent the whole weekend trying to help, to give voice to, to make matter . . . were the ones behind all this?

How in the ever-loving fuck-all hell did I manage to miss the mark by that much? I drove out here thinking I had it all figured out. Finally. After a thousand fits and starts, I needed to protect Lakshmi, I needed to save Hamilton Baine and help Joey, and I could do it all by way of making sure Stacy Adams was about to go to a very small cell for a very long time.

I was so far off we might as well have ended up in Montana.

Hamilton opened the door—I couldn't see how with his backside between me and the knob—and waved us through. Joey let go of his elbow and put a protective arm around me. Two injured limbs, and he was still trying to be the hero. I slipped one of mine around his waist and squeezed, but edged in front of him when Hamilton closed the door and crossed to us, Lakshmi standing just inside the room, her gun no longer raised.

Hamilton raised a brow and grinned at me. "Spunky, aren't you?" He laughed. "I like some spunk in my bitches, don't I, Lala?"

She didn't answer, and I didn't take my eyes off him.

He tipped his head forward. "Well done, I must say. Since Joey here wasn't on the need-to-know list, I imagine it was you who found us here, Miss Clarke, was it not?"

I didn't move, even to blink.

He nodded. "It's helpful, when you get right down to it. I have you out of the way, and there's one more thing for your friends Agent Miller and Agent Chaudry to worry about when they can't find you two." He swept an arm through the air around him. "Welcome to Hotel Hamilton," he said. "Not the most comfortable accommodations, I'm afraid, but you'll make do for a day or two, won't you? You two might be useful if your federal agent friends are smarter than I thought they were."

He began pacing the width of the long room. "Now I know you're wondering what will become of you after we've returned the leadership of this country to its rightful owners." He wrinkled his nose. "Women aren't worthy of high office—sniveling, cheating, lying, emotional creatures. And I'm going to make this right." He clapped his hands together and turned a beaming smile on us. "But what fun would it be if I told you that now?"

Sweet Jiminy Choos, he wasn't depressed—he was crazy.

And I didn't catch it because I saw what I wanted to see. The way he looked at Lakshmi in the photos wasn't love. It was disdain—he was half glaring at a piece of meat. Stacy's comment about him not being good with women wasn't cute, it was telling. Because Hamilton didn't trust them. Us. Any of us.

Governor Baine's panic-stricken insistence that Aaron find his son made a whole different sort of wickedly frightening sense. He wasn't afraid the kid was in danger. He was afraid the kid *was* the danger.

Would've been nice to put all that together a couple hours ago.

Lucky for us, I had ridden this roller coaster a time or seven. I cleared my throat. "So, you're going to kill the president. Solid plan, except for the part where the Secret Service knows you're coming."

Baiting the crazy guy is pretty safe when he's not the one holding the gun.

He shook his head, clasping his hands behind his back.

"They know no such thing," he said. "They know there's a threat at her speech, exactly as I wanted them to. I've watched Thomas's security detail for over a year now. They get laser-focused on one thing that becomes their mission, whether the actual issue has anything to do with their thing or not." One side of his mouth twisted up in a grotesque mockery of a smile worthy of a comic book villain. "But we're not waiting for the speech. And they'll never see us coming." He crossed to me, crooked a finger under my chin to tip my face up to his, and leaned in. I felt everything in Joey go still and coiled behind me, and I blindly reached a hand back to keep him where he was. It seemed two could play the baiting game here, and I couldn't let Joey get himself shot diving for this cheap, smelly little worm.

Hamilton's ten o'clock shadow brushed my cheek, his lips hovering close enough to my ear to tickle the lobe. I kept rigid, determined not to flinch, scream, or vomit until he was out of sight.

His breath was humid and sticky hot on my ear and jaw, his words sluicing chills through me I wouldn't give him the satisfaction of reacting to. "Everything about this has gone according to plan, except the part Joey here mucked up saving the day. Hell, I told people she was dead before I found out he'd decided to play the hero. You played your part perfectly, Miss Clarke. Much appreciated. Now, before you get me bragging on my brilliance and somehow parlay that into my downfall, I have important chores that need my attention. Y'all sleep tight, you hear?"

I swallowed hard.

He withdrew, striding back to the door and patting the side of his thigh as he walked past Lakshmi. "Come," he said, like he was talking to Darcy. "We're done here, and we still have work to do."

She followed him out the door, his voice muffling to almost nothing when it shut behind them.

I listened to the lock slide home and shrank back into Joey. Furious, terrified tears stung my eyes, blurring the stark white walls and cold gray concrete floor into a fog of colorless despair. But the anger stopped halfway up my throat and stuck there, a hard, scorching, bitter ball of resentment I wanted to hurl at someone.

Except the person I was the maddest at . . . was me.

Joey and I were stuck in a hole in the ground, and they were going to kill the president, and Kyle and his friend were looking in the wrong fucking place. None of it was entirely my fault, but my attempt at helping had failed more spectacularly than a line of Christian Louboutin flip-flops.

Now what?

31

Three hours passed before I figured it out.

Or thought I had.

Again.

"It's not the speech, it's the breakfast," I said, spinning back from the wall for the thousandth time.

Joey tried to look at me from his spot on the floor in the corner, raising himself up on his good elbow and tipping his head to one side.

"What?"

"Hamilton said that Kyle and Chaudry were thinking they were going to kill the president at the speech, but they're not. The hotel is too easy for the Secret Service to secure. Nobody will ever get near her unless they have someone on the inside, and if they had that she'd probably already be dead with all the crazypants revolution bullshit he was spouting. Tomorrow morning, she's supposed to stop at a school and read to the kids, talk with the staff and students at the medical school about the future of the health-care system, and then go to a breakfast at the Coliseum with donors. There will be caterers at the breakfast. It'd be easiest there to slip an extra person into the room."

"Easy? To get past the United States Secret Service?" Joey shook his head. "I don't think that word means what you think it means. Don't you think one of the stops is a better target?"

I shook my head, the way Lakshmi's neck stayed angled toward the floor gnawing at me. "I don't. Lakshmi is . . . well, she's apparently a few things I didn't have any idea she was, but at the end of this long, murderous day, I don't think she's evil. Setting off a nuclear explosion in a school or a hospital is a bridge too far for most people, even awful ones."

"But in a big room full of average people, it's totally fine?" Joey sat all the way up. "I'm not sure I agree with you here, princess."

"They're not average people. Not to him. Didn't you hear him? They've paid to hear President Denham speak, which makes them the enemy. And we have no way to warn them."

He stood, crossed the room, and laid his forearms on my shoulders, staring straight through my eyes into my messy, scattered thoughts in that way he had that made me feel like things would work out okay somehow.

"I know you think you've done something wrong here, but you haven't." His voice was soft. "I know you feel like you have to fix something, but you don't. Not every story ends with the good guys saving the day, baby."

I shook my head. "How about with us living to save another day? I'd take that right now."

"That little weasel is not going to kill us." Joey shook his head. "You could take that guy any day without me even in the room."

"When it's a fair fight, probably."

"I'll make sure it's fair," he said. "And I'll be the one doing the fighting."

I snorted. "With two bum arms. Okay." I rested my forehead against the cool cotton of his shirt, the warmth from his shoulder beneath coming through after a moment. "I'm telling you. It's the breakfast. It has to be. The law of simple averages says I'm due to be right about something today. Yesterday. Whenever it is."

"And you're sure Miller was wrong about the bomb thing? Because he said they couldn't make a bomb from the stuff you were talking about yesterday."

I leaned back against the wall and sank to the floor, watching him inspect the door before he returned to prowling the perimeter of the room like a hunting jaguar, stalking a way out that flat didn't exist but unable to sit still.

"Stacy Adams is selling people on this reactor for electricity because it's a salt reactor that uses thorium—a mineral the US holds almost a fifth of the world's supply of—as an energy source. As a bonus, it doesn't have the by-product plutonium that's so dangerous to the surrounding area."

"And that people can make bombs from," Joey said.

"Right. Except. It turns out there's a way to use thorium in this reactor that creates a weaponizable by-product called U-233. Something they can make bombs out of. Big bombs, with not much material. So the reactor doesn't even have to run for long to create one."

"And that's the thing you think Rey Drake discovered when he worked for the federal government?"

I nodded. "I can't say that for sure, but I'd bet my shoe closet on it. And, by extension, that this is the thing Grayson was after when he got himself involved with Lakshmi. Here's what I can't figure out yet: Angela Baker is dead. She was, as far as I know, the only person who knew why Grayson wanted to know Lakshmi. But given what we've seen here so far, why would that get her killed? I've been sure since Saturday morning that Grayson was the mastermind behind this mess. Yet Hamilton was crowing about his plan and he never even said anything about Grayson. They can't be angling for Grayson to be president—he's a convicted felon. I can't see how Angela's murder fits in here."

"She was in prison. Things happen," Joey said slowly.

I shook my head. "That's too big a coincidence. There has to be another link in this web I'm not seeing."

He sighed. "I don't know, baby. I wish I did."

I watched his face carefully. He wasn't lying. So what did he know? And why was he on a first-name basis with the crazy on the other side of the door?

I pulled in a slow breath, steeling myself to ask the question I had batted my lashes at and flirted with for hours now without actually saying the words. "Why did he know you? Hamilton Baine. You tried to get him to let me go, and then he said you didn't need to know about this place . . . What aren't you telling me?"

As soon as the words were out, hanging heavy in the air between us, I wanted to wad them up, stuff them back down where they came from. I'd rather live with that knot in my gut than see what the question did to his face.

It twisted. Not unlike when Lakshmi whacked him with the gun. Not mad. Not scared. What I saw on his face was pain. His hand went to his abdomen, his head shaking. "I'm—" He stopped.

I kept my eyes on his face. He was a good man, with a good heart. He knew bad people and had done some questionable things, but I knew who he was.

He trusted me. Loved me. And I loved him.

It was time to go all in. Past time, maybe.

"Just tell me," I said. "Please. I know you—you wouldn't be a part of anything like this."

I shoved the memory of his stricken face when I said I was going to cover the speech back into a dark hole in my brain and locked the trapdoor.

He wouldn't.

His face closed off right in front of my eyes. Cold. Stoic. Unreadable. "I can't." His voice was just as flat and icy, stopping my breath. "I'm not supposed to tell anyone, even you. Please, know that I would if I could. And that I will work for the rest of my days to earn your trust."

Chips down. Cards to his vest. I had been wrong about enough shit today. I'd believe him until someone gave me evidence I shouldn't.

"I trust you," I said, squeezing his fingers. "You'll tell me when you can."

I didn't bother with a question mark at the end of that.

"I can't get us out of this," he said.

"I don't think I can, either."

He nodded. "The breakfast, huh?"

I tapped my finger on my knee, pulling out my phone to check in vain for a signal to materialize under a thousand tons of concrete, clicking the recorder off when I saw it was still running. Yay, I'd hit the buttons right. At least if Kyle found my phone, he'd know what had happened here.

"I swear. That has to be their target."

"How much time is left?"

"Nine hours until she arrives at the facility," I said.

He stood and walked back to the door, waving me over.

I stopped behind him, following his gaze to the top right corner.

"What is that?" I asked, spotting the three unobtrusive little lines in the edge of the frame.

"I'd say it's a speaker." Joey sighed. "Recording us, maybe?"

Holy Manolos.

I flapped one hand, backing away as the other clapped over my mouth. "Stacy Adams," I whispered, the high-tech elevator voice ringing in my ears. "Just like the elevators. That's how he opened it. It's voice activated."

"Great. My impressions suck, I'm afraid." Joey turned and put his back to the wall behind the door, shaking his head. "So, we wait for them to come back and see if we can surprise them, get the jump on her, and get the gun, maybe?" He raised his brows. "You need the restroom? That's cliché and ridiculous, but we could give it a shot."

I shook my head, holding up my phone, the voice recorder app still open on the screen.

"We don't have to. If he opened it with something he said when they left, I've got it right here."

Nine hours. Maybe all hope wasn't lost just yet.

32

.

All I had was a string of half-muttered gobbledygook, because Hamilton hadn't been facing me.

I pulled the phone away from my head, closing my fingers tight around the plastic of the case so I wouldn't chuck it across the room.

"Why is it that every single break I think I see coming with this bullshit evaporates faster than Eunice's armadillo eggs at the sports desk the second I close in on it?" I asked, falling back to the floor and pillowing my head with one arm, blinking back frustrated tears and trying to focus on the ceiling.

I closed my eyes, the tears leaking out and trailing across my temples into my hairline anyway. Joey's footsteps crossed the concrete and stopped next to me, his hand cradling my jaw, thumb wiping them away.

"It'll be okay," he said.

"How? We're stuck. This was the last hope I had of getting us out of this room, certainly in time to stop their presidential assassination plot—*presidential assassination plot*, Joey." I paused, shaking my head. "How am I even saying this? And that's not considering that we may not make it out of here alive at all. If they're harvesting that shit in this building, we could die of some kind of radiation poisoning even if we manage to see daylight again."

His hand moved to my arm, his fingers trailing slow, soothing circles on my skin. "That doesn't sound like you," he said. "Doom and gloom isn't your thing. You're a fighter to the core. Come on, baby. What's wrong with your recording?"

I opened my eyes, the overhead light searing my corneas and making me shut them again. "They were facing away from us across the room, and he wasn't talking to me. The phone was in my pocket. Apple's engineers are good, but they're not wizards." I pinched the bridge of my nose. "It's so muffled I can't even make it out. If I could remember what the hell he said, even, that would maybe help." Of all the times for my photographic memory to retreat into panic.

Joey nudged my hip with his knee, tickling the tip of my nose with one finger until I opened my eyes. "What?"

"He said, 'We're done here, and we still have work to do.'" He grinned. "See? I've learned something, hanging out with you so much."

I sat up, blinking, the words filtering back through my brain in Hamilton's voice. "He did." I nodded. "And right before that, he was talking to Lakshmi like she was a dog. 'Come,' I think is the command he used. He even patted his leg at her." I wrinkled my nose. "Jackass." I tapped the phone screen to life, going back to the beginning of the long recording clip and hitting "Play," laying a finger across my lips as I wished for a pen.

There it was. I hit "Pause." "Rewind." "Play."

Again.

Checked the screen. "Remember eight fourteen," I said, raising the phone back to my ear and hitting "Play," hearing Hamilton say "Done, I must say" for the fourth time.

I kept searching, another hour and a half passing as I found and noted the time of each word. When we had them all, I looked at Joey as I clicked open the GarageBand app I was suddenly thrilled I'd never gotten around to deleting and selected the file to load. "You remember them all?" I asked.

"Eight fourteen, twenty-three thirty-one, and twenty-six fifty-three," he reeled off. "What're you doing?"

I held up one finger and set about isolating each clip, then dragged them into order, crossed my fingers, and pressed "Play."

"We're done here," Hamilton's voice said from the speaker.

"Making a key, I hope," I said, pumping my fist in the air and laughing when Joey sucked in a sharp breath and then leaned forward to capture my lips in a kiss that was far too hot for our current predicament.

"Hold that thought, will you?" I asked, shooting to my feet and crossing to the door, pressing one ear to the inside.

I didn't hear anything.

Which might be good and might not. And there was no way to know. Suck it up and throw the very large loaded dice.

I felt Joey's hand land on my shoulder. "You ready?" he whispered.

"No. But we have six hours and we're two from the Coliseum. So I don't have time to not be ready."

I raised my phone to the speaker in the doorframe, whispered a fast prayer, and pressed "Play."

The lock hissed as it slid back, the door hanging loose on the hinges. I pulled it open a crack.

The hallway stretched in front of us, longer than I remembered, but empty and silent. I scooted through and felt Joey step up beside me, his fingers closing around mine.

"Let's go save the day?" He flashed a smile that told me he was more nervous than he wanted to sound.

"I'll settle for getting out of this building right now," I whispered, squaring my shoulders and moving purposefully toward the stairs, so thankful for my silent, rubber-soled sneakers on the concrete floor, I could almost kiss them. I scanned the entire hallway with every step, my ears pricked for the slightest sound, keeping my center of gravity low so I couldn't be knocked off balance easily.

Halfway to the steps, I pulled my keys from my pocket and laced them between my knuckles, gripping the pepper spray canister tight and finding the trigger with my index finger. It made for an awkward fist, but two quasi-weapons were better than nothing.

We were twelve of about a thousand stairs toward the top when I heard a round slide into the chamber of a gun behind us.

Joey froze next to me, his head turning in tandem with mine, our eyes meeting for a split second as we spun back. I raised the pepper spray. He nodded, a bare flicker of movement someone not looking for it would miss.

I kept turning, raising my arm in the same motion, my finger tightening on the red trigger as my hand came up.

Too much happened at once, my brain running a delay processing the information my eyes were sending it.

Lakshmi.

Maybe three stairs down.

She had a gun.

But she was holding it by the wrong end.

Her fingers were tight around the barrel, extending the butt Joey's way.

Wait.

What?

He reached for it as the spray permeated the stairwell, sending us all into a coughing fit and sending Lakshmi to her knees, her eyes closing, her head shaking. She waved a hand in front of her face.

I let go of the canister and stepped backward, pulling Joey with me, the gun hanging useless at his side thanks to his bilateral battle injuries.

He tried to raise it and winced, shaking his head. "I can't," he coughed, looking up at me and holding the thing out. "Take this."

I shook my head. "I'll shoot you on accident the way this day has gone," I said. "Just hang on to it. At least she doesn't have it."

He shoved it into my hand more insistently. "It's just like laser tag. Remember when we went to play laser tag?"

I kept shaking my head as my fingers closed around the metal, warm from his hand. "I don't like guns."

"Nichelle, please." He bent his head and caught my gaze. "You can do this."

I handed him my keys so I could wrap both hands around it. It wasn't like I'd never shot one. And I'd seen twenty thousand action movies and watched my cops handle guns up close and personal.

He was right.

I could do this. Brandishing a handgun beat the hell out of dying.

I rested my right index finger on the trigger guard like I went to the range four times a week.

"There you go." Joey leaned in, his lips close to my ear, fighting back a cough. "Make sure the safety is off." He nodded to the barrel. "That little button there."

I clicked it.

"Now, just point it at anyone you think will try to hurt you and pull the trigger. Aim lower than you think you need to."

I nodded, my eyes on Lakshmi, who was crawling up the steps under the fog of pepper spray floating toward the vertigo-inducing high ceiling.

"Stop." I tried to sound forceful without being too loud.

Joey leaned into my shoulder. "Wait." He gestured to the gun. "Something isn't right."

I cut my eyes to him. No kidding. I just didn't want her close enough to reach us until I knew what and why.

She did what I said, raising a tearstained face to us that I couldn't attribute with any certainty to the pepper juice.

Keeping her crouched position, she tried to widen her eyes and had to reach up to swipe at them, highlighting the angry red mask around them. If she wasn't going to shoot us, I'd feel at least a little bad for trying to blind her. She shook her head, pointing up. "Get out of here. Before it's too late. Just go." Was that a cough or a sob?

Joey put one foot on the next step down, coughing and crouching under the pale cloud of paper spray. "Lakshmi, what the hell is happening here?"

She shook her head. "I can't. My dad . . ." The way her face collapsed told me everything I needed to know.

"It is his research they used to make their weapon." I didn't bother with a question. Hamilton told Mrs. Powers he had reasons she wouldn't understand for being with Lakshmi. But it wasn't all Romeo and Juliet, written-in-the-stars blind love—she was a tool, a means to get what he wanted from her father.

She nodded. "The reactor is here. Stacy got a private donor to build it. He was so proud of himself, going to use statistics from a fully operational reactor to sway the governor to his side. And it worked. Baine wants to start his own version of the WPA and build these all over the state, which sent the coal companies into fits. They went to their old buddy Ted Grayson, who jumped at the chance to set Baine up to take a political fall. Wyatt connected Grayson with Hamilton, who wanted to take his dad and President Denham both down—he hates the president because he believes women are good for little besides sex and procreation. He hates his parents because of something to do with his mother and a big secret, but he never told me what it was. He knew about Stacy's reactor, and he knew about my dad, about what he'd found at his old lab. He decided it was the perfect weapon, new and secret and something nobody will see coming. There's no metal, so detectors won't work. They told my dad they'd kill me if he didn't help them with the ionization process that produces their bomb. And they told me they'd kill him if I didn't do what they said." She turned her face to Joey. "What you walked into the other night . . . Hamilton set me up. I thought he was coming to meet me, but the guy who walked in said Hamilton sent him as a 'gift.' He was drunk, and so angry. Hamilton told me when he shoved me out of my apartment Friday with a gun in my back that I was supposed to die in that office. So thank you." She sucked in a deep breath and coughed.

I believed every word. Her story made this whole damned thing finally make some sort of sense. And Hamilton Baine had some balls, handing her a gun and ordering her around. That was confidence that he was in utter control of the situation, right there.

"Please, before he figures out you got the door open." She whisper-shouted, "Go."

She couldn't open it because of the voice key. But once we did, she was trying to help.

Dammit. I couldn't leave her there. And I knew that vein poking out of Joey's forehead meant he wouldn't, either. How much could one person be expected to handle? She looked on the verge of falling to a zillion tiny pieces in front of us, and I wouldn't blame her a bit.

"No. Come with us," I said.

She shook her head so hard she sent herself into a fresh coughing fit.

"Sorry," I said.

She waved a hand. "I can't. He'll kill my father. You have to"—cough, cough—"tell someone. Stop them. There's not much time left." She stood, her whole long frame trembling. "Please. He's crazy, Nichelle. He thinks President Denham is going to destroy the republic because she has a vagina. Women can't be trusted, he says, because his mother did something once that he can't forgive her for. We cannot let this happen. Go."

It was an impossible decision. She had been battered and demonized and finally broken, by her love for her family. How could we leave her?

I could tell looking at her that she wouldn't leave her dad any more than I would leave my mother with a madman. And there was a national tragedy brewing that only we knew enough to stop. Maybe.

That's how.

"The good of the many over the good of the one." Joey did it again, whispering what I was thinking as he stood up straight and started up the stairs backward.

I held Lakshmi's gaze for another half minute. "Take care of you. I'll send help, I promise."

She nodded. I spun, edging in front of Joey and holding the gun out in front of me, wondering how I'd keep that promise. Everyone was focused on protecting the president, including us.

One stair at a time.

Outside first. In the car.

Then I could figure out who to call.

33

Every one of the last fifty steps made my legs burn hotter. Even Joey, who ran six miles every morning along the riverfront, was huffing by the time we got to the door.

Which had a pin pad bolted to the wall next to it.

"Of course." He let his forehead drop to the cold steel wall next to it. "Any ideas?"

"Actually . . . yeah." I closed my eyes, rifling through my memory for Hamilton's social media pages.

There.

I took one hand off the gun and lowered it. "Stacy built this place and he seemed pretty gone over Hamilton."

"Too bad for him," Joey snorted. "That kid isn't more interested in anyone than he is in himself."

Exactly.

I punched the keys for Hamilton's birthdate.

The green light at the top of the pad flashed and the door slid back.

Joey bolted upright, waving me through. I raised the gun again and flipped around the opening, flattening my back against the outside wall like I was Charlie's fourth Angel.

"Nice," Joey said, pulling in a lungful of clean, cool, predawn air. "With the door."

I was too busy gulping air myself to reply. Rotten wheat never smelled so good.

Finally, something was going our way. I glanced at Joey's watch.

A little less than five hours, and we were two from the city.

I put my arms straight out and started jogging. "You still have the keys, right?" I called softly over my shoulder.

"Yep." He came up alongside me, easily matching my stride. We dived into the withering stalks, not slowing down.

We were maybe fifteen yards from the car when the first shot fired.

I stumbled, taking one hand off the gun and raising it to examine the chamber.

Shit.

Not mine.

I turned to warn Joey just as he put his shoulder into mine, sending me flying into the wheat stalks with a shove that would do a professional line-backer proud.

I screamed, because I knew what was coming.

And I couldn't move fast enough to stop it.

The peaceful morning exploded around me. Joey staggered backward like he'd taken a good right hook to the gut.

Except it was his shoulder where the black-red stain bloomed out from the little hole, spreading faster than he fell.

I scrambled backward, crab style, putting a few yards between me and the general direction of the bullet before I got my footing well enough to half stand. Creeping low through the stalks and moving slowly, I rested my finger on the trigger instead of the guard, the safety still off.

I couldn't look at Joey, because panicking wouldn't help anyone, and my heart wouldn't stay under my rib cage if I saw him lying there bleeding.

Like Aaron.

Like Grant.

I'd been shot in the shoulder once. He'd be okay. As long as I managed to keep my head straight and get him out of here.

These assholes thought they were dealing with a reporter. They wanted me to freak out and run.

Time to show off what two years of digging myself into trouble chasing stories had taught me.

I'd sidestepped about ten feet when I spotted Hamilton through the stalks.

Holding a rifle to his eye like he was on safari.

With Ted Grayson trailing his heels, hiding behind the kid like the weasel he was. So much for that ankle monitor. Either he got it off or he figured nobody was watching it with the threat to President Denham. I couldn't see his feet clearly enough to be sure.

Bastard. Hamilton Baine had a warped worldview and a serious lack of conscience, but Grayson was calling the twisted shots here.

I saw them before they saw me, but not by much. Grayson's arm flashed up, pointing.

Behind the gun, Hamilton's cold smile stretched his face farther than should've been possible. His finger moved to the trigger.

But mine was already there.

I heard Joey in my ear: *"Aim lower than you think you need to."*

I kept my eyes open as I squeezed.

Hamilton crumpled, the rifle pointing up toward the sky before it fired as he fell.

I rushed forward.

Grayson, close enough now for me to see the nose hairs he really needed to trim, locked wide eyes with me.

His right arm came up, the early light glinting off a small silver revolver.

My heart hammered so hard I wasn't sure it could keep it up much longer. Blood rushed in my ears, muting everything around me. There wasn't time to think, even if I could've managed coherence through the adrenaline-spiking survival instinct.

I aimed.

Fired.

Grayson fell on top of Hamilton.

I didn't move to see if I'd killed anyone, keeping the gun on them as I backpedaled double-time to Joey.

"You okay?" he asked, trying to sit up.

"I got them both." I didn't have to try not to sound proud. It was horrifying. I shot someone. Two someones. My hands shook such that one of us might be third if I didn't put the damned gun down.

But I was still alive, and had no doubt I wouldn't be if I hadn't pulled the trigger.

I knelt next to Joey, pressing the gun into his hand. I wriggled out of my hoodie, threw it down, and pulled one tank over my head, shivering under a single thin layer of cotton and a whole damn lot of adrenaline in the chilly morning air. Taking the hem in both hands and yanking until I heard the stitches give, I bunched up the length and wrapped Joey's shoulder. Pulling as tight as I could, I finally managed to force my trembling fingers to tie it off on the third try.

He grunted. "Thanks, princess." He managed a smile. "I may have to come up with another nickname. You're kind of a badass."

"Do badasses feel like they're going to puke in these situations?" I stood, reaching for his punch-broken, non-shot hand and pulling him up, ducking under his arm to make myself a human crutch as he wavered, blinking.

"Whoa."

"Easy," I said. "Almost there."

One painstaking step at a time, with me turning to look for a terrorist over my shoulder every five seconds, we made it to the car.

I hit the unlock button about fifteen times, belted Joey into the passenger seat and leaned it back, then sprinted around the hood and slid behind the wheel, cranking the key.

Clock check. Four hours and change. Shit.

I slammed a foot on the gas, spinning a U-turn with one hand as I fished my phone out of my pocket with the other.

"Hey, Siri, find the nearest hospital." The phone binged. Flashed an address. For St. Vincent's, in Richmond. Shit. No houses or schools meant no health care nearby.

I held the car steady and touched Kyle's name in my call favorites.

His voicemail picked up on the fifth ring.

"Hamilton Baine and Ted Grayson are bleeding in a field, and Lakshmi

Drake is locked in a nuclear reactor. It is a bomb, Kyle. No metal. And it's not the speech, it's before—" I stopped short of saying "the breakfast," because I couldn't be wrong. Not about this.

"I have to get Joey to a doctor, but please, please call me when you get this," I said.

Clicking the call off and dropping the phone in the cup holder, I glanced at Joey. He was pale, but his breathing was smooth and even. "Hang on, baby. I'm going."

"Where the hell is Miller?" he asked, trying to hide the pain that made his voice thready.

I shook my head. "I even sent him a pin. He knew where we were, and we've been gone all night." I tried to keep the irritation out of my voice. Kyle was busy. And we'd be okay.

I hoped.

Laying my foot on the gas, I focused on the road. Ten miles from the silo, I reached for the phone again, this time dialing Landers.

He picked up on the third ring. "Do you know what time it is, Clarke?"

"Can I trust you, Detective?" I asked, not bothering with an apology for the hour.

"Of course," he said. "Are you"—he cleared his throat—"are you okay?"

"I am not. But a whole lot of people aren't going to be in a little bit if I'm right." My brain was dropping puzzle pieces faster than I could keep up, processing the events of the past few hours as my heart rate came down. My stomach tightened a little more with every mile of blacktop behind us.

"How do I help?" Landers asked.

For all his blustery asshat facade, he wasn't a bad guy at crunch time. And I loved Aaron, but today, I was sure Landers wanted to do the right thing. Aaron might be too blinded by politics to see the right thing if it gave him a lap dance.

"I'm going to send you a map pin. Take four officers you trust and go there. Hamilton Baine and Ted Grayson are in the hayfield, they've been shot. Lakshmi Drake is locked in the back silo. With a nuclear reactor."

"A bomb?" Landers's baritone exploded from the phone's tiny speaker. "Christ, I thought Miller was being dramatic."

"No, I think the bomb has left the building. I just hope I can catch up in time to stop it."

"Did Grayson shoot the Baine kid?"

My fingers tightened around the steering wheel, my voice shaking. "I—uh—I shot them both. I'll explain later."

I clicked "End" and sent him the location pin, nodding when he replied with a thumbs-up.

Joey snored softly from the passenger seat.

I spent the next hundred or so minutes shattering no less than a dozen traffic laws, whispering to myself as I worked out the rest of what I thought had happened in the past few days, and praying I actually had it right.

I was out of time for being wrong.

And the weight of the world—the free world, anyway—was really damned heavy around my shoulders.

34

The tires squealed, the air filling with the hot, acrid smell of burned rubber when I slammed my brakes in the ambulance bay at St. Vincent's. Two orderlies strolled through the automatic doors shaking their heads.

"You can't park here, miss," the shorter one said.

"I'm not parking," I said, rounding the hood at a run on sore, shaky legs and throwing the passenger door open. "He has a gunshot wound to the right shoulder. It's been almost two hours. He's bleeding and pale, but breathing well. I'm pretty sure he's been unconscious for about an hour and a half."

The tall one scrambled back through the door shouting, returning with a gurney and three burly nurses. Tears welled and spilled over before I could stop them as I watched them lift Joey onto the rolling bed and rush him inside.

I slammed the passenger door and slid back into my car, the stocky orderly who had yelled at me before tapping on the passenger window. "Park over there"—he pointed to the small lot—"and come in through the doors around the side to registration."

I shook my head. "Please take good care of him."

I couldn't say anything else without dissolving into a puddle of adrenaline and tears, so I rolled the window up and put my foot on the gas, leaving the orderly waving his arms in the rearview. Just twenty-four hours ago I'd have said there was nothing that would keep me from Joey's bedside in an emergency.

Turned out there was one thing.

Clock check: ninety-one minutes. The Coliseum was fifteen west of me in traffic.

Kyle's office was five to the east. Kyle was a planner—he'd be getting ready for what he thought was coming tonight.

I took the left on Monument and sped toward the tall modern building that houses federal offices in Richmond.

He wouldn't answer his phone, so I'd go tell him in person.

I clicked on the local NPR station.

Top of the hour, and the president was arriving at Jefferson Elementary.

I checked both ways and ran the light at Hamilton Street, swinging a U-turn and parking in front of a fire hydrant. Shooting two people before coffee made a parking violation seem pretty damned inconsequential.

Running into the building, I spotted Kyle's friend John at the desk next to the metal detectors. I waved. He jumped to his feet, his eyes widening with alarm. "Miss Clarke?" His voice was a full octave too high.

Lord, what must I look like? Bloody hands, bloody shirt, hair that had seen many cleaner days half sticking out of my ponytail. A girl could probably walk away from the zombie apocalypse with a less alarming appearance. Nothing to be done for it. There wasn't time.

"Here to see Kyle, John." I didn't break stride as I crossed the lobby.

He stepped around his desk, shaking his head. "He's in a meet—"

Nope.

I kicked it into high gear, sprinting through the detectors and betting John wasn't in good enough shape to catch me before I got in the elevator. I tried not to think about the very real possibility that I might land back in jail after today if I didn't get myself killed first. One crisis at a time.

Hitting the up button, I turned to see John standing at the end of the hall, his head swiveling between me and the doors. He threw up his hands and shook his head at me, returning to his post. Good. I'd apologize later.

If anyone still cared.

The elevator binged open to reveal Agent Chaudry and Wyatt Bledsoe.

I stumbled backward.

Chaudry barely looked at me, and Bledsoe flinched when the doors first opened, then looked between Chaudry and my bloody hands and walked past me, reaching for his phone.

I watched until he was out of sight, another question rifling through my brain. Was Governor Baine in this after all? Grayson might not have a shot at the White House, but Baine was beloved. Cool in a crisis. And a hell of an orator.

Dammit. Because I needed yet another reason to doubt myself today.

I shook it off. There'd be time to figure out who was into what tomorrow. I just had to get to Kyle and make sure there was a tomorrow.

I punched the button for his floor hard enough to jam my finger, leaving a red smear on the plastic. Reaching up, I pulled the elastic band out of my hair and tried to smooth it back. It was slightly better when I retied it. What I really needed was about four showers. Long, hot ones.

Later.

The numbers ticked up on the overhead display, my fingers tapping on my thighs as I moved into a starting-block stance when the elevator stopped. Kyle's office was straight down the hallway on the right.

The doors whispered open to a commanding voice barking orders. I was four strides toward Kyle's office before it registered that he was behind me, running down a plan.

"I've just gotten word our best informant is in surgery at St. Vincent's with a GSW, so we're going on information that's more than twelve hours old, but it's all we've got. We're looking for this man, Stacy Adams, and he may be in any form of disguise. He's armed and highly dangerous, and . . ."

I rounded the corner into the room without really realizing I had moved that way.

Gasps and murmurs rippled through a dozen agents, front to back, and Kyle whirled, his head drawing back and his eyes flying wide when he saw me.

"Nichelle, my God, what—"

I shook my head. "It's not Adams. It's Hamilton Baine. And I think Jerry Stickley is carrying the bomb into the breakfast this morning for them."

"Jerry Stickley? That guy couldn't find his ass with two hands and a flashlight," Kyle said. "He's nothing but a small-time thief. No way he's into anything this complicated."

I leaned back against the wall, my knees finally giving. "He knew Hamilton, Stacy Adams told me. Those guys, the trailer explosion, the trial. The weight loss and hair loss and tomato-red skin. They weren't cooking meth. They were building experimental nuclear bombs. But meth is a way lighter rap than terrorism. That's why the case was such a slam dunk, why they copped to the charges Friday. Why Jerry turned on them and he's still breathing. Because it was planned that way from before you guys ever made it to the scene. Kyle, I swear."

An agent in full tactical gear crossed the room and dragged a chair over next to me before he extended a hand to help me into it.

"Can we get a glass of water here?" Kyle barked over his shoulder as I sank into the chair, shaking and fighting for air.

"I know all that," he said. "Why do you think I tried so hard to get you as far away from this as I could after Craig Terry called me on Saturday when you started asking him questions? We couldn't charge those guys with terrorism without tipping our hand before we got to whoever was really running the show. But Jerry Stickley is no assassin. What do you mean, he knew Hamilton?" He pressed a cold glass into my hand. "And what the hell happened to you?"

I closed both hands around the glass. "I shot them. Both of them," I said, raising my eyes to his. "What you said before . . . your 'best informant.'" I choked on the last word. Raised the glass to my cracked lips as Kyle's disappeared into his goatee. "Kyle. Who?"

He put a hand on my shoulder, not seeming to care that I was covered in blood still. "He'll be okay, honey. He's strong."

Oh my God.

What Joey couldn't tell anyone, not even me.

I closed my eyes, pushing the panic back down, down, down until I could breathe.

He wanted me to move in with him.

I said our lives were too different.

And now he was bleeding on an operating table.

There wasn't time to think about this now.

He would be okay, because he just goddamn had to.

And I would sort this out later.

I opened my eyes. "We only have an hour. We have to go. It's Jerry, I swear. His stringy, thinning hair, the constant runny nose. I don't know why he flipped on them, but he was closer to this than you think, and he's stayed in it while his friends have been sitting in cells. He walked up to Hamilton Baine in a public place Friday night like they were old friends. Does that sound like the timid, backward Sticks from the courthouse? He's your guy."

Kyle pulled me to my feet. "Drink that," he said, tapping the glass. I complied. He set it on a table and ushered me out the door, pressing on a little wired plastic piece behind his ear. "Nichelle is going to have to go in with you if we've got the perimeter. She says she knows who you're looking for." He paused. "I'm sure." He glanced at me. I nodded. "Yeah. We're sure. Meet me out front, I'm leaving now."

He pushed the button to call the elevator.

"I'm sending you in with Chaudry because I don't have a choice," he said. "My team is holding the perimeter in case something goes wrong and the perpetrator makes it out of the venue. We need someone who can ID the subject, and I never even questioned that guy. I've seen exactly one grainy newspaper photo. Point him out and get the hell out of the room."

"How can they just let people walk in here? Why is she even going to be there?" I asked. "Can't they lock her in the hotel or something?"

"She wants to go," he said. "They told her. She doesn't believe it's going to actually happen, and the event is important to her."

I didn't get that. She wasn't just endangering herself anymore.

But it didn't matter.

Nothing mattered except getting there in time, and being right for once in this whole lousy mess.

35

Chaudry paced a small square of concrete between the Coliseum doors and the corner. Kyle hadn't stopped the car before I clicked my seat belt catch and kicked the door open, landing on the curb when I jumped out.

"Nicey!" The urgency in Kyle's voice caught me off guard and I spun back, eyebrows up.

"Make sure you get back out of there, okay?" Pained lines rimmed his blue eyes. He didn't want to let me do this.

I nodded. "Welcome to my world, Special Agent Miller," I said, reaching to grab his hand. "I'm proud of you, you know that?" I wasn't sure why I said it, really. I wasn't as scared as I probably should've been. But I wanted him to know. Just in case.

"Back at you, friend."

I nodded, letting his fingers go. "Do your thing. Keep your head down."

He smiled. "You too."

Chaudry stepped forward. "Getting tight, guys."

I shut Kyle's door and backed toward the squatty concrete building, watching his Explorer disappear into traffic. Chaudry touched my elbow with two fingers. "This way. Miller said you know who we're looking for. How?"

"I spent the night under three tons of concrete next to a nuclear reactor courtesy of the governor's son, who seems to have a different view of women and politics than most people," I said. "Hamilton thinks killing the president returns the country to its rightful owners. That's what he said. I haven't stopped to work out the political beneficiaries web, but I'd bet you're in a better place to do that than I am, anyway. They've been making test bombs for at least a year, in a trailer park on the edge of nowhere. They have something security won't pick up, they think, but I'm betting they're angling for the breakfast and not the speech tonight, because there are more ways in."

He pulled the door open and waved me inside, nodding.

"Here." He pushed open the door to the stairwell. I followed. We made it up two long flights, my legs protesting every step, before he ushered me into a long, dim empty hallway.

I turned. "Is the kitchen—" The words died on my lips when I saw the gun.

"Oh, you've got to be fucking kidding me." The words slipped out before I could stop them.

He was an excellent liar. None of us had guessed.

The president was still on her way here because she didn't know a damned thing.

Kyle was setting his team up blocks away. Joey was on an operating table. Aaron was AWOL for reasons I still didn't understand. Landers was on his way to Nukes 'R' Us, hours from here.

I was on my own.

Staring down a gun in the hands of an expert marksman at point-blank range.

Objectively, I didn't like my odds. But damned if I was going out without a fight.

"So you were their inside man," I said. "Did you and Hamilton meet on some sort of homegrown terrorism web forum, or is there a local chapter?"

He shook his head. "I've known Hamilton since he was a kid. Former state police."

Of course. He'd even told me that, in my kitchen. And I was so busy freaking out about Joey killing someone I didn't manage to hold on to it. That was it. Someone who knew how the governor's detail worked, how the

ATF worked, and how the White House worked. Chaudry was my patient zero, the center of this whole messy web of secrets and death, and I'd followed him right into a neat little indoor blind alley.

Nice one, Nichelle.

I stepped forward, the blade in my pocket hard and cold against my leg. 'Don't bring a knife to a gunfight' was a cliché for a reason, but I had zero options. I had to get close enough to touch him, and I needed surprise on my side.

Keep him talking.

"Why did you come get me? Yesterday afternoon? Why not just let me sit in jail?" I raised an eyebrow. "I have a bit of a reputation for being a pain in the ass for guys like you."

He snorted. "No lie. But Miller told me to go after you while he talked alone with your little snitch friend. I couldn't say no without possibly blowing my cover. So . . . here you are. I told Hamilton to take care of you last night when I saw on Miller's phone that you were on your way to the silo."

I blinked.

"Your message came up while he was in the can. I deleted it, I texted Hamilton. But." His hand tightened around the butt of the gun. "If you want something done right, you do it yourself."

"How did you get Hamilton into this?" I blurted, stepping to the side and forward.

He rolled his eyes. "This, the bomb part, was Hamilton's idea. All I came in knowing was that I wanted Katherine Denham under the turf at Arlington National with my baby brother. Women have no business sending soldiers into harm's way. Wyatt Bledsoe knows a couple of my old buddies from the state police who knew how I felt about our commander in chief. So Wyatt accompanied the governor to the White House last year and found me, told me about Grayson's plan: take down Denham and pin it on Baine by way of Hamilton. Saved me from having to do it myself, and Grayson and I get a fat retirement payday from Standard Coal, too. All I had to do was get Denham here and keep Miller off Hamilton until today. He's not quite all there, that kid. I think the thing with his parents kind of fucked him up from an early age, really, but he's handy. Nothing like a zealot to make sure a plan goes off well." He gave me a once-over, his eyes lingering on the bloodstains still on my shirt. "Though it seems he underestimated you. I won't make that mistake."

We'd see about that.

"Anything you want me to tell anyone?" he asked. "I am sorry it had to come to this, believe it or not. I will of course have chased you up the stairs when you took off after a hunch, only to have arrived a split second too late." He cast his eyes down, his voice going soft. "She died in my arms, man. I'm so sorry. She said to tell you . . ." He looked up at me with a cocked brow. "What?"

He blinked at my proximity. I'd slipped right up next to him during his little dramatic performance, palming the blade of Joey's knife.

Flipping it forward, I closed my hand around it tight, biting down on a scream when the teeth sank into the meat of my palm. "Tell him people like you always underestimate me," I said, wrapping my other hand around the first and jabbing as hard as I could, the blade sliding into his side so effortlessly it took the blood pouring out over my hand to make me sure I'd gotten it deep enough.

Chaudry sucked in a sharp breath, raising his big right fist and swinging hard at my face. I leapt back, managing to just catch the back edge of his massive class ring on the tip of my temple instead of the full force of the blow.

But I stumbled, landing on my ass.

And the knife clattered across the linoleum, disappearing behind me.

Shit.

Chaudry was bleeding pretty good, but it wasn't slowing him down much. He stepped forward.

"How about I just tell him you loved him?"

He raised the gun.

I pinched my eyes closed, pulling in a deep, calming breath.

36

Shoving with everything I had in both arms, I vaulted myself back to my feet and sprang at Chaudry, a scream ripping up my throat from some primal place I didn't know I had.

I hit him square in the center of his sternum with the top of my head, pain exploding down my neck as we tumbled to the floor.

The air rushed out of his chest when we hit the ground. I knew that gave me a split-second biological advantage. His body would focus first on getting oxygen back.

Scrambling to an upright position, I straddled his thighs and spotted the open gash in his side, balking for a half tick.

Could I do this?

His chest started to expand again.

If I wanted to live, I had to.

Sinking both thumbs into the wound, I twisted and scratched, swallowing the bile that rose up my throat at the warm, squishy feel of something I didn't want identified under my bare fingers. His whole torso wracked, a low, growling scream twisting his face into a mask of fury and pain. "You bitch!" he howled, banging his fists on the floor before he swung them blindly at me.

The metal end of the gun swooped so close to my face I felt the air move around it, but didn't hit me.

Before I could process the near miss, Chaudry's meaty left hook collided with my shoulder, pain skating out from the blow in every direction. I tightened my abs and stayed upright, my eyes still on the hand clenching his sidearm in a grip I had no hope of breaking.

No time for pain. No room for squeamish disgust. I set my jaw and pulled outward in opposite directions with both thumbs.

His flesh tore, blood flowing faster over my hands. His arm fell to his side on the floor, his back arching off the floor and forcing me to clamp my knees around his legs to hold my position.

Oh God.

I couldn't. I was going to puke.

But I had to, nausea be damned. It was either him or me and everyone in five city blocks.

I pulled harder. He screamed again, this one high and long, his fingers relaxing on the butt of the gun.

That was all I needed.

Yanking my hands out of his middle, I dived, Kyle in my ear lecturing me on how to disarm an attacker. One hand tight around the barrel, one pushing up from the bottom of the butt. Pull, push, twist, all in one motion.

I threw my whole body backward when I felt the gun coming loose, landing on my back across Chaudry's feet, his weapon in my hands.

Gripping it tight, I rolled left, because Kyle said people usually move right, coming up on my knees over him and checking the safety on the gun. Off.

Resting a finger on the trigger, I aimed it at him.

"Stay there, Agent."

He writhed on the floor, both hands covering the wound in his side. "Shoot me," he said, turning his head toward me, a thin trickle of blood running from one corner of his mouth.

I rose slowly, keeping the gun on him. "I've shot enough people for today."

"I won't go to prison. You do it or I will," he said. The blood trickle thickened. Damn.

"No dice," I said, looking around for something to cuff him to.

The door to the stairs had an old-style crash bar. That was probably sturdy enough.

"Give me your cuffs," I said.

He shook his head. "Shoot me, dammit!" he roared. His face melted into something else altogether, a desperate, livid, terrified mass of skin that didn't even look half-human.

I swallowed hard.

If he was strong enough to get up and come at me, he would have. The black-red pool under him oozed outward over the dirty floor at an alarming rate, and the trickle from the corner of his mouth was getting thicker. He wasn't going anywhere. But I had a job to finish.

I backed toward the door.

"You win," Chaudry called. A thick-sounding cough sent blood droplets spraying into the air. "If you can find him."

Whirling and hitting the crash bar with my free hand, I didn't look back. I sprinted down the stairs, shouting for help. The lobby was filling with people dressed in their designer runway best. A security guard raced through the crowd when I screamed, reaching his hands out and then drawing them back when he got an eyeful of all the blood.

"There's a federal agent in the hallway two flights up those stairs, I think he's bleeding to death. Call the PD, ask for Aaron White, and tell him this man is trying to kill the president." I spit the words out fast, trying to sound authoritative and realizing I both sounded and looked batshit crazy.

"What?" He fumbled for his radio. "Who are you? What do you mean someone is trying to kill the president? I think you'd better come with me."

I backed out of arm's reach. "Just call Detective White, and don't go up there alone," I said. If he didn't call Aaron, that was his problem.

Spinning toward the first-floor hallway, I ran.

The breakfast was in the Madison room.

The service staff would have to be in the next one over.

I read the signs on the doors as I pushed through the growing crowd headed for the huge ballroom, indignant shouts peppering my wake.

There.

I turned, running smack into a woman holding a Burberry-outfitted toddler on one hip. "Sorry," I said, ducking past her. I yanked the door open and stopped short, nose to nose with Wyatt Bledsoe.

His wide eyes narrowed, his mouth screwing into a scowl.

I didn't have time to think. One step back, base foot planted. I jumped, sending my best *ap'chagi* flying at his stomach. He hit the ground and I sped past, ignoring the recoil cramp in my quadricep as I scanned the room.

People spun. Whispers turned to murmurs. Trays crashed to the tile.

My eyes kept moving.

Until they lit on the one person who didn't look shocked by my appearance.

I started for him at a dead run, the room erupting behind me as the security guard zipped in with a half-dozen Secret Service agents who actually wanted to do their jobs.

"There she is!" I heard over the shouts and murmurs.

"Miss? Miss!" A chorus of deep baritones drew close on my heels, but I couldn't focus on anything but Jerry, who was frozen to the floor faster than a supermodel in a throng of paparazzi.

My hands hit his tray first, flipping it up into his face. He stumbled backward, swinging the tray and nodding when it connected with my stomach, doubling me over.

An agent put a light hand on my back. "You're going to have to come with me, miss," he said.

I pointed. "Him. It's him. He has a bomb."

Didn't matter if they thought I was crazy. I just needed them to follow the lead, and they would, because they don't take words like that lightly.

Three other agents closed around skinny little Jerry. A different sort of murmur went through the crowd. I crumpled to the floor, turning my head in time to catch a glimpse of a perfectly coiffed trademark chignon atop a slender neck, heading for the next room.

"You're too late." Jerry cackled from behind the agents. "You'll never find it before she does."

The agents reacted as a unit, one hollering into the mic in his cufflink about securing Eagle, one twisting Jerry's arms up behind him so hard and fast I was pretty sure I heard something crack before Jerry yelped, and the other two shoving a path clear and sprinting for the door.

I pulled in a shaky breath and looked up at the security officer.

"The guy at the police department said to find the Secret Service," he said. "The ambulance is out front. Man, that dude is bleeding."

I nodded.

My phone buzzed in my pocket. I pulled it free.

Bob: *We have a staff meeting.*

I laughed. Way too loud and way too long to be in the same county as appropriate. Monday morning, and Nichelle is late for the meeting.

Normal.

I shook my head, my thumbs moving over the screen.

I don't have a job anymore. I think. Send.

Buzz. *I didn't say I was at the* Telegraph. *Where are you? Coffee?*

I dropped the phone and rested my forehead on my knees. I was out of words, out of brainpower for solving riddles, and just so. Damned. Exhausted.

"Miss?" That was the security guard again. I looked up to find him with his radio to his ear, three of his colleagues herding people toward the exit with calm voices. "We have to exit the building."

I nodded, getting slowly to my feet.

He started to offer a hand, looked me up and down, and changed his mind. Couldn't blame him.

He followed close behind me as we moved to the exit. "So . . . who are you?"

I smiled. "Nichelle Clarke." I checked his name tag. "Nice to meet you, Frank."

"Are you a cop?"

I shook my head. "I'm a reporter." Whether I had a paper to work for or not.

Frank twisted his lips to one side. "You look like you just walked out of the end of *Die Hard.* Must have been some story."

"You wouldn't believe it, Frank. Right now I'm not even sure I do."

We filed out into the light. Raising up on tiptoe, I spotted a huddle of Secret Service-issue suits, moving together and depositing President Denham into the back of a waiting limo.

"Nichelle!" I turned and practically fell on Kyle, who was ready to catch me as he pushed through the crowd of disappointed political aficionados.

His arms didn't close all the way around me before tears flooded out of my face like a levee had shattered. Shaking my head, I tried to make words but couldn't manage more than a string of gibberish and sobs.

Kyle stroked my sticky, greasy hair. "Joey's fine," he said in my ear. "He's in recovery in the ICU, but there were no complications, and he's stable."

I nodded, catching my breath.

Whatever else the universe had ready to hurl at me, Joey was fine, Kyle was fine, I was mostly fine, and President Denham was fine.

That was enough for today.

37

I closed my fingers tighter around DonnaJo's, watching the closed door. "What's taking so long? This can't be good, right?"

She covered my hand with her free one and returned the pressure. "Honey, I'd be more worried if it wasn't taking a while. Calm down."

She picked up the paper on the table in front of her, the president's face on the cover floating over a photo of a smiling crowd waving signs for Congressman Speeks. "This was a good piece. Way to come out swinging in the new digs."

I nodded. "Thanks. Bob makes it easy. He's a good editor."

"I can't believe Bob Jeffers left the *Telegraph*," she said. "It's been the talk of the courthouse all week. Well, that and the gas leak that caused the evacuation at the president's breakfast. Always some sort of drama."

I tapped the cover of *RVA Week*, running a finger across the red letters of my name under the headline.

Gas leak.

Kyle's idea.

The bomb was in the podium at the front of the banquet hall. Not huge, but not small—Kyle said the plastic case held enough clumsily made U-233 to take out six city blocks. Sticks and his friends were thorough. Stupid enough to give themselves likely fatal radiation poisoning and end up living out their days in a state hospital, but thorough. The agent who found their home-baked nuke was still being treated for exposure, but was supposed to recover.

Chaudry was in a private cell in the VIP block at Cold Springs with Hamilton and returning guest Ted Grayson. Treason topped the list of charges: apparently the coal company's cash wasn't enough, since they were ass-deep in illegal weapons trading with a Russian radical group, the leaders of which were plenty pissed that they didn't get their bomb supplies. Plus, Grayson was on the hook for murder for hire, having paid off the inmate who got Angela Baker with a shiv fashioned from soaked and hardened sanitary pads. He said he didn't even know she'd talked to me. He just disliked loose ends. Quite a guy, our ex-senator.

Lakshmi Drake was in fact dead—according to the United States Government, anyway. She and her folks were on a beach in Florida with new identities, faculty jobs waiting for Lakshmi and her dad at Florida State after their hard-earned vacation.

Governor Baine had made the rounds on the major local morning shows airing his family's dirty laundry, apologizing for denying that Lakshmi had been found dead in his office, and twisting the week's events around to make himself the victim, which might be the most honest thing anyone was saying about the whole damned mess: turned out Hamilton had set an alcoholic congressman with a penchant for violence from the southwestern corner of the state on a bender and tricked Lakshmi into meeting him, with every intention of framing Governor Baine for her murder. Once Hamilton had his weapon, his key to getting it had become a liability. But Joey, who had been at the capitol chatting Bledsoe up trying to get Kyle an in on the weapons ring, threw a massive wrench into Hamilton's plan. And then I tossed in the rest of the toolbox.

People seemed eager to forgive their governor for what Dan Kessler called "being human" at his sit-down with Baine: the governor's poll numbers were steady in the fifties.

The general public went about their lives with no idea how close we'd come to the unthinkable—with a little help from me by way of my new job. Bob had in fact gone hiking—with the new publisher at the local newsweekly, an independently wealthy venture capitalist who wanted to invest in meaningful reporting from people who cared about good journalism. Bob agreed to take the job as editor in chief, as long as he could bring Parker and me along with him.

And the first story I wrote for them was a thirty-five-hundred-word lie about the president's visit to Richmond and the upcoming midterms.

I put the paper down, my eyes going back to the closed door, then to the shot of the smiling crowd from President Denham's speech on our first cover.

Kyle was right. Aaron said so, too—he'd worn a wire to our meeting because Baine gave them security footage showing Lakshmi walking out of the capitol in the predawn hours Friday, so he thought someone was lying to me. Since he needed Baine to think they were still on the same team, he figured coming in with the wire and making me think he was after Kyle would get me to give up the real culprit. Smart play, but looking back, I wished he'd just asked straight out. But Kyle and Aaron were right about the endgame: sometimes, people don't need to know how close they come to death erupting in waves of fire on a sunny Monday morning.

The truth folks believe is the one that counts.

Now I just needed to know which one the prosecutors in that room were going to choose.

"Are you sure? Why is this a hard question?" I uncrossed and recrossed my legs.

"A sitting United States congressman disappears for three days and turns up dead in a burned-out car, drunk off his ass with a fifth of whiskey in the passenger seat—and your friend's DNA under his nails," DonnaJo said. "They want to know why they were having dinner. Why your friend let the congressman leave. How he got scratched. And why he was in the hospital for three days last week."

Joey got scratched by flailing defensive slaps as he punched the congressman's face in. But of course, nobody else knew that. He'd called Kyle from his cell when the congressman stopped breathing, and Kyle ducked in and hustled Joey out before anyone started asking questions.

"I told them he was with me Thursday night," was all I said to DonnaJo.

Kyle had helped us work out that story, sitting around Joey's bed in the ICU. Funny how abhorred I was at the idea of him covering Lakshmi's murder for Baine, but I didn't blink when he offered to do it for Joey. Perspective changes the rules.

"Having our relationship compromised at this point won't be good for either of us," he'd said, alternating his pointing finger between himself and Joey.

Their pretty long relationship, it turned out, had started after Kyle shot Don Mario more than a year ago. Joey asked Kyle to lunch and offered to play double agent inside the Caccione organization in exchange for immunity when Kyle eventually busted them—so he could stay with me. When I thought back over the past fifteen months, I felt like Bruce Willis in *The Sixth Sense*: astounded at everything that one truth explained.

"All we need is for the prosecutors to dismiss the case," Kyle had insisted. "This will work. It costs money to bring these kinds of charges, and with an alibi from a respected journalist and a superstar federal agent"—he smiled—"they won't do it."

I'd squeezed Joey's hand and nodded, shushing his objections to me perjuring myself to save his ass. I'd done worse in the name of keeping people I loved safe, and after a week of too many nightmares and too much coffee and a lot more introspection than was likely healthy, I was still wrestling the demons, but there wasn't a single choice I wouldn't make again to get to the place I was sitting.

Provided that door opened to smiling faces, anyway.

DonnaJo patted my knee. "It will be fine," she said, her eyes sliding sideways. "You know, I don't remember you saying anything about a date. On Friday, when I saw you at the courthouse."

I shook my head. "Do you tell me about all your evening engagements? We were watching TV."

She nodded. "Yeah."

We sat in the quiet for a few beats. "Did you know that Jerry Stickley was running guns for Hamilton Baine? During the trial?" she asked.

"I would've told you," I said. Every word true. "You know me better than that."

"Yeah. We've seen a lot, haven't we?" Another pause. "I just can't figure out why he'd be running drugs for the meth outfit if he had that going. There's way more money in weapons."

"He's not the smartest guy I've ever met." I kept my voice even.

She was smart. Really smart.

And she didn't quite buy our story.

I hated lying to her, but there was too much at stake for me to slip now. DonnaJo was my friend. If her boss and the federal prosecutor on the back side of that door believed us, she'd let it go. I hoped.

The doorknob rattled. I sat up straight. Her fingers squeezed mine. "It's fine."

The door swung inward and Kyle stood aside as Joey walked out, shooting me a wink.

"Gentlemen, thank you for your time," Kyle said, putting a hand out for commonwealth's attorney Jonathan Corry to shake.

The dark-suited lawyers nodded. "Sorry to drag you through all this, Mr. D'Amore," The one who wasn't Corry said. "I hope you understand."

I blew out a long, slow breath.

We did it.

They traded a few more pleasantries and the lawyers turned for the elevators. DonnaJo squeezed my shoulder and followed them. I jumped to my feet, my Manolos clicking on the marble floor as I scurried across the hall and threw my arms around Joey, careful to avoid jostling his sling.

"Thank God," I said, the words muffled by his jacket.

He hugged me tight with his good arm, his lips landing warm and soft on the top of my head.

I stepped back, smiling at Kyle. "Thank you."

He and Joey exchanged a look over my head. The kind that said there was something I didn't know. Again.

"Don't thank me yet," Kyle said, shuffling his feet and folding his arms across his chest.

I stepped back, putting myself across from the two of them. "What?"

Joey reached for my hand. "I just have to go away for a while, is all," he said. "It'll be okay, princess."

Wait.

My eyes shot back and forth between their faces, panic twisting my middle again. "But they believed you. I heard the guy apologize to you."

Kyle nodded. "And that's good. But we're not the only people who know what happened—and didn't happen—with this case. There are loose ends to tie up, some legal and some . . .not so legal. Joey could be in danger until we get any potential Caccione leaks taken care of. Now that he's out of the hospital, we need him to be somewhere safe for a while." He rocked back on his heels. "I'll work fast, Nicey. I promise."

My hand flew to my lips, my head nodding even though all I wanted to do was scream *no* until Kyle stopped talking. I fluttered my lashes. Lowered my hand. Tried to smile.

"I'll be back before you know it," Joey said. "You have your new job, and your friends—when's the last time you and Jenna had a girls' night?" He grabbed my hand and raised it to his lips. "I'll see you soon."

Kyle patted my shoulder and turned with another look at Joey. "We should get going."

Joey pulled me close and kissed me until I almost forgot what was happening, Kyle shuffling his feet and clearing his throat next to us.

Pulling his face up from mine, Joey dropped another kiss on the tip of my nose. "I'll see you soon. I love you."

"I love you." I managed to get it out without sobbing, trying for a smile. "Be safe."

They turned for the elevator.

I watched them go before I squared my shoulders and picked up my bag.

He'd be back soon.

I'd settle into my new job, which was actually pretty cool so far: Bob and Parker and me getting to run what we pleased and write what we cared about, without Rick Andrews or Shelby Taylor or a money-minded board cutting another position every week. The only downside was that Rick had, of course, given Shelby my old beat. But even that was merely annoying. Shelby couldn't beat me to a headline with four interns and a caffeine IV.

Life would return to normal. A new normal, maybe, but not a worse one.

That was the truth I chose.

HIDDEN VICTIMS: Nichelle Clarke #8

A letter from a dead man catapults Nichelle Clarke into the biggest story of her career...if she can stay alive long enough to report it.

Nichelle Clarke needs a big break.

With a new job and a new boss, she's under pressure to find a story that will send papers flying off the racks—and money flying in the door.

When she learns that the widow of a beloved athlete is entangled in the opioid crisis, Nichelle sets out to track her down. But the story takes a turn when her interview prospect becomes a suspect—for murder.

Detectives have found a dead body, along with a letter addressed to Nichelle. Determined to uncover the truth, she jumps into the race to find the killer—even as it turns into a police manhunt for the the now-missing widow.

But this story leads Nichelle deep into a mystery where nothing is what it seems, and the truth behind a brutal murder is just the beginning.

ACKNOWLEDGMENTS

It was such fun to be back in the newsroom with Nichelle, and with such an exciting story to work as a bonus. I am endlessly thankful to the fabulous readers who have sent me kind notes and messages for the past two and a half years asking about more Nichelle stories, and I hope this is your favorite yet.

Also grateful to my fantastic agent, John Talbot, who had faith in me when I didn't, and to Andrew Watts, Jason Kasper, Amber Hudock, and the rest of the amazing team at Severn River Publishing for helping Nichelle reach readers and being such fun to work with.

Special thanks this time to my favorite (former) US Secret Service Agent, JJ Hensley, for answering all my questions about presidential security. My thanks also to the book advocates and bloggers who help readers find my books, and to all of you who read them so faithfully.

My wonderful husband, Justin, and my littles, who never complain when socks don't match or we're ordering pizza again because I got too wrapped up in my imaginary friends—I love you right up to the moon, and back. As always, any mistakes are mine alone.

ABOUT THE AUTHOR

LynDee Walker is the national bestselling author of two crime fiction series featuring strong heroines and "twisty, absorbing" mysteries. Her first Nichelle Clarke crime thriller, FRONT PAGE FATALITY, was nominated for the Agatha Award for best first novel and is an Amazon Charts Best-seller. In 2018, she introduced readers to Texas Ranger Faith McClellan in FEAR NO TRUTH. Reviews have praised her work as "well-crafted, compelling, and fast-paced," and "an edge-of-your-seat ride" with "a spider web of twists and turns that will keep you reading until the end."

Before she started writing fiction, LynDee was an award-winning journalist who covered everything from ribbon cuttings to high level police corruption, and worked closely with the various law enforcement agencies that she reported on. Her work has appeared in newspapers and magazines across the U.S.

Aside from books, LynDee loves her family, her readers, travel, and coffee. She lives in Richmond, Virginia, where she is working on her next novel when she's not juggling laundry and children's sports schedules.

Sign up for LynDee Walker's reader list at
severnriverbooks.com/authors/lyndee-walker
lyndee@severnriverbooks.com